The Underground

ROXANNE BLAND

BLACKROSE PRESS
BALTIMORE, MARYLAND

Other Books by Roxanne Bland

Invasion

The Moreva of Astoreth

The Underground

Published 2019 by Blackrose Press
Book and cover design copyright © 2019 by Blackrose Press

Book interior by Vyrdolak, By Light Unseen Media

ISBN-13: 978-0-9967316-2-1
ISBN-10: 0-9967316-2-8
Library of Congress Control Number: 2019949658

A Blackrose Press Original

Blackrose Press
P.O. Box 18402
Rosedale, Maryland 21237
www.blackrosepress.com

This is a work of fiction. All characters, locations, and events portrayed in this book are fictional, and any resemblance to real people, locations, or events is purely coincidental.

For
Don Gerrard

"A gentle man is a dead man."
—*Xia'saan proverb*

CHAPTER 1

"Stay human. Stay human. Stay human."

Parker Berenson, alpha of Seattle's werewolf pack, slammed the door to his aging brown Chevrolet Caprice. "Stay human. Stay human." Hands clenched into fists, his feet pounded the icy pavement leading from the driveway to his blue-gray stucco house. Though the February fourth night was unusually bitter and he wore neither overcoat nor jacket, he didn't feel cold. Sweat streamed down his face and neck. His white dress shirt was soaked, as were his trousers. Tiny tendrils of steam rising from his muscular shoulders made him look as if he were smoldering.

His wolf's hard push against the mental bonds that held him inside their shared body and mind made Parker stumble. *Fuck staying human. I want out!* he roared.

Regaining his balance, he ignored his beast as best he could and kept walking. "Stay human. Just stay human."

I'm—

"At least wait until we get inside," he said through his teeth.

The porch light was out again, but Parker could see by the streetlamps' ambient glow. He shoved his key into the front door lock and gave it a savage twist. The bolt didn't move. Using more pressure, he tried again and nearly snapped the key in two. "Open, you sonofa..." he muttered, jiggling the key in its slot.

That's it, his wolf snarled and gave another hard mental shove. *Tear the sucker off—*

"No!"

The key finally turned. Parker threw the door open, stormed over the threshold, then banged the door shut.

One day, I swear-to-God, I'm gonna kill that—

"You and me both." He leaned against the door, panting. "Now calm down, will you? Calm——"

Calm down? After what he did to us tonight? Again? Calm down my——

"Shut up. We need a drink."

I don't need a drink. I need——

"Shut up, I said."

His wolf didn't reply. That was a good sign.

Parker strode away from the small patch of faux-slate tiles that served as a tiny foyer. The room he marched across comprised nearly all of the main level. White walls supported glass and metal sculptures with jagged edges sharp enough to carve a holiday roast. These stood in stark contrast to the rest of the sparse furnishings—the clean, straight lines and ninety-degree angles formed by industrial-grade steel pipe. The black leather cushions on the sofa and chairs did little to soften the interior's threatening appearance.

The decor wasn't pretty but it had its uses. The lack of furniture allowed enough space for all of his wolves to sit when the pack met at his place. And in case his neighbors discovered what he was and decided to do something about it, the wall hangings and furniture could be broken into makeshift but lethal weapons.

Parker headed for the freestanding bar about twenty feet away. He grabbed the jumbo-sized Jack Daniel's bottle from the counter and then snatched a double shot glass from a nearby rack. Pouring the glass full, he drank it in one gulp, ignoring the liquid fire searing his throat. He tossed down two more shots.

After his fourth drink, he felt at least some of the tension leave his shoulders. Holding the glass in two large, strong, and trembling— but very human—hands, he set it down on the upper counter. Leaning against the marble, he closed his eyes. "Okay. We're okay now. Right?"

His wolf remained silent. Another good sign. The last thing he wanted was to morph into his other, a gargantuan man-wolf eight feet tall. A forced morph was triggered in werewolves by the full moon and sometimes, like now, by powerful emotions. And the greater the size differences between the human and *were* selves, the more agonizing the change. Parker-the-human stood six feet, six inches tall in his stocking feet. Morphing into his eight-foot *were* hurt like a knife-wielding bitch.

Parker had been just about to let out a sigh of relief when he caught a whiff of cologne clinging to his shirt. It wasn't his. He ripped the still-wet shirt off and threw it across the room. His broad, hairy chest heaving with anger, he watched the discarded garment land in a crumpled heap about ten feet away.

No, we're not okay, his wolf growled. *Human, when are you going to wake up and smell the blood? That bastard is driving us insane.*

"That bastard" was Kurt, the vampire Master. Old and extremely formidable, Kurt extended preternatural protection from Seattle's human horde to just about every exotic—zot—that lived there. The smell Parker had picked up was the vampire's favorite scent.

He poured a fifth shot of whiskey into the glass. "Quit calling me 'human.' Besides, what do you suggest we do about it? We're Kurt's servant. Bound to him by blood. Day or night, he calls, we come, and then we do whatever he wants." He downed his drink and grimaced. "Like we're his damned dog or something."

His wolf's anger surged. *Guess you like it, huh? Like this, maybe?* A mental picture flashed in their shared mind's eye, one Parker would rather not have seen. Kurt's grinning face was poised above him. He heard the seductive whispering in his ear and felt the sweet ecstasy of fangs piercing his flesh.

Parker's face reddened. "You think I wanted to go down to Kurt's nightclub tonight?" he shouted. "You think I wanted his hands on me? No. You know what he does. Takes over my mind and twists my head around until I'm practically begging for it." He tossed down a sixth shot. "And while he's doing it I sure don't feel you trying to stop him."

That's bull and you know it.

"Shut up." He poured himself an seventh shot and drained it, which was followed by an eighth. But Jack wasn't doing the job. The humiliating images of what had happened to him and his wolf in Kurt's office beneath the vampire's Last Chance nightclub refused to fade.

Parker gripped the shot glass harder. His blood pressure skyrocketed. Rivers of sweat burst from his pores and ran down his face and chest. His wolf's snarling inside their shared mind swelled into a howl. He started grinding his teeth, a sure sign he was going into a forced morph.

"Oh, shrrit!"

CHAPTER 2

After a Herculean effort of will, Parker managed to keep his wolf at bay. He slammed the glass down on the bar's marble countertop. It shattered, and a shard gouged the base of his right thumb. He didn't notice.

"I know how to get Kurt outta my head," he muttered. Dropping into a squat, he yanked open the doors to all of the lower storage cabinets, unaware of his cut thumb spattering blood on the floor. Knocking various objects out of the way, he rummaged for the marijuana stash he thought he'd put there.

"Shit." Leaving the cabinet doors hanging open, Parker ran to his study. Hurling inside, he kicked at the pile of software magazines on the floor, sending them flying. He rooted around for whatever stash he might have left in his desk and file cabinets and even looked under the cushion of his desk chair.

Nothing.

"Where is it?" he shouted to no one. His wolf's growling inside his head grew louder. On top of everything else, his frustrated searching was making it harder for him to stay human. Then he had an idea. "Maybe it's…" Whirling, Parker dashed back into the great room, sprinted upstairs, and blew into the master bedroom. He flipped the switch and the bedroom flooded with light. Four long strides brought him to his bureau. With its intricate pattern of colored wood and mother-of-pearl inlay, the piece was worthy of an Erté print. He'd found it at a yard sale.

"Okay, okay…where?" He tore into the drawers' contents. After several minutes, he still hadn't found what he was looking for. Nothing— not even an old, dried-out weed stem. He stepped back, his gaze sweeping over the rumpled king-size bed and the nightstands on either side. "I can't have gone through a quarter pound of weed in less than two weeks." He scratched his chin. "Could I?"

Giving up the hunt, Parker stumbled across the frayed, room-sized blue braided rug to an overstuffed chair near his bed and fell onto its cushions. He blew out a heavy breath. Propping his elbow on the armrest, he rubbed his eyes and tried to think.

"Ya smoke it all again, Park?" a voice from his past echoed in his head. It belonged to Frank Suggs, his werepanther friend in Arkansas who'd been skinned alive when the boys were fifteen. At thirteen, the two had discovered a small patch of weed growing wild in the woods behind their houses. In those last years of Frank's life, Parker's buddy had said that to him a lot. "Hey, Park—ya smoke it all again?"

Parker snorted at the memory. "Guess I did, Frank."

The telephone rang. Pinching the bridge of his nose and squeezing one eye shut, he glared at it, willing it to stop. The phone rang twice more. Grimacing, he snatched up the receiver. "Berenson," he growled.

"Alpha?" a young child's timid, sexless voice said. "Alpha, it's me, Susie."

Despite his desperate state, Parker's face relaxed and the murderous look in his eyes softened. He smiled into the handset and crossed his legs. "Hey, Susie." His voice was gentle, showing no trace of rage. "Whassup?"

Parker-the-human and Parker-the-wolf were very fond of this darling, precocious little werewolf girl, one of the few children in his pack. Parker-the-human thought it was because the child was a lot like him at that age. Parker-the-wolf thought it was because this girl cub just might turn out to be an alpha someday. Female alphas were rare.

"Alpha, are you coming to my birthday party on Saturday?" she said, her voice sounding relieved now she knew Alpha wasn't mad at her.

"'Course, honey. Wouldn't miss it for the world."

Susie had just taken a breath to say something else when Parker heard the faint sounds of a scuffle. The anxious voice of a young woman replaced the child's. "Alpha, I'm sorry," Susie's mother said. "Susie knows she's not supposed to call you but she picked up the phone while I was out of the room and—"

"Hey, it's okay, Janet," Parker reassured her, keeping his tone light. The child had broken an important pack rule—no one under the rank of Third could contact the alpha wolf directly outside of dire emergency. Anyone who did was subject to punishment. Even Susie's mother wouldn't have called him since she was a Sixth.

"She's only four years old. Okay, almost five. The cub's excited about her party. Can't blame her for that." He shifted in the chair, back to his original position.

"But Alpha—"

"No, Janet." Parker's voice was firm. "Susie broke a pack rule but she's too young to understand what it's for. You can punish her for it any way you like but I won't. I'll see you guys on Saturday. Stay human."

Parker dropped the phone into its cradle, annoyed. *She dared to question me.* But it soon faded. He stared at the ravaged bureau drawers without seeing them, thinking. *Maybe I should have been more polite?*

You asking me? I would've—

"No, I wasn't asking you. It's just that—look, just because Janet is one of the lowest-ranked wolves in my pack doesn't mean I have to treat her like it."

Why not?

"Oh. So you would've pulled a Slade on her, right? Maybe beat her to a pulp while Susie watched?" Darrlyon Slade was the old alpha Parker had defeated in a death-match almost three months ago.

He felt his wolf's anger rise. *Don't wanna think about him.*

"Fine. So let's just relax, huh? Think good thoughts. Say, what about our last pack hunt, when we caught those deer?"

His wolf calmed. *Uhrrm. That was great, wasn't it?*

Parker sighed in relief. Between his wolf's rage and his own, he'd had enough trouble staying human tonight. He stretched out his six-foot-six-inch frame in the chair and tented his hands over his stomach. Closing his eyes, he willed forth the memory of the deer herd he and his pack had brought down and the feast they'd enjoyed afterward.

It didn't work.

CHAPTER 3

Parker tensed in his chair. Instead of the pack's last hunt, his inner movie screen played his memory of the night of last December third, an endless rerun of a torturously bad horror film in which the wolfman was the star.

"*Come on, Park,*" his mental soundtrack played. *The voice belonged to Garrett Larkin, a witch and the woman he loved. "You have to do this. You haven't got a choice. So you might as well get it over with."*

Walking along an alley, they reached the Last Chance nightclub's back door. "I don't see why. Kurt already knows you. You two have known each other for years."

"Yes, but this is different." Garrett made a face when Parker sighed. "Look, Park—this introduction's just protocol. You don't like Kurt, but you know the rules. You're alpha of the wolfpack, and the alpha is Kurt's servant. I'm your new freyja. That doesn't make me his servant but I'm in charge of the pack in case something happens to you."

"And if something does happen to me?"

He watched Garrett's jaw set. "I won't be Kurt's servant, Parker. Master or not, I've better things to do."

The remark stung, but Parker said nothing. He turned away and searched for the loose brick near the door's jamb. Finding it, he pulled it out and thrust his hand into the open space, ignoring the mortar scratching his skin. His fingers brushed against the hard plastic button and mashed it. The door's lock clicked. The two entered and he led Garrett into the nightclub proper.

Kurt, alone in the club, stood on the far side of the hardwood dance floor, waiting for them. Parker and Garrett crossed until they stood about ten feet away. "Master," he said as politely as he could, "I present to you Garrett Larkin, my freyja and the mother of my pack. She is my equal in all things."

Back home, on his private movie screen, Parker could almost feel how tight his throat had been while choking out the next line of his formal recital.

"Ask of her whatever you would ask of me, and it shall be given."

"Thank you, my servant. You have chosen well."

He cringed. The inflection had felt like a knife twisting in his gut.

Kurt's amusement at Parker's discomfort was plain to see. Turning to Garrett, his gaze traveled up and down her small, willowy body, lingering on those parts he apparently found intriguing. He gave her a beatific smile and held out his hand. "Come with me. Let's go over here, hmm?" he said, pointing to a table and three chairs abutting the dance floor.

Garrett took it without hesitation.

Sprawled in the overstuffed chair, Parker winced hard, not wanting to face the shame he always felt at his galling weakness before the vampire. He remembered his dismay when Garrett dropped her hand from his and accepted Kurt's. He'd tried to keep her hand in an iron grip but his strong fingers had loosened like overcooked spaghetti. Kurt's telekinetic power over Parker meant the former could take control over the werewolf's body whenever he wished. Exploiting that control, Kurt had freed Garrett's hand by forcing Parker to let go.

His inner movie kept rolling.

Walking Garrett to the table, Kurt turned and looked over his shoulder. "Stay there."

"The hell——" Parker took a step forward but that was as far as he got. Kurt had immobilized him, putting him under a stasis so he could neither move nor speak. With a smile, the vampire removed Garrett's cloak and began massaging her shoulders. "You are a beautiful woman," he purred. "I'm pleased my servant has such good taste."

Garrett smiled, her eyes shiny and vacant. "Thank you, Master."

Parker gripped the arms of the overstuffed chair. He'd known what her look meant. He'd seen it before in other zots. The bastard had hypnotized her and now she'd do anything he wanted. He remembered how surprised he'd been that she'd succumbed so easily. Garrett wasn't just a witch—she was a mage. He'd seen her stare down vampires who'd thought she'd be easy prey. *Why didn't you fight him, Garrett?* he thought for the thousandth time. *Why?*

His movie resumed.

THE UNDERGROUND

"I've never had a mage servant before," Kurt said, glancing at Parker. "Humans, weres, elves, and even witches. But never a mage." He turned to him. "I want her. Frankly, I think she'd be happier with me than with you. Wouldn't you, Garrett?"

"Yes, Master."

Kurt smiled, a grin of triumph. Parker tried to break the stasis by repeatedly throwing his mind against it but the vampire's hold didn't budge. He was furious enough to force morph but dammit, he wasn't able to move.

His master walked over to him. "I know how much you hate to share, wolfman," he cooed in Parker's ear. "But you'll just have to get over it, hmm? Of course, I'll lend Garrett to you whenever you wish as long as I'm not busy with her. I do respect she is your freyja, Parker. I really do." Kurt took a few steps backward. "To show my respect, wolf, I will even ask before I make her mine." He smiled again. "Garrett, would you consent to be my servant?" he said without turning around.

To Parker, it sounded like some kind of sick marriage proposal.

"Yes."

Kurt returned to where Garrett stood. Looking over his shoulder, he gave Parker a lascivious smirk, took her into his arms and sat her on the table. Then he sank his fangs into her neck. When he had his fill, he looked up, his mouth stained with her blood. He slowly licked his lips. "Mmm...like nectar. Let's see if the rest of her is just as sweet, hmm?"

To Parker's horror, Kurt lifted Garrett's dress and fucked her on the table in front of him. He took her from the front, from behind, and every other which way he chose. Parker could only stand rooted to his spot, forced to watch while his woman gave herself to the vampire. He wanted to scream but couldn't.

At home, he could and he did. "Gawwrooo!" he let loose with a howl of pure misery. Clapping his hands over his mouth to stifle the second howl welling up in his throat, he leapt from his chair and started pacing.

When the urge to howl passed, he removed his hands from his mouth and gripped his head. "Stay human, stay human, stay human..." he chanted, striding around in circles. The pressure in his chest was almost unbearable.

After his breathing returned to something approaching normal, Parker fell into his chair a second time. Closing his eyes, he pinched the bridge of his nose. "Oh, God...why did I have to see that shit again?" He gritted his teeth at the few tears that leaked from under his eyelids.

"There was nothing I could do. Nothing."

He slouched in his seat, feeling sorry for himself. Then he noticed his wolf was quiet, too. The memory—and the hurt—of that horrible night had taken the wind out of its angry sails.

Parker sat up. "Screw this. I gotta do something." Looking down, he saw the healed gash in his right thumb. He licked at the dried blood, thinking. He'd planned to spend a quiet evening at home—for a change—but after all he'd been through tonight, that plan was history.

He slouched in the chair again. *I was a good boy at Shanty's Bar last night. That dude was being an asshole but at least I didn't throw him through the window like I did to that other guy at the Lion last week.* He nodded once. *Okay. Shanty's it is.*

What about the blonde? his wolf growled. *Remember her? She might be waiting for us to show up again.*

Parker scowled. He'd almost forgotten. Sitting eight stools away from him at the bar counter, the blonde woman kept giving him the eye, obviously wanting him to buy her a drink. Maybe lots of drinks. He hadn't, though. He knew he was built like Hollywood's version of a hairy Norse god—werewolves like him often were—but he'd have bet his werewolf's hairy balls the woman was a lorelei. Loreleis were humans who specialized in outing exotics. After gaining a zot's trust by pretending to be a zymp—zot sympathizer—the lorelei would turn a lover over to the police. When that happened, the exotic in question disappeared, never to be heard from again.

So what should he do, then?

I'm starving, his wolf blurted.

He blinked in surprise. The two of them had been so pissed off at Kurt their shared stomach's distress hadn't registered until now. Whatever else they did tonight, eating had to come first. A werewolf's metabolism was way off the human charts. That extraordinary metabolism was also the reason why it was so hard for a werewolf to get drunk.

"Me too. Lunch was a long time ago. And we've lost a lot of blood tonight." He thought for a few moments. "Okay. This is what we'll do. We go to Tina's on Southwest Thomas for dinner. She always gives us extra big helpings, and we can sit in that booth way in the back in case we see any loreleis. After we eat, we make a score for a new stash, then come home and finish that program before our client fires us. Sound good?"

Uhrrm. Let's do it.

Rising to his feet, Parker's sensitive nose caught another whiff of Kurt's cologne. He shoved aside the memory of how the scent had gotten onto his skin. "Shower first," he muttered. "No way I'm going out smelling like him."

After showering, he dressed while humming a paean to his expected meal. Tina's was casual, so he wore an Oxford cloth shirt, jeans, and a pair of loafers that hadn't yet seen better days. Parker turned out the bedroom light and loped downstairs. Pausing at the base of the staircase, he decided against wearing a coat. The night was arctic but he wouldn't be outside long—just enough to get in and out of his car.

He'd just started to turn the front door's knob when a familiar trance overtook him. His eyes narrowed and his jaw tightened.

What does he want now? his wolf growled.

The door vanished. Parker gasped as if he'd been sucker punched. His mind's eye had filled with an intimate view of Kurt sodomizing a young man.

But that wasn't even the worst part. The young man was Gerald, a minor member of his wolfpack who'd been kept as a sex slave by a human family from God-knew-when until he was fourteen years old. From what Gerald had told him, they'd used the werewolf boy for themselves, their friends, and anyone else who'd been willing to pay.

He couldn't believe what he was seeing. Eighteen years old now, Gerald had been so traumatized by his human abusers that he appeared more or less unable to care for himself, which was why Parker had placed him with the vampires, much as he'd hated having to do so. In Kurt's colony, someone—human or not—was always around.

A wave of protective concern for this junior member of his pack surged through him. Gerald, he was sure, hadn't consented to Kurt's attentions.

Parker's hand gripping the doorknob started to shake. Soon the quivering spread through his body. The door rattled in its frame. Even if he was in the room with them, he could do nothing to stop Kurt from taking as much pleasure as he wanted from the boy, nothing at all. And he knew Kurt was putting on this—this *show*—for his benefit. To remind him of his impotence.

His wave of concern turned into a tsunami of fury. What was the point of being alpha if he couldn't protect even the least of his pack from this sort of abuse, the very thing he'd thought the poor cub had been rescued from?

Then Kurt's contemptuous, echoing voice filled his mind, silencing him. *You may be king of your wolves but really, you're just another of my little pegboys like Gerald.*

The vision disappeared. For a full five seconds, Parker stood frozen in shocked disbelief.

He couldn't take anymore. His wolf erupted. A lava flow of *were*-strength blasted through his arms, then through the rest of him. His human eyes glowed his werewolf's green. He heard and felt his clothes rip. He was morphing.

Hardly aware of what he was doing, Parker ripped the knob from the door. Spinning around, he hurled the brass piece across the room. It shattered a large mirror that had, until very recently, reflected his remarkably still-human image.

"I. Am. Not!" his maddened beast roared. He tore the door open, nearly taking it off its hinges. Leaping over the threshold, Parker slammed the broken door shut and fled into the freezing night.

CHAPTER 4

While Parker burned rubber out of his driveway, six thousand miles to the southwest of Seattle, Melera, Shen'zae of Xia'saan and Domina of the Third Galactic Sector, lay on her couch twitching in the throes of a nightmare.

She stood on the observation deck inside her captured yacht, watching with mounting fury as Akkadian starlegions herded her ship's seventeen-member crew—prisoners now, judging by the manacles and chains they wore—down the yacht's boarding ramp and into the huge docking bay.

Seran Rhys betrayed us.

Yes, her czado's cold, four-toned voice echoed in her mind. We and the captain were the only ones who knew the coordinates for our jump.

Melera's lips tightened. Her czado, or shadow, shared her body and mind, the conscious remnant of a twin she'd absorbed while developing in their mother's womb. And it was right about Seran Rhys's betrayal. Her czado was always right.

The other ship, breathtakingly vast, had been waiting for them after they'd reentered third-dimensional space. Rhys had ordered their immediate surrender. Melera's warrior instinct told her they should fight and for a moment she was tempted to override his order. But logic prevailed. Her yacht boasted enough firepower to fend off a pirate attack but it was no match for the Yprés-class dreadnought that now held it in its iron grip.

The swishing sound of the deck's automatic doors made her turn. Mag Beloc, Jahannan warlord of the Akkad Protectorate, strode into the small room with ten of his starlegions crowding in behind him.

"Your Majesty," Beloc rasped, inclining his bald, pale blue head.

Melera glared at him. "What gives you the right to seize my ship? I could have you—"

"No, you could not. The Fourteen Sectors—"

"Fourteen? What are you talking about? There are fifteen sectors."

Beloc smiled. It wasn't pleasant. "That's why I'm here. The Fourteen have declared your Third Sector forfeit. And you, Shen'zae, are under arrest."

Melera gaped. "For what?"

The Jahannan warlord's smile faded. His three eyes narrowed. "Don't play coy with me. Treason—for aiding the Vst in their rebellion against the Akkad." Before Melera could protest he barked a command and the legions swarmed over her. She fought as hard as she could but it was no use. On the crowded deck, there was too little room for her to maneuver.

Grappling with a legionnaire over the plasma pistol strapped to her thigh, she squeezed off one shot before falling to the deck in a sea of armored fists.

The loud zzzzt! from the plasma pistol's charge exploding against the ceiling woke her. Wide-eyed and panting, she struggled to sit up. Her head swiveled left and right. There were no legions, no Beloc. It had been a nightmare. Again.

The acrid smell of molten rock filled her nostrils. A grating sound from above her made her look up. A big, smoking piece of her hidden island fortress was falling straight for her.

"Jakk," Melera shouted, her five-toned voice echoing about the cave. Clutching her gun, she threw herself off the couch and landed on her knees. A moment later, she peeked over the cushion's edge. The superheated stone had landed near the middle of her bed and was melting another crater in the couch's inflammable wadding.

"Damn." She squeezed her eyes shut and smacked her forehead against the cushion. Looking up, she surveyed her bed and grimaced. "I've had this jakkin' dream so many times my couch looks like the back end of some misbegotten moon." She scanned her bed again then blew a heavy breath. *Ph'uk it. I've had it worse.*

Hauling herself from the floor, pistol in hand, Melera sat on the couch's edge with her head hanging. She began to tremble. Elbows on her thighs, she dangled the gun between her muscular legs. Her chest hurt from a muscle she must have pulled leaping off her bed. Staring at the weapon, she waited with dread for what often followed one of her nightmares. She began stroking the gun's matte black barrel with shaking fingers. Maybe she should just use the pistol on herself. Considering what was about to happen, it was tempting.

Moments later, a sad half-smile formed on the dream-haunted warrior's lips. She stopped her stroking. "Not today, my friend," she whispered at the gun. She couldn't do it. Mag Beloc—her nemesis—would see her suicide as an admission of defeat and in more ways than one.

Still...

Melera sat up. *No. Beloc will not win.*

Her tremors disappeared with her new-found resolution. She hurled the gun across the cavern with every ounce of her alien strength. Following its trajectory with her eyes, she watched the weapon discharge upon hitting the far rock wall. The plasmatic explosion took out one of the arc lamps attached to the huge metal grid suspended from the cave's ceiling.

Get ready, her czado said.

Melera scooted in about two feet from the edge of her bed. Leaning back, she crossed her legs beneath her and then sat forward. She knew how to escape the worst of it. Taking slow, deep breaths, she pushed her consciousness down until she'd settled into a profound trance. She kept pushing. She was almost there, to that special, secret place deep in her psyche. Hiding in what she'd always visualized as her very own cozy and warm dark hole would shield her mind from the worst of the torment. Which, she was sure, would begin at any moment.

As Melera had expected—but not as she'd hoped— when she reached her inner psychic sanctuary, she couldn't get in. The way was blocked, as it always was now, by a mental barrier she couldn't break through—a solid wall of gray, soft and pliable as limp rubber yet unyielding as the hardest stone.

It took three seconds for her to break the trance. "Damn you, Beloc. Damn you." Tears of resigned anticipation began rolling down her cheeks. She squeezed her eyes shut.

They popped open a few minutes later after she realized she felt no pain. She let out a little gasp. Maybe this time there wouldn't be any.

"Please?" she whispered to the cave. But no, there it was. Deep in the center of her brain, a minute vibration had begun, so gentle she could barely feel it. Then it became a soft buzzing in her left ear and soon the pulsation spread to her right.

Melera tensed and gripped her knees. Would she make it through this time?

The buzzing grew stronger and louder. In seconds it had filled her entirely, becoming an infinitely complex pounding rhythm that threatened to burst her skull. The buzz's pitch began to rise. It became a hum and then, rising higher, it turned into a spine-freezing whine. The searing vibrations stripped apart the very fibers of her being.

Clapping her hands to the sides of her head, she keened in counterpoint to the devastating, insistent whine. She began to rock, faster and faster. Spasms rippled her muscles. The tremors hurled her off the sleeping couch and she struck the floor with a sharp, smacking thud she didn't feel. Each convulsive tic of sinew and tendon brought pain so exquisite it sang.

When the drilling whine in her head sharpened to where it felt like an iron bore tunneling through her brain, Melera screamed with enough force to break the small blood vessels in her throat. Thrashing and roaring, she tried in vain to dislodge the ravaging bore as well as the worms eating through her from the inside out. Writhing on the smooth floor, she clawed at her flesh and howled. Her agony seemed eternal.

Then she felt nothing.

CHAPTER 5

Melera opened her eyes only to be blinded by the glare from an arc lamp's triple suns overhead. She groaned in pain.

Little by little, her brain started functioning again. *What happened?* was her first coherent thought. *Where am I?* Then, *who am I?* She concentrated hard but the answers wouldn't come. Her eyes widened in fear. She started to get up. A fireball of pain exploded through her. "Augh," she grunted, falling back to the floor.

When her feeling of being charred had subsided to a mere burn, her amnesia began to lift. "Oh...yeah," she croaked, her quintuple voices sounding like a chorus of broken bassoons. She'd had another seizure.

Staring at the cave ceiling, Melera felt a few tears trickle from the outer corners of her eyes and slide down her temples. The trickle became a torrent. "I don't know how much more of this I can take."

Toq! You are a war machine. Machines endure.

"Well, this machine is wearing out."

Her czado said nothing. She stared at the ceiling a few minutes longer then closed her eyes. "The seizures are getting worse, aren't they?"

Yes.

"How many more of them, do you think, before they kill me?"

I do not know but you are not dead yet. Clean yourself up and get back to work.

"Your sympathy warms my heart." But she knew her czado was right. Gathering what little strength she had left, she struggled to her feet, ignoring the wave of nausea that washed over her. Once stable, she headed for the bath.

Best to make sure you and I remember everything, her czado said as she staggered across the cavern. *Amnesia can be tricky.*

Melera stepped over one of the translucent, glowing power cables that festooned the cave's uneven walls and smooth floor. "Good idea." Her voice, hoarse from her screaming, sounded tired. "Why don't you start?"

Very well. Who are you?

"I am Melera Shen'zae of Xia'saan. I am czado, a warrior elite."

What else?

"I came here to find the battlestar war fleet my father, Tarq Shen'zae, hid somewhere in this solar system."

And?

She tripped over a large exhaust hose. Stumbling forward, she grabbed at the seven by four feet replicator to keep from falling. "To find the fleet, I have to decipher the code he left behind," she said, lurching upright. "When I find it, I'll...I'll..."

Think!

A vision appeared in her mind's eye. Once again she hung naked from a metal beam attached to a ceiling in one of Beloc's "playrooms." The Jahannan warlord held one of his favorite toys—a zaprod—a foot-long laser he used to burn holes into prisoners' flesh. In their more intimate moments, like the one she saw now, he'd been especially fond of taking her from behind and skewering her breasts, cooing sweet nothings into her ear while she screamed.

The answer came to her. "I'll turn it over to the Vst so they can fight the Akkad."

Excellent. The memory function is intact.

Leaning against the replicator, she exhaled a heavy sigh of relief. But then her jogged memory slipped in one last recital.

Xia'saan—home—is gone...

Fighting back her tears, Melera tottered the rest of the way across the cave floor, down a short tunnel, and into the bath.

Back inside the main cavern, she slid onto the bench facing her siitheer, the instrument she used to break Tarq's code. "I'm not ready to do this," she muttered. "I feel like I've been tranked. I can hardly think straight."

THE UNDERGROUND

You must. Every minute is precious. If you do not solve the code soon, the Vst will lose the war.

Instead of answering, Melera ran her long, lean fingers over the siitheer's seven rows of twenty-five round, blue buttons. Then she fondled the three rows of twelve silver knobs located on a panel perpendicular to the one with the buttons. They seemed like old friends. She stared at the panel's centermost knob, her thoughts spiraling around the mystery of her father's and her beloved Ruri's deaths. A tear formed in the corner of one eye and trickled down her cheek. *Why? How did Beloc find out Tarq, Ruri, and I were—*

Work, her czado boomed. She flinched. Nodding, she wiped her tears. It didn't matter how Beloc had learned the three were supporting the rebellion. All that mattered was that she'd loved Tarq and Ruri with everything she had and now they were gone, leaving a dark, empty hole where her heart had been. She pushed thoughts of her father and her lover aside and focused on the concave screen above the silver knobs. She noted its pattern of scrolling rainbow colors. Good—the siitheer was still in tune.

Melera regarded the three-sided panel monitor displaying fifteen staves of Tarq's musical puzzle. Staring at it, her determination crumbled. "What in jakk makes me think I can crack this code?" she cried, her quintuple voices breaking with despair. "It's a damned symphony. And I don't have the key." She dropped her head into her hands and burst into tears. "I...I can't do it. I just can't do it!"

A year ago, it would have been unthinkable that Melera Shen'zae—the finest interstellar assassin ever to serve His Majesty's government and the last hereditary Queen of Xia'saan—would have felt so unsure. Unsure if she was good enough or smart enough or strong enough to finish this last task Tarq had left her. Unsure of who she was. Unsure of everything.

Stop. Tarq pledged the fleet to the Vst. Tarq is dead. You gave our ka on that promise and now we are bound to keep it.

"Then you solve jakkin' thing!"

I cannot. I am tone-deaf. You know that.

Her tears eventually dried. Her czado was right again. She couldn't just quit and her twin couldn't help her. She harbored no love for the Vst—nor they for her—but being ka-bound gave her one of only two choices: either break the code and deliver the fleet or die trying.

Melera looked up at the screens again and tugged at a moveable tray holding a trapezoid-shaped keyboard. With a heavy sigh, she took up where she'd left off earlier and continued her deciphering.

CHAPTER 6

After a long while, Melera rose from the siitheer's bench, stretched, and then headed to her sleeping couch. Plopping onto its pock-marked cushion, she looked around at the gargantuan, rough-hewn cavern she called home.

Her isolation was complete. She'd made base on a smallish planet, the third of at least eight she'd counted orbiting an ordinary yellow star. Her barren, volcanic rock island lay in the middle of a vast blue ocean, thrusting into the air like a gigantic insult. The planet was diurnal but inside her fortress, she had no real sense of day or night unless she went outside to look. Most times she didn't bother to do even that.

With a small groan, she leaned forward and hid her face in her hands. *What am I thinking? How can this tomb ever be home?* Home could only be Xia'saan, with its vibrant, teeming cities and the edgy, earthy nature of the people who lived there. Home was her clan and their communal lives. Home was her beloved Ruri, with whom she'd been promised in heartfast. But like everything else important to her, all of that was gone. All she had now was this hole inside an alien mountain, with nothing but the dull drone of machinery for company.

Jakk, I might as well be in prison.

The realization jolted her. She sat up with a jerk. *Wait. I don't have to stay in this cave. I only came here because too many people in Maqu are looking for me. But that's in Maqu.* She snorted in disgust. Her paranoia about being out in the open had gotten the best of her for far too long.

The last Shen'zae jumped from her couch. "I'm out of here." She strode to the commcen, the cluster of machines that served as her means of communication with the Vst. "But before I go…"

When Melera first encountered this world in the deep-space

transport that had brought her, Tarq, Ruri, and their equipment, it had been obvious to her that the dominant bips—bi-pedal species—were intelligent, judging by the satellites and other debris orbiting the planet. For that reason, they'd kept the transport's stealth shields activated, in case the hardware was part of a planet-wide defense system. Other than the bips' intelligence though, she knew nothing about them.

"I don't even know what the bips call this planet." She halted before the quantum receiver, taller than her six feet, two inches. Always on, it monitored for messages from the Vst. Each of the fourteen colored bands of light pulsed with the different frequencies the rebels used for contact.

Shutting the receiver down, she watched the colored lights fade and go dark. That she'd just severed her only connection to the Vst didn't bother her much. Having been Beloc's captive wasn't exactly a badge of honor with them. The Jahannan warlord's methods of breaking prisoners were highly successful and a select few ended up infiltrating the rebel ranks. After her escape, she knew better than return to the Vst. They wouldn't immediately execute her as an Akkadian spy. They'd imprison her until she'd cracked the code and delivered the fleet. Then they'd execute her. The Vst hadn't learned she was free until after she'd liberated her corvette from one of their off-planet base stations.

Melera stepped over to a black cube rising about three and a half feet from the floor. On its flat surface were two clear panels. The rightmost panel emitted a fluorescent-like glow. The other, now dark, provided a heads-up display of messages received. She placed her hand on the lit panel and watched it sink below its surface. The commcen's security program measured her neural impulses and compared these to the ones stored in its memory. The panel's color changed from bluish-gray to orange. Through a direct connection to her nervous system, she now controlled the commcen by thought. She directed the receiver to reactivate in standard mode.

Before making planetfall that first time, Melera, Tarq, and Ruri had spent a month orbiting just outside the planet's atmosphere while the transport's cameras had clicked away, feeding data into the ship's computers to create a minutely detailed three-dimensional map. Sometimes she and Ruri had kept themselves entertained by switching on the viscreens to watch the planet's fauna and flora go by.

"Some of those towers we saw on our fly-bys have got to be for long-distance communication. All I have to do is find the right frequencies." Looking at the column, she watched its topmost band change from white to deep purple and then to dark blue while she adjusted for wavelength.

The audios exploded with gibberish. The frequency indicator glowed deep red. "That's number one." She muted the noise and adjusted the next locator until she heard more gibberish. Listening for a moment, her musician's ear could tell the speech coming through this audio was different from the one she'd heard before. She frowned. "That means they don't have a common language. How in jakk do they talk to one another?" She pondered it for a few seconds and then shrugged. That wasn't her problem.

After reprogramming all fourteen channels, Melera directed the commcen's computers to analyze the planet's languages for common speech structures with Xia'saan. From those cross comparisons, the commcen would translate, as much as possible, the languages into her native tongue.

Now that the receiver had been programmed, she headed to the holo projector about ten feet away. Ovate in shape and opaque like milk glass, it rested on a translucent cube about two feet high. She looked around. "Where'd I put the remote?" Spotting it on a nearby chair, she grabbed the black wand and returned to the projector.

She pressed a small button. Almost instantly, a holo of the planet blossomed in mid-air. Pressing and then holding down another button, the floating image began to rotate. She stopped it when a spot of white light like a tiny sun came into view. The spot pinpointed her base. "All right, here I am. Now, where should I go?"

Melera paced a circle around the planet's image, inspecting the large landmasses hovering on the blue seas. Every so often, her body rippled and morphed into another being. Her czado enabled her to do this. Without much thought, she could morph into anything she wished and often did it simply because she could.

"I want to go someplace temperate." Scrutinizing the largest landmass, she morphed into a tyraticin, a two-legged beast of burden from the planet Mylatha. Then she morphed into a wakul, a winged monster inhabiting a nameless planet on the fringes of Maqu.

An hour and twenty-four morphs later, she'd decorated the holo planet with fifteen pink stars—all possible candidates. "Now for a closer look." She adjusted the map's focus. Five of the pink stars she eliminated because the areas didn't have the technological infrastructure to support her or her work.

Melera had narrowed her choices to three when the commcen chirped. She hurried over to it. Scanning the frequencies, she soon found the chirping channel. Sinking her hand into the fluorescent-like panel, she accessed the commcen's message. The display floated before her eyes. It was the linguistic analysis she'd wanted.

"The bips call themselves...hum...ans?" Her quintuple voices sounded uncertain. "Mmm...maybe it's hu-mans." Then she shrugged. She'd have plenty of time to figure out the pronunciation later. "The name of this planet is 'Dirt,' which"—she frowned—"is also what they call the soil." She raised her brow. "Not very imaginative, but I suppose it's accurate enough." There was nothing more. Disappointed, she disconnected and returned to the holo projector.

Melera had thought she'd have to start all over again when she found where she'd set up her new base. It would be located on a huge and narrow landmass that spanned almost one entire side of Dirt. The spot she'd chosen was at the edge of its upper quadrant.

Homing in, she saw a verdant landscape with mountains in the distance, some snowcapped. The blue sky arching over all made it seem magical. She zoomed in closer. The land was dotted with cities here and there, some so close together she couldn't tell if they weren't in fact only one metropolis. It didn't matter. She could see the area had everything she needed to live and work in comfort.

She zoomed in on the largest city and then adjusted the perspective so it appeared she was at ground level. None of the buildings were very tall. She guessed the tallest probably wasn't more than seventy-odd stories. It wasn't what she was used to, but after being holed up in this mountain, the city looked like heaven.

Scanning more images, she found one of two hu-mans on a street. One was male, with dark hair and ruddy-looking skin. His mouth was open in what she supposed was a laugh since he wasn't carrying any weapons. The other was female. Her skin was brownish and unlike the male, her hair was yellow. The male wore baggy, tan trousers and a colorful, one-piece shirt with short sleeves. A loose, short length of fabric that appeared to hang by two strips of material, one over each shoulder, covered the female's torso. Her lips pursed. *His pleasure-slave, obviously.* Both wore open shoes strapped onto their feet. She stared at the images. During their fly-bys, she'd caught glimpses of hu-mans on the viscreens but she really hadn't paid attention. Now, though...

"They don't look that much different from me. Good. Makes it easier to blend in." She smiled. *I wonder what the hu-mans call this place.*

Flipping through the images, Melera felt her old self returning, her brazen, take-no-prisoners attitude slipping over her like a well-worn glove. Finding the picture with hu-man writing, she studied it for a while and then let out a little snort. "Like I'm supposed to know what this means."

Then she had an idea. She looked around and spotted her electronic tablet and stylus on a small table near the holo projector. Grabbing them both, she pulled up the chair. "I'll just scan this into the commcen and see if it comes up with a match." She reset the machine's input mode from speech to manual. Picking up the stylus, she began copying the mostly angular markings onto the backlit screen. "Wonder if they're letters or numbers...guess I'll find out soon enough," she whispered.

W-E

"So far, so good."

O-M-E

"Hmm..."

T-L-E

"Done." Melera looked at what she'd written.

W-E-L-C-O-M-E T-O S-E-A-T-T-L-E

CHAPTER 7

On February first, Garrett Larkin coasted along an unnamed service road at northern Seattle's watery edge, looking for a place to leave her maroon Altima since the parking lot was full. Parallel parking was something she'd never been very good at, so she pulled into the first open spot that looked twice the car's length.

Slamming the door shut, she leaned against it and looked around. She stood atop a ten-foot-high earthen embankment, two hundred feet or so inland from the black waters of Puget Sound. The seagulls' arcing swoops over the water in search of breakfast reminded her she hadn't eaten yet, either. A rising westerly wind tousled her hair. With each gust, she felt it lift off the nape of her neck. It was cold, and the light rain that pelted her felt like tiny knives of ice.

Her gaze settled on a huge, decrepit, windowless warehouse forty feet from the water's edge. On the icy breeze, she could hear the building's aged wood siding creak, as if protesting the wind's rough treatment. She tilted her head and listened to the eerie sound. *All the despairing souls.*

Casing the warehouse, she could see much of the wood on the windward sides had split. A few pieces looked as if the next hard storm would blow them away. Rusted oil drums and unidentifiable machine parts were strewn about like discarded toys.

"Abandon hope all ye who enter here," she intoned. Then she giggled. That shopworn joke never failed to amuse her.

The wind blew harder. Garrett shivered and grabbed the edges of her black wool cape, clutching the heavy material close for extra warmth. She started picking her way down the slope. The unpaved road leading to the complex lay seventy-odd feet to her left, but she didn't bother with it. She hated the cold and this shortcut, treacherous as it was, would get her to the warehouse that much faster. She slipped a few times. The soles of her sneakers couldn't get a firm grip on the oily brown dirt.

Reaching level ground, she stopped and surveyed listless weeds doing their best to survive. Then she turned, smiling at the figure she'd caught sight of from the corner of her eye while navigating the slope. It was Pinkie, the youngest member of the coven. She had a personality as bubbly as her name.

"Hey, Garrett. Wait up!" the twenty-three-year-old witch called.

Garrett waited. She liked Pinkie. The young woman had a way of brightening the world around her. Even this bleak place seemed cheered by Pinkie's boundless good nature. Pinkie's coat was open and as usual, the eccentric witch was dressed in layers of loose, brightly-colored clothing much too big for her. Not long ago, Pinkie had told her she dressed the way she did because she liked carrying her stuff in her pockets instead of a purse. So she'd sewn extra pockets, some large, some small, into all of her oversized clothes.

They greeted each other with mutual kisses on both cheeks. Pinkie gave her an inquiring look. "Can you feel it?"

"Oh, yes. The tension's gotten much worse in the last few weeks. It feels like a pot about to boil out here."

She frowned a little. "Seattle isn't always this way, is it? I'd always heard the city's humans were pretty mellow about zots."

"They are, usually. Humans like to pretend zots don't exist but they know how it works. The old spell's energy dissipated with the election and the coven has to renew it. The longer they have to wait, the more nervous they get."

Pinkie squinted at her. "Do you feel it more because you're a mage and not just a witch? I mean, I've never known a mage before, and…"

"I don't feel it any more or less than you do. The main difference between a witch and a mage is that mages have greater powers to summon the elemental forces and bend them to our will. Otherwise, witches and mages are pretty much the same."

"Oh." Pinkie looked down and dug her toe of her boot in the gravel. She said nothing for a few moments. Then she looked up. "You nervous about this morning?"

Garrett shrugged. "Yeah, I guess so…I mean, who wouldn't be?"

Her lips stretched into a half smile. "It's funny—I've done this so many times, but each time it always feels like the first."

Pinkie looked surprised. "Really? This is my first time. Don't tell me I'm always gonna feel this way."

Her smile broadened. "Only if you're not human."

They linked arms and chatted while they strolled toward the decrepit hulk looming in the distance. Actually, Pinkie did most of the talking. Garrett just made the usual, noncommittal sounds. She had other things on her mind.

They made for an odd sight, two women walking against the wind amidst the desolation of the abandoned buildings. The warehouse's wretched appearance was deceiving. Underneath the decayed siding, sturdy creosote-coated wooden planks an inch thick had been fitted together and nailed to the studs. The minute spaces between the planking had been caulked with sealing compound and then covered with tar, and the whole building, from inside the walls to underneath the raised floor, had been packed with dense fiberglass insulation.

Far from being abandoned, the property was owned, as it had been for decades, by W.B.C., Inc. The letters stood for "Witches of the Balthus Coven," although that name didn't appear on any corporate documents. The coven had christened and dedicated the warehouse "Temple of Balthus," a sea-god and principle deity of the Llachlan, an ancient seafaring people. Naming the Temple for the old god didn't mean they were his followers. "Balthus" had been chosen because of Seattle's proximity to the ocean.

They reached the Temple's entrance. Garrett had started up the three wide stairs leading to a set of oversized double doors when Pinkie startled her out of her half-listening reverie.

"I hope I don't get to be IT," the young witch said, sounding grave.

She stopped. "Why not? I mean, it can be hairy, yeah, but..." Curious, she frowned and tilted her head. "Would it bother you to be chosen?"

"Oh, no. I mean, it's just that..." Pinkie shook her long, brown curls. "Lord and Mother, Garrett—Jim Russell's a pig."

James C. Russell had been elected mayor of Seattle the previous November.

Garrett laughed at Pinkie's comical expression. The scowling young woman looked surprised. Then she too started laughing. "Oh, you know what I mean."

"Pinkie," she said between chuckles, "I agree Russell's a pig, but remember, pigs can be people too." Still laughing, she skipped up the remaining steps and held open one of the oversized double doors for the younger woman to enter first. Following, Garrett pulled the door closed, shutting out the cold that tried to blow in behind her. She licked her lips. Her lightheartedness hid how she really felt.

She wasn't just nervous. She was scared.

Me too, Pinkie. I hope IT doesn't choose me, either.

CHAPTER 8

Garrett smiled when she saw Paul Mendiz sitting at a small desk in the reception area, rummaging through its drawers. The Balthus Coven didn't have a hierarchy but all the witches recognized the trim Filipino as being the coven's "elder" and high priest because at seventy-two years old, he was the eldest witch.

"Hello, you two," he called and stopped his rummaging. "Go on in. Maira made our cakes this morning and everybody's mostly here. If you want some, you'd better hurry." Maira was Paul's wife.

"Oo, cakes," Pinkie cooed. She pulled off her boots and bolted through the double doors leading to Balthus's Lair, where the coven made its magick.

Garrett stopped beside the desk. "Hi, Paul. How are you?"

"Nervous, of course. But otherwise fine." He smiled.

"Good. I'm going to see if I can grab a cake. Don't be too long—I'm sure the coven is anxious to start." She gazed for a moment at her friend. Genetic differences between zots and humans meant the former aged far more slowly than the latter. At seventy-two, Paul could pass for a man in his mid-forties, even in bright light.

Slipping off her sneakers, she pushed open one of the doors and entered the Lair. Three cakes left. Her steps quickened. She reached the table just in time to snag the last one. Munching on her treat, she headed toward the big pile of mismatched pillows the coven used for sitting during a gathering. Choosing a pillow with a floral pattern, she half-carried, half-dragged it across the floor to a spot not far from where Mark sat.

Garrett finished the last of her cake and looked around. The Lair was a huge square room, fifty by fifty feet, and almost two stories high.

Each of its four walls lay in one of the cardinal directions—east, west, north, and south, and each had been painted in its associated color: yellow for the east, blue for west, green for north and red for the south.

She could see the coven was nervous. Pinkie chattered about nothing to anyone who was listening. Others paced, seeming lost in thought. The tension was thick enough to cut with the proverbial knife. Her lips tightened. The coven was about to take the first step on a perilous journey. Once started, there was no turning back.

From the corner of her eye, she saw Paul enter the room. When the rest of the witches noticed he'd joined them, silence descended like a stage curtain coming down. He hurried over to an almost hidden cabinet set in the yellow wall. Opening it, he reached in and retrieved a small brown suede bag. He walked toward where the coven sat on their pillows and sat in an open space between Bertie and Sam.

This morning, the witches met to prepare for casting the Saperet spell three days hence. On February fourth, Mercury, Venus, and Mars, visible in the winter sky, would be aligned with each other. It would be an especially auspicious time. The spell drew down from the cosmic plane an aspect of I AM so that it appeared in PERSON to spread its blessing. This particular blessing was in the nature of a vaccine, lowering humans' susceptibility to zots' preternatural powers.

Garrett had always thought that the Saperet was the real reason why humans tolerated—if only barely so—witches and their magick. Saperet-shielded humans could usually withstand a vampire's seductive invitations long enough to avoid becoming a meal and they were also less likely to become therianthropic, or shape-changing, if bitten by a *were* in animal form. The spell even provided protection against elven power. Elves wielded glamour, clouding human minds so to make illusion and reality indistinguishable.

Paul opened the soft leather bag. Right now, the coven would cast lots to determine which of them would serve as the vessel through which I AM manifested. The lots were round, flat, quarter-sized stones painted turquoise except for one that had been painted white. There were twenty-seven stones for the twenty-seven Balthus witches.

"All right," Paul said in a strong, firm voice.

The coven stared at him with tight, tense faces.

"As the bag is passed, reach in and grab a lot with your hands. Don't look at it or let anybody see it. When we all have one, we'll see which one of us I AM has chosen to channel IT during the ceremony. Remember, just because Jim Russell is a man doesn't mean IT won't choose one of us males to be the vessel, so be prepared for that."

Garret watched him reach into the bag and hesitate, his face filled with trepidation. He plunged his hand the rest of the way into the bag. Withdrawing his hand in a fist, he passed the bag to Bertie.

Imitating the elder, Bertie drew a stone from the bag and passed it on. When the bag had made its way back to Paul, it was empty. He took the bag from Sam and looked up. "Okay, who's got the baby?" In the hushed room, everyone looked down and uncurled their fingers. Garrett checked her stone. Her stomach clenched in horror. The stone was white. I AM had chosen her to be the Goddess of the Saperet.

"You the lucky one, Garrett?" Paul called.

With hard effort, she managed to squelch her fear. Tearing her gaze from the stone, she looked up and smiled. "Sure am."

He smiled back. "Congratulations," he said, applauding with the rest of the coven. Then he looked around at the circled witches. "That's it for now but we need to get ready. I've put a sign-up sheet on the bulletin board in the kitchen. We need ten volunteers for two cinquets to do the prep work on Garrett and Jim. My name's on top, so we need nine more for the cinquets. We also need volunteers to prep the Lair. And please sign up to help construct the magick circle, too."

The coven stood, relaxed and talkative now that the lot casting was over. Before rising, Bertie had picked up the leather bag from the floor. Amid much laughter and conversation, the witches crowded around her and dropped in their stones, Garrett included. After putting the pillows away, the coven broke up. Most went for the door to the vestibule but some witches headed for the kitchen.

She walked over to where Paul stood and tugged on his shirtsleeve. He turned. "Garrett."

"Paul, listen. If I'm going to be staying at the Temple for the next few days, I have to go home and take care of a few things. I should be back by oh, noon or so."

"Sure, take your time. It's only eight now. Just don't eat anything."

She affected a stricken look. "I know, I know, gotta fast." Then her face broke into a grin. "Goddess or no Goddess, I'm glad I got a piece of Maira's cake first."

Paul chuckled. "Know what you mean, Sister." He leaned closer. "I had four of 'em at home before I got here and I still had the nerve to eat two more after everybody started arriving. And then Pinkie went and saved the last piece for me, too."

She laughed. "Careful—if Maira finds out you've been eating all her cakes, she'll cut you off."

Paul laughed, too. Then his expression turned serious. "I saw the look on your face when you found out you'd been chosen. You didn't look too happy. Anything wrong?"

She gave him an innocent look. "No, why?"

"Must've been a trick of the light, or maybe I'm just getting old." He gave a little shrug. "Okay. Go do what you need to do. I'll probably still be here when you get back but if I'm not, you have a key, don't you?"

"Sure. Don't we all?" She smiled again then leaned forward and gave him a light peck on the cheek. "I'll see you later." She turned to leave.

"Wait," Paul said.

She turned back. The elder looked uneasy.

He glanced toward the kitchen. "I'm a little concerned about Pinkie. Has she ever talked to you?"

Garrett frowned. "About what?"

"About what should be done about zot/human relations. She thinks zots ought to revolt. Rise up and demand the same legal rights humans have. And we should do it by any means necessary."

"Where did you hear this?"

"I overheard two of our Sisters talking about it."

She shook her head. "No, Pinkie hasn't said anything like that to me."

Paul nodded. "Okay. Sorry to keep you."

"Look, I'm sure she didn't mean anything by it. Rise up? Humans outnumber us by Mother knows how many to one. They'd crush us in a minute."

"I'm sure you're right." But he still looked uneasy.

Garrett smiled and kissed him again, then crossed the main hall and slipped through the swinging door. Heading for the oversized exit doors, her thoughts of Pinkie melted away and her terror at being chosen to lead the ritual returned. A spell like the Saperet could go wrong in any number of ways, with resulting disasters differing only by degree. A worker in her position had to be mentally and emotionally free from outside influences when she focused the magick. If she wasn't, at best the only ones to perish would be the high priest and priestess of the Saperet, the prime players whose bodies and minds magnified the magick being wrought. At worst, the entire coven would perish with them.

Her lips tightened. She couldn't tell anyone what was wrong, or why she was the worst choice to channel Goddess. A knot formed in the pit of her stomach.

The only thing she could do was pray everything would be all right come the fourth of February.

CHAPTER 9

On the evening of February first, Kurt, vampire regent and Master of Seattle, stood across the street from The Grey Whale. He'd never been here but he'd overheard a few of his human servants talking about it.

His gaze roamed the bar. The place was a dive. On the sidewalk level, three rows of eight large, thick glass bricks passed for a window. One of the windows on the third floor had been boarded up. The old building itself seemed to sag. Menacing-looking people milled about, most dressed in jeans, bulky leather jackets, and engineer's boots. Spikes and chains seemed to be de rigueur.

Kurt, wearing a hand-tailored cream silk suit, stuck out like a sore thumb. He sighed and crossed the street.

He had curled his fingers around the door pull when the police arrived. Lights flashing, the two cars screeched to a halt. Four burly men jumped out, Tasers at the ready. They ran toward him. In a moment, he was surrounded by a ring of dark blue and Kevlar.

"Good evening gentlemen," he said in a voice like smooth velvet. "Thank you for coming but it's not necessary. I'll handle this."

"Sir, you can't go in there," said a policeman to his right. "We got a call that there's a huge fight going on. At least six men. You'll get hurt."

A muffled crash came from inside the bar.

Kurt gritted his teeth. "I'll be fine."

"And you are, sir?" said another policeman.

"Masters. Kurt Masters."

The policemen looked startled. They knew who he was—in his human guise, anyway. "All the more reason why you can't go in there, Mr. Masters," the policeman furthest to his left said.

Kurt smiled. "You don't understand. You see, I received a call, too.

My nephew's in there and his parents would be mortified if they learned he was involved in something as common as a bar fight." He looked at each policeman in turn.

"Just point him out to us and we'll get him to you," the policeman on the right said. "No one will know he was there."

Ah, but you will. And that's something I won't tolerate.

The policeman nearest the door reached for the door pull. Still smiling, Kurt waved his hand. The four policemen froze, one with his arm in mid-air. His smiled broadened. "Be right back."

He entered the bar and ducked to avoid a flying chair. It crashed against the wall, leaving a deep dent in the plaster. Straightening, he took in the scene. The place was a shambles. Every mirror on the wall had been smashed. So had many of the bottles behind the bar. Broken furniture littered the floor. In the middle of the mess stood Parker, fending off seven attackers.

One of the men, a recent recipient of Parker's left hook, stumbled past him and fell against the bar. The man shook his head and looked up at him, bleary-eyed. Kurt raised his brow. The man's eyes crossed. Then he slid to the floor, unconscious.

He eyed the insensible man and tightened his lips. Looking up, he chopped the air with his hand and everyone in the bar turned to statues. Except for Parker.

The wolf looked around, blinking. "Hey, wha' happened?"

Feet crunching on broken glass, Kurt walked over until he stood almost nose to nose with the other man. "Come on, Parker. It's time to go home."

Swaying, Parker stared at him with glassy, bright green eyes. "Don' wanna go home. Wanna drink. Wanna fight."

"I think you've done enough drinking and fighting for tonight, hmm?"

"Naw."

Kurt grabbed his arm but the wolf twisted out of his grip. "Said I'm not goin' home."

"Oh, yes you are." In a lightning move, he reached up and gave Parker's temple a light tap. Parker went down. Squatting, Kurt hefted the big werewolf over his shoulder. Swiveling his head, he stared for a second at each combatant, the bartender, the owner, and the knot of women huddled in the corner, erasing Parker from everyone's memories. Then he cloaked the two of them in invisibility and walked out the door.

He stood before the four still-frozen policemen and gave each a look. "You may go in, now. And I and my nephew were never here." He instantly dissolved Parker and himself into mist and floated up. Hovering, he watched the four policemen burst through the door. There was a moment of silence. Then the noise of several people shouting at once wafted from the bar. Satisfied, he flew with his burden across the city to Parker's house.

Kurt slipped them under the front door and materialized in the great room. He slid the wolf's body off his shoulder and dumped him on the floor. Staring at Parker's inert form, he shook his head and left the room.

He entered the study and walked to the desk. Studying the large blotter calendar, he saw Parker had a job tomorrow. He looked at his hand-made Swiss watch. *Today, rather.* "Better go find his car," he muttered. It wouldn't be hard. As many times as he'd seen it, he'd know Parker's battered old hulk anywhere.

Dissolving into mist again, Kurt headed back across town. Reaching his destination, he saw that though the lights were still on, The Grey Whale was quiet.

He floated high over the neighborhood looking for the familiar car and spotted it about three blocks away from the bar. Descending, he made sure no one was watching and materialized beside the driver's side door. He grasped the handle. Looking around a second time, he misted the car and himself and flew away.

Back at Parker's house, he noticed that a number of houses to the left and right had lights on in the windows. Humans were still up, even at this hour. He decided to leave the car in the alley. *Less chance of being seen that way.* Floating to the house's rear, he materialized the car beside the eight-foot privacy fence. Chore completed, he misted and returned to the great room.

The wolf hadn't moved.

Kurt checked his watch again. He needed to get back. His nightclub, Last Chance, would be closing soon and he had to total up the night's receipts. Then he had to go over the architectural plans that had been delivered to Smoot Construction, another of his enterprises, before his meeting with his client at nine a.m.

He knelt beside the passed-out werewolf. Caressing Parker's sweaty brow, he stared at him, his forehead creased with worry. *I was almost too late.* A few minutes later, he let out a sigh and stood. Dissolving into mist, he left the house and headed to Last Chance.

Inside his office beneath the club, the first thing he noticed was the plate of cubed cheese, sliced apples, and a freshly decanted bottle of his favorite merlot someone had placed on his enormous, hand-carved mahogany desk. He smiled. Lily, one of his human servants, was at it again. A warm, motherly type, she'd taken it upon herself to cater to him, especially if it involved food. He'd told her over and again she didn't have to do this and had even punished her several times for her disobedience but she'd been undeterred. "I raised five boys, Master," she'd said, rubbing her chafed wrists after the last time he'd punished her. "I don't care if you're a vampire. I know a man who needs looking after when I see one. And you need looking after." Lily had cocked her head. "Haven't you ever been in love with a good woman, Master? One who took care of you?"

Kurt had smiled but said nothing.

He pulled up his chair, poured a glass of wine, and dug into his snack. Ordinarily, vampires cannot eat or drink because they choke on human food but Kurt was no ordinary vampire. Still, he didn't need to eat anything. Blood was his source of nourishment. He ate because he liked it.

He bit into an apple slice and chewed. There were so many things he could do that other vampires couldn't. Eating was almost the least of them. But that wasn't widely known. Except for his colony, no human or zot in Seattle knew his secrets. He'd made sure of that by laying a psychic block on all of his vampires as well as his human and zot servants from speaking of it, even with each other. Kurt preferred it that way. It made it easier for him to operate behind the scenes, helping him maintain his control over Seattle's zots and providing them with a measure of protection against the city's human horde.

He popped a cheese cube into his mouth. *Except for Parker. He's the only one of my servants who doesn't know. Neither does Garrett.* Of course, they'd find out someday but only after Garrett's plan had succeeded.

Finishing his meal, he pushed the plate away and pulled his computer keyboard toward him. The screen showed an electronic spreadsheet, the night's take. He'd started on the first column when what Lily had said about being in love came back to him. Leaning back in his chair, he pursed his lips and gazed at the ceiling.

In all the centuries I've lived, there have been any number of times I've been in lust and in like. But I've been in love only twice.

Kurt sat forward and reached under the desk. After a quick search, his fingers found a depression in the wood. He pressed it. A small, shallow drawer popped out, just beneath the desktop's lip. Drawing out a square gold locket, he fingered its cover and then opened it. *Only twice,* he thought, gazing at a miniature portrait of a dark-haired woman richly clad in early sixteenth-century attire. *Once when I was alive, with my darling Marguerite.* He stared at her portrait for a few moments longer, then closed his eyes. *And once after I was dead, with—*

He cut off the thought. Closing the locket, he returned it to its tiny prison and pushed the drawer back into place. Pulling the keyboard closer, he took a deep draught of wine and began going over Chance's accounts.

CHAPTER 10

At nine a.m. on February second, a cinquet of five witches arrived to fetch Garrett for the first of her many ritual baths. They discovered her sitting naked in a half lotus on the floor, deep in a meditative trance.

She'd been awake for hours. She'd had too much on her mind the night before and hadn't slept well. At five, she'd gotten out of bed and showered. After that, she'd meditated on the silk prayer rug next to the bed, hoping she could replace at least some of her lost sleep. The last thing she needed was to be incapacitated by fatigue when she channeled Goddess.

The cinquet waited in respectful silence until she came out of her trance. Her gaze settled on Paul. "Good morning, Garrett," he spoke for the other four witches.

Rising from the prayer rug, she stepped over to Paul and kissed him on both cheeks, then did the same to the others. Pinkie presented her with a pair of soft indoor moccasins. Georgia held up a white, silk-lined satin robe and helped her put it on.

Paul smiled. "Ready, my Lady?"

"I'm ready."

The elder turned and with Garrett walking behind, led the group out of the bedroom to the purification room. The room's most prominent feature was a square, white, marble Jacuzzi large enough for two people. One side was set into a wall covered with a slab of marble that rose halfway to the ceiling. Neck-sized indentations had been scooped out along the tub's upper edge. From there, the tub sloped to its bottom, providing back support.

The rest of the wall to which the tub was attached, as well as the room's other three walls, was covered in dense, dark blue carpet. The floor was laid with waterproofed linoleum in the same color. A series of wall sconces provided a dim light.

I love being in here. The room always evoked in her a sense of inviolate safety, a comfort she never felt outside the Temple's walls. *This must be the way a baby feels in its mother's womb.*

When Garrett and the cinquet entered, the tub was already filled with a piping hot solution of water, baking soda, and non-iodized sea salts. Standing at its edge, she slipped off her moccasins while Pinkie helped her out of the robe. She stepped in and sank into the tub's depths until she was immersed. The water's heat and the stinging salt felt good. Already she could sense the solution drawing out toxins lodged in her flesh. Leaning back, she let Pinkie—or maybe it was Georgia or Paul—guide her neck onto a pillow and smiled when whoever it was gave her neck and jaw a final caress. The Jacuzzi's jets were turned on. At its lowest setting, the hum of the whirlpool's motor couldn't be heard. The only sound was the soft, muted whoosh of swirling water. "Sweet dreams," someone whispered into her ear.

Then the cinquet left her alone to soak. After spending a few moments reveling in the luxury of her bath, she thought about Kurt and Parker. She hadn't the slightest idea if or how they might be affected by her channeling Goddess. Her brow creased. *Mother, the three of us might not survive this.*

Questions and worries tumbled about her mind like rolling dice. Assuming the link did expose them to Goddess's power, would it matter if they hadn't been cleansed? For Kurt, it might not matter. Vampires were dead, and dead tissue didn't absorb toxins. His body wouldn't spontaneously combust for that reason. But there were other ways in which Goddess could destroy.

For Parker, having a proper cleansing could be a matter of life or death.

"I should have thought of this before," she whispered. Then she sighed. There was nothing to be done about it now. At least she'd gotten a chance to warn Kurt. *But Parker...*

Her lips tightened. His and her blood connection to Kurt had opened up an emotional and telepathic link between the three of them. She'd tried to talk with Parker telepathically—like she'd done with Kurt—but he'd refused to respond. She'd left a message for him on his answering machine before she left her house for the Temple yesterday. It was risky because one never knew who might be listening to a recorded phone message but there hadn't been an alternative.

Considering the problem, Garrett ran her wet fingers along her hairline. *I'm going to try again. It's too dangerous not to, and I can't afford to lose him.*

Unfocusing her gaze, she pictured Parker in her mind. Projecting her will into the image, she then scanned the ether with her inner ear. There—she had him. The image in her mind's eye disappeared. Though she could no longer see him, she could "hear" his vibration.

Parker? she called. There was no answer.

Park, look. I know you can hear me, so please listen. I'm going to be channeling a very powerful spirit two days from now. When I do, I don't know if the energy will bleed through my astral field into yours. If it does, I don't know what'll happen. Take care, Park. Don't leave yourself open. The night of the fourth, you need to put up your psych shields and keep them there until morning, okay?

Still no answer. Garrett broke the connection and sighed. She'd done what she could and prayed it would be enough. Yawning, she pushed the two men and the rest of her fears from her thoughts. Closing her eyes, she returned to concentrating on the delicious feel of the hot water and stinging salt on her skin. The gentle rocking and soothing gurgles of the Jacuzzi's churning waters carried her toward slumber.

She was fast falling asleep, much faster than she usually did. *Did someone slip...*

Sleep claimed her before she could finish her thought.

Inside her Temple bedroom, Garrett finished the last page of the latest bestselling thriller and put down her electronic reader. She automatically looked up at the clock on the wall. It wasn't there. "Mm," she grunted. She'd forgotten. Not having access to clocks was part of her ritual preparation, meant to give her a sense of being suspended in time. But her internal clock was still working and she knew it was February third. She just wasn't sure if it was day or night.

She decided she needed more juice. The concoction, made with various herbs, cleansed the toxins from inside her body, just as the ritual baths cleansed her outside. Rising from her chair, she grabbed her tall glass and headed for the kitchen. Once there, she opened the refrigerator door, took out the pitcher of juice, and poured her glass full. She'd taken a sip when she heard voices coming from the Lair. Curious, she exited the kitchen, crossed the narrow hallway, and then cracked open the door to the Lair and peeked inside.

About twelve of the coven were milling about the huge room, eating cookies and drinking out of plastic cups. Garrett knew why they were there. The witches were about to build the mandala, or magick circle, for the Saperet ritual. She'd helped build the circle in years past and it had been fun. Disappointment that she couldn't participate this time washed through her. She decided to watch, even though she wasn't supposed to be outside her room.

"I see you, Garrett. Come on out," Paul called.

Feeling a bit sheepish, she pulled the door wide. "How'd you know I was there?"

"I saw the door open."

She smiled. "Guess I'd better get back to my room, then."

Paul shook his head. "It'll be all right. We'll just give you an extra bath." He looked around. "Somebody get Garrett a pillow."

Stepping inside the Lair, she watched Tom walk to a cabinet and pull out a pillow, then head in her direction. He held it out to her. Taking it, she dropped it on the floor and sat, being careful not to spill her juice.

"Let's get started," Paul said in a loud voice.

Seven of the coven gravitated toward a large pile of bundled sticks in the Lair's middle. This was the mandala's mold. While the witches snapped the pieces of wood together, Bertie made a sand paste in huge bowls, each bowl holding a different color. Once she'd finished, Paul helped her ladle the paste into buckets. He gave one to each of several witches, who then filled the mold.

Now they had to wait for the sand to dry. The coven returned to chatting and eating cookies. Garrett noticed Pinkie wandering about, inspecting the mold but not really talking to anyone.

"Pinkie," she called. "Come sit by me."

The young witch walked over and stood before her. "Are you sure? I mean, don't you have to stay——"

"It's all right," she said and patted the floor. "My next bath will take care of any toxins I've absorbed by being here."

"Okay." Pinkie sat and began twining her long curly hair about her fingers.

Garrett smiled. "How's school coming along?"

"I love it. My class on cosmic underwater basket weaving is super."

Garrett burst out laughing. A few witches turned their heads in their direction.

Pinkie giggled. "No, really. It's great. And I've met some fab people—besides the coven, I mean."

"You said you come from a small town of mostly zots. Seattle must feel huge to you. Are you finding it hard to be around so many humans?"

Pinkie shrugged. "Garrett, I don't have a problem with humans. They have a problem with me."

"But——"

"But I think the world's changing," Pinkie talked over her. "Pretty soon, humans will stop thinking of us as monsters and start treating us like we really are—people."

Garrett recalled her and Paul's conversation about Pinkie's radical notions. Dismissing it, she gave a little shrug. "Maybe."

"Sand's dry," Bertie announced.

Pinkie frowned. "How will they get the mold off the floor without messing up the circle?"

"Watch."

While the rest of the coven moved away from the mandala, four witches stood together on the circle's far side, holding hands. Garrett knew they were linking energies. A minute passed. Then two minutes. "Rise," they finally intoned.

The mold lifted from the floor and hovered for about ten seconds. Then it began to float toward the far side of the Lair, where it finally settled with a soft ker-plop. Left behind was a blue circle, thirty feet in diameter. Inside, the five points of a pentagram, its arms alternating red and yellow, reached the circle's edge. The pentagon in the star's center was white.

She gave Pinkie a sideways look. "What'd you think?"

The younger witch stared at the mandala with wide eyes. "That was…awesome."

"It was, wasn't it?"

"Okay, everybody," Paul called. "Thanks for helping out today. Be here tomorrow by five—we consecrate the circle at six."

"That's my cue," Garrett said, rising from the floor with empty glass in hand. "Better get back to my room."

Pinkie stood, too. "I'll grab the pillow." She paused. "Guess the next time I see you will be after the Saperet."

"Well, actually you'll see me—"

Pinkie rolled her eyes. "You know what I mean."

Garrett chuckled. "Yes. I'll see you then." She turned and headed for the kitchen. Fasting made her thirsty and she wanted another glass of juice. After getting her drink, she walked along the hallway, thinking about what Pinkie had said about humans treating zots as people.

She paused before the door to her bedroom. "Don't worry Pinkie. It'll happen. Soon." Her lips stretched into a small smile. Opening the door, she stepped inside.

CHAPTER 11

That evening, the half-empty tumbler of Jack Daniel's had just touched Parker's lips when the doorbell rang. Letting out a heavy sigh, he set the glass on the desk. He rose to his feet and looked down, staring at the golden brown liquor. Then he snatched up the tumbler, drained it, and wiped his mouth on the sleeve of his ratty green sweater. He glanced at the wall clock. Five minutes to eight p.m. He sighed again and left his study.

Amidst the sounds of low laughter and quiet conversation, Parker waded through forty-nine of the fifty-six members of his wolfpack sitting on the floor in his great room. They moved out of his way as best they could but even so, he couldn't help kicking three or four of them as he passed by. He didn't apologize. As alpha, he didn't have to. Besides, he didn't want to. He didn't want them here. He wanted to be alone.

From the corner of his eye, he spotted Tasha, one of the pack's Fourth-ranked werewolves, emerging from the kitchen. He turned his head. "I'll get it, Tash. Go find someplace to sit. It's almost time to start."

The bell rang again just as he reached the door. Scowling, he opened it to see Tran Nguyen standing on the porch. Tran was the pack's beta wolf, second only to Parker in power and authority over the pack. "'Bout time," Tran growled. "My butt's freezing out here." He stepped over the threshold.

"Too bad," Parker growled back.

Tran looked surprised. "Hey, dude, lighten up. I was just kidding."

Parker didn't reply. He took Tran's coat and threw it on top of the large pile of outerwear lying on the gray carpet. Tran leaned forward and gave Parker's lips a light stroke with his tongue, the lupine gesture of greeting and submission. After pulling away, Tran stared at him with an unreadable expression. "Good to see you, Alpha."

"Yeah, good to see you too, Tran. Beer and munchies are in the kitchen."

"Whatcha got?"

"The usual. Meatballs, beef cubes, cocktail ribs, stuff like that."

"Done rare, I hope?"

"Took the horns off and wiped the ass. What'd you expect?"

Tran raised his brow. "My, we're in a good mood tonight, aren't we?"

Parker ignored him. "You want something warmer than beer, there're a couple of bottles of Jack behind the bar."

"Ah, good old Jack. Always there when you need him." Tran turned and headed deeper into the great room, stopping every now and then to greet his packmates.

Eyes narrowed, Parker watched Tran's retreating back. He was pretty sure that had been a jab but with Tran, it was often hard to tell.

He swept his gaze over the forty-nine wolves present. The seven that were missing had been excused from this meeting. Two were the mothers of the four cubs in his pack, too young to attend, and the seventh was away from home. For a moment, he was tempted to order everybody out of his house. But he couldn't blow this off any longer. The moon was already past the first quarter. Tonight's meeting should have been held over a week ago, at the new moon. With the full moon less than a week away, rescheduling now would put many of his pack in danger of being outed to the police.

Wading through his wolves a second time, Parker almost planted his bare foot into a bowl of bloody beef cubes that had been placed on the floor. He glared at Donny, the werewolf who'd been eating from it, and bared his teeth at him. Paling, Donny picked up the bowl and tucked it into his lap.

Reaching the stairs, he climbed the first four and sat. Tran sat on the stair below him and Rhonda, the pack's secretary, sat below Tran, her laptop at the ready. From his elevated position, he could see everyone. Some of his wolves looked indifferent. Others looked skeptical. A few looked downright hostile.

He ignored all of it. "Let's get this over with. First up—who's going out of town?"

For the next two and a half hours, Parker slogged through the mundane administrative chores of running a wolfpack. In urban areas like Seattle, the alpha wolf did much more than lead the hunt at the full moon. He assigned specific duties, usually on a rotating basis, like serving as emergency contacts for those who ran into trouble, cub-sitters, or drivers to take wolves without transportation to the pack's hunting grounds. He mediated disputes not serious enough to merit resolution by combat and meted out punishment for pack rule infractions. The penalty for trespassing on another pack's territory was death, so he liaised with the alphas of foreign territories to negotiate visitation rights. Modern pack life was far different than it had been in the past.

Parker finished conferring with Rhonda and looked up. "Okay. Last item. The mayoral election was last November but Balthus Coven hasn't yet cast its spell. Humans are antsy. I've solid information that at least sixty people were outed to the police last month and after running the genetic screening test, seven turned out to be zots. We—"

The telephone rang. He frowned. "Hang on, everybody. I'll be right back." He would have let his answering machine take the call but he'd turned it off this afternoon. Standing, he looked around and decided to take it in his bedroom rather than wade through the pack a third time to get to the kitchen.

He reached the telephone on his nightstand just after the fifth ring and picked up the handset. "Berenson." He listened for a few minutes. His throat tightened. "Thank you," he whispered and returned the receiver to its cradle. Parker stared at the window without seeing it. Then he took a deep breath, let it out, and left his bedroom. Reaching the staircase, he walked down a few steps and resumed his seat.

"That was Ferdinand Michaels, alpha of the Tacoma pack," he said, looking at his feet. "They—the police—picked up Jaime five minutes ago." Jaime was the seventh wolf he'd excused from tonight's meeting.

The pack sat in stunned silence. "No," a wail rose to his right. "Jaimeeee—oh God, noooo!" He looked over, knowing who had screamed. It had been Jaime's mother. Tears streamed down her cheeks.

"Nora," he said, trying to stem his own tears, "I'm sorry. I tried—"

"And just how hard did you try, Alpha?" Nora's wolf roared. "Where were you when my Jaime needed you? Where are you when any of us need you?" A Fifth, Nora didn't have the control over her *were* that a wolf like Parker had. She went into a forced morph. Eyes glowing her wolf's yellow, Nora's red and black checked-flannel shirt and jeans ripped apart, exposing her shaggy, dark-brown pelt. Her nose and jaws lengthened into a snout. A minute later she'd become a four-legged wolf, almost five feet tall at the shoulder.

Parker sat stone-still, fighting to hold back his own wolf. As alpha, he could have torn out Nora's throat for such disrespect. But his human side understood the mother's rage and grief and that helped him maintain his human form. It also helped that deep inside him, he wondered if she might be right.

After regaining full control over his body, he looked at the distraught she-wolf without expression. "Nora, as alpha of this pack, I don't have to justify myself to you, or to anyone else. But I tried my level best to save Jaime's life. Yes, I failed. But I did try. And you know it."

Nora howled. The werewolves sitting closest crowded around her, stroking her pelt, kissing away her wolf tears and licking her slavering jaws, comforting her. He watched for a few minutes. "Jill," he called after Nora had calmed a little. Jill turned a tear-stained human face toward him, her arms entwined around Nora's shaggy neck. "Take Nora to the mud-room off the kitchen. There's a chest back there with some extra clothes in it."

Jill stood. "Come on, Nora," she said, her voice soft. She tugged on the she-wolf's brown fur. "Come with me, cubby." Nora rose with effort, nearly dwarfing Jill's human form. The two disappeared into the kitchen.

No one spoke for a long while. "So when's Balthus planning on doing the spell?" Sheldon broke the silence. "Alpha, I've been on sick leave from work for going on three days and my human boss is getting suspicious."

He nodded. "I understand, Sheldon. I have it on good authority that it'll happen tomorrow, February fourth."

"Your authority is our mage freyja, I suppose," Dan, a First-ranked werewolf said. His tone dripped with sarcasm. "By the way, where is our freyja? Wouldn't the vampire Master let her come out tonight?" He smirked. "And, oh—if I might ask—when are you going to choose another freyja? A real freyja, I mean."

Parker leapt. A second later, he stood in front of Dan, holding the other wolf by the throat with one taloned paw. Lines of blood dripped down Dan's neck. "No, you may not ask," he growled, his wolf-green eyes glowing like hot coals. "Garrett's whereabouts is none of your business. And she is my freyja until I say she isn't. Do not disrespect her again."

He released the other man's neck. Dan fell back a step and then sat on the gray carpet, his puncture wounds already healing. Parker stood over him, licking Dan's blood from his claws. "Don't worry, Dan. I'll choose a new freyja," he said in a human voice, "and when I do, I'll make sure you're the last to know."

Dan said nothing. Bloody but obviously unbowed, he glared at the alpha wolf with undisguised contempt.

Morphing his wolf's paw into his human hand, Parker started back across the room.

"So what do you want us to do right now?" Tran said after he'd returned to his seat.

"Nothing that we're not doing already. But from now until February fifth, I'm suspending the no-contact rule for Fourth-ranks on down. If you hear or see anything unusual—anything at all—report it to me or Tran." He looked around. "That's it. Anybody got anything else?"

"Yeah," a voice piped up from the back. It was Gerald. "Why do we have to put up with this human crap, anyway? We're just as good—no, we're better than they are. Why don't we just—"

"Gerald. Who have you been talking to?" Parker looked at the young scrum werewolf through narrowed eyes. He'd heard this sort of thing before. It was idle talk—he'd certainly done his share of it over the years—but someone with Gerald's background and emotional problems might think differently.

Gerald ducked his head. "Uh, nobody."

"Nobody who?"

"Um, a girl I know."

"What's her name? Where'd you meet her?"

Gerald didn't answer at first. "Her name's…Pinkie. I met her at the university. At the coffee shop where you got me that job."

Parker tightened his lips, wondering if that silly name could possibly be real. He'd never known Gerald to lie but there was always a first time. He decided to let it ride. "Uh-huh. And Pinkie—she's the one who told you this?"

Gerald nodded.

Parker didn't say anything for a minute. "Gerald, is Pinkie zot?"

Now Gerald looked frightened. "Yes. I mean, no. I mean, she might be. I don't know."

"Does she know you're a werewolf?"

Gerald's face reddened. "I'm not a werewolf," he shouted. "I'm a piece-of-shit scrum!"

Parker's look softened. "No, Gerald," he said, bothered that his pointed questions had crumbled the young man's rare show of self-esteem. "You're scrum, but you're not a piece of shit. You're one of us. Right?" He looked around at his pack. Most faces wore concerned looks but a few—including Dan—sneered. He raised his brow and the sneering looks disappeared. "Right?"

"Right," about half of the pack chorused, while others bobbed their heads. Dan, he noticed, stared at the ceiling.

He turned. "Gerald, you say you don't know if Pinkie's zot. It's important to know these things. If she's human, she might be a zymp but she also might be a lorelei. Do you understand? If Pinkie's a lorelei, then we're all in danger."

Gerald hung his head.

"I don't want you talking with her anymore, Gerald." Parker's gentle tone had become stern. "If she comes into the shop, be polite, but otherwise don't talk to her. Find some other work to do, okay?"

"Yes, Alpha."

"All right." He closed his eyes. He was trying to do his best by Gerald but he often wondered if the kid would ever overcome the trauma of his horribly abusive childhood. He'd taught him to read and write a few years ago and it seemed to have helped. When Gerald had turned eighteen, he'd thought maybe the scrum's having a job might help even more. Now he wondered if the job at the university's zymp-run coffee shop had been such a great idea after all.

Grocery store might've been better. I'll look into that later.

Parker let out a minute sigh and pinched the bridge of his nose with his thumb and forefinger. After Nora, Dan, and Gerald, he'd had enough. "Okay, everybody. We're done. You can go. G'night, and stay human." Without another word, he descended the stairs and headed for his study—and his bottle of Jack.

Inside, he didn't bother turning on the lamp. The waxing moon gave plenty of light. He went to his desk, filled his tumbler, and crossed the study to the window. Had he really done his best to save Jaime?

Parker had been on his way to a job when Jaime had called his cell, saying he'd been outed. After hanging up, he'd handled his client, saying he'd had a family crisis. Hanging an illegal U-turn, he'd rushed over to Seattle's north side to pick up Jaime. He'd thought about hiding Jaime in his house but had decided the Third-ranked werewolf would be better off out of the city. He'd called Ferdinand while they were on their way to Tacoma, not knowing whether the old alpha would agree to hide Jaime on his territory. Ferdinand had instructed him to take Jaime to a safe house, go home, and wait for his call. Parker had done just that. Not forty minutes ago, Ferdinand had called to say Jaime had been picked up. What had happened in the hours between his dropping Jaime off and Ferdi's call?

An alpha is always willing to die for the sake of his pack. That was what Willie Becker, alpha of the wolfpack he'd belonged to back in Iowa, had told him years ago. He looked down into his glass. If the police had traced Jaime and him here, they'd both be dead right now. Was that why he decided to take Jaime to Tacoma instead of hiding him in his house—because he hadn't been willing to die for his packmate?

He thought about Gerald's outburst. In some ways, the scrum reminded him of Frank Suggs, his werepanther friend who'd been murdered when they were fifteen. Frank hadn't been the brightest bulb in the box but Parker knew his buddy had been a lot smarter than he let on. He understood why. It had made things easier. Like Sheldon, the wolf on sick leave, Frank had been one of those *weres* who, when in human form, didn't look quite human. Playing dumb had been a disguise to make everyone think he was just another inbred hick from the backwoods. It had worked, too—until it didn't.

Parker wondered if the same might be true about Gerald. It had been over three years since he'd found him living in a dumpster on Seattle's east side. He wouldn't expect Gerald to be completely normal—not now or ever—but was the kid as much of an emotional wreck as he seemed to be? Or, like Frank, was he just playing dumb?

The sound of approaching footsteps made him turn. Tran stood in the doorway. "I need to talk to you."

He took a gulp of whiskey. "So talk."

"It's about Dan," Tran said in a low voice. "Park, that dude's gonna challenge you someday."

Parker grunted. "Yeah. I know."

Neither wolf said anything for a few moments.

"Think you can beat him?" Tran broke the silence.

"I can."

"Even without torching him?"

He didn't answer. Pyrokinesis in *weres* was rare, but he didn't flaunt his ability. It was too dangerous. Werewolves were jealous of pack rankings, and among the highest-ranked wolves, any unusual advantage was perceived as a threat. A wolf with Parker's talent was usually challenged to a death-match and by enough numbers to guarantee defeat. Of his pack, only Tran and Garrett knew about his pyrokinetic gift.

"I can take him, Tran," he finally said. "Even without the fire."

"But—"

"I can take him, Tran."

Tran bit his lip. "Okay. But Dan's just using Garrett as an excuse, you know. He wants to be alpha. The pack's divided into God-knows-how-many factions as it is over her being freyja but if you don't choose, it'll just bring more of them over to his side."

He shook his head. "I hear you, Tran, but it's too soon. Divided or not, the pack—"

"Park," Tran talked over him. "Are you sure this is about the pack?" He paused a beat. "Or is it about you?" Without waiting for a reply, he turned and left the study.

He heard the soft squish of Tran's shoes on the carpet and the soft thumps when he'd reached the tiled foyer. The front door opened and shut. His wolf-hearing didn't pick up any other sounds of movement. Good—everybody had gone. He was alone again.

Parker stood at the window for a long time. He thought about what Tran had said about Dan and about his having to choose a new freyja. Tran was right on both counts but right now Parker wasn't sure what he would do about it. Or if he even wanted to do something about it.

Fuck it. I'll think about it tomorrow.

He finished the last of his drink, set the glass on the desk, and went to bed.

CHAPTER 12

On February fourth, at the same time Parker was speeding homeward after his unexpected rendezvous at Kurt's Last Chance nightclub, the cinquet tending Garrett gave the high priestess of the Saperet her final ablutions.

It was a quarter past eight in the evening. After bathing her, the witches laid her upon a large, generously padded table and began anointing her with oils, herbal tinctures of marapuama and morning glory that filled her with hot, raw desire. Other oils expanded her mind, giving her a peculiar feeling of being inside and outside her body at once, blending her senses until she could no longer tell one from the other. Like a sensory symphony, she could see/hear/feel/smell/and taste the warm-colored sweetness of the ritual purification room and the Gregorian-like chanting in the main hall.

A mask was placed over her face, and then she became aware of her body rising from the table. The telekinetic energy tickled her fevered skin, making her moan in ecstasy. The cinquet floated her out of the purification room. Once in the corridor, they turned and headed toward the Lair.

Inside the huge room, twenty-one masked and barefoot witches wearing hooded robes slowly shuffled counterclockwise around the recently consecrated mandala. Glowing like the embers of a dying fire, the circle pulsed as if breathing, slow and deep. The rest of the Lair had been transformed. Forty-eight large beeswax candles illuminated the ritual space. Snug in heavy, antiqued silver holders on the floor, their golden light imparted a cozy atmosphere to the hall, masking the winter cold and darkness outside. At the mandala's heart lay the Saperet altar, a round pillow seven feet wide and covered in black satin. At its easternmost arc, two more large candles stood inches away from the black material. The candlelight's reflection shimmered in the heavy, shiny fabric.

Mayor Russell lay sprawled across the altar, his face covered by an eyeless, dark silver mask. His skin, sweaty and slick with the same libidinous and hallucinogenic oils used on Garrett, had flushed a deep red. Spasms coursed through his ample body, the movement rubbing the tip of his veined and purple erection against his protruding stomach. With each twitch, soft groans issued from behind the mask.

"Aummm-ni-mah-ter-ah, aummm-ni-mah-ter-ah," the witches sang while they danced. Their hypnotic, singsong chanting made the air tremble like heat waves rising from concrete baked by the sun.

The cinquet, with Garrett floating in their midst, entered the Lair. The rest of the coven stopped dancing around the glowing circle. They stood, chanting and swaying, while the solemn procession crossed the main hall.

A witch wearing a red robe, not one of Garret's cinquet, stepped to the blue line's edge and pulled a handmade split-blade athame, or ritual knife, from the folds of the garment. Tip pointed toward the floor, Red Robe symbolically cut an opening in the circle by slashing the athame across the sand. One by one, the witches outside the circle stepped through the doorway and took up positions as before. Finally, Garrett and her cinquet crossed the glowing blue line. While the six witches proceeded to the altar, Red Robe slashed the circle closed.

"Aumm-nimah-ter-ah, aumm-nimah-ter-ah, aumm-nimah- ter-ah..." the witches chanted faster.

After she'd crossed the circle, Garrett's personality was immediately swept into the embrace of Goddess and merged with Her until she and Goddess became One. For one ecstatic moment, she was no longer Garrett Larkin but Goddess herself, come across the cosmic worlds yet never having left this one to inhabit the fleshly Temple offered for Her use.

An instant eternity later, she felt removed from Goddess's embrace. Now there were two personalities inside her. Goddess, unfathomable and unknowable, dominated her body and most of her mind. Garrett Larkin was merely a conscious veneer, watching the proceedings as if she were a spectator at a parade.

Although her synesthesia had allowed her to see after being masked, once she was inside the mandala, her vision improved exponentially. With Goddess's power flowing through her, Garrett saw everything. She could see through the witches' robes, through to their naked skin underneath, through to their internal organs, and all the way into their souls.

A light tug on her astral hand caught her attention. Garrett turned. Through Her eyes, she and Goddess watched Russell writhing and groaning on the black pillow. A long while later, She deemed the mayor to be ready for Her, and Garrett watched herself kneel on the pillow.

Starting at his chest, Goddess began stroking his hot and fevered skin. Pictographs appeared in the wake of Her fingers, etched deeply into Russell's flesh as if with a razor. Rich, dark red blood welled in each slice and spilled under Her caresses. Garrett watched Her write on the Mayor as if he were a blank slate, memorializing Her covenant with the humans who had asked for Her blessing and protection from preternatural power. Each gentle touch of Her fingers elicited grunts and moans of what Garrett knew were moments of unbearable pleasure and pain.

When finished, her Goddess-controlled body straddled Russell's thighs and took his trembling cock in both hands. Wrapping her fingers around it, she held it against her abdomen. In moments, thick rivulets of blood began leaking through her clasped fingers.

Russell let out a thin scream. Garrett let go. Where she'd touched him, eight bleeding pictographs spiraled around the shaft of his erection. Rising to her knees, she took his blood-slicked penis in her left hand and positioned its tip at her opening. Then she lowered herself until she was sitting on the mayor's hips. Rocking slowly, she felt sparkling tingles radiating through her groin. The slickness and smell of the mayor's blood— the life energy that Goddess needed to shape the spell—was intoxicating.

As Goddess gave Jim Russell the fucking of his life, Garrett's astral body floated in and out of the magick being worked, getting lost in the sensations, smells, and sights of the ritual and the power in the room. Her synesthetic state made her dizzy. She felt/smelled/saw/tasted and heard the air pressure inside the circle growing denser, as was the pressure inside her head and deep within her womb.

Blood, the Mother's milk that nourished the embryonic spell, began leaking profusely from her nipples. It ran down her torso and drenched through her mons to mix with the blood that had begun to flow from her womb for the same purpose. As her and Russell's blood blended, the embryonic spell grew into a fetal one. The mayor thrashed on the pillow, bellowing. Garrett felt his pleasure and his pain, and Goddess smiled.

A moment or three later, Garrett knew something was wrong. When she'd entered the circle, she'd seen the tumor nestled in Russell's brain like a squat, malignant evil. She could feel his life slipping away. His thrashing had become a combination of ecstasy and death throes. Now his screaming was growing weaker. It frightened her. She couldn't heal him right now, not while channeling Goddess. Whether She saved the mayor's life was not up to her.

A sudden wave of ecstasy swept away her fear. She rode the tide, higher and higher when a bolt of pure rage tore through her consciousness. The conflicting energies of hate and love collided and like matter and anti-matter, annihilated each other in a blinding flash.

The collision set her ablaze. Her mind was burning, as were her internal organs. She screamed. In minutes, the smell of her charring innards filled her nostrils. She would become a smoking, blackened husk and later still, a pile of ashes.

The mage and the mayor would die together.

No! Mother, it can't end this way. Please!

Goddess answered her plea. Love is always stronger than hate, and Her love for Garrett, Russell, and all that there is and will ever be acted like an umbrella, shunting the hateful rage aside and channeling it into the sacred pentagram where it then sluiced into the ether. As the rage dissipated, Garrett saw and felt her and the mayor's spirits being hauled from the brink of death.

Goddess possessed both bodies now. Garrett and Russell, imbued with Her essence and strength, went at each other with renewed passion, expressing Her joy at the lives She had saved and the new life She was creating.

Garrett climaxed again and again, while the mayor howled and bucked beneath her. There came another blinding flash. Unlike the other, this one contained no heat.

It was Goddess's blessing, being born.

While Garrett and the mayor screwed each other into oblivion, Goddess sent Her progeny out into the circle, past it, and into the Lair. Flying through the Temple walls, the protective blessing spread over Seattle, where it settled like a thick, invisible fog.

Goddess smiled again.

CHAPTER 13

Russell and Garrett finally lay still.

Little by little, she felt Goddess retreat from her mind and body, leaving behind an emptiness that was a combination of physical exhaustion and sadness at being only Garrett Larkin again. Just before Goddess left completely, She spoke in a whispering echo Garrett knew only she could hear.

IT IS A MOST DANGEROUS GAME YOU PLAY, DAUGHTER. HAVE A CARE—IT IS NOT ONE YOU WANT TO LOSE.

Then She was gone.

Garrett was too spent to react to Goddess's warning. Still straddling the mayor, she managed to rise to her knees. Doing so took all the physical strength she had left. Instead of gracefully climbing down from her mount, she merely fell onto the pillow.

Red Robe, the witch who had opened the magick circle, stepped forward. "The Goddess has given Her promise," he told Russell in a deep, otherworldly voice. "It has been written upon your body and it has been written upon your soul. The blood and seed you have sacrificed tonight have given life to the blessing She has granted. You and yours are now under Her protection for as long as you shall rule."

Red Robe paused. "Go now, and be at peace. Blessed be."

"Blessed be," the coven echoed as one.

All of the candles flared at the same time. For a moment, fifty suns blazed forth, bathing the lair in a dazzling white light.

The mandala's light erupted, too. Throwing its colors toward the ceiling, it became a ring of garishly stained fire silhouetting everyone inside the circle.

Then the Lair went black.

CHAPTER 14

The fifty candles relit themselves. Guttering at first, each flame grew stronger, driving away the room's utter darkness like the dawning of a new day.

The coven began to hum a slow, simple tune of five notes— da-dah-da-da-dah—a song more ancient than the Saperet itself. The mandala no longer glowed. Its magick spent, the vibrant colored sands had paled into ghost-like pastels. As the witches hummed, the two cinquets symbolically cut two doorways in the tired blue line on opposite sides of the mandala. They floated Garrett and the mayor out of the circle, and into the purification rooms where their wounds would be soothed and healed.

Mayor James C. Russell would carry the scars of Goddess's covenant on his body for the rest of his life. A personal badge of honor, they marked him as a man of courage willing to sacrifice himself for humanity's greater good.

After her cinquet had helped her into the Jacuzzi, she asked Sam to find out from the other cinquet whether the politician still had a brain tumor. Sam's expression turned horrified. "Russell has a brain tumor?"

"Yeah," she said, her voice weak. "I first saw it after I floated into the circle. Look on the right. It's pretty big—I'd say he has a couple of months at most."

"Lord and Lady," Paul said. "It's a wonder the spell didn't kill him."

Sam scurried out of the purification room. He was back in six minutes. "Robert and Dana did a laying on of hands," he reported. "The tumor's gone."

Garrett smiled a little at Paul's heavy sigh of relief. The cinquet washed hers and the mayor's dried blood from her body. After her bath, they anointed her again with aromatic oils—curative rather than libidinous this time. Then they brought her to the bedroom and made her comfortable. Letting her head sink into the pillows, she and Paul discussed the Saparet ritual. She didn't tell him about her near-death experience.

In less than two hours, every cut and bruise on and inside Garrett's body had healed. It took another hour before she'd recovered enough to stand without getting too dizzy. Rising from the bed, she began to dress. Pulling her knee-high black leather boots over her woolen tights, she could feel Paul's eyes watching her.

From the corner of her eye, she saw his concerned expression. "You sure you want to go so soon? I know how hard the Saperet is on a body. Maybe you oughta stay here for the night."

Garrett waved the suggestion away. "I'll be okay," she assured and donned her black cape. "Besides, I'd really like to sleep in my own bed tonight." Not wanting any more conversation, she pecked him on both cheeks and left the Temple.

Four minutes later she was in her maroon Altima, driving to Pioneer Square. All she wanted to do was go home and crash for a week but she had other urgent business to attend to first. Her head swiveled left and right. It was after midnight and despite the late hour and the intense cold, people seemed to be everywhere on the streets—young singles rushing to and fro and older couples walking serenely, holding hands. Entire families were out plying the sidewalks. Some pushed strollers carrying sleepy infants bundled against the raw weather.

In contrast to the anxiety-ridden air of five days ago, the atmosphere was festive, almost giddy. All around, she saw smiling faces and heard gay laughter through her car's closed windows. She knew why. The humans were feeling Goddess's blessing. Though they hadn't known of the Saperet's casting tonight, they'd intuited Her nurturing warmth and felt Her promise of safety from those they feared.

From experience, Garrett knew the party mood would last about a week. Then it would be back to the usual tension, just not as much.

She yawned and wondered how many of the people on the streets were zots. "The ones not laughing," she muttered. That reminded her of what Goddess had said earlier. A pained look crossed her face. "I know, Mother," she said in a low voice to the stop sign in front of her. "I know how dangerous the game is and how it could destroy us all. But if we win..." She shook her head. "Mother, if we win the game, it will have been worth it, whatever the final cost. Even You must see that."

"Beep-beep! Be-e-e-p!"

She jumped. Behind her was a white Honda and its frowning driver. She waved her apology and stepped on the accelerator. As she crossed the intersection, her lips tightened. *And if I lose the game, then at least I'd have tried.*

None of the coven knew about her blood connection to the vampire Master—or that she was freyja of the werewolf pack, for that matter. If any of them discovered these connections, they would be duty-bound to give her over to the human authorities and she'd be summarily executed.

That had been part of the deal witches cut with humans over a millennium ago. Humans agreed to stop killing witches simply because they were zots and in return, witches would protect humans from other zots. Part of the deal was the uncompromising stipulation that the life of any magick worker in an alliance with any zot other than a fellow witch was forfeit, even if the zot in question happened to be a blood relation. The last execution of a witch for a forbidden alliance had occurred in Pennsylvania only five years ago. He and his rat-woman partner had been burned at the stake.

The light at the next intersection turned red just before she reached it. "And me, I'm not just tied to one zot, but two," she whispered.

Garrett had plotted her strategy with care, chasing down every thread of possibility she could think of and spinning it out until she'd reached its end. True, her relationships with Kurt and Parker meant all three—if they were discovered and captured—were liable to be executed. But even if only one of them was caught, that death would most likely lead to an all-out war between the witches and the rest of the zots. The vampire colony and the pack would go to war with the coven. The remaining zots would side with the undead and the werewolves.

The coven wouldn't fight alone, though. They'd call up an army of demons to fight with them and these would bring legions of their own. Humans, caught in the crossfire, would respond to the zot war with their own weapons of mass destruction.

Seattle would be leveled. And there was always the possibility the war would spread beyond Seattle. She pursed her lips. The prospect of civil war was certainly worrisome but she also thought it unlikely. *No. No war. All of us—zots and humans— have way too much to lose.*

Garrett thought about what had happened during the Saperet. She didn't have to guess where that bolt of inhuman rage had come from.

The vampire must have been playing head games with the wolf again.

"You sonofabitch," she muttered, speaking about both Parker and Kurt. The more she thought about how close to death she'd come tonight, the angrier she became. In a minute, she was too mad to be tired.

Garrett pulled up next to the service alley that would take her to the back door of Last Chance. Stopping her car hard by the alley's entrance, she noticed the red and white sign anchored to a metal pole.

NO PARKING ANY TIME—LOADING ZONE.

She snorted and parked. *Screw it. I'm not going to be here that long.* Slipping between the buildings, her boot heels clicked purposefully against the bricks, echoing off the building walls. By the time she reached the club's back door, she was ready to ream the vampire a new asshole.

Garrett searched for the loose brick near the door's jamb and yanked it out. She pressed the hard plastic button it had hidden. Then she shoved the brick back into the wall. When the lock released, she threw the door wide and headed for Kurt's private office. She burst inside without knocking.

Kurt lay naked on a padded, foldaway table where a young female vampire in the same attire was giving him a massage. The girl's head snapped up when the door flew open. Kurt didn't move, except to roll his head in Garrett's direction and open his blue eyes.

The Master's stare was cold enough to freeze blood.

The masseuse looked to be about fourteen years old but Garrett knew for a fact the child-woman was nearing the half-century mark. "Get out," she said through her teeth.

The young middle-aged vampire resembled a deer caught in headlights. She quickly donned a loose white robe and scuttled from the office.

Kurt had turned over onto his side. Supporting his head on one hand, he regarded the two women with an insouciant smile. Once the girl had gone, his brow darkened. "Do I have to teach you how to properly enter your Master's rooms, servant? And who are you to give orders to what is mine?" he said, his voice sounding low and dangerous.

Before Garrett could reply, his face brightened. "Ah, well. Just because you choose to be rude does not mean that I must be too, hmm?" Hopping off the table, he sauntered over and tried to worm his right hand inside her cape while his left snaked around her shoulders and pulled her closer.

She pushed him away. "Get it through your pretty head, vampire— I'm not your damned servant. And I sure as hell didn't come over here tonight to fuck you."

A hurt look crossed Kurt's face. She knew it was feigned. "No?" he pouted. Before she could stop him, his hands found their way inside her cape again and slipped up under her gray wool tunic. "Then why ever are you here?" he whispered into her hair while one hand roamed her spine. The other grabbed a handful of her ass and squeezed.

Garrett pushed him away a second time. "Listen. You and your bullshit with Parker nearly got me killed tonight. What did you think you were doing?" She narrowed her eyes. "If you knew you weren't going to protect me, couldn't you have just left the wolf alone for one mother-damned night, Kurt?"

The amused look in Kurt's eyes melted into annoyance. Instead of answering, he strode over to a liquor cabinet. In the soft light, she noticed the sheen on his back from the massage oils. When he turned, he held an exquisite cut-crystal decanter and a glass. His annoyed look was gone. "Would you care for some wine, Garrett?"

She glared at him. "Stop trying to change the subject."

Pouring himself a glass, Kurt sighed and turned back to the wall. His struggle to maintain his gracious demeanor was obvious. "And what subject is that, dear Garrett?" he seemed to ask the deep red, velvet-flocked wallpaper. "What on earth are we talking about, hmm?" His tone was still pleasant, but with a sharp edge.

"You know exactly what we're talking about."

He turned to her but said nothing.

Garrett threw up her hands and began to pace. "Kurt, I told you a week ago the coven was casting the Saperet tonight, and three days ago I told you I'd been chosen to channel Goddess. I'm sitting on the mayor's cock, almost through with the ritual, when this—this blaze of hate comes out of nowhere. Nobody but you or Parker could have done that to me, and I know it wasn't you."

She whirled before he could reply. "Motherdammit, I almost died back there, Kurt. You were supposed to shield me from Park's emotions, but no—you left me completely open to him. If I still hadn't been channeling Goddess, I would've been crisped."

He shrugged. "But your Goddess saved you." His light tone suggested that since She had, there wasn't anything for Garrett to be so upset about.

Hearing it, her fury skyrocketed. "Yeah, She did. No thanks to you!"

The look of equanimity fled from his face. Gripping his wine goblet, he said icily, "Garrett, please calm yourself. There is no need to shout. I can hear you quite well. And keep a civil tongue in your head, servant."

"Fuck you!"

In a split second, Kurt was standing less than an inch away from her. She never saw him move, but she'd long gotten used to his undead way of transporting himself. He grabbed her hair, yanked her head back, and savaged her mouth. After he pulled away, she stared into his fiery blue eyes. "Yes, you will fuck me, my witch," he said through his teeth, "but I'm no longer in the mood." Releasing her with a little shove, he took a step backward.

"Is sex all you ever think about?" When Kurt didn't answer, she threw up her hands a second time and walked away, trying to ignore the heat that had flared in her face and crotch from the vampire's kiss. That she'd reacted with such passion angered her even more.

Once she was sure her face wouldn't give her away, Garrett spun around. "Listen, Kurt. We agreed that I'd bring you the wolf, and I did. I spelled him to fall in love with me. I convinced him to take on Darrylon Slade in a death match so he could become Alpha." She pointed at him. "You were supposed to get him to join us. You said it'd be easy since the alpha of the wolf pack is your *were* servant and he'd do whatever you told him to do. Just in case you've forgotten, Kurt, let me remind you—a tryst needs three. Three! So where is he?"

Kurt looked furious. "Stop it, Garrett. You know as well as I do Parker isn't the docile little lapdog we thought he was." He tossed his head. "Yes, I could compel him to join us but you said that wouldn't work. You said he had to come to us of his own free will."

"So how come you haven't convinced him yet?"

"You damned well know why. Parker detests being my servant. If I called him here right now, do you really think he'd come waltzing in ready to listen to what I have to say about your tryst?"

She knew this was true, but she wasn't about to let Kurt off the hook. Her lip curled. "Your plan, as I recall, was to break him down so he'd quit fighting you. If I recall, you said it was a matter of getting the wolf to understand that he can't beat you, so he might as well join you." She glared at him. "Well, in case you haven't noticed, your plan isn't working, Kurt."

Neither zot said anything for a long moment. Sighing, Garrett ran her fingers partway through her hair. "Look, Kurt," she said in a quieter voice. "You're no ordinary vampire regent, and I'm not just any witch. I'm a mage. As for Parker...we might not know everything Park's capable of doing with his power, but we do know it's extraordinary. I mean, how many pyro *weres* do you know?"

She paused. "Zots like us don't happen every day. You and I have known each other for fifteen years, and we both know the chances of just the two of us being in the same place at the same time are astronomical. Throw in Parker and the odds are damned near impossible. This is our only chance to be a tryst—and to use what we have to turn Seattle, and maybe the entire state of Washington, into a place where zots know they're safe." She regarded him with a steady gaze. "That's all I want, Kurt."

Kurt's eyes narrowed. "You haven't seen much of Parker since last December when you two became my servants, have you?" His tone dripped with sarcasm.

"I'm not your servant. And except for pack meetings, Parker acts like I don't exist."

"Perhaps so, but he misses you. Did you know that? Well," he shrugged, "since the wolf is still so enamored, perhaps you ought to pay him a little visit one night, hmm? Spread your legs as eagerly for him as you do for me, and I'm sure he'd be happy to join our little threesome."

Furious, Garrett stamped up to him and poked her index finger into his chest. "Listen up, Master. Do something about the wolf, or our little deal is off. I'm not playing a duet with you, Kurt. And don't think you'll make me just because you've had a bit of my blood, either."

Kurt didn't answer. He stared at her with that unearthly stillness only the undead could achieve.

Without waiting for his response, she turned on her heel and black cape billowing, swept out of the office.

CHAPTER 15

Kurt drained the glass of wine he'd poured. "That little bitch," he muttered, shivering as if to shake Garrett off. He poured another goblet and sipped at it. "Is any of this even worth the headache those two give me?"

I truly forgot about her little spell tonight. His lips tightened, annoyed with himself. Garrett had told him what might happen if he didn't shield her from the wolf's emotions. He knew the magnitude of the powers she often dealt with, and he also knew they were deadly if not handled properly. He should have protected her.

He raised the wine goblet to his lips and grimaced. Garrett Larkin's atrocious manners irked him. Kurt belonged to a collateral branch of the Stauffen dynasty, who'd dominated the throne of the Holy Roman Empire for several hundred years. When alive, he'd ruled a secular principality in southern Germany during the early sixteenth century.

"One would think, being such an accomplished actress, she could at least pretend to have *some* breeding," he complained into his wine. Garrett was one of the lead actors in permanent residence at the Kenneth G. Stohlman Center for the Performing Arts, a venerable and highly respected West Coast theatrical venue.

Raising the glass to his mouth again, Kurt pursed his lips into a half-smile. Garrett might give him a headache but he had to admire her toughness. No other zot in Seattle would have stood up to him the way she had tonight. He rolled his eyes in mock exasperation and his half-smile widened into a full-fledged grin. *All right, all right. I like her fierceness, too.*

Then his smile disappeared. Right now, Garrett wasn't his problem. *Parker…what am I going to do about him?* He took a quick sip of wine and set the goblet on the cabinet. He started to pace. "Damned if I know."

It was maddening. Kurt wanted the tryst as much as Garrett did—if not more so. When she'd made her proposition, he'd fathomed its potential immediately and had agreed to it even before she'd finished talking. Of course, he'd made her wait a few months before actually saying yes. But the benefits of Garrett's plan were tremendous. From the way she described it, a trinity of Parker, Garrett, and he would render him the greatest vampire un-alive. He would be a true prince again, with absolute power over every human and zot in Seattle.

He stopped his pacing. Settling on the chaise, he stared at the impossibly beautiful man who stared back from the enormous, gilt-framed mirror hanging on the wall. Just shy of six feet tall, Kurt was Michelangelo's David come to life. Smiling, he ran his fingers through his thick, golden yellow curls. He winked. His azure eyes, the same shade as a perfect September sky, almost always sparkled with sly amusement, as if the world were a joke only he understood.

Kurt chuckled, forgetting his Parker problem for the moment. There were only a very few like him, vampire regents who could be seen in mirrors, who could consume human food and drink without harm, who could enjoy being in the sun and playing in the surf on a pristine beach.

A long time ago, he'd heard tell of a well of blood whose properties rendered any vampire who drank from it just about invincible. Against his Mistress's rules, he'd abandoned his colony and spent the next fifty years tracking down every lead he found, ending up in the Amazon jungle. He knew he was close when about ten primitive-looking vampires had seized and bound him. They'd herded him through the forest until they came to a large vine- and leaf-thatched hut. Another vampire with an intricately woven headdress had emerged.

I knew what he was the moment I saw him, Kurt remembered.

At a signal, he'd been unbound, stripped naked and tied to a wooden post. Then the vampires retreated, leaving him to face the rising sun.

A vampire trapped in sunlight takes hours to die. When the sun's rays had hit him, his skin had begun to blister and smoke. After his skin had split, the rays had begun eating into his flesh, shriveling his muscles.

Kurt had refused to scream or plead for mercy. Gritting his teeth, he'd stared at the colony's Master with defiance. The other vampire had stood in the sunlight unaffected. His hunch had been correct.

He remembered fainting and reawakening in blind agony. A small portion of sanity left to him knew his death was imminent.

Kurt hadn't felt his head tip backward and a cold liquid poured down his throat. Within moments, his agony had ceased. The sun no longer burned him. He'd opened his eyes and could see. The Master had stood before him, nodding and smiling. He'd felt his flesh reknit.

For a minute or so, he'd wondered why the other vampire had saved him. Then he'd understood. Because of his dogged refusal to plead for mercy, the Master had rewarded him with a cup of his blood. Kurt had stayed with the colony for two weeks, getting used to his new powers. After leaving, he'd lost all memory of where his ordeal had taken place.

Now, the mumbo-jumbo Christianity and any other sect used to banish vampires were useless against him. The power of the cross, willow branches, garlic, or other protections humans had used over the millennia to keep the undead at bay held no sway over him. Thanks to the blood from the Amazon Master, there was very little Kurt could not do and few powers he did not have.

"Except get Parker into the tryst." He sighed. Garrett had been right that his plan to break the wolf down wasn't working. When they'd begun their campaign, they had agreed the easiest way to get Parker into the tryst would be if he were the pack's alpha wolf since the alpha automatically became the Master's *were* servant. It should have been easy for him to manipulate him into agreeing to help manifest the tryst. Except it wasn't. The only way to get Parker to do anything he wanted was through brute psychic force.

That kind of mental capability was enough to give a vampire regent pause.

Kurt had then concocted the plan to pretend to turn Garrett into his servant. He knew how deeply the werewolf loved her and that he would do anything for her. If Parker thought she'd become Kurt's servant, it stood to reason that might make him easier to persuade. The only means to get her back would be to join the tryst. Unfortunately, the plan had the opposite effect. These days Parker dealt with her only when pack business required it, or when Kurt forced him to make sex-magick with her.

He frowned. *Maybe I went too far with the sex-magick. It's not as if Parker needed to be the catalyst for whatever spell Garrett was casting. It was just another way for me to exert my power over him.*

Relaxing his brow, he stared at the ceiling, remembering the night Parker had shown up at Last Chance the first time. The werewolf had just moved to Seattle and per Kurt's law on new arrivals and guests, had to be introduced to the city's Master. Upon meeting him, Kurt had immediately been taken by his intelligence, easygoing demeanor and sense of humor. He'd tried repeatedly to make friends but to no avail. Kurt had finally realized Parker didn't like him, and the other's willingness to engage in conversation was nothing more than a show of his good manners.

Then Garrett had come to him with her plan, and Kurt had seen an opportunity of a different sort.

He jumped from the chaise and began pacing again. "I thought it would be so different. I thought if Parker became my servant, if I could show him how I feel..." He shook his head. Once Parker had discovered that by becoming pack alpha he'd also become the Master's servant, he'd turned cold and distant. Through their mental connection, he'd tried to melt the wolf's icy demeanor but it hadn't worked. Without Parker's friendship—or something more—he knew he'd never be able to persuade him to willingly join Garrett and him in the tryst. He'd thought and thought, trying to figure another way but there hadn't been. And he wanted the tryst so badly. His desire for the tryst and his longing for Parker's friendship had warred in him until the tryst won out. It had pained him but to get Parker into the tryst, he'd been forced to fall back on the only course of action a sixteenth-century prince knew. He had to break him.

Kurt stopped pacing and turned to his reflection. "Maybe I should just tell the wolf?"

He rolled his eyes, knowing he was grasping at straws. "Oh, right. Tell Parker I'm in love with him? I can hear it now. Fuck you, asshole," he said in a perfect imitation of the alpha wolf's growl. He plopped back onto his chaise. His inability to break Parker down was bad enough, but he had a more immediate worry.

The werewolf was out of control. What had happened the other night in The Grey Whale had been just one of a long string of escapades Parker's drinking had caused during the last two months. And Kurt, or one of his servants, had always come to the rescue.

But if this keeps up, one day the police will get there before I do. Kurt tightened his lips. He didn't see he had a choice. Much as he hated it, there was nothing for him to do but continue battering at Parker's psyche in hopes the wolf would someday surrender. In the meantime, he hoped his luck would hold and he'd continue arriving to extract Parker from a scene before the police did.

Thinking about his Parker problem prompted him to wonder what the other was doing now. He closed his eyes, telepathically tuning in to his servant. In seconds he could see where Parker was and what he was up to.

The werewolf was busy demolishing a living room in someone's house. He was also shit-faced.

Dammit, Parker. Not again. Blowing an exasperated sigh, Kurt dressed in the clothes he'd worn earlier during Parker's visit, a black collarless silk shirt and butter-soft lambskin trousers in the same color. He dissolved into mist and following his mental link, flew to the house where Parker was and drifted inside.

Maintaining invisibility, he resumed his human form and leaned against the large doorway to the room the alpha was systematically destroying. Parker ripped gaping holes into the walls, broke furniture and windows, and terrorized the people, all human and male, who cowered in the room's corners.

One of the men pulled a gun. Kurt telekinetically jammed the trigger. He doubted the gun held silver bullets but the last thing these humans needed was to find out regular ammo would barely slow Parker down. He gritted his teeth. All the more reason to get him out of there.

"Stop." His voice echoed like it was coming from someplace far away.

Parker heard. He ceased tearing up the sofa and looked around as if trying to figure out where the voice had come. Reading his mind, Kurt discovered why he was at this particular house and sighed. He didn't understand Parker's fascination with the stuff he called "weed" but he'd noticed it went a long way to calm him down. Until he'd figured a better way to deal with Parker if smoking weed made the wolf happy then as far as Kurt was concerned the other should have as much of it as he wanted.

79

Spotting a small cabinet, Kurt scanned its contents. It held what Parker had come to this house for. "Go to the cabinet on the far wall," he instructed. "Take whatever's in there and go home."

Parker obeyed. Leaving the shattered sofa, he marched over to the cabinet and took out a large, bulging brown grocery bag.

Must be at least six or seven pounds in there. Kurt watched the alpha head toward him and frowned. Something about Parker's clothes didn't seem right. Aside from being bloody, his cotton Oxford shirt was wrinkled and there were dark, greasy-looking stains on it and on his jeans. He would expect him to be disheveled, given his current drunkenness, but...

As Parker passed him, Kurt looked more closely. The shoulders of his shirt had been torn at the seams, partially exposing the wolfman's brawn. A few of his shirt buttons had popped off too, revealing his broad, hairy chest and washboard abs. And wasn't that a tear in the cotton cloth down the middle of his back?

Either he did that while ripping this place apart or a forced morph began and he stopped it... He stared at the retreating werewolf with wide eyes. No *were* could stop a forced morph once it had started.

Could they?

Kurt remembered how furious Parker had been when he'd left the club earlier tonight. He'd been able to feel his rage without trying. He also knew how much more furious the other had been after being forced to watch his antics with Gerald.

If the wolf is strong enough to stop a forced morph—

The sound of the front door's slam yanked him back into the moment. He followed Parker outside just in time to see him stumble down the stairs and then stagger onto the cracked concrete sidewalk. Kurt looked around. The wolf's playground was in a seedy and rough part of the city.

He watched Parker stagger along the sidewalk until he reached his car. He fished in his pockets for the keys. It took him a good two minutes to fumble the right one into the door lock but he finally managed to open the thing. Holding his grocery bag, he almost fell into the driver's seat. When he didn't move after that, Kurt repeated his earlier order.

"Go home, Parker!"

Nodding as if he'd just remembered that was exactly what he'd planned to do, the wolf drove away. Weaving along the pavement, he miraculously avoided the parked cars lining both sides of the street.

Kurt watched until he saw the Caprice turn a corner two blocks away. Sighing, he broke his connection with his errant servant and returned to the house Parker had torn up. Gliding inside, he could see the men in the living room were starting to recover from their shock over his *liebchen's* carnage. Four of them scrambled over wrecked furniture to reach two others, who lay in bloody heaps against what was left of one wall.

Sinking into a squat, he examined the two injured men, inspecting the damage Parker had inflicted on their soft, human bodies. A broken femur protruded from one man's leg. The other lay still under a large piece of drywall that had fallen on him during the rampage. He reached out with his senses and knew the drywall-flattened one had fallen into a coma.

Not that he cared. Kurt stood in one fluid motion. He was fairly certain none of the men in the house had known Parker, but he erased their memories just the same. *After that performance, they'd almost have to know their guest wasn't human.*

Finished with the job of cleaning up after Parker yet again, Kurt left the house and stood on the tired front porch, ignoring the loud curses coming from inside. His lips tightened into a grim line. *Garrett is right— and enough is enough. Parker must be dealt with.*

But how?

Less than five minutes later, he had the answer. *Appeal to the wolf's ridiculously human sense of decency and fairness. Why didn't I think of that before?*

Kurt dissolved into mist again and flew across the city to the International District to pay a late-night call on the pack's beta and Parker's second in command, Tran Ngyuen.

CHAPTER 16

Parker's phone rang the next morning before dawn.

A shapeless mound covered by pale blue sheets shifted on the bed. From the mound's bottom, a hirsute, muscular arm shot from under the sheets and went for the telephone. Parker snatched the receiver from its cradle. The handset disappeared under the sheets. The rest of the unit crashed to the floor.

"What," he snarled.

"I heard what you did last night," a voice on the other end said. It was Tran.

He opened one eye. "What?" He didn't give a wererat's ass what he'd done last night, nor the night before, nor the night before that.

"Alpha, you've gotta stop this...this madness. Keep it up and you'll bring us all down." Tran sounded like a patience-strained parent scolding an erring child.

Parker half sat up and opened his other eye. His sleep-tangled dark copper hair hung in his face. His brow furrowed. "Okay, give. What're you talking about?"

"You don't even remember, do you?" Tran cried. "Park, you not only nearly killed those two thugs, you had to go and take the dealer's house apart, too?"

He squeezed one eye shut again and frowned.

I did?

He tried to remember.

Uh-uh. Nope.

Closing his other eye, he furrowed his brows harder. Images of what remained of a room inside a house started worming their way to the forefront of his sleep-and-alcohol-fuzzed memory. He saw in his mind's eye the broken walls and windows and the furniture in pieces. It looked like a hurricane had gone through the place.

Oh…yeah…

Parker tried unsuccessfully to hold his head and an armful of pillow at the same time. Giving up, he opened both eyes and rolled onto his back. Now he remembered the thugs—sort of. "Yeah, well."

The pictures in his head became clear and he finally remembered what he'd done and why. His rage rekindled. "Fuck them. They tried to kill me."

"Will you listen to yourself?" Tran yelled into his ear.

Parker winced and pulled the receiver away. Last night, he'd managed to guzzle God-knew-how many bottles of whiskey and whatever else he could lay his hands on. Now he had a hangover. It'd be gone in an hour or so but right now his head pounded like someone had decided to use it for a bongo drum.

"You looking for another werehunt? You wanna get your ass skinned?" he heard Tran's tinny shout. He put the receiver back to his ear but said nothing.

"Look," Tran said in a softer tone. "I don't care if you wanna drink until it's coming out of your ears or blow enough smoke until you choke. But for the pack's sake, you just can't keep going like this." He paused. "Lemme tell you something else, dude. Dan's not the only one in the pack itching to challenge you. And don't get me wrong but Kurt's even suggested I do it."

The mention of Kurt's name was usually enough to send Parker's wolf into paroxysms of rage but this time it had the opposite effect. Closing his eyes, he gave his hand a tired wave. "You wanna be alpha, Tran? You wanna be Kurt's servant? You wanna be his boy toy and goddamned blood cow whenever he wants a goddamned taste?" He let out a heavy sigh. "Go ahead," he offered in a weary voice. "I don't care. Pick a place and time and we'll have at it. Fight to the death. I'll make sure you win, okay? Just throw what's left of me into Elliott Bay."

"Come on, Park. Don't do this. The pack's been through enough already."

Resting his right hand on his forehead, he opened his eyes and stared at the ceiling.

"Park? You still there?"

"Yeah," he muttered. "I'm still here."

"Park, look. I know how much you're hurting. And what Kurt makes you do with Garrett—the sex-magick, I mean— isn't helping. But like I told you the other night, the pack's about to disintegrate. If we do, what happens to us then? And no matter what he's doing to you, Kurt works to keep humans mellow enough to leave us alone—most of the time. You know that."

Tran hesitated. "Park, in the last four months we've been through a werehunt Kurt didn't lift a finger to stop, an inter-pack war, and then you went and chose a mage as our freyja. Don't you think we've been punished enough?"

Parker's brow furrowed. "You see my choosing Garrett as a punishment?"

"No," Tran sighed. "I didn't mean it like that. I—"

"I know what you meant," he growled and then decided to let it go. He imagined his second pacing the small apartment in the International District where he lived.

"You know something else?" Tran said. "You might be ready to make that big leap over the moon but the rest of us sure aren't." There was a moment of silence. "Park, you have to stop it. Most of us can't survive being what we are anywhere but here. That might not be saying much but this is all most of us have. Do us a favor. Don't fuck it up for everybody."

Parker closed his eyes. "Um."

"You know, maybe you should take a vacation or something. Get away for a while. I can take care of everything and while you're gone, I'll make sure the pack still respects Garrett as freyja, even though she's not officially anymore...oh, you know what I mean."

He knew. Technically, Garrett was no longer his or the pack's freyja. Though she'd sworn to protect and serve the wolves, her repudiation of him—and the pack—by taking up with Kurt amounted to the same thing as dissolution of marriage by death. He also knew the reasons why the pack was still willing to acknowledge her as his lifemate. One was because he hadn't given them permission to kill her. Two, many of his pack were still trauma-scarred from the werehunt and the inter-pack war and they needed her healing powers. And three, after all that had happened within the past four months, none of the possible contenders for pack alpha had the stomach to take him on in a death-match.

His thoughts flashed on Dan, the First-ranked who'd come within a wolf's hair of challenging him the other night. *Not yet, anyway...*

"Park," Tran said, his voice sounding tired. "I can't keep the pack together forever. Not without you. And you know, I don't exactly want anybody challenging me, either."

He grimaced. Tran was right. Just because Garrett had deserted him for a dead man didn't mean he had the right, even as his pack's tangible god, to take them all to hell with him. "Okay, Tran." He rubbed his forehead. "I'll figure out something. In the meantime, I'll try to behave, okay?"

"Thank you, Alpha," Tran whispered. The relief in his voice was plain.

Parker's eyes popped open. He realized for the first time since their conversation began how deeply frightened the other wolf had been. Not only did his behavior carry with it the possible extinction of the pack, but it also threatened Tran. Like Tran had said, most of the pack couldn't survive anywhere else but Seattle. Unlike the rest of them, he could always return to Iowa. He'd inherited a huge chunk of working farmland from his human grandmother, and the local wolf pack would welcome him. Few other zots enjoyed the luxury he had to make such choices.

Beyond that, Tran was also right in pointing out that whatever Kurt was doing to him, he was still alpha wolf. He had a pack to take care of.

He shook his head hard. It hurt like hell. "Parker?"

"Yes, Tran."

"Park, didja ever think maybe Garrett isn't worth what you're doing to yourself?"

His throat tightened. "Never," he whispered of the woman who, despite her crushing, humiliating loss to the vampire, was still his lifemate, his freyja, and the only woman he wanted. Tears leaked from under his closed eyelids, wetting his temples and hair. Without waiting to see if Tran had something else to say, he pulled the receiver from his ear and hung his left arm over the side of the bed.

Parker let go of the phone, not hearing its soft thunk when it struck the rug-covered floor.

CHAPTER 17

One night during a period the hu-mans called "the ides of March," Melera wandered through Pi-oh-neer Square, looking for a place she could make into her base.

Frowning, she swiveled her head left and right. *See-at-tell is a strange place. The tension—I can feel it. It's so thick I could poke holes in it with my laser knife. I wonder what's going on.* She pondered it for a moment and then shook her head. *Well, whatever it is, it isn't my problem.*

Melera twitched her shoulders, trying to readjust the itchy golden neck collar she wore underneath her close-fitting, zippered shirt. It was uncomfortable but vital to wear because it had a personal stealth shield, now activated. She had no intention of interacting with the natives and the best way to do that was not to be seen.

She threaded her way through the crowds on the sidewalk. Despite the city's edginess, the hu-mans she encountered seemed relaxed enough. Many appeared drunk. Loud laughter and animated conversation filled the air. Music blared from a couple of the buildings she passed. It was night in the twenty-four hour period hu-mans called Sat-ur-day, which apparently was a party time.

Melera stopped at the corner of an intersection. A narrow street bracketed by two dark buildings beckoned from the street on which she now stood. She'd seen a couple of streets like this, which unlike the wider streets, carried no hu-man or vehicular traffic. There was just one light, near the narrow street's entrance. The quiet and darkness suited her. *I need to think.*

She crossed the street and entered the dark space. When she'd reached about halfway along the narrow street's length, she saw it was a dead end. *Perfect.* She kept walking. Near where the street ended at a brick wall, she spotted a door. There was no banner overhead, nothing to indicate what lay behind it. A small frown creased her brow. *If this is a market, the owners can't get much trade, not all the way back here.*

By now she'd reached the end of the street. She sat with her back against the wall, her knees drawn up to her chest. *We aren't having any luck, are we?*

No. Maybe we should try another city, her czado said.

Melera tightened her lips. *There's got to be someplace around here we can hide out.*

Her czado didn't answer. She tipped her head back until it rested on the wall and let her mind go blank. Presently, her thoughts focused on the door. She looked at it. Curiosity filled her. *Wonder what's behind it? I mean, what kind of market could it be?*

Would you like to find out?

Sure, why not? Rising to her feet, Melera walked to the door. She grasped the knob and tried to turn it. Not surprisingly, the door was locked. *Think you can open it?*

Of course.

She mentally stepped back and let her czado take control of her mind and body. The alley, formerly drenched in gloom, now appeared as if it was full daylight.

Her twin inspected the doorknob. *There is no locking mechanism on the door.*

Then it must be somewhere else.

Melera's czado-controlled body took a step backward. Her gaze roamed the door. Nothing. She expanded her search to the bricks immediately surrounding it and inspected them one by one. Then she saw it. About halfway along the door's height, there was a sliver of brick jutting out from the rest.

That one.

She stepped forward, placed her fingers on the brick and pushed. The brick depressed, then popped back into place. A second later, the lock clicked. She grinned. *Let's go in.*

Her czado retreated and Melera was in full control again. She turned the knob and pulled. The interior was pitch black. She stepped across the threshold. Behind her, the door closed with a soft thunk and locked itself.

Looking around, she wondered why she'd even bothered. It wasn't as if she could see anything. Her lips pursed. *Want to take over?*

No. Even I cannot see in utter darkness.

Melera extended her arms before her, palms up. Nothing. She slowly widened her reach. A few seconds later, her hands came into contact with rough walls. Fingering them, she figured they were brick. She closed her eyes, imagining her current position. *Must be some sort of hallway. Maybe there's a light switch along here somewhere.* She slid her hands back and forth on the brick, but there was nothing.

Turn on the collar's light.

Not yet. I don't want to wear out the battery. I forgot to charge it before we left the ship. She thought for a second. *Better turn off the stealth shield, too.* She unzipped her shirt, exposing the flexible metal collar. Fingering it, she located the shield's manual control and turned it off.

Melera stretched her arms out from her sides again. A moment later, the rough brick scraped the palms of her hands. She'd just lifted her foot to take a step when the hallway unexpectedly lit with a bright, bluish-white light. Startled, she lost her balance and toppled forward. She put her foot down to stop her fall but there was nothing. Her eyes widened. "Jakk!" Gritting her teeth, she fought gravity's insistent pull and managed to right herself. Melera looked down and was glad the lights had come on. She wasn't standing in a hallway. She was standing at the top of a long, steep stairwell. If she'd stepped forward, she would have tumbled to the bottom. She probably wouldn't have broken anything— Xia'saan warriors are tough—but it sure would have hurt. She let out a slow breath. *Thank the Dark.*

Let us go, her czado said.

Moving slowly in case the steps were rickety, Melera started her descent. The stairs seemed solid enough. She quickened her pace. At the stairway's bottom was another door. She tried it and the door swung open. From the light behind her, she could see it was another stairwell.

She stepped onto the landing, and before she could close the door, the stairwell lit up. She looked around. Here, the ceiling was much lower. She stepped off the first stair. Surer of her footing now, she moved faster along this staircase. At its end lay a third door. She opened it and was surprised to find more stairs.

Melera clattered down these steps, too. A fourth door beckoned. She kept going. She reached the fifth door and pulled it open, expecting to find another staircase. But there wasn't. An expanse of brick greeted her. She'd reached the bottom.

She stuck her head through the doorway and looked left and right. There was no one. Easing through, she shut the door. She took a few steps and stopped. Turning in a slow circle, she could see she was on a street, not unlike the one she'd left earlier. Tall black columns lined the far side of the avenue, each topped by a ball of the same bluish-white light encased in what looked like glass. Both sides of the street were crowded with large, attached buildings, two stories high. The building's windows were dark.

Melera started walking along the street's middle. She walked for several blocks, turning corner after corner. Once, she thought she heard a scraping sound. She scurried around a corner and pressed her back against the building, listening. The sound didn't repeat.

Probably wasn't anything but I should get off the street. She decided the building she leaned against would make a hiding place as good as any other. Peeking around the corner, she then tip-toed around the building to its door. She tried it. The door swung open and she stepped inside. Like the stairwells, the darkness was pitch. She waited for the lights but there was nothing. Fumbling in the dark, she tugged at the collar, re-orienting it until her fingers touched a long straight bar embedded in the metal. "Mehtak."

Light flooded from the collar. Looking around, Melera saw she stood in a vestibule. On her right was a solid door. Before her, stairs beckoned. She started climbing. At the top of the stairs stood another door, this one half-glassed. She opened it and stepped through.

Now she was in a hallway, with doors lining each side. Moving forward, she reached the third one and decided to see what lay behind it. She pushed the door open, took two steps in and stopped. Pivoting, she saw she stood inside a huge room, measuring about thirty by twenty feet, in her estimation. Except for her, it was empty. A satisfied smile appeared on her lips. *This is perfect. Plenty of space for everything I need.*

Melera walked to one of the room's wide, unshaded floor-to-ceiling windows overlooking the street. Ambient light from the lamps lining the brick pavement spilled inside. It occurred to her she should black the windows out. It had been hours since she'd found her way here and she hadn't seen a single hu-man. But a city was a city, whether on Dirt or some other planet and she knew that just because this part of See-at-tell seemed abandoned didn't mean no one was about. The last thing she wanted was for the hu-mans to discover her.

Turning away from the window, Melera looked around the room again, visualizing her set up. *I can put my—*

She sneezed. She thought nothing of it until she sneezed a second and then a third time. Moments later, she was wracked by a violent coughing fit that drove her to her knees.

What the jakk—?

CHAPTER 18

Inside the fifth dimension, a uthyrisis had just captured its prey when it was sucked into an immense vortex.

Bright shards of colored light pierced its misshapen, balloon-like body. The next thing it knew, it had slammed into something completely beyond its ken. Firm, but soft. Mostly.

The uthyrisis opened its eyes and was startled to find it only had two of them. Disoriented, half-blind and off-balance, it started to sway. Then it fell, landing on something hard and smooth. It closed its eyes.

Time passed. When the uthyrisis opened its eyes again, the dizziness had almost stopped. It could see a little better, too. It was sore in places from its fall but it didn't hurt too much.

"Welcome to the third dimension, demon," a disembodied voice said.

The uthyrisis said nothing. It didn't understand.

"This is your new body. For a while," the voice came again. "Explore. Get to know it."

The uthyrisis lay still. It had no idea what to do. A few minutes later, it became aware of another presence. It sent a thought-form, its usual mode of communication. There was no response. It had been about to send another when the presence sent a thought-form. The uthyrisis studied it. This thought-form was primitive and hard to decipher. A moment later, it realized the presence was trying to teach it to communicate. The uthyrisis let the thought-form penetrate its mind. It worked.

Who are you? the uthyrisis said.

My name is Janice.

Janice?

Yes.

Where am I, Janice?

You're in the third dimension. Inside my body.

Where...wha...I...? the uthyrisis sputtered, stunned.

It's okay. Relax—I'll help you. We'll start with the basics.

All...all right.

First, I'm female. I'll explain more about that later. Then the Janice lifted one of her body's appendages. *This is my arm. I have two of them. At the end of my arm is my hand.* She wiggled her fingers.

Arm...hand.

Next, the Janice lifted one of her lower appendages. *This is my leg. I have two of these, too. At the end of my legs are my feet.*

What do you do with your legs and feet?

I walk—it's how I move my body from place to place.

I see.

Try lifting my arms.

The uthyrisis concentrated. Its movements were jerky.

You're doing well. Now bend them.

How do I do that?

There's a joint in the middle of the arm. Lift the lower half.

The uthyrisis concentrated again and lifted the Janice's forearms.

Great. Now bring them up to my head. Where my eyes are.

The uthyrisis soon touched a hard surface with a supple outer covering. It explored with the Janice's fingers. It touched something soft. *What's this?*

My hair.

The uthyrisis grabbed a hank and pulled hard. A stabbing pain. *Ow,* the Janice said.

More time passed.

Do you think you can stand up, now?

I will try. With the Janice helping to keep its balance, the uthryisis got to its feet.

"Very good," the other voice said.

The uthyrisis opened the Janice's eyes. Another body stood before it. It glanced down at the Janice body and then at the other body, and knew that body was female, too. "Who are you?" The uthyrisis's voice came out as a croak.

"My name doesn't matter, demon."

The uthyrisis had a flash of insight. "You brought me here. From the fifth dimension."

"Yes."

"Why have you done this?"

"I have a task for you."

The uthyrisis said nothing at first. "What is it you wish me to do?"

"I want you to go hunting. For a human."

"A human? What is—?"

"Humans are the dominant species in this dimension. I want you to kill one."

"Why?"

"Never mind why. I command you to do it."

Anger surged through it. "I am not yours to—" Sharp, bright pain slashed through the Janice's head. Both it and the Janice cried out. And then the uthyrisis knew. It had to obey.

The pain was gone as quickly as it had come. It stared without expression at the female standing before it. "Very well."

"I will leave the details to you and Janice."

The evening of April third, the uthyrisis and the Janice stood outside a door leading to what the Janice called a "bar."

"This is where we'll find our human," the Janice whispered. "Do you remember the plan?"

Of course.

"Then let's go in."

The Janice pushed the door open. It was a big room, overrun with three-dimensional humans. Almost all seemed to be drinking some sort of liquid in varying colors out of clear cylinders. Near the ceiling, panels with moving pictures on them held the rapt attention of many. Every so often, the three-humans watching the panels let out a simultaneous roar.

That one, the Janice thought.

The uthyrisis looked. A three-human—male—sat in a small, half-walled space. He stared into a clear cylinder filled with a golden liquid. He was alone.

The Janice walked over to him. "Excuse me."

The three-human male looked up.

"Do you mind if I share this booth with you?" She looked around. "It's pretty crowded tonight."

The male pointed to the empty seat across from him. "Sure. Sit down."

The Janice scooted into the booth. "My name's Janice."

"Derek."

"Pleased to meet you, Derek. And thank you."

The Derek shrugged. "No problem."

A three-human female walked over to them. "What can I get you?" she said to the Janice.

"I'll just have what he's having."

The female nodded and walked away.

There was a short silence. The uthyrisis sensed the Derek was feeling uncomfortable. He picked up his glass of liquid and took a sip. "So what brings you here tonight?"

"I was working late and decided to stop for a beer before going home. I'd forgotten there was a game on."

Now the Derek looked curious. "What do you do?"

The Janice smiled. "I'm the Director of First Impressions at the Lydol Corporation."

The Derek looked puzzled.

She laughed. "Oh, all right. I'm the receptionist."

The Derek laughed, too.

Neither said anything for a minute. The uthyrisis sensed the Derek's discomfort growing again. Another roar came from the bar's front. "What brings you here?" the Janice said when the noise had subsided.

"Business. I'm an engineer."

"Where from?"

"Chicago."

While the two made small talk, the uthyrisis watched the Derek's thoughts hovering over his head. It fed this information to the Janice.

The Derek's eyes seemed to light up. "Really? I love jazz and blues, too. And Chicago's got great places to hear some really good stuff."

The Janice nodded. "I know. I'm particularly fond of FitzGerald's and the Green Mill."

The Derek's jaw dropped. "Same here," he said, sounding awed. Then he cocked his head. "Where did you say you were from?"

"I didn't. I'm from downstate. Cuba."

"Never heard of it."

"Would've been surprised if you had. The town's only got about a thousand people, if that many."

The Janice and the Derek talked until the three-human female who'd brought them their drinks said it was time to leave.

"I'm not ready to go back to my hotel," the Derek said.

The Janice smiled. "Why don't we go for a walk in Magnolia Park? It's not too far and it's really beautiful at night."

The Derek hailed a cab and the two rode to the park. When the cab had departed, they walked inside.

"I've had a lovely time tonight, Derek," the Janice said. "It's so hard to believe we've just met. I feel like I've known you for ages."

"I feel the same, Janice. You're an amazing woman."

They walked in companionable silence. "You know, we really shouldn't be here," the Derek said. "The park's closed."

"Well, I won't tell if you won't."

The Derek chuckled.

They walked further. "It's so peaceful," the Janice said. "I—"

"I just hope we don't run into any zots. We wouldn't stand a chance."

"I don't want to think about that. Let's go to the bluff," the Janice said. "There's a gorgeous view of Puget Sound. Though I don't think we'll be able to see much. The moon's not that bright."

"Okay."

The Janice took the Derek's hand and they resumed their stroll. Neither spoke. A few minutes later, they reached the bluff. The Derek sat and patted the grass next to him.

The Janice sat and leaned into him. The Derek placed an arm about her shoulders. "Tell me what it's like to live in a town with no zots."

She shrugged. "Not much to tell. I mean, it's a really small place. Everybody knows everybody. A zot wouldn't be able to hide for long."

"Must be great."

"It is if you don't mind everybody knowing your business."

The Derek laughed and kissed her hair. "Oh! I'm sorry. I didn't mean—"

"It's all right, Derek. I…I liked it."

They sat in silence. About five minutes later, the Janice let out a nervous giggle.

"What's wrong?"

"I have to pee."

"Well, where—"

"It doesn't matter, Derek. I have to pee. Now."

"There are some bushes over there." He pointed to his left.

"Fabulous. I'll be right back."

"I'll come with you."

The Janice shot him an odd look.

"I mean, to stand guard. Just in case."

She nodded. "Hurry."

The two rushed over to the bushes the Derek had pointed out. The Janice disappeared into the foliage. She smiled as she stripped out of her clothes. She didn't have to pee.

It's time, the Janice said. *Are you ready?*

Yes.

Then let's switch.

Janice's uthyrisis-controlled body emerged from the bushes, stark naked. She laughed when she saw the Derek's jaw drop.

He stared at her, saucer-eyed. "J-Janice, what are you doing?"

The Janice laughed again. "I'm seducing you. What does it look like?" She cocked her head. "Don't you want to?"

"I…I—"

"Come on, Derek. It's not like there's anyone around."

The Derek blinked. "Aren't you cold?"

The Janice stepped forward. "Yes, but I have you to warm me up." She blew him a kiss. "Come on," she whispered.

The Derek took a step toward her.

In an eyeblink, the Janice's body morphed into what looked like a giant, misshapen butterfly, the uthyrisis's three-dimensional form. She leapt. Wrapping the Derek tight in her wings, her momentum tumbled them to earth. Lying on his back, he stared at her in horror. "W-what are you?" his voice quavered.

She grinned. "I guess you might say I'm a zot."

The uthyrisis's feeders, like stiff tubes, shot from the Janice's flattened body and tore through the Derek's jacket and clothes. He screamed so the Janice covered his mouth with hers. The uthyrisis began sucking out the Derek's blood. Pieces of fabric lodged in the holes it had made and slowed the blood flow, but not enough to make much difference.

Two minutes later, the uthyrisis had drained him. It retracted its feeders and morphed back into the Janice's form. It stared at the Derek's body, at his torn clothes and the look of terror still etched on his exsanguinated face. It smiled. "You were delicious," it said in a low voice.

The uthyrisis returned to the bushes and donned the Janice's clothes. It stepped out from behind the foliage. Giving the Derek's bloodless body one last look, it laughed a final time and sauntered out of the park.

Two days later, the Janice didn't go to work. "I don't feel so good. I feel like I'm burning from the inside out."

The uthyrisis said nothing. The Janice had control over her body right now and it felt her body's distress. But it didn't know what was wrong.

"I need water." The Janice got up from the bed, grabbed the empty glass on the nightstand and hobbled into the bathroom. She filled the glass from the sink and looked up. Her jaw dropped. "Oh, my Lord. Look at me!"

Black, flaky lesions covered her face. The Janice took off her robe. More lesions covered her arms and the rest of her body. "What's happening?" She sounded frightened.

I do not know.

Then the pain started. Burning, burning agony. The uthyrisis and the Janice screamed and dropped to the floor. The Janice body writhed on the tiles. A minute later, her body was dead.

The uthyrisis was hurled out of the Janice body and sucked into the vortex. The next thing it knew, it was home.

It took a while for the uthyrisis to re-orient itself to the fifth dimension. When it had, it decided its third-dimensional adventure would make a splendid story to tell the Mighty Ones when they gathered next year. The Mighty Ones, whose experiences in dimension-hopping made them the objects of awe and veneration by the uthyrisis' kind, might even make it one of Them.

But that wasn't until next year. It tucked thoughts of its recent adventure into the recesses of its mind. Right now, it was hungry. It was time to feed.

CHAPTER 19

In late May, nearly four months after promising Tran he would behave himself, Parker checked his watch and scowled. It was only three-thirty in the morning. *Two and a half more hours.* Taking a deep breath, he blew a heavy sigh.

The alpha wolf was dog tired. He hadn't slept well the night before and had put in a full day programming a client's new security system and on top of that, had spent the last ten or so hours on patrol—or 'rolling as his pack called it—walking, walking, and walking until his feet felt like lead.

Seattle's usual rain had stopped a few hours ago and the skies had cleared. Just now, a cool breeze blew inland and rustled the tree leaves, smelling of the sea and caressing his face like a lover's hands. The light cast by the waning gibbous moon bled all color from the landscape, turning the green park into an eerie montage of black, white, and gray.

Well, at least it's been quiet. As quiet as can be expected, anyway.

Except for a few members, everybody in the pack pulled 'rol duty at least once a week. The wolves' territory included all of Seattle. Every night, alone or in pairs, ten or more wolves took to the streets on foot, watching the humans, watching other zots, soaking up the mood of the city and comparing notes when they met up with each other or if not, by cell phone. Tonight his wolves had reported nothing too unusual—a bike-and-car accident downtown, a shooting on Meserine Avenue—all involving humans. No word about gruesome murders. For that, Parker was grateful.

A normal 'rol shift lasted twelve hours—sometimes longer—depending on what was happening around town. This was supposed to have been Harold's shift, but his she-wolf Shirley had borne their first cub—the fifth in his pack—early yesterday afternoon. He could've ordered Harold to go anyway, but this 'rol had been a heaven-sent excuse to get out of his duty visit with Ted and Jane Roberson last night.

Duty visits were a way for an alpha wolf to keep tabs on what was happening within his pack. Visits like these always involved food and he and the First-ranked Robersons were supposed to have had dinner together. That would have been fine except that Ted insisted on doing the cooking and a meal from Ted's paws was culinary torture.

Parker sniffed the night air, not smelling anything out of the ordinary. He smiled. Harold's 'rol territory covered the northwest part of the city. Discovery Park, where he was 'rolling, was one of his favorite hangouts. Ambling under the trees, he noticed an old oak not far from a bluff overlooking Puget Sound. He decided underneath its branches would be a good place to take a rest.

Sitting under the oak, his thoughts wandered until they settled on Frank Suggs, his werepanther friend who'd been skinned when they were fifteen. His lips stretched into a sad smile. After all these years, he still missed his best buddy. He reminisced about how he and Frank were forever getting themselves into one sort of trouble or another and when they did, how he usually managed to talk their way out of it.

"Park, yore a real silver-tongued devil, ain'tcha?" he heard Frank's voice in his mind. Frank always said that after Parker had gotten them out of one of their scrapes.

He snorted. *Yeah, Frank. I was a real silver-tongued devil but we both know my being Judge Berenson's son sure didn't hurt.*

His smile died. Judge Berenson. His father. Parker hated him because he was the reason Frank was dead. The three men who'd actually done the killing—Pitt Jackson, Tom Gaines, and Jake Walther—had been nasty characters in their own right but that time they'd been acting on his father's order. *Wonder if any of 'em are still around. Hope not—and if they aren't, I hope somebody skinned them, too.* His eyes flew open and he gave his head a little shake. *Doesn't matter. Frank's gone, so why even think about it? Besides, I'm still on 'rol. I gotta get back to work.*

Focusing on his job again, he scanned the terrain and saw he wasn't alone. About a hundred yards from where he sat, someone walked along one of the park's numerous trails. With his wolf-sight, he could see the person was almost as tall as he was and moved with a self-assured awareness that made him think *zot*.

Vampire, maybe. If so, the vamp really needed to think about getting home. It'd be light soon.

Parker sniffed, matching sight for sound for smell, searching for odors that didn't belong with what he saw and heard. He caught a whiff of something that might have belonged to the walker. Three hundred feet was certainly close enough for him to catch the man's scent but the breeze kept mixing up the smells.

Absorbed in the other's progress, he twitched, startled, when the walker was pulled off the path and into a stand of fir trees. *What the...?* Silence reigned for a half-minute. Then his wolf hearing picked up the unmistakable sound of flesh being beaten. He jumped to his feet. *Oh, no. Don't let this be what I think it is. Not another one.*

The victim hadn't cried out when he'd been pulled from the path but someone was screaming now. He'd just taken a step to run when his wolf's hard mental shove threw him off-balance.

And you're going where?

But—

Stop acting like a human. It ain't our problem.

But—

No dice.

Parker wavered. His wolf was right. He'd been about to break a cardinal pack rule: *Whatever's happening, don't get involved unless directly threatened.* The rule was callous but practical. Getting involved might lead to a discovery of what he was, which could be fatal—for him and the pack.

But what if it wasn't an ordinary mugging? What if it was something far worse?

An agonized scream, cut short, decided him. Kicking his wolf into the background of his mind, he sprinted toward the trees, running fast enough that his sneakers were hardly dampened by the rain-soaked grass. But the fight was over by the time he got there. The tree stand and the grassy clearing it enclosed were quiet.

Too quiet.

He stood motionless, listening at the breeze soughing through the fir branches and hearing the high-pitched squeaks and groans of bruised and trampled grass. Other than that, there was nothing. No panicky birds. No chattering squirrels alerting all and sundry to the danger on the ground. All animals became quiet in the presence of death and Parker's wolf sensed death was near.

He began a slow pivot, watching for anything out of the ordinary. Three-quarters of a turn later, he spied a human-sized lump lying in the grass about fifteen or twenty feet away. His heart skipped a beat.

Parker had just taken a running stride toward the victim when a blow caught him in the middle of his back. "Whumpf!" he grunted and stumbled forward. From somewhere over his head, something large and heavy crashed onto his shoulders, propelling him further. He managed to take two more reeling steps before the weight shifted and a vise clamped his thighs together. Pitching forward, he flung out his arms to break his fall. The weight rode his back while the ground rushed up to his face.

He'd intended to hit the dirt on all fours but his hands skidded out from under him. Then his head was pushed into the ground. He choked on the wet grass. His attacker grabbed a hank of his hair and pulled hard, jerking his head and neck backward.

That hurt!

Parker started morphing without thinking. His temperature sky-rocketed and a reddish-colored pelt, two shades darker than his human hair, sprouted along his arms. "Urrghhh," he growled in fury and pain while his bones and sinews stretched to the breaking point and then beyond as his body began changing from human to animal.

The sharp thwick! of a switchblade knife locked in for the kill. Its tip dug into the hollow just behind his right ear.

Parker's glowing werewolf eyes went wide. Bearing down on his wolf's fury, he forced his body to stay human. Morphing was absolutely the worst thing he could do right now. The change could send the knife sliding into his neck without his assailant having to do a thing. If the blade cut his carotid artery, he might bleed out before his body had a chance to heal.

Finally able to lie still, his first coherent thought coincided with the frisson of fear arcing down his spine.

Holy fuckin' shit!

Fear ratcheted into terror. *I thought he was zot, but...!*

Zots don't need to carry weapons.

I'm going to die!

Heart pounding in his chest and the knife at his neck, Parker tried not to imagine what was coming next when the pre-dawn silence was broken by a soft, mellifluous, almost baritone voice. "You look for someone?"

This guy's a woman? an inner voice squeaked. The knifepoint bit harder into his neck. In his haste to respond, he swallowed his mouthful of grass. Its bitter taste almost gagged him. "Uh, no. No, I'm not," he managed to stammer, his voice sounding squeakier than the one in his head. "I...I thought someone needed help."

The woman said nothing.

Parker squeezed his eyes shut and silently recited every prayer he knew.

"Ohh-kay," she finally said.

His shoulder muscles relaxed. *ThankyouthankyouthankyouGod.*

He opened his eyes a minute later, puzzled that the woman and her knife hadn't yet budged. His neck hurt. He'd expected her to get off him when she'd decided he wasn't a threat. The unpleasant thought that she might kill him anyway tickled at the back of his mind. "Um...may I get up now?" he said, trying not to suck in more air than necessary.

To his surprise, the strange woman began to laugh. Her low, sensuous chuckling vibrated through his body, sensitizing him to the warmth of her thighs and knees squeezing the sides of his chest. Not only that, her scent was an airborne aphrodisiac to his beast. His wolf's erection, pressed into the rain-dampened earth hurt as much as his neck did.

Uhrrummm, his wolf purred.

This ain't the time, pal.

"Mmmmm...yes," the woman said as if mocking him. In a moment, the knife's pointed pressure was gone from his neck and her weight from his back.

Parker rose from the wet ground, keeping his back to the woman so she couldn't see the look on his face. His wolf might want to fuck her, but right now she was fucking with him and it was pissing him off. He started brushing at the grass and dirt clinging to his clothes and scowled at his hard-on. Thirteen throbbing inches of his wolf's dick had bulldozed its way past the waistband of his jeans. It lay against his stomach, bulging through his light cotton T-shirt. He tried to will his beastly erection into submission but it remained defiant.

He gritted his teeth. *Well, I can't just stand here and wait for it to go away.* He started to turn. "Look, lady. I heard someone being attacked and thought I should—"

From the corner of his eye, he saw dark movement. He spun the rest of the way around only to discover seven finely honed inches of the biggest pigsticker he'd ever seen poised to slide between his ribs and into his heart.

Parker froze.

"Jesus!" he hissed. His head snapped up and he was looking into a pair of huge, dark amber eyes inches from his.

"Gyaah!" he shouted, almost in a scream. His wolf-erection died, shrinking into his jeans while his balls tried to find a new home inside his pelvis. He stumbled backward—away from her—and fell onto his butt. Chest heaving, he stared at the woman in confused horror.

She appeared highly amused. One side of her mouth stretched into a scornful-looking smirk. Then she started snickering.

Parker went ballistic. All the rage he'd kept pent up exploded through his veins—rage over every humiliation as the vampire Master's servant, rage over all the looks he constantly got from the pack, looks that questioned whether he was fit to be the alpha wolf.

Rage over losing Garrett to Kurt.

And now—now this!

Blood roared in his ears. *Cunt, I'll wipe that smile off your face.*

The woman had closed her blade and was slipping it into her back pocket when he sprang. "Unmph!" she grunted when his head rammed into her stomach. He and the woman went airborne, his weight driving them backward.

"Ughh!" she grunted again when she landed on her back. They bounced, throwing him to the side. He grabbed at her. Twisting left, the woman rolled twice, evading his grasp. Once on her feet, she came at him low and fast.

Parker leapt into a defensive crouch. Just before she barreled into him, she jumped. He raised his arm to block too late. Her kick to his chest bowled him backward. Before he could rise, his opponent was upon him, her fists flying. Fending off as many blows as he could—the bitch hit hard—he contorted until he got onto his stomach. She was sitting on him again, but at least her punches now landed mostly on his back.

He endured her assault. Leveraging his weight onto his legs, he shot to his feet and threw the woman over his shoulder. The soft groan she made when she'd thudded to the earth was music to his ears. He turned just in time to see a roundhouse kick coming straight for his head. Parker jerked back, dodging the woman's boot by mere inches. Catching her ankle, he hurled her across the clearing. She twisted in midair to land on her feet.

Snarling, he rushed her. She was just turning away from him when he took one final leap...

And smacked face-first into something solid.

His knees buckled. *How...how'd this tree get here?* In his dazed state, he felt more than saw the woman's arm lash around his neck. At first, he thought she was trying to keep him from falling but then she squeezed. It was hard to breathe in the fierce headlock and that brought him to his senses. In his stooped position, he couldn't get a firm hold on her and she was squeezing his neck harder.

The woman loosened her grip just enough for him to twist his neck and look up at her. She grinned. Then she kneed him just under his ribs. While he gasped for air, she released his neck, only to catch him on the chin with a right uppercut that sent him flying back to land on his ass.

Parker slowly sat up and shook his head. The blow had nearly knocked him cold. A second later, he remembered how he'd ended up on the ground. He jerked into a squatting position, ready for her next attack.

Instead of coming at him, she stood with a hand on her hip, still grinning. She started snickering again.

Fury boiled Parker's blood. She'd finally pissed off his wolf self, too. With a roar, he leapt at the woman. She fought harder than a First-ranked werewolf but he was determined she wasn't going to get away from him again. Maneuvering behind her, he wrapped his arms around her midsection and pinned her arms.

She stomped on his instep and kicked his foot out from under him.

"Aggh!" He fell but brought the woman down with him. He twisted

ROXANNE BLAND

so this time she landed face-first in the slick grass. "Mmm…tastes good, doesn't it?" his wolf growled in her ear.

Her response was to heave her ass into his groin. It felt delightful but he knew there'd been nothing sexual in her move. She was trying to get to her knees to shake him off. He used his weight to force her back down. They rolled over and over in the grass. When they stopped, he had her just where he wanted her. Spread-eagled beneath him, she didn't have enough leverage to rise.

She'd lost their fight and they both knew it but that didn't stop the woman from trying. She squirmed and bucked beneath him.

"Uhrrrmm," his wolf purred. "Keep that up and you're gonna make me cum, honey." The woman stopped struggling and stared up at him, her lips slightly parted. Parker stared back with a leering grin. "Now who's fucked?"

She didn't answer. He'd just decided he'd rather kiss her than rip out her throat when the woman's eyes widened and she drew a gasping breath. His grin broadened. "That's right, sweetheart. Your ass is mine." He lowered his head to her exposed neck.

The woman sneezed. Twice.

He snapped his head up to avoid the wet grass spewing from her mouth and pressed his lips together when the little green shards stung his jaws and neck. Then he glared down at her. *Shoulda made you swallow it, bitch.*

The woman's expression seemed surprised. She held his stare for a moment and then closed her eyes. He braced for another sneeze.

She disappeared instead.

His jaw fell open. A soft pop of air filled the vacuum where the woman's body had lain. He dropped to the ground. "Ooof!" he whooshed, landing on his stomach.

Face pressed into the dirt, Parker decided if grass was going to be a regular part of his diet, he'd at least like it with a little sugar.

108

CHAPTER 20

While Parker lay in the grass in Discovery Park, Melera hurtled through a rip in the universal fabric.

She hit the floor with her shoulder. Rolling twice, she ended up on her back with splayed arms and legs, the same position she'd been in just seconds ago in the park. Panting and shivering, she stared at the ceiling. "Acksh-choo! Tchoo! Tchoo!" she sneezed, hard enough to lift her back and legs from the floor. Trying to finish the job her sneezing had started, she struggled to sit up.

"Ughh," she groaned. Drawing her thighs close, Melera hugged her knees to her chest and rocked back and forth. She started giggling, which soon erupted into full-fledged laughter. "Whooo-chukt-hoo," she hooted, her quintuple voices sounding like a chorus of trilling flutes. It had been ages since she'd felt so good, so alive. Battling that hu-man in a bare-knuckled fistfight—it had almost been like being back home in the 'drome, taking on all comers, khikt-ou-khikt, and the first one jammed gets jakked!

"Yiow hahoo…ckugh! Ckugh! Ckuuugh!" Her laughter dissolved into a coughing fit. Viscous tears flecked with silver streamed from her burning eyes. She rubbed at them while she hacked.

"Fook," she croaked when her coughing had finally stopped. Light from four column lamps, one in each corner of the large room, came on low.

Jakkin' allergies. Her throat felt raw and her clogged sinuses made her head feel wrapped in dense foam. She started to get up but dizziness kept her on her knees. Head hanging, she crouched on the floor and waited for the spinning to stop.

"Fook," she croaked again. The four lamps burned a notch brighter but that didn't help her any. Her tearing eyes made it impossible to see a thing. She began crawling across the floor, hoping she was heading for the corner where she'd strung her hammock. "Ow," she grunted after bumping headfirst into the siitheer. "Clowth enough." She felt her way around the instrument until she found its bench and then hauled herself onto it. Drained by her effort, she sat with her head in her hands.

"Brr-rrgh!" Melera squealed, jumping like she'd been jerked on a string. Occasional flashes of intense cold were side effects of having skipped through the Void. For short distances—three hundred or so miles—all she had to do was picture in her mind the place she wanted to be next and step into it. The cold flashes would stop soon. Skipping might be an efficient way to get from one place to another, but it was hardly pleasant.

Her runny nose didn't feel pleasant, either. Rubbing her eyes clear, she spotted a roll of soft paper cloths—tissues—on a nearby table. She leaned forward and misjudging the distance, nearly fell off the bench trying to reach it. Finally grabbing the roll and ripping off a length, she blew her nose. "Dizzgustinck," she muttered after wiping her face. But she wasn't finished. Ripping another piece, she blew again, soaking this paper too.

A starfarer faces numerous perils when visiting an unknown planet and a wise one who intends to survive plans accordingly. Melera had visited so many planets both inhabited and uninhabited that taking precautions was second nature. Dirt had been no different. But the last thing she'd expected was to be allergic to the damned place.

She felt awful. "Fook," she said. "Fook, fook, fook." The four lights were now at maximum brightness.

Before her eyes could tear again, she scanned the top of her siitheer, looking for a medium-sized red, green, and gold box. Spotting it, she withdrew a long and slender brown cylinder with one rounded end. Then she picked up a mangled book of matches.

Brows knitted, she concentrated on detaching one of the paper stems from the rest. *Careful, careful—don't rip it apart.* Melera was extraordinarily strong by Dirt standards, in part because the planet's gravitational pull was weaker than Xia'saan's had been. Unfortunately, it meant she often destroyed the things she handled without meaning to do so. She could have lit the thing with her czado's pyrokinetic ability but in the throes of an allergy attack, she couldn't see very well. Last time she'd tried it she'd almost burnt a hole in her thigh.

This time she must have done something right because the match flared into flame after one strike. Bringing it to her face, she lit her see-gar. Inhaling long and deep, she felt a warm, fuzzy feeling spread through her body and rush into her head. She savored it, floating, then took another drag.

This tow-bac-co is the Dark's mercy. No wonder hu-mans smoke so many of these. She had discovered tow-bac-co by accident, looking for what hu-mans called a drugstore to help her allergies. Some of the remedies sympathetic hu-mans had suggested—the pills, mostly—made her feel worse than the allergies did. Other treatments hadn't worked at all.

About a month ago, while walking downtown, she'd been attracted through watery eyes by a row of brightly-colored boxes in a store window. It had been a tow-bac-co store, one that sold see-gars. She'd asked the clerk what see-gars were and how they worked. When he'd told her, she'd asked why people smoked the brown sticks. Grinning, the clerk had offered one for her to try. He had even lit it for her. After her first few puffs, all of her allergy symptoms had disappeared.

She'd been elated. See-gars were the only things she found that worked. While the clerk had babbled on about his stock, her czado had given his mind a small push. The clerk's eyes had glazed over for a moment. Then, face splitting into a cheerful grin, he'd handed over three boxes of see-gars—with his compliments.

Melera smiled. She could feel her sinuses clearing and her eyes had stopped itching. The light buzz she got from smoking tow-bac-co was nice too, though it lasted only a few minutes. But its symptom-eliminating effects lasted for hours. How long she couldn't say since the time always varied but as long as she smoked regularly, she'd be fine. This morning she'd forgotten and when a see-gar's effect wore off, it really wore off. Her allergic reaction to Dirt was immediate, which was what had happened in that park.

She leaned against the siitheer's keyboard. Smoke curled around her head in lacy tendrils. Jumping from the bench, she began to pace. "He's not hu-man," she murmured, thinking about the tall male with the reddish hair. Hu-mans were like the one she'd killed before the redhead had shown up. She hadn't meant to kill him. They just broke so easily.

Taking a drag from the see-gar, she ran her fingers over the siitheer as she passed it by. "He can't be hu-man. If he was, he should've been down for good after I swung from that tree branch and kicked him." She paused. "And that last hold he caught me in…I couldn't break it. I'd just been ready to morph when my allergies started acting up." She snorted at the irony. The redhead had been surprised when she'd sneezed. Her unexpected allergy attack had saved her.

And do not forget, he started melting while you sat on him, her czado said.

She raised her brow. None of that—the redhead's strength, his morphing—fit with what she'd learned about hu-man physiology before she left her island. Comparatively speaking, the bips' strength was limited and she'd found nothing in the electronic databases to suggest they were a malleable species.

Melera stopped her pacing and commanded the lights to turn to the lowest setting. Walking to one of the room's two windows, she stared at its blackened panes without seeing them.

Is it possible he may be half hu-man? her czado said.

"Maybe." There was always a chance Dirt had been colonized by alien life forms. She stood motionless, thinking on it. *No. There's no colony here. That space station I saw is nowhere near big enough to handle interstellar transports, even the short hoppers. So…maybe his sire was a junker looking to make a few chits?*

She took another drag on her see-gar. Exhaling, she gave her head a slow shake. "I doubt it. If that little space station says anything, it says hu-mans have barely made it off-planet, much less into hyperspace. So there's nothing here to sell. A junker would pass Dirt by without a second glance."

Which made the answer to what the redhead was obvious. She wasn't the only starfarer in See-at-tell. Beloc had discovered the wormhole, the shortcut to this galaxy, and had sent one of his trained hounds to bring her back.

An unbidden memory surfaced in her mind's eye. Covered in blood, she'd cowered in a corner of her cell, trying in vain to fight off the dense cloud of stingers. She'd swatted at the tiny, wasp-like robots, crushing them with her hands and body but there had been too many of them. They'd stung her everywhere, even crawling into her mouth when she screamed.

She shoved the memory aside and grimaced. "I'll be jakked if I let Beloc get his hands on me again." She had to find that redhead and dispose of him. Then she had to figure out a way to fool Beloc into thinking that she was someplace in Maqu. A soft, exasperated hiss escaped her lips. This was one complication she could do without.

Her thoughts drifted, settling on the hu-man male whose body still lay in the clearing. *I should go back and dispose of him, too.*

She wondered whether the redhead had contacted Beloc yet. If he had, Beloc might even come for her himself. She hissed again. If Beloc came after her, Dirt was in deep jakk. The Jahannan warlord wouldn't come alone and against a fleet of Akkadian warships, this planet was defenseless.

Melera's jaw tightened. She had to find that redhead and soon, before Dirt and its people found themselves pawns in a war that would destroy them all.

CHAPTER 21

Bewildered, Parker picked himself up from the ground. "Will someone tell me what the hell just happened?"

Nobody answered.

Maybe it's some kind of trick? Spinning around, his eyes searched the moonlit clearing but he couldn't see the woman. He couldn't hear her, either. He sniffed the air. Even her scent was gone.

Parker scratched his chin. He hadn't imagined it. The woman had been here, lying under him, and now she was not. He shook his head. "Fuck it. I'm going home." Turning, his eye caught the human-shaped lump on the opposite side of the clearing.

The stench of death was stronger, now. He approached the downed figure and knelt. He poked it. The body didn't move, not that he was expecting it. Pushing hard, he rolled it over. His jaw tightened. It was a man and as he'd known, he was dead.

The moonlight illuminated what was left of the man's face. One eye had popped out of its socket and lay like a bloody grape on his smashed cheek. Where his nose had been, there were only shards of bone. His lower jaw, no longer aligned with his upper, canted to the left at an odd angle.

Parker's gaze traveled past the man's face down to his neck and then his trunk. Grossly misshapen, his ribs had been broken. Inspecting the damage further, he realized the strange-looking bulge at the base of the dead man's neck was his heart. Remembering the woman's knee in his chest, he knew with sickening certainty how it had gotten there.

"No way she's human," he murmured as if he'd any doubt in the first place.

Neither are we, his wolf growled. *Let's get out of here.*

"Yeah." He stood and peered back through the trees. From what he could see, the path was still clear of people but the earliest of the early morning joggers would be out soon. He picked up the dead man.

What're you—look, we gotta go.

"Getting rid of the evidence."

Why? She's the one—

"Shut up. I know what I'm doing." Hefting the body over his shoulder, Parker ran for the bluff. He lifted it high overhead and calling on his wolf-strength, threw it with all the force he could muster. The body crashed into the Sound about twenty feet out. After it sank from view, he blew a heavy sigh of relief. He glanced at his watch and was surprised to see it wasn't yet four-fifteen.

He turned and started walking. About ten yards later, he looked down at his dirty and bloody clothing and stopped. It would take him at least forty-five minutes to walk home and by that time, it'd be almost full daylight.

I can get us home twice as fast. Hard to spot a running wolf in the dark.

"Good idea."

Behind a nearby tall bush, he stripped naked, securing his watch and keys in his clothes. After neatly folding them up, he slipped the bundle under his arm, closed his eyes, and morphed.

Looking around, Parker-the-wolf made certain no one was about. Then, using the bushes and trees for cover, he loped homeward.

While his wolf crouched behind a large bush near the end of an alley a few blocks from the park and searched for signs of human activity, Parker thought about Seattle's most recent unsolved murders. The newspapers had dubbed the killer "The Seattle Slayer." Contrary to the moniker's implication, according to his source in the mayor's office, the police were almost certain the murders had been the work of more than one person. But aside from that, they didn't know whether the killers were zot, human, or both.

Nobody here or on the street.

So let's move. His *were* ran down the alley, keeping to the shadows.

The distinction between whether the killer was zot or human was important. No exotic would ever count the law as a friend but the police didn't want a zot pogrom on their hands any more than the exotics did. Pogroms sometimes incited humans to riot. More than once in Seattle's civic past had the National Guard been called out to pacify the city.

At the end of the alley, his wolf dove into a gigantic manicured hedge.

What the—

Shh. Look.

Silent, the two watched while the hedge's owner jogged across her lawn. The middle-aged brunette deposited several trash bags into a bin, then jogged back to her house. They kept watching until she'd disappeared inside.

Parker's wolf exhaled the breath he'd been holding. *That was close.*

Yeah. Too close.

They took off running again. Though the authorities had publicly announced that no one should assume the killers were zots, most humans—and zots—had, anyway. The city's tension over the unsolved murders had been running high for weeks, a powder keg waiting to explode. That was one reason why 'rolling was so vital. It was also a very good reason not to risk the possibility of the police or anyone else discovering the body of the man that strange woman had killed.

Make sense now?

Uhrrm. But you still broke the rule about minding your own business. I'll have to punish you.

Shut up.

A few minutes later, his wolf stood panting in another alley. His house was only thirty yards away. *Want your body back? It's getting on full light.*

Parker thought for a moment. *No. I'd have to put these bloody clothes back on and I know Lieutenant Carlson will be leaving for work any minute. He's the last person we need to run into.* The policeman lived two houses down from him.

He won't be the only human up at this hour.

But it's still so early. Besides, if anyone sees us, we'll be moving so fast they might decide they're dreaming.

It's your call. His wolf took one last look around. All clear. He streaked toward the eight-foot privacy fence and vaulted over it in one heroic leap. Landing on his feet behind the tall hedges his human side had planted, he dropped into a crouch.

Okay, I'll take over now. Someone still might see us but in our own backyard it'll be a helluva lot easier to explain being outside and naked than it'll be to explain being outside and a wolf.

Got that right.

Parker felt his wolf retreat from the forefront of their shared mind. Willing himself back to human form, he set his clothes bundle on the ground and fished for his house keys. Tucking the bundle under his arm again, he jogged across the wet grass to his back door and slipped inside.

You're welcome.

He blinked. "What? Oh. Thanks, pal."

Uhrrmph. Humans.

He ignored the insult. Not bothering to turn on any lights, he stumbled his way to the bedroom and threw his dirty bundle of clothes toward the open closet. Keeling over the bed, he hit the pillow face-first. *I could stay like this forever.* But the stale smells of blood, sweat, and fear were nauseating him. He needed to shower.

Parker wasted no time. He ran to the bath and six minutes after rising from the bed, he was again lying face down in the pillows.

The need to get more comfortable compelled him to shift position. Rolling over, he gathered the rumpled bedclothes and rearranged them. He settled in, crossed his arms behind his head and closed his eyes.

He opened them a few minutes later. He couldn't stop thinking about her.

The only zots I know of that can disappear like that are vampires. But the woman wasn't a vampire. Parker turned his head to the left and snuffed at his bicep. His keen olfactory sense detected the woman's lingering scent even now, after his shower. "Vampires don't smell like that," he whispered.

A tactile memory of holding the woman in his arms while she'd struggled and the fierce heat that had poured off her body started his groin tingling. *They don't feel like that either.* Then he thought about that blast of bitter cold after she disappeared. In that instant, he would've sworn the temperature had dropped below freezing. He gave a little shrug. It was probably just his body's overreaction to the sudden loss of heat after she'd vanished. The night had been warm but the breeze had made it seem much cooler. Plus, he'd been on top of her and by then they'd both been sweating hard.

He stared at the ceiling, mentally reviewing their fight. Recalling how the woman had been spread-eagled beneath him made his thigh twitch.

I wanna bite her all over, his wolf purred.

Shut up.

Oh—like you don't?

"That's not the issue. Now shut up and let me think."

Uhrrmph. Don't hurt yourself.

Parker rolled his eyes but his wolf said nothing more.

He knitted his brows. *She isn't* were *either. I couldn't make her.* All werecreatures can detect, or "make" each other, when in close proximity. The energy enabling transformation crackled and tingled like weak static electricity. Much like his groin was tingling now.

Studiously ignoring it, he stared at the ceiling and frowned. "So maybe she's some kind of elf?" *Could be.* Like humans, elves came in all shapes, sizes, and colors.

His frown deepened. That didn't fit, either. Most elves were pretty tough characters in their own right but they used glamour to confound an opponent. *Wait a minute. What about that tree or whatever it was I ran into?* That was the kind of thing an elf would pull but she'd only done it once. An elf would have kept psyching him until the fight was over.

Parker slowly shook his head. The woman had pretty much kicked his ass—he winced at the truth of it—with nothing but brute force and skill.

And carrying that switchblade... He thought about the man the woman had wiped. The Seattle Slayer victims had been found full of holes and drained of blood. He blinked at the ceiling. The wounds didn't fit with someone using a switchblade. They were more like vampire bites.

Who says she always uses a blade?

True.

The woman's image appeared in his mind's eye. He'd been too busy to notice while she was whipping his butt, but she'd been drop-dead gorgeous. Remembering the feel of her thighs squeezing his chest and her hips grinding against him set his groin tingling harder.

Will you stop it?

Hey, dickhead—that's you, not me, his wolf chuckled.

Exhaling a small sigh, Parker rolled onto his right side, grabbed another one of the pillows and stuffed it under his chin. He closed his eyes and started to doze off. But they flew open thirty seconds later.

The woman disappeared before she had a chance to get rid of the body.

And he was a witness.

His jaw tightened. She'd come after him next. It didn't matter that she didn't know where he lived. She'd find him. He was sure of that. And the way she fought? He stared at the wall. He'd make it as hard for her as he could but between her weapon and her skill, he was pretty sure she could take him.

Not me.

Parker didn't respond. Letting one's *were* loose in public was a dangerous proposition. Like earlier this morning, when they'd had to hide from that woman taking out her trash. There was always a chance the wrong person might see. But in this case…

"It might come to that," he whispered. "Unless we find her first."

He closed his eyes a second time and finally went to sleep.

CHAPTER 22

The following night, the uthyrisis again stood facing the female who had called it. This was its eighth foray into the third dimension and it was eager for the hunt.

It looked down. The body it wore this time was male. Reaching out with its mind, it sensed the body owner's presence. *Who are you?*

The presence didn't answer.

Do not be afraid.

Uh...Gerald.

Very well.

The uthyrisis raised the Gerald's legs, first one and then the other. It lifted the arms over its head and stretched. It twisted from side to side. The uthyrisis had learned that though these three-dimensional bodies were similar, they did not move precisely alike. This body pleased it. *You are stronger than the other bodies I have been given.*

Um...thank you.

"Are you ready, demon?" the female said.

The uthyrisis looked up and stared at her. "Yes."

"Good." The female waved her arm. The uthyrisis had also learned until she did that, it could not walk but a few paces in any direction. It stepped forward.

"You will return here after you have killed," the female said.

"Yes."

"Then go."

The uthyrisis stepped out into the night.

The uthyrisis and the Gerald wandered the streets, looking for someone to kill. Not many three-humans were out tonight.

Where shall we go? the uthyrisis said.

Let's go down to the railroad yard. There's usually somebody around there.

At the Gerald's direction, the uthyrisis headed for Seattle's south side. Along the way, the Gerald spoke of many things it did not understand, like oppression and revolution. During a lull in the Gerald's monologue, the uthyrisis was ready to ask a question about three-humans when the Gerald spoke.

Do you like sex?

What is that?

It's like we have these holes in our bodies you can stick things into. It's fun. Everybody likes it.

What makes you think I would like it?

Just try it, okay?

They walked on and soon reached what the Gerald had called the railroad yard. They clambered down the embankment. At the bottom, the uthyrisis stripped off the Gerald's clothes and began to walk. It wasn't long before they found their victim.

"Hey," a male three-human shouted. "What're you doing here?"

At the Gerald's prompting, the uthyrisis ducked behind a large silver box with what looked like its feeders sprouting from the top. The three-human followed. As soon as the three-human rounded the corner to the box's rear, the uthyrisis sprang and wrapped him in its wings. An acid-like substance secreted from its retracted feeders melted the three-human's clothes for easier feeding. Then its feeders came out in full. The Gerald told it where the three-human's holes were. The uthyrisis shoved a feeder into both of them. To stop the three-human's screaming, it thrust a feeder into his mouth.

While feeding, the uthyrisis felt the Gerald's teeth morph into much larger ones, then chew on the three-human's face. After it had drained the three-human's blood, the Gerald took full control of his body and morphed his arms. He ripped off the three-human's hand and shoved it into the hole in his backside.

They left the three-human's body where it lay. Finding the Gerald's clothes, they left the railroad tracks. The uthyrisis was content to let the Gerald have control over the body. But it was curious about something.

122

Why did you do that? Chew the male's face? And rip off his hand and put it in his backside?

Revenge.

What is revenge?

It's when you get back at someone who did something bad to you.

But that three-human did nothing to you.

I didn't say it had to be the same person. The Gerald paused. *I'm tired of being kicked around like I'm a nothing. I'm tired of being laughed at. Used. Abused. I'm somebody, dammit! And pretty soon everybody is going to find out I'm nobody to mess with.*

The uthyrisis said nothing. Sex, oppression, revolution…to it, this three-human Gerald was growing more intriguing by the second.

I'm not a three-human. I'm a zot. I'm way better than any human.

You are all three-human to me.

You gotta lot to learn about the third dimension, Uthie. And I'm just the one to teach ya.

Yes. Perhaps you are.

The two reached their destination and walked inside, where the female waited for them.

CHAPTER 23

A few nights later, Garrett stood at the stove in her kitchen, making a cup of chamomile tea. It was a little after midnight and the soporific would help her sleep.

The doorbell rang. Her brow creased. *Who could that be?* She put down the teapot, left the kitchen and headed to the front door. Garrett wasn't afraid that it might be the Slayer or some other criminal. She could protect herself. *Maybe it's one of the coven.* Sometimes a covener came over to talk about something that was bothering them, or just to talk, and the time of day or night was given little consideration.

Garrett opened her front door to find Parker standing on the porch. Her jaw dropped a little but she quickly recovered. "Parker. Come in." She opened the door wider.

He stepped over the threshold. She closed the door and turned. "What can I—"

"What happened in Chance that night, Garrett? You're a mage. How come you gave into Kurt so easily?"

Her eyes widened a fraction. She hadn't expected this. She looked into his face, thinking fast. "He took me by surprise, Park. Our ritual introduction was supposed to be just that, right? There was no reason for me to think I'd need my psych shields." Garrett shrugged. "Kurt just bulled his way into my head. I tried chanting a spell to make him release me, but by then it was too late—he'd gotten too far inside. Trying to get him out was like trying to move Mount Everest."

Parker stared at her but said nothing. Neither did she. A minute passed. She took a breath. "Why don't we sit—"

"Kurt ordered you not to come back to me, didn't he?"

She looked him in the eye. "Yes."

Parker's lips tightened. He nodded, then bent down and planted a light kiss on her cheek. "I gotta go. I'm on 'rol."

"Okay." She let him out the door, watched him run down the stairs and jog away.

Garrett closed the door and fell against it. Her heart beat faster. Parker, speaking to her again? This was momentous. It could mean...

She hurried into the kitchen, all thoughts of tea and sleep forgotten. She sat at the kitchen table and splaying her fingers, pressed her hands against its surface.

Closing her eyes, Garrett sent a telepathic message to Kurt.

Four nights after Parker had shown up on her doorstep, Garrett sat in a chair in the party room at KM Entertainment Inc.—one of Kurt's many businesses—growing more annoyed by the second. He had called this last-minute meeting and it still hadn't started.

She shivered. "Damn these hot-blooded *weres*. Somebody turn off the air conditioning. It's polar in here," she muttered.

Feet tucked under her, she huddled under her heavy cotton shawl. It helped warm her some but not much. She looked at her analog watch and saw the numbers on the dial's date window turn from June fourth to the fifth. Sighing, she prayed this meeting would hurry up and begin. She had a dress rehearsal this afternoon for the play she was starring in and the rest of her day was going to be busy, too. She'd at least like to get some sleep.

"I'm ready whenever you are, Kurt," a woman's voice called.

Garrett turned. The speaker was Mandy Stewart, Mayor Russell's chief of staff and a First-ranked she-wolf. A well-built blonde of medium height, Mandy stood before a large easel festooned with some of the grisliest photographs she had ever seen.

The latest Slayer victim, she surmised. The man had been murdered a week ago. After the story had hit the papers, the atmosphere in Seattle had become as taut as a tripwire. Most people assumed the killer was zot. In case humans started retaliating, zots needed to make plans for their survival. That was why Kurt had called this meeting.

None of it has to happen. There is a way. If we could make the tryst, we could stop the killings, stop the humans' hatred of us...we could stop everything. Zots could finally live in peace.

She, Kurt, and Parker would talk about that after the meeting was over.

The room was crowded. Even from her elevated position, the small army of zots sitting at Mandy's feet obscured her view of the other woman's legs. Those not sitting on the floor had draped themselves over chairs and conversation couches that had been arranged in a rough half-circle. She took a discreet look around. These were the titular kings and queens of the assorted clans, mobs, packs, pods, and parliaments that called Seattle and its surrounding waters home.

Next to her, Kurt rose from his seat and clasped his hands behind his back. "My friends," he said in his velvety voice, "thank you for coming on such short notice. We have some unfortunate business to discuss. As you all know from the papers, another human fell victim to the Slayer seven nights ago. What you don't know—and neither does the press—is that there's been one more murder since then." He paused. "This time, the victim was zot."

Everyone began talking at once. "Oh, no," someone said. "Shit," came another voice. "Goddammit," a third voice shouted. Garrett mentally counted her coven. She'd spoken with several yesterday but not with everyone. The victim could have been a witch. Her heart beat faster.

"It was my daughter," a deep voice boomed from the middle of the room. "My daughter, Katy. And I want to know what's going to be done about it!"

She looked up. The speaker was Isadore Drummond, Chair of the Grand Elven Council. A morran, he was built like a bull and almost as ill-tempered. He jumped from his chair, face contorted with rage. His head swiveled left and right.

Kurt held up his hand. He stared at Drummond, his blue gaze intense. "Isadore, Isadore." Though he spoke in a soft, soothing tone, Garrett could sense the power behind it. "That's why we're here. To figure out what we can do."

It worked. After a few moments, Drummond calmed and retook his seat.

He refocused his attention on the crowd. "So as you can see," he went on, "every one of us now has a vested interest in bringing this murder spree to a halt. I—"

"Why should I care what happens to a wererat?" Trina Jamison, prime minister of the wereraven parliament cawed. "They haven't done me or mine any favors."

Garrett saw Kurt's jaw tighten. "Because we're all in this together, Trina." His voice had gained an edge. "As long as the killer is out there, none of us is safe."

Steve Coleman, headmaster of the wereshark school, narrowed his eyes. "All in this together, huh? So where were you during last year's werehunt? Just about everybody in here lost somebody. You did nothing."

"Yeah," someone shouted. "That's true," came another voice. The room filled with angry murmurs of agreement.

Kurt's gaze turned cold. "I had my reasons." His voice, razor-sharp, cut through the babble. The room quieted, but whispers could be heard.

"And what reasons—aggh!" Steve clutched his head in obvious agony.

"I said, I had my reasons. That is all you need to know."

The big room went silent. The angry tension now held an undercurrent of fear.

Kurt smiled. "Let's move on, shall we?" He paused. "As you know, most humans assume the killer is a zot. We—"

Garrett looked around, not bothering to be discreet this time. The zots she made eye contact with looked away. She knew why. Humans were the zots' enemies. Witches protected humans. Therefore, witches were the enemy, too. Her lips tightened. *The tryst will change all of you. We will all live in peace, not just with humans, but with each other.*

In her half-listening reverie, she sensed someone watching her. She looked to her right. Parker was staring at her, his bright green gaze soft. They smiled at each other.

She felt her customary wave of relief. With Parker speaking to her again, it shouldn't be hard to persuade him to join her. Their reconciliation meant she'd almost reached the end of an arduous journey she'd begun half a lifetime ago. One that had taken her from the south of France to Paris, then to London and New York, and had finally brought her to Seattle. To get here, she'd broken quite a few promises, lost more than a few friends, and had made even more enemies. But none of that mattered. Not anymore. Thinking on it, Garrett's heart began to pound.

At last—she would have her tryst!

CHAPTER 24

Sitting beside Garrett, Kurt scanned the sixty-odd faces in the party room. His decision to involve Seattle's zots in the hunt for the Slayer was two-fold. He didn't care about the human victims but he did care about the murders' effect on his nightclub business. Frightened Seattleites weren't going out after dark and Chance's nightly receipts had fallen over twenty percent since mid-April.

And now the Slayer had killed one of their own. His jaw tightened at the thought. Seattle's zots were his to rule over. To him, the murder was a personal affront. So he'd decided zots needed to do a little investigating for themselves. Obviously, the police needed all the help they could get.

"The investigation is completely stalled," Mandy said. "The investigation team isn't sure they're dealing with one or more than one killer, much less whether they're zot or human. Not only that, the medical examiner doesn't even know what kind of weapon was used to kill the victims."

A wave of incredulous murmuring filled the room. He couldn't blame them. Like everyone who'd been following the news and other gossip, he'd assumed the condition of the bodies meant the Slayer was zot.

Mandy held up her hand for quiet. "The Chief's office has been feeding the papers those dribs and drabs about the case's 'progress' to buy time. You all know what it's like out there. This city feels like it's going to blow any moment."

"Damn right it feels like it's going to blow," Mario, king of the wereagles, shouted. "I got eaglets who're afraid to go outside! And now you say—"

"That's enough, Mario," Kurt said. "Let Mandy continue."

Mandy shot him a grateful look. "The only thing the eight victims have in common is that all were discovered full of holes and drained of almost all their blood. Nearly everything else about the bodies' condition is different. The first vic was the only one who was clothed. The weapon—or weapons—used on him had punched right through the fabric. Number two looked like she'd been beaten before being cored. Numbers three and four had been found with their heads crushed, and numbers five, six, and seven were, except for the obvious, relatively intact."

She took a breath. "Number eight, the last one reported, appeared to have been raped with some kind of large, hollow blade, though no one except the police—and now us—know about that." Her brow creased into a small frown. "Two blades, actually. Aside from the large one that had sliced up his rectum, a smaller one, about the size of a large needle, had been inserted deep into his urethra like a catheter."

Kurt and every other man in the room winced.

"More than that, his left hand had been torn off below his wrist and shoved into his ass, and half his face looked to have been eaten." She paused. "The ninth, Katy Drummond—no one but the police know about her. Her body was discovered"—Mandy checked her watch—"yesterday morning. From what I've been able to find out, she'd been raped too, with three blades this time, two large and that small one I've mentioned. Beyond that, a message had been carved into her back, which I'll get to later."

She looked around the party room. "The police aren't going to release any information on Katy, and yes, for the usual reason. But even if they were so inclined, they also know that if humans found out the latest victim was zot, it would probably be open season on us. You know how humans are. Killing one is a license to kill us all." She wrapped her arms about herself as if cold and began to pace. "Not that they'd care anything about that but while they're running around checking out every dead body their resources would be stretched in so many different directions they'd probably never find out who's doing this." She let out an explosive breath.

Kurt narrowed his eyes, wondering. *Oh, yes. Last year's werehunt. Her younger brother and his cub were skinned.* He watched the blonde woman paced in a tight circle. For her, it seemed as if the room and its occupants had ceased to exist. "Mandy," he heard Parker's voice. He looked over. The wolf's expression was of benevolent concern.

Mandy started. "What? Oh—I'm sorry." Her brown eyes were wet. "I…"

Kurt rose from his chair. "These are photos Mandy so kindly brought for us to see," he said, indicating the easel behind her. "As she's told us, the police investigation is going nowhere. Since we're going to be doing a little investigating of our own, I asked her to show them so we could perhaps get a better idea of what the police—and we—are up against." He sat.

Mandy smiled a little. "Thanks, Kurt." Her voice carried a slight rasp. She shook her head as if clearing it and then turned to the first photograph. "Look here. This is Number Eight, the one killed a week ago. As I said before, most of the right side of his face appears to have been eaten."

It did. Patches of flesh had been ripped away, exposing muscle and bone. What was left looked to have been chewed by something with large teeth. Missing the right eye, the gory face resembled a grisly caricature of an old-fashioned pirate.

"The M.E. can't figure out what might have done this. What's confusing is that some of the bite marks were obviously made by fangs but the rest seemed to have been caused by human teeth."

Kurt raised his brow. "A justborn vampire *could* have done that. They get a little—enthusiastic—when they feed." His eyes sought out Daniel, his executor.

No, Daniel mouthed.

Kurt nodded. His ironclad rule against rebirthing vampires without his permission hadn't been broken. "But of course, all of my justborns are accounted for." He cocked his head and gave Mandy a curious look. "Does the M.E. have any idea what those fangs might have belonged to?"

"Not really. Her first assumption was that a vamp had done it but a closer look made her reconsider. The shape isn't right. The M.E. isn't sure but she thinks they might belong to some kind of *were*—probably an immature one—but the marks don't fit with anything they have on file." She paused. "The closest she can figure is maybe—*maybe*—a wererat."

Everyone turned to look at Limousine Jack, one of Seattle's two King Rats.

Kurt had always thought it unfortunate that Jack resembled his *were*. Wiry, with a long pointed nose, beady eyes set too close together, and small ears jutting from the sides of his head, Jack was a homely man.

Jack shook his head. "Not from my pack. We got some litters on the way but we don't have any juvies." He turned to the man next to him. "What about you, Roy?"

Roy was the city's other King Rat. He and Limousine Jack looked like they could be twins. The second rat-man shook his head, too. "We got some pups, yeah. But none of 'em are over ten years old. They're way too small to take on a grown human."

"What else does the M.E. think might've chewed this dude up?" Tyrell, raj of Seattle's weretigers said.

"Frankly, Tyrell, it could be any *were* with fangs," Mandy said, "and that means most of us. Like I said, a wererat was just her guess."

Isadore Drummond leapt from his seat again. "This is an outrage," he bellowed. "Why are we bothering about him?" He pointed at the easel. "Who cares about some dead human? What about my Katy? Why aren't we talking about her?"

Kurt jumped to his feet. "Isadore. Sit down and be quiet!"

Isadore gave him a wild stare. Chest heaving, he looked like a bull about to charge. A minute passed. Then his face crumpled and he seemed to deflate. Falling into his seat, he leaned forward and held his head in his hands.

Kurt glared. "None of us cares about the humans, Isadore. But if we're going to catch your daughter's killer, we need to learn as much as we can about all the murders, not just hers."

The big room went quiet. He watched Isadore through narrowed eyes, ready to lay a stasis on the morran if he so much as twitched. He didn't.

Kurt sat.

Mandy turned back to the easel. "The rest of the photos show the puncture wounds. Look at the different sizes. They range from something like a swizzle stick to a half-dollar." She pointed to the second and third pictures. There were so many holes in the corpse the man's body looked as if he'd suffered from some kind of pox. "And they don't look alike, either. Some are round, others are square—and look at the ones with the ragged edges. And—"

"What does the M.E. say?" Andy said. Andy was a machinist. Tall and lanky, in his off hours he was sometimes a grossly outsized king cobra.

Mandy shrugged. "Again, they have no idea. Ice picks? Large-bore drill bits? Fangs? A bird's beak? You name it."

"I vote for the bird," Limousine Jack called. "Looks like a were-raven's beak to me."

"What?" Trina Jamison shouted. "You little shit!"

Kurt fought the temptation to roll his eyes. *First Isadore and now this.* "What are those discolorations around the holes?" he said before Trina or Jack could say anything further. Being a vampire, he knew what they were. He'd just wanted to keep them quiet.

Mandy swiveled her head. "Bruising. It means the victims were alive when they got skewered." She looked around the room. "So what do you guys think? Was it one of us? Humans?"

While the debate raged around him, Kurt thought about Garrett's tryst once more. She seemed to believe the wolf would jump at the chance to participate but he wasn't nearly as sanguine about the prospect. She wouldn't—or couldn't—see that Parker hated him. The alpha was civil enough when necessary. But one didn't have to like someone to be civil.

He let out a little sigh. He'd given up harassing Parker about a month ago after it had become beyond doubt that he would never break the wolf. He'd brooded over his nonexistent options and then Garrett had reported she and Parker were on speaking terms. He hadn't thought much of this development but she obviously did. For four days, she'd pestered him about inviting Parker to tryst. He'd finally agreed because he hadn't found a better alternative.

Kurt stared at the intricate pattern in the Persian carpet. Given the wolf's feelings, he had no illusions about the other's probable reaction. It would take a miracle for Parker to willingly tryst with them.

And just now, the Master was fresh out of miracles.

CHAPTER 25

"Now for Katy Drummond," Mandy said, casting a wary glance at Isadore. "Her body was found by the docks." Katy's father, head still in his hands, didn't move.

Garrett tightened her lips. She wanted to see Katy's killer caught as much as anyone did, but she was sick of all this talk about murder. She tried instead to concentrate on the rain pattering against the room's tall windows.

"Katy had been hung upside down on an old lamppost by one leg with her hands tied behind her back. From what I'm told, her position mimicked one of the cards in the Tarot—The Hanged Man."

Garrett sat up, feeling uneasy. *Witches use the Tarot.*

"When she was cut down, the police discovered the phrase 'thou shall not suffer a witch to live' had been carved into her back in runic script. The mutilation had been done after she was dead. The M.E. is pretty sure the runes were made with a long, narrow-bladed knife, maybe a switchblade."

Her eyes widened. Had that message been meant for the coven?

"Could someone have mistaken Katy for a witch?" Sheila Graham, the leopard queen, purred. A murmur rippled through the room.

"What do you think, Garrett?"

She looked up. Kurt had asked the question and now everyone was staring at her. The hostility radiating from the others was palpable. She opened her mouth but no words came. Then she closed it and tightened her lips. *Screw all of you.* She took a shallow breath. "I don't think it matters whether the killer thought Katy was a witch or some other kind of zot. I also don't think it matters what the M.E. thinks about who or how many killers there are out there or what they're using to make the kills."

She paused. "What's really important is that somebody's trying to spark a pogrom. The humans are planning to massacre us."

Kurt and a few others frowned at this. "How so?"

Garrett sighed. "Think about it. Except for Katy, all the victims were human. But the condition of all the bodies implicates zots." She looked around at a sea of confused faces and threw out her hands as if in supplication. "Don't you get it? Humans kill each other all the time, but they don't bother to make it look like one of us did it."

Everyone in the room still looked confused. She gritted her teeth. "Do I have to spell it out for you? Look, we're being set up. Kill humans in a way that makes it look like we were somehow involved, and then kill a zot to make it look like humans retaliated." She leaned forward and swept a defiant stare over the crowd. "Can anyone think of a better way to spark a pogrom?"

No one said anything. She slumped back into her seat.

"Oh, come on," Sheila purred. Her lip had curled into a sneer. "There hasn't been a pogrom in Seattle in over thirty years. Why now, all of a sudden?"

"Why not?" Garrett shot back.

"If someone's trying to pogrom us," Kurt said, "then I'd like to know why it hasn't started already. Eight humans is a large number of dead. It usually doesn't take more than one or two to set them off." He cocked his head, staring at her as if he were expecting a very interesting answer.

"The coven cast the Pax Omnia—a peace spell—when the murders started last April. We've been maintaining it ever since." She let out a tiny sigh. Kurt would probably be annoyed that she hadn't told him but it hadn't seemed necessary. Grumbling swelled through the room—something about witches and humans she couldn't quite catch.

"I'm sure we're all grateful to Balthus Coven for their protection," Kurt said, his hard gaze sweeping about the room. The whispering ceased. He turned to her. "But you and your coveners can't keep it up. It's a powerful spell, yes, but it won't hold humans forever."

She nodded. "That's right. The spell's being pushed to the limit as it is. If humans learn there's been another murder, the casting will probably fail."

"Look, I know what it's like out there—I get that we could be pogrommed any minute. But nothing you've said explains why someone would want to start one," Sheila purred in her skeptical tone. "This is Seattle. After all this time, there's got to be a motive." She eyed her. "But I won't pretend to be an expert on human behavior."

"And I won't pretend to be one either," Garrett snapped. She understood the leopard queen's insinuation. Witches were born from zot/human unions, so technically they were half-human. But no witch would ever admit she had the taint of human blood flowing through her veins.

"Don't be too quick to dismiss the possibility," Kurt said. "Garrett could be right."

She saw Mandy's nod. "The I-team is checking out that angle, too."

Kurt's eyebrows twitched. "I've seen enough pogroms to know there doesn't have to be a reason for one to spark and the years don't matter either. When the horde wants to kill, it will kill." He tapped a finger against his upper lip. "We should get Underground ready just in case. Garrett, please make sure your coveners know Underground is open to them, too."

A wave of hostile muttering swept the room. Kurt's face turned furious. "Cease," he shouted. He slammed his fist onto a small side table, cracking it in two with a sound like a rifle shot.

The room went silent.

"You know as well as I do how the humans treat witches. When it comes to pogroms, witches die just like the rest of us. That's why Underground was built in eighteen eighty-nine—and that's why it was built with their help." His hard glare seemed to settle on Sheila. "And if I hear one more thing from any of you about the coven, I will take it personally. Is that understood?"

The tiniest of smiles appeared on Garrett's lips. Sheila looked as if she'd just shit her pants.

"This meeting is over," Kurt said. His voice had calmed but it still carried a sharp edge. "For now, I'm going to assume someone's trying to pogrom us. All we can do at the moment is get out on the streets, find out what we can and keep each other informed." He tilted his head toward Mandy, still standing by the easel. "Mandy will be the contact point. Anything you get, report it to her. She'll let me know and I'll take it from there." He slapped his thighs and then stood.

Watching the zots sitting closest to her make ready to leave, Garrett got nervous all over again. She closed her eyes and tried to meditate her growing fervor away. This might be the moment she'd waited for all these years but to be successful she needed to stay calm and marshal her thoughts so she could convince Parker to join her. If she managed it, she could create the sanctuary she'd dreamed of since she was a child, a place where she could walk freely without always looking over her shoulder.

"Parker, come here, please. Garrett and I need to talk to you," came Kurt's smooth voice.

She opened her eyes. Everyone else had gone. She watched Parker close the party room door. Moving closer, he flopped into a chair about ten feet from where she and Kurt sat. He looked as if he'd rather be someplace else.

Just be cool.

Kurt turned to her and nodded once.

She took a deep breath. "Park, about twenty-five years ago, when I was an apprentice mage in France, I came across an old reference book about the Craft that had belonged to my mage mentor."

As she spoke, Garrett fondly remembered Feodor's library, with its hundreds of ancient tomes, some written in long-dead languages known only to the oldest and wisest of mages. "This book described something called a tryst. Essentially, it's a way of pooling power into something greater than what any individual zot could ever possess." She thought for a moment. "Think of it as sort of like a computer network. By linking computers together, you can increase the capacity and speed of each machine without having to upgrade the components."

Parker looked skeptical. "It can't be that simple."

She dipped her head and smiled. "No, it's not. But that's the simplest way I can think of to describe how a tryst works."

"Uh-huh," Parker said. "But a computer network..." He frowned. "Wouldn't that mean if one unit goes down, the system crashes?"

Her smile died. "I'll get to that part later." She glanced at Kurt. He stared at her with narrowed eyes. She hadn't told him, either. "Anyway, we—the three of us—can do that, too. Network, I mean. The Book tells me how. We—"

"What kind of power are you talking about?"

"Well, we could change human attitudes toward zots, for one thing."

"And?" Parker said. "You and Kurt can do that already. Besides, didn't you say Balthus cast that Pax...peace spell?"

"Yes, but as a tryst, we'd cast the Eall Tholia. There's a world of difference between it and the Pax Omnia. Both spells operate on the psychic level but the Eall Tholia operates on the physical level, too. The Eall Tholia would actually change how humans *feel* about us, which means it's permanent." She leaned forward in her chair. "Think of it, Park. No more pogroms. No more werehunts. No more living in fear of some human finding out what we are and forming a posse to hunt us down."

Parker stared at her. The look in his eyes had turned cold. Nobody said anything. The silent minutes seemed to stretch into hours. Undeterred, she opened her mouth to explain further but he spoke first. "What does this tryst thing have to do with last December?"

Garrett let out a tiny gasp. She hadn't expected this.

Oh, no. Don't tell me he's figured it out.

CHAPTER 26

"I—" Garrett said.

"I'm afraid that was my fault," Kurt said. "Let me explain." This was exactly what he'd thought would happen. Parker was highly intuitive, and he was no *dummkopf,* either.

Our moment of reckoning, hmm? All right—here goes...

He heaved a deep sigh. "Garrett came to me with her proposition about the tryst not long after you two met."

"Kurt—" Garrett began.

He turned. "Garrett, don't you think it's time we told him? He'll find out anyway, especially if the three of us merge like you say we will. If our connection is going to be that deep—well, frankly, I'd rather him know now than later."

She glared at him but remained silent. Pulling her shawl close, she looked away and then at Parker.

Kurt pursed his lips. "According to Garrett, a tryst is composed of a mage, a vampire regent, and a *were,* all of whom—by themselves—must possess extraordinary power." He smiled. "That certainly describes the three of us."

Parker said nothing.

The wolf's silence was unnerving, but he had no choice but to plow ahead. "One of the requirements for this tryst is that each has to be willing to join forces with the other two." Kurt's gaze turned serious. "I know how much you despise me, Parker. You think me cruel and capricious. You hate the way I rule my colony and how I treat other zots."

Parker didn't reply. He didn't even acknowledge Kurt had spoken. The wolf had eyes only for the mage.

Kurt waited a few moments. "Anyway, knowing you would never

have joined us on your own, I thought persuading you might be easier if you were my servant. So I had Garrett convince you to take on Darrylon in a death-match. You did and you won."

He watched the two closely. Garrett stared at the wolf with a wooden expression. Parker was still pretending not to hear.

Kurt leaned back in his chair and closed his eyes. "We underestimated you, Parker. Before you became alpha, you seemed so easygoing, so pliant. Both of us thought you'd be no trouble to convince." Heaving another sigh, he opened his eyes and sat forward, his lips twisting into a wry smile. "As long as I'm confessing, let me tell you something else. Garrett's being a mage"—he shook his head—"I could only turn her into my servant if she allowed it." Still smiling, he turned first to Garrett and then to Parker. Neither responded to him.

Will one of you say something?

They didn't.

His smile died. It was too late to stop now. "So we—I, really—came up with a plan. I'd pretend to seduce Garrett and make her my servant and you...well, once you saw that, you were supposed to fall in line like a good boy. To make the tryst, it would have been the same as if you'd agreed." He looked from one to the other and made a small grimace. They might as well have been statues.

Kurt's expression turned apologetic. "I'm sorry, Parker—and I think Garrett is, too—for what happened, for what we did. It was wrong, but knowing how you feel about me..." His head dipped a fraction. "There just didn't seem to be any other way."

He waited for the werewolf's reaction. There was none.

Kurt stared at the other man. "So, Parker...I know it seems presumptuous, especially now, but Garrett and I are asking if you will tryst with us."

CHAPTER 27

Garrett watched the look in Parker's bright green eyes go from cold to sub-zero. It frightened her.

"Let me get this straight." His voice sounded colder than the look in his eyes. "You two want to make this tryst but you need me to be the third, right?"

His stare transfixed her as if he'd laid her under a stasis.

"Yes," Kurt answered for both of them. He sounded eager.

"So instead of just asking, you two decided to trick me into joining you."

No one said a word. Parker rose from the leather chair. On his feet, he simply stood there, like a piece of granite. The only time she'd seen Parker this angry was the night he'd ripped Darrylon Slade to shreds. She braced herself, ready to hurl a paralyzing bolt of magick if he made a move toward her.

But he didn't. Silent, he stared at her for a few moments. Then his brow furrowed a little. "You know, I can understand you two maybe wanting to get rid of Darrylon." He paused. "And I can even understand your thinking that I was the only one in the pack who could do it." He paused again. "But what I don't understand," he said, his voice rising, "is why you thought you had to fuck me over like this to get your fucking tryst!"

Parker's hands clenched into fists. Still staring at her, he felt his way around the chair until he'd cleared it. Without turning, he began walking across the room, his backward steps slow and measured until he bumped against the door.

"Parker——" Garrett said.

"Do you have any idea what you've done to me?" he shouted. "Do you? Do you have any idea what this blood-sucking bastard"—he jerked his head in Kurt's direction—"has put me through? All so you could have your stupid tryst?"

He took a deep breath. "You two have a lot of goddamned nerve." His voice had quieted but there was no mistaking his barely-controlled fury. "You…" He stopped as if there were nothing more for him to say.

"Parker, I—" Garrett tried again.

"You know something? You want your tryst, right?" Parker's eyes were like green ice. "Well, I'll tell you what. The two of you can just kiss my hairy werewolf ass!"

He glared at Garrett a moment longer. Then, hurling the door open, he leapt over the threshold and was gone.

CHAPTER 28

The sound of the door Parker had slammed rang in Kurt's ears. "My word. That didn't go very well, now did it?"

Garrett burst into tears. "Oh, Mother," she wailed. "I've failed, I've failed, I've failed!" She buried her face in her hands and sobbed.

He watched her, puzzled. In all the years he'd known her, this was the first time he'd ever seen Garrett cry.

A few minutes later, he lifted her from her seat and held her close. She was limp as a rag. Kurt looked down at her face, at the tears that ran from beneath her closed eyelids. For all her fierceness, right now she seemed so small, so...vulnerable.

An old memory surfaced. Something twinged deep inside him.

He kissed away the salty drops. "Garrett, dear, it'll be all right. We'll just let Parker cool off a little while, and then we'll try again, yes?"

She shook her head. "No," her voice hitched. "He'll never—"

"Shh. We'll think of something."

She stopped her crying and looked up at him. "Will we?"

"Yes, we will." Then he smiled and gently kissed her lips. "Come. Stay with me tonight. Things will look better tomorrow. They always do."

Garrett's eyes narrowed. "How come you're being so nice to me?"

He shrugged. "A weak moment, no doubt." Looking deep into her hazel eyes, puffy and red from her crying, he suddenly felt more than just a twinge inside.

"A...very...weak...moment," he whispered, lowering his lips to hers. He kissed her with a passion he hadn't felt in an exceptionally long time. Ending their kiss, he stepped back and took Garrett's delicate hands into his. He gave her a little tug. "Come."

She nodded. Slipping an arm about her waist, Kurt led her to a door opposite the one Parker had slammed. Why was he being so nice to her?

And then he knew. *Garrett, I never dreamed anyone could…right now, you remind me so much of my darling Marguerite, dead these long centuries.*

But he wasn't going to tell her that.

CHAPTER 29

Parker hardly remembered leaving the party room and going outside. He stood in the alley, oblivious to the downpour beating on his head. Had he stumbled into somebody else's nightmare? If so, he sure wished the guy would wake up.

He didn't. Stuffing his hands into his pockets, he began to walk.

Parker had no idea how long he wandered in the rain. With each step, the enormity of Garrett and Kurt's hoax loomed larger and larger. It became like an unbearable physical weight, squeezing his chest until he couldn't breathe. He reeled onward, his crushing burden growing heavier and heavier until his feet slowed to a stop.

Parker had thought no pain could be worse than what he'd felt that night last December when he'd been forced to watch the vampire seduce and win the woman he loved. But to have learned not only was that night staged just for him but his love affair with Garrett had been entirely one-sided from the beginning...

He'd been wrong. The pain he felt now was worse. Far worse.

Without warning, a bolt of pure fury from his *were* exploded through his body. Balling his hands into fists until his fingernails bit into his palms, Parker inhaled a lung-bursting breath, threw his head back, and...

"Ahhhrrhhoo-oohrrgh!"

His anguished howl reverberated against the old brick buildings. It wasn't the cry of a natural wolf. Deeper and throatier, it echoed as if coming from the depths of hell. He howled a second time, pouring into his cry all his heartbreak. He'd been played for a fool, cruelly used, and he was powerless to do anything about it except walk away.

The howls had brought Parker's enraged wolf close to the surface. Determined to wrest control from its human self, his *were* surged to the fore of his conscious mind. A flash-fire of white heat blazed through his body. On its heels came the blade-like agony of his human form starting to shift. His light sweatshirt tightened into a straitjacket. A distant roaring rang in his ears. He'd gone into a forced morph.

"Shrrit!" Parker's human side reasserted itself. The only thing he could do was run, run like the wind in hopes of diverting the energy generated by his *were's* rage from fueling his change. He took off. Barreling through the rain, the soles of his expensive English loafers smacked against the flooded pavement, sending up sprays of water with each long stride.

Little by agonizing little, Parker's human side regained control over their shared mind and body and the wolf-madness subsided. His running slowed. But he didn't stop.

"Whmpf!" he grunted a few minutes later. He'd fallen over a large, heavy object. Blowing like a spent racehorse, he looked to see what he'd collided with.

Whose goddamned ride is this?

Sprawled over the car's front end, he blinked at the old brown vehicle, thinking it looked awfully familiar...

Oh. It's mine, he realized, panting softly.

Parker pushed himself up off the car hood and stood upright. His legs hurt. *Go,* a small voice inside his brain whispered. He fished for his keys. Using the car for support, he stumbled around to the driver's side, unlocked the door and fell inside.

He sat behind the leather-wrapped steering wheel, not seeing the rain-splattered windshield. Water from his soaked hair dripped down his face. He rested his forehead on the perforated cowhide. Clutching his belly, his broad shoulders shook with silent sobs. The car's windows fogged over. *How could I have been so stupid, so fucking blind?* he screamed inside his head. He wanted to die.

"I loved you, Garrett," he said in a strangled whisper. And he had. That he eventually would have had to choose another freyja was immaterial. His heart belonged to her and that was what counted.

Parker lifted his face and stared miserably at the foggy windshield. All this time, somewhere deep in the back of his mind, he'd been hoping against hope that Kurt would release her from his psychic grip and she'd come back to him. But even that had been taken from him. She'd never been his from the beginning.

Unexpectedly, the voice of Caril Draper, a werewolf who'd been blessed—or cursed—with extraordinary psychogenetic abilities like his broke through the numbness in his brain. Nearly twenty years older than he, she'd been one of his mentors during those difficult years after he'd become a werewolf.

"Watch out for other wolves, Parker," he heard Caril say. He sat up in his seat, remembering. Caril's face materialized in the foggy windshield. "Never let anyone see how strong you are or what you can do. Your size alone is enough to make any pack alpha nervous. Anything more and jealous alphas won't give you a chance to challenge them to a deathmatch." She shook her head. "That goes for other zots too, Park. We like to think that because of what we are, we can trust each other implicitly but we can't. Zots are no better or worse than humans and won't hesitate to use you as a pawn in whatever little game they happen to be playing." She paused. "Be careful, Park. Don't let that happen to you."

He'd taken Caril's words to heart, knowing that she'd spoken from bitter experience. He'd kept himself closed tight like an unpeeled orange, aloof and untrusting, alone even in the midst of his pack. Until Garrett, that is—until he'd fallen in love with that two-faced cunt. With her, he'd hoped to prove Caril wrong, but instead, Garrett had proven to be just what his she-wolf mentor had warned against.

"Oh, God...what do I do now?" he whispered at the rainy windshield but it held no answers.

Go home, his inner voice urged. He didn't want to go home. But he couldn't just sit here, either. Feeling leaden and weightless at the same time, his trembling hand fumbled his key into the ignition. The Caprice's powerful engine roared to life. Pawing at the dashboard, he managed to switch on the car's defroster and windshield wipers. He waited for the glass to clear.

Parker drove aimlessly through the streets. The rain's toneless drumming against the car's metal roof seemed to repeat her name—*GarrettGarrettGarrett*. A pressure built in his chest until he couldn't stand it.

He stomped on the brakes. The Caprice screeched to a halt in the middle of Halpine Avenue. During the daytime, it was one of Seattle's busiest transportation arteries. This time of night, the avenue was completely deserted. His white-knuckled hands gripped the steering wheel. "You goddamned bitch," he roared, rattling the windows in the close confines of the stationary vehicle.

His wolf, sensing the weakening of its human side's control over their shared mind, burst forth a second time. "No," Parker shouted, his human eyes flaring into his wolf's glowing green ones. His foot slammed the accelerator to the floor. The tires on the old brown car spun against the rain-slicked asphalt, screaming as the intense friction burned rubber.

They took off. Man and wolf rocketed along the avenue, accelerating from forty to fifty, and then to sixty miles an hour. Parker's eyes changed rapidly from his wolf's to human and back again. His *were's* need to vent its fury was overwhelming. It needed to kill and was determined to do just that—to hell with the consequences.

Parker-the-human's mental bonds over his creature snapped. His wolf had almost full control over the body. It was all he could do to hang on by a wolf's hair and stay human. Again and again, the human inside hurled its will against the beast driving the car.

Streetlights strobing past, the Chevy sped its erratic way along the avenue. "Nnrrooh," Parker's human side managed to shout again. His voice was deep, gravelly, and not human.

Discovery Park loomed on his left. Parker jerked the steering wheel in that direction and the car skidded across the asphalt. They slewed onto Discovery Park Boulevard. The Caprice jumped the curb and then Parker and his *were* careened midst the greenery. The rain-softened earth slowed the car from sixty, then to forty, and dropping further still, to thirty miles an hour.

He tried to lift his foot off the accelerator but his wolf wouldn't let him. Tires churning the turf into mud, the big brown car fishtailed over the grass. Headlight beams bounced and stabbed through the darkness. Spinning every now and then in one hundred eighty or even three hundred sixty degree turns, the Caprice looked as if it were dancing, an impromptu ballet of destruction.

The Chevy's frame squealed ominously from his wolf putting it through maneuvers it was not built to perform. They rocketed over the edge of a low rise in the earth. For a moment, the car was airborne. Crashing to the bottom, Parker heard something beneath the car snap.

Its eyes like green fire, his wolf laughed with maniacal glee, rejoicing in his ruinous creation. As the car spun in yet another one hundred eighty degree turn, something thumped the car's left fender. Surprised, his wolf allowed the car to rock to a stop. Both he and his human self watched whatever it was that hit them fly over the hood to land in the churned earth about twenty feet away.

They sat with jaw hanging open, staring in shock. Parker-the-human reacted first and mentally kicked his wolf into the background. The green glow in his eyes went dark.

"Goddammit," Parker yelled in a human voice, "you crazy-ass shit, we just hit somebody!"

Ignoring the persistent rain, he sprang out of the car and ran toward the inert lump. With his car's headlights illuminating the surreal scene, he knelt in the mud beside the body, gasping with fear. He placed his fingers on the person's neck and was rewarded by a steady pulse. His breath whooshed out in relief. He gingerly rolled his victim over so he could get a look at the face.

"Jesus!" He tried to leap backward but slipped in the mud and fell on his butt. It was her—the woman who'd jumped him in this very same park ten days ago.

Parker stared with saucer-like eyes at the strange woman's mud-caked face, his mind whirling like an out-of-control carousel. For a moment, panic obliterated his common sense but then his brain jump-started itself and started working again. *What do I do now? Should I just leave her here? Wait. I can't do that. She's killed nine people.* He blinked a few times. *Okay, I know. I'll take her to Kurt.* Then he shook his head. *No, that's no good, either. I...I can't go back there. Not after tonight. Shit.*

It was still raining hard. The cold drops pelting the woman's face washed away some of the mud, leaving dark streaks on her forehead and cheeks. Groaning softly, she stirred and rolled onto her stomach. He watched in disbelief while the woman pulled herself onto all fours. Her flexing fingers dug into the muck. She was trying to crawl away.

She didn't make it. Without another sound, the woman dropped face-first into the mud.

That's it. He scrambled over to where she lay. *She's hurt. I can't just leave her.* Blinking the rain out of his eyes, he rolled the strange woman

151

onto her back, sat her up, and then began scraping the more of the mud from her face.

She never moved.

Parker slowly rose to his feet, bringing the woman with him. Slipping an arm behind her thighs, he cradled her against his broad chest. Despite the mud still clinging to her face, the woman's exquisite beauty shone through. She was even more gorgeous than he remembered.

He carried her to his car, seeing not only had he left the door wide open but he'd left the engine running, too. "'Bout time something went right tonight," he grumbled. The rain had soaked the driver's seat as well as the carpet underneath. The passenger's side had remained largely dry.

"Well, mostly right, anyway." He sighed. Between the rain and the mud that he was about to smear over the seats, he'd have a hell of a cleaning job to do later. Holding the woman by her slim waist, he maneuvered her through the car's doorway and pushed her across the bench seat to its middle.

"Ow," he muttered as he rapped his left knee against the steering column while climbing in. The car's headlights revealed that his way was clear to the street. He switched them off. "Okay, sweetheart," he whispered into the darkness. "Let's get you out of here."

Gripping the steering wheel in his left hand, Parker tentatively pressed the gas pedal. The rear tires spun uselessly at first but then found purchase in the mud. The car rocked forward.

Thank God for small favors. For a moment, it had looked like he'd have to get out and push. Driving over the wet grass, he saw the downpour had died down, though not by much. *Another small favor.* Dawn was just a couple of hours away and as long as it kept raining, it wasn't likely he'd be spotted off-roading through the middle of the park.

At the edge of the street, Parker stopped and peered left and then right. Seeing no one, he eased over the curb and drove home.

CHAPTER 30

Arriving at his house, Parker pulled the Caprice around to the back rather than park in the driveway. His rampage through Discovery Park earlier might make today's news. Though he doubted anyone would notice brown mud on his brown car, even in daylight, he didn't want to take the chance.

The woman nestled under his arm was still unconscious. He wrestled her out of the car. Hefting her over his shoulder, he unlocked and then slipped through the gate.

In the mud room off the kitchen, he propped the unconscious woman in a corner on the floor and flipped on the light. "Okay, honey, let's see what we've—jesusfuckingchrist!"

Parker fell to his knees beside her. The woman looked as if she'd been dragged through a bale of concertina wire. Her lightweight black shirt and trousers had been reduced to rags. Through what was left, he could see deep gouges in her golden brown flesh. Most were bleeding, rewetting the drying mud that covered her. Had she been attacked? By who? Or rather, by what? Did this mean she wasn't the Slayer?

The woman was losing more blood. He checked her pulse again. It was steady but fainter than it had been before. He tore off the remains of her clothes and then stripped off his own. Gathering the unconscious woman into his arms, he ran upstairs to the bath. He carried her to the tub and manhandling her as tenderly as he could, he maneuvered them both inside. Then he turned on the shower. Water cascaded around them like the rain outside. Rinsing the filth from her body, he tried not to see the aquatic battle between red and brown sluicing into the drain.

Inspecting the woman's now more or less clean wounds, Parker winced at one particularly nasty set of four furrows that started at the top of her left shoulder and gaped over her breast, almost down to her stomach.

Soaping her, he couldn't help but notice the woman's firm flesh. She seemed to be all muscle, without a trace of fat. Fingers sliding along her slick skin, he took in the ridges and valleys of her corded forearm while he rinsed her. She had beautiful hands, her four fingers and thumb tapering like elegant candles from her large palm. Pretty, perfectly rounded nails covered her fingertips.

They were dirty. He brought the woman's arm toward his face so he could see them better. The mud had been ground in deep. Then he realized there was more than just mud underneath her fingernails. He took a closer look and gasped. *She did this to herself!*

Caught between the nail and the underlying skin was bits of bloodied flesh. Parker glanced down at the four stripes on her neck. She must have inflicted not only these but most of the others, too.

Why?

He couldn't begin to fathom it, and the unconscious woman wasn't telling. He concentrated on getting the rest of the woman clean. His soapy fingers played over her skin, cupping her breasts to get at the mud that lay in the crease underneath and then sliding down to clean away the mud that had gotten into the folds at her crotch.

Finishing their shower, he hauled the woman out of the tub, swiped a towel hanging on a peg and dried them both as best he could. With satisfaction, he saw her wounds had stopped bleeding. He carried her into his bedroom.

"You'll be okay," he murmured, laying the unconscious woman on his bed. He turned to the nightstand and switched on the small lamp. "You're with me, now. You're safe." He knew she couldn't hear him, but it made him feel better to say it.

Parker gazed down at her, at the swell of her generous breasts with their large, dark brown nipples. His eyes traveled along the woman's flat stomach to her flaring hips and then further down, lingering on her long, well-muscled thighs. Mesmerized by her body, her terrible wounds barely registered in his brain.

She had the biggest clit he'd ever seen, almost like a small penis. He licked his lips without realizing it.

Go on, his *were* purred. *You know you wanna—*

His wolf's whispering jolted him to his senses. "Shut up. I'm not gonna do anything to her, understand? And neither are you." He set his jaw and moved to the foot of his bed. Grabbing the top sheet, he pulled it up to the woman's chin.

Parker had just finished arranging the white covering when she opened her eyes and seemed to look at him. He gasped and took a step back. *Her eyes. . .look at her eyes.*

The woman's orbs were snakelike—all irises with vertically slit pupils—but that was where the similarity ended. Their predominant color was gold but there were other colors too— purple, red, green—a rainbow of colors that flashed like little sparkles of glitter in a kaleidoscope.

Then she closed them. He watched for a while but the woman didn't stir again.

With a small sigh, he went to his closet and pulled on a pair of jeans. Then he crossed the braided rug to the overstuffed chair near the bed and sat. Elbows digging into his knees, he gazed at the unconscious woman, hypnotized by the slow, rhythmic rise and fall of her chest.

"Who are you?" he whispered in the pre-dawn darkness.

The woman didn't answer.

Parker stared at her for a minute longer, then leaned back and stared at the ceiling.

He never remembered falling asleep in the chair.

.

CHAPTER 31

Melera had made it halfway to full consciousness when she sensed something was wrong. Floating in her personal darkness, it dawned on her that she felt a profound loss as if someone or something beloved had died. *What...?* That jot of mental clarity disintegrated into a jumble of nonsense and she fell back into oblivion.

She woke again and gazed upon a glacial expanse of white ceiling. She wondered to whom it belonged. Then her body woke up. Melera wished it hadn't. She felt mangled as if she'd been run through a rock crusher. Trying to lift her head inundated her with vertigo. Lying back in the pillow, she squeezed her eyes shut. Then she noticed the air held a heavy, musky scent that gave her a shivery feeling.

Well, she wasn't going to worry about that now. *All right. What's...* Then she knew. Her memory was gone. She couldn't remember anything—who she was, where she was, or what had happened to her.

Remain calm, her czado intoned inside her head. *It will come.*

"Right. Remain calm," she murmured, working to quell her rising fear. "I can't remember jakk and you tell me to remain calm?" She didn't know to whom those cold voices belonged but she knew it was right. Panicking would only make her situation worse.

After she'd quieted herself, Melera craned her neck and took in the rest of her surroundings. She occupied a sunny and sizeable pale blue room, the walls of which were punctuated by two sets of large, double windows. She'd been laid out on a bed that appeared big enough to comfortably sleep three people. A cool sheet of thin, white fabric swathed loosely around her, exposing most of her golden brown skin.

She frowned upon seeing her ugly bruises and torn flesh. The ghastly sight triggered her memory. *Jakk. Another seizure.* Closing her eyes, she recited her mnemonic litany and then squinted at the ceiling. *I'm forgetting something. I know I am, but I can't*—

The door to her room opened. Her eyes widened. It was the starfarer with the reddish hair.

Beloc's hound!

Melera reacted before her czado could stop her. She hurled herself from her prone position into a flying somersault over the bed. Her plan was to knock him aside and then get the jakk out.

But the seizure had left her too weak to perform even this simple maneuver. Instead of landing on her feet, she tumbled off the bed and fell to the floor in a heap, hopelessly tangled in the white material. "Ughhh," she groaned, struggling to get up. Her nerve endings were on fire. Screwing her eyes shut, she strove to dampen her agony before she fainted.

A moment later, the redhead was cradling her in a pair of strong, hairy arms. She tried to push him away but her arms might as well have been made of putty. Disgusted, she relented and let him help her sit.

"Jesus, sweetheart," Beloc's pet said, lifting her onto the bed. "What were you trying to do? Just take it easy, okay?"

Melera opened one bleary eye and then closed it again. *Jakk off, ph'uka,* she thought, annoyed by his concern. She knew what he was up to, and wasn't about to be fooled by that old ruse.

The dog kept up a running monologue while busying himself getting her comfortable. "My name's Parker. Parker Berenson. This is my house. I—"

Her ears tuning him out, her eyes took him in. The hound wore a pair of faded blue trousers—*jeans*—no shirt, and no shoes. Holding her close while he untangled the sheet that had wound around her left leg, she noticed his broad shoulders and chest—and the way his hard muscles bulged beneath his skin, rippling each time he moved.

The redhead's dense chest hair tickled her nose. Looking up, she saw the strong planes of his face, his high cheekbones, and squarish chin. He had beautiful eyes. A startling shade of green, they were nearly the same color as a newly hatched ky'un, a vicious reptilian-like creature that had been popular house pets among her people. Back home, she'd always kept a pack of the little savages and had loved them all. The jakker even had a ky'un's smile. That pleased her.

Hmph. At least Beloc sent a pretty one.

She was also keenly aware of how gently the redhead handled her while he rearranged the white sheet and how his body heat soothed her blasted nerves. It had been so long since anyone had touched her, she'd almost forgotten what live contact felt like.

Once she was settled, he sat on the edge of the bed and gave her a small smile that died a moment later. "Oh, jeez," he said with a pained look. "You're bleeding." Melera looked down and saw red spots where the sheet had blotted her blood.

The hound shook his head. "I'll get a cloth," he offered and stood.

"What do you care?" she said in Toro, the official language of Maqu. An artificial tongue, Toro was spoken galaxy-wide. Without it, interspecies communication would be just about impossible.

The redhead had been ready to take a step when she'd spoken. He stared down her with huge eyes. "Uh, what was that?"

She didn't answer. *Cut the jakk,* she thought with a tiny, tired frown.

Silent minutes passed before the hound spoke again. "Umm...don't you speak English?"

Melera narrowed her eyes, trying to figure his advantage in continuing to play hu-man. She couldn't think of any. *All right, jakker,* she told her enemy. *I don't know what you think you're singing, but I'll sing along—for now.*

CHAPTER 32

Parker stared at the woman lying on his bed. He'd have sworn he'd heard her speaking English that night in Discovery Park.

"Yes," she said after a few very long moments.

"Oh, good." He smiled. "For a minute there, I thought I was in trouble."

The woman said nothing, nor did she return his smile. She glared at him with whirling, slit-pupil eyes. Her look made him feel as if he were being dissected. That, in turn, reminded him the woman was probably a psycho—and a murderous one at that.

"Here," he said, hoping he didn't sound too jumpy. "I'll go get that towel." He headed for the bathroom. When he came back, wet washcloth in hand, the woman had come out from the sheet and was sitting up. Ogling her, he nearly tripped over the rug's frayed edge. Reaching the bed, he handed her the cloth and then stepped back. He dared not sit again. She'd already kicked his ass once. The woman might be weak right now but he'd bet his werewolf's hairy balls she was far from helpless. God knew what she'd do to him if he got too close.

The woman wiped the drying blood from her breast, arms, and legs. The ugly tears in her flesh had disappeared. Her golden brown skin was smooth and unmarked as if she'd never been wounded. He nodded a few times. That she was a self-healer didn't surprise him in the least.

When she'd finished, she handed him the washcloth. He took it and threw it toward his closet. Backing away a little further, he fell into the chair beside the bed. She stared at him, inscrutable.

Parker stared back. He had so many questions—like who she was, what she was, where she came from, whether she was the Seattle Slayer, and if she wasn't, whether she had a boyfriend.

Ask about her boyfriend first, his wolf growled.

"So what's your name?" he blurted.

The woman rolled her eyes and grimaced as if he'd said something infuriating. Then she sighed. "Melera."

He didn't quite catch it. "Mel—what?"

The woman sighed again. "Melera," she said, louder this time.

Melera. Odd name. "Nice to—"

Before he could say anything more, she erupted into a violent sneezing fit. Then she began to cough—deep, bronchial spasms that made him think *asthma.* Her golden eyes watered and she clawed at them as if they itched. Falling back onto the mattress, she drew herself into a fetal curl, her body convulsing with each cough and sneeze.

Parker jumped from his seat and fell on the bed. He gripped her shoulder. "What's wrong?" he shouted as if the attack had maybe made her deaf, too.

Choked by a particularly brutal fit of coughing, Melera didn't answer. "Tow-bac-co," she wheezed at last. "Me—ckugh! Ckuuugh! Need tow-bac-co."

His head jerked in surprise. "What?"

"Get me—choo—tow-bac-co!"

"You want to smoke?" He slowly wagged his head, thinking she must have hit hers when she'd fallen off the bed earlier. He smiled like a parent to a confused toddler. "Sweetheart, I don't think—"

"Tow-chugh! bac-co! Ckugh-shoo!"

He blinked, taken aback by her insistence. "But I don't..." Then he had an idea. "Wait here." He stood and ran out of his bedroom, racing down the stairs and into his study. Last night, he'd rolled a bunch of joints and had smoked some while going over his program notes. Maybe he had a few left.

He could hear Melera's hacking all the way down here. It sounded terrible. He yanked the desk drawer open. There—he had three. Grabbing them, he raced back upstairs and barreled into his bedroom. On the bed, he scooted next to her, stared at the tip of one of the joints and torched it.

"Ack—ack-shoo!" she sneezed.

After making sure it would stay lit, he helped the stricken woman to sit up. Holding her close, he proffered the joint. She tried to take it, but her fingers shook too hard. Batting her hand away, he placed the cigarette between her lips.

Melera inhaled a huge hit and held it for a few moments before letting it out. To his amazement, her coughing fit stopped. She sneezed once more and took another drag. After the third, she pulled her head away. He held onto the joint, watching her.

She looked at him through half-lidded eyes. "Not tow-bac-co," she said, exhaling smoke.

Still holding her close, Parker brought the burning joint to his lips, took two hits and offered it to her again. "No." He let out a smoky sigh. "But it's all I have." They finished the joint in silence. Putting out the ember by pinching it between his thumb and forefinger, he popped the now-cooled roach into his mouth and swallowed. Now pleasantly high, he gave in to his urge to stroke Melera's long black hair and was delighted when she didn't object. "So, tell me. What happened to you just now?" he said, his voice low.

Leaning into him, she rested a forearm along the length of his thigh. Parker let his right arm fall from her shoulder and slipped it about her waist, grinning when she didn't object to that, either.

"Al-ler-gies." Her breath warmed the skin on his neck.

Startled, he stopped his stroking. *A zot with allergies? That's weird.* Zots were immune from nearly every human affliction imaginable.

Melera squirmed out from under his arm and straddled his thighs. She smiled, a wide, warm grin that made him go all gooey inside. Her upper canines, slightly longer than the rest of her teeth, gave her a deliciously feral look. She started giggling. Then she began to laugh.

He stared, fascinated. He would've sworn he heard at least five different voices coming from her throat. *Whoa…this weed's better than I thought.* High or not, it didn't keep those dulcet tones from sending thrills up and down his spine. He started giggling, too.

Rising halfway to her knees, she twined her arms partway around his neck and pushed, forcing him onto his back. The feel of her skin against his was maddening.

"What," she started, but erupted into another fit of giggling. "What give—whoo-hoo!—give you me—heh-hee?" she demanded.

"Ah-hah! Weed," he said, trying to stem his own giggles without success. "Don't worry—a-hum—it's harmless. I mean, I don't smoke tobacco. That stuff can kill you."

She chuckled. "Ishti mara," she said in that odd language of hers. Her eyes seemed to whirl, first one way and then the other. She started giggling again. It was infectious. Soon they were both laughing as they had a minute ago. They rolled on the bed, chortling at each other. Parker wondered if all psycho killer bitches were as much fun as Melera.

When their rolling had stopped, she was straddling him again. Her breath coming almost in gasps, she stared down at him with her full lips slightly parted. He wanted to chew those lips.

Then, to his astonished delight, Melera kissed him.

CHAPTER 33

Parker's cure for Melera's allergy attack—weed, he'd called it—had also acted on that part of her brain governing her libido. The last thing she wanted was to fuck this jakker but she couldn't stop herself.

The drug had banished her lethargy, too. She felt energized as if she'd awakened from a long rest. Deep into their kiss, she briefly wondered if weed was a derivative of one of the countless drugs Beloc had used to make her more—amenable—to those he wanted to impress or reward.

Her qia swelled until it resembled an inch-long penis peeking out from her vulva. Her crotch had drenched. Kissing him again, she wrapped her serpentine tongue around his shorter, stubbier one and stroked it. He groaned. Then, uncurling her long pink snake, she slid it down his throat. "Ahhmm," he uttered, a strangled sob. She retracted her tongue and flicked it around the inside of his mouth, licking his teeth and gums.

Parker grabbed her shoulders and pushed her away, their lips making an audible pop on parting. He stared at her, gasping.

Melera sat up. Watching him through narrowed eyes, her lips curved into a sly smile. Starting at the base of his neck, she traced her index finger down the length of his trunk, over his chest and stomach, past his navel and down to his jeans. She loosened the button. His erection burst forth, parting the zipper on its own. She looked down and her smile widened the tiniest bit. *Mmm.* The jakker's brlk was about nine inches long and looked to be at least six inches around. Thick, purple veins bulged in stark relief and a drop of pre-cum glistened at the tip of its plum-sized head.

Reaching for Parker's hugely swollen member, she dug his balls out of his jeans, cupped them in one hand and gently squeezed. Then, curling her fingers around the shaft, she lightly stroked him. He felt heavy, like a stout club.

Parker whimpered.

Scooting up a few inches, she lowered her hips and slowly rocked, sliding her wet kynt back and forth along his length while staring into his startling green eyes. With his slack jaw, he was the one who appeared to be drugged.

"Talit kar erya u Beloc?" she said, speaking Toro. "Is this what he promised you for coming after me? A piece of my royal Shen'zae ass?"

Dog, I'll make you wish you'd stayed in Maqu.

Rising to her knees, she placed the tip of the jakker's brlk at her opening. Towering over him, she watched him pant for a while. Then she sat.

"Aaaagh!" he screamed.

He tried to shove her up off of his brlk but she held fast. Squeezing him tighter, she rode her bucking, bellowing mount while wagering how long he would last before begging her to free him. "What's the matter?" she sneered. "Surely you knew. Isn't that why you wanted to jakk me? Isn't that why everybody in Maqu wanted to jakk my kind?" She chuckled. "My friend, everything you heard is true. We bite!"

Barely able to hear herself over his yelling, Melera watched a river of tears stream down his cheeks. Her upper mouth stretched into a grin of pure malice while her lower one continued to chew.

Then she began to laugh.

CHAPTER 34

IthurtsithurtsgetthisbitchoffmehercuntsgotteethohGodshesbitingmyfuckingdick-off!

The pain was unbearable. Parker's human self could no longer maintain control over his inner beast. His wolf burst forth so fast he wouldn't have felt it even if he'd been paying attention.

Parker-the-human didn't fight Parker-the-wolf. Black nose twitching at the end of his long snout now, he pulled his lips back from two inch-long fangs and laughed—a grumbling snarl—at Melera's shocked expression.

The wolf roared with delight when she threw her head back and screamed. He started bucking again, spearing her with his now thirteen-inch long prick. She'd humiliated him with her biting cunt. But he was the wolf-king and he wasn't about to take her bullshit. He narrowed his glowing green eyes. "You want sex? Fine. I'll fuck you until you learn to show the proper respect."

She tried to rise to her knees.

"Oh, no, you don't." He grabbed her by the hips and, sinking his talons into her flesh, pulled her back down on his cock. Fresh blood spurted from the holes his claws had made and trickled down his furred arms. The scent was intoxicating.

"Uhrrm…you feel real good now, bitch." He was so big she couldn't squeeze his enormous wolf prick. Her inner teeth now only scraped him gently, adding to the pleasure. Like being jacked off by someone wearing a French tickler on her finger.

His length had forced her wide open and the top third of his dick lay inside her womb. Now that really felt good—as if he was fucking a second pussy, sans teeth.

She moaned.

"You feelin' it?" He raised his hips up from the bed. Her weight, balanced on his groin, pushed him deeper into her.

Melera doubled over and buried her face in his abdominal fur.

Parker laughed at her obvious pain. "Like my wolf-dick, don't you?" he growled, wiggling his hips to maximize her agony.

She raised her head and howled.

His wolf went at her. He sank his fangs into her golden brown flesh again and again, into her luscious tits, her ass, her thighs—everywhere. Her blood was like nectar. Taking her from behind, he carved his human name into her back with a cutlass-sharp claw. He fucked every hole she had and took especial delight in watching his cum splash over her face.

The bed was ruined. Parker's dark red pelt and Melera's black hair were matted with blood and semen. She'd fought him for hours, but now she put up no resistance. His wolf wasn't sure she was even conscious. Sensing his victory, he roared in triumph.

Just when he'd decided the bitch had taken as much punishment as she could stand, the house began to shake.

Melera knew how to deal with this kind of pain. After that first plunge into agony, when Parker's form had shifted from hu-man-like into the red-furred giant, she'd embraced her pain, letting it envelope her until the hurt became an ecstatic, bottomless bliss.

Like pebbles dropped into a pond, each time he ripped into her flesh or impaled her with his monstrous brlk, waves of pleasure rippled throughout her body, tumbling over and merging with one another until it was almost unbearable.

Tossed onto her stomach, a super-hot steel rod was shoved into her ass. She cried out at its sweet sting. A pair of clawed hands grasped her hips and dragged her a short distance over the bed. Her rump was in the air and the furry red giant was slamming into her. His heavy balls smacked at her opening with every stroke, teasing like an outrageous flirt.

As she pumped her hips, her penis-like qia rubbed over his pelted thighs and the smooth bedsheet tickling her hardened nipples sent surges of ecstasy to her brain and kynt.

Then she went limp. Most of her strength had deserted her. She couldn't have stopped him from jakking her even if she'd wanted. She listened to his growls and snarls. Every now and then she felt the creature's snout at her ear and shivered under his tongue's rough caresses. She reveled in his searing body heat scorching her back.

The giant deserted her ass for her kynt, breaking into her womb and splitting her wide again. She opened her mouth to scream with delight but nothing came out but a deep rumble, almost a vibration rather than an actual sound.

Melera had fallen into an alternate state, a rapturous delirium in which she was only aware of an intense pressure building within her. Then she did something she thought she'd never do again.

Opening her five-chambered throat wide, she began to sing.

CHAPTER 35

Earthquake! the small portion of sanity left to Parker's human self yelled inside his and the wolf's shared mind.

A second later, he realized it wasn't the house that was shaking——it was him. In the next moment, he'd been wrapped in a blast of tone that rattled his bones, an un-sound that threatened to split his skull. Then he was dumped into a giant blender, the thing's slashing blades chopping him into tiny pieces until he was a puree of flesh, blood, and agony. Dimly, he knew this was Melera's doing. He screamed for mercy but she gave no quarter. All he could do was roll with her and endure his unending misery.

Just when he thought he would die, he broke through to a marvelous heaven. There was no more pain. He was being propelled through a wondrous sea of sound and color that stroked and tickled him like the softest silks and satins, inside and out. Tumbling head over heels as if buffeted by a river current, his form alternated between human and wolf. His fingers sprouted the familiar dark red pelt and claws and seconds later they would change back to human fingers. *It doesn't hurt,* he thought, awe-struck.

Then he saw Melera swimming alongside. Enveloping him in her arms and legs, she kissed him with fiery passion. They swam together through the endless sea, parting and merging, over and over until he couldn't tell where she left off and he began.

Howling his joy, Parker watched, astonished, as myriad hues of blue, green, and purple issued from his mouth. The cool colors washed over her as if he'd painted her with a brush. Smiling, she opened her mouth and a mélange of reds and yellows surrounded him. The various colors swam like flickering ropes of light and twined around and within the two of them like living vines. In the midst of all this color, she kissed him again.

There came a blinding flash. Parker exploded into billions of tiny bits. Each shard hurtling through eternity, each piece a seed to colonize a new universe. He couldn't see or hear Melera anymore but that was okay. He knew she was with him, in all her billions of bits too, and together, like a cosmic Adam and Eve, they would create a whole new breed of beings, beings that were more than human, more than exotic, beings that were more than God in all His selves...

CHAPTER 36

After their simultaneous climax, Parker didn't pull out of her and she didn't want him to. He lay draped over her back—insensible, it seemed.

Melera crouched on the bed, enjoying the feel of his brlk becoming flaccid while the last vestiges of song vibrated her cells. Eventually, his weight forced her to lie flat on her stomach. He sounded winded. Each huff pressed his chest against her shoulder blades and his hot breath tickled her left ear. She felt and heard a kiss and then his weight was gone.

She rolled onto her side, facing him. At some point, he'd changed from the red-furred creature back to the hu-man-looking one. She wondered which of them was his true form.

Healing herself of the gashes and bruises of love, Melera stared at him, thoroughly confused. She'd always thought only her people could make song. More than that, as far as she knew, she was the last Xia'saan alive in Maqu. She should not have been able to sing.

Yet with him, she had. They both had.

It put her situation in a whole new light. Parker might really be of this galaxy and of Dirt. If so, he couldn't belong to Beloc, which meant the Jahannan warlord hadn't discovered the wormhole to this solar system. Of course, the other possibility was that Beloc did know about the wormhole and then, after discovering what he could do, had sent him from Maqu. If this was true, Parker was a dead—whatever he was. But she had to be sure.

At that moment, Parker opened his eyes. He turned his blood-streaked face toward her. His lips stretched into a lazy, satisfied-looking smile. "Wow. Sweetheart, that was... you're..."

She frowned. "What 'sweetheart' is?"

He gave her an odd look and then shrugged. "It's just a little name to call someone you really like."

Now it was she who gave him the odd look. "Me you like?"

"Very."

She raised her brow. *After what I did to you? Interesting.*

"C'mon." Parker sat up and scooted off the bed. "Let's get clean and then I'll make us something to eat. I'm starving."

Melera didn't know what "starving" meant but she knew the word "eat" and she was very hungry. He took her hand and led her into a narrow, brightly lit room. She watched him fiddle with a clear knob jutting from the center of a silver disk set into a tiled wall. Water fell from a nozzle near the ceiling.

They showered and dried each other off with large, soft, and fluffy cloths—*towels,* she remembered. Then they returned to the sleeping room. Inside, he opened a door in the wall across from the bed. Reaching into a dark, smallish space, he took out a pair of light-colored drawstring pants.

She stood naked in the room's middle and watched him dress. *Beloc doesn't allow prisoners to wear clothes.*

He reached into the little dark room a second time and withdrew a collarless, full-sleeved white shirt made of some kind of lightweight material. To her surprise, he came over to where she stood and helped slip it over her head. The shirt's fabric felt smooth and cool against her skin. It was fairly long too, hitting her legs at mid-thigh. The loose sleeves allowed for plenty of air circulation and plenty of movement. It was quite comfortable.

Parker stepped back a pace. His startling green gaze slowly traveled over her body, as if appraising a particularly fine pleasure-slave. Flushing from head to toe, she felt her nipples swell. Her body's heated reaction felt like a betrayal. She'd been in prison. This wasn't the first time she'd been scrutinized by males, females, or in-betweens and she'd always remained cold as steel. Why should this male be any different?

"What?" she said. She'd tried to sound gruff and irritated but only managed a soft and husky murmur.

He stepped forward and gazed into her eyes. Sliding his hands over her tits, he lightly massaged her hardened tips underneath the soft cloth.

I will not give in to him, I will not. She began to tremble.

"You look lovely," he whispered. Slipping a hand between her legs, he gently probed her kynt with his fingers. She gasped. Her crotch immediately soaked and her knees went weak. But she refused to shut her eyes.

Withdrawing, he probed her parted lips with two sopping fingers. Then, his gaze still locked on hers, he licked his hand clean. He smiled and took her trembling hand in his damp one. "C'mon. We have a lot to talk about, but first, let's eat."

She blinked, bemused by the sudden change of subject. "No." Pulling him back, Melera caught herself at his smug expression. *Jakk—I almost—he thinks he can play me like that?*

"No...what?" he said, caressing her cheek with his dry hand.

With a small smile, she curled her fingers around his wrist. Then she turned her face into the fleshy part of his palm and bit.

"Yaagh!" He tried to snatch his hand away, but she held fast. He watched his blood rivulet over her golden brown skin. She brought his hand to her mouth again, this time to lick away his blood. By the time she finished, the wound had healed. She smirked.

Parker chuckled. "Touché, sweetheart."

He led her out of the sleeping room. Trailing him, she stared at his heavily muscled back. This game they played had taken a lot of unexpected twists. Descending a flight of stairs, Melera raised a black brow. Parker had mentioned there was a great deal they needed to talk about after they'd eaten.

He was right about that. Parker Berenson indeed had a lot of talking to do.

CHAPTER 37

Though it was well past dinnertime, Parker prepared a sumptuous breakfast for the two of them and was gratified to see Melera devour her food almost as fast as he. He liked women who liked to eat—psycho killers or not.

When they moved into his study to talk, he noticed her hesitate and then look about the room with the air of someone who hears a noise they can't identify. Frowning, he listened too but heard nothing unusual.

She shook her head as if deciding she must've hallucinated whatever it was she thought she'd heard. She smiled at him.

"Sit here." He pointed to an overstuffed chair similar to the one in his bedroom. While Melera made herself comfortable, he pulled his old padded chair with the cracked leather seat away from his desk and rolled it forward. Then he sat, too.

She gave him an inquiring look.

Parker wasn't sure what he should say, so he decided to start with an apology. He took a deep breath. "Look. I'm sorry if I hurt you before…I mean, when we were upstairs." His mouth twisted into a sheepish smile.

She didn't answer at first. Then she smiled back. "Is ohh-kay. Liked it." She leaned forward, her eyes spinning at slow speed. "Sorry too, you me hurt."

He started to smile. Without warning, his study disappeared and he was sucked into the depths of her two golden whirlpools, drowning in them and perfectly content to do so. A moment later, his study returned as abruptly as it had disappeared. A sense of temporal dislocation flashed through him. His eyes widened in confusion. *What the hell just happened to me?* He stared at her for a second and then gave his head a minute shake. He'd worry about it later. Right now there were more important things.

Letting out a breath, he shifted in his chair. "So anyway, we need to talk about…" Then he gave an embarrassed laugh. "I don't even know where to begin."

She raised her brow. "Beginning?"

He shrugged. "Good as place as any, I guess." Looking at the floor, Parker thought for a moment and then looked up. "Do you remember the night we met? About ten days ago in Discovery Park?"

"No."

His jaw dropped. "You don't?" he blurted, his eyes wide and disbelieving. "But…" He frowned. "If you don't remember, how come you recognized me when I walked into the bedroom?"

Melera looked away. "Remembuh you, yes," she said, her voice sounding soft and hesitant. "Where from, know not."

His eyes narrowed. *Amnesia? Maybe…I hit her pretty hard. But she could be faking it.* He decided to give her the benefit of the doubt, at least for now. "Well, that's where I found you last night. In the park. I brought you home because you'd been hurt bad. But more than that…" He stared at her a moment. "You killed a man that night ten days ago. A human."

"Me do?" Melera frowned. "Me…hmm…" She gave a little shrug. "Tsen he deserve, yes."

Speechless, his jaw dropped again. His amnesiac guest gazed at him with golden, untroubled eyes.

"Ohh-kaay, let's talk about something else." He gave her a pointed look. "What do you know about the Seattle Slayer?"

She frowned a second time. "See-at-tell Slay-er? What tsat is?"

"Who, not what." Parker took a deep breath. "The Slayer is a killer. He or she—or they—have murdered nine people since last April. I've seen some of the crime pictures, and they looked pretty nasty. All of the bodies were full of these holes, and most of their blood had been drained." He took another breath. "We—I mean, a number of others, including me—have been looking for him," he paused, "or her, and—"

Melera still looked confused. "You tell me why?"

"Well, uh, because…"

She sat forward. "Tsink you me Slay-er, yes?" she said, sounding incredulous.

"Uh…well, no, I mean…"

She started giggling. Soon she was clutching her belly, laughing hard.

Her laughter made him feel like an idiot. "What's so funny?"

Melera didn't answer at first. "Me?" she snorted when she could speak. "You silly silly, yes." She shook her head. "Pawkher. Me do? Could, yes. But never you find dead hu-mans. Fook, you know not tsere be killings."

He had to think about that one. Melera's English was so bad he almost always had to decipher what she'd said. "Now that I can believe," he muttered when he'd figured it out. But where did it leave him?

"Pawkher?"

He looked up. "Yeah?"

Melera pointed to her chest. "Question?"

"Sure."

She strode to a small closet on the opposite side of his study and yanked the door open. Reaching inside, she took something out and slammed the door shut. Marching over to where he sat, she stood just out of reach and held up a large rock with myriad striations. Her eyes spun like a kaleidoscope gone mad. She looked furious. "Where get?" she demanded. "Who you, troots? Tell, or kill me will."

Parker stared. He'd no idea why his rock should've made her so angry but he had no doubt—if she didn't like what he told her, kill him she would.

CHAPTER 38

Eyes narrowed, Melera glared at the man sitting before her. The stone she held was all the proof she needed. This jakker calling himself Parker Berenson was in fact Beloc's hound, and everything he'd told her—from finding her in that park and bringing her here, to this so-called Slay-er stalking See-at-tell—was nothing but a pack of lies.

"I, uh…I—" the dog stammered.

"Tell!" She raised the rock higher.

Parker sat still and said nothing, but the look in his startling green eyes had turned from confused to ice-cold. "You dare threaten me in my own den?" he snarled.

"Me do, yes. Say who you is not troots. Who jakk you is?"

The frost in his eyes melted and he looked confused again. "I…who am I?" He blinked a few times. "I told you. My name's Parker Berenson."

"Is? Tsen how get?" She pointed at the rock.

"I…I found it." He shook his head. "Look, Melera, if you really wanna know, fine. I'll tell you." His eyes turned frosty again. "But you have to sit down first—and dammit, stop threatening me."

They glowered at each other in silence. She slowly lowered the rock and without taking her stare from him, backed into her chair.

Parker let out a small sigh. "I've had that rock since I was a kid. Fifteen, to be exact."

Melera shook her head. "Kid, fifteen…words me know not. 'Splain you."

He blinked. "A kid. You know, a child."

Her brow twitched. His explanation meant nothing to her but she remained quiet.

"And by 'fifteen,' I mean that's how old I was when I found the rock. I'm twenty-nine now." He cocked his head. "Get it?"

She pursed her lips and looked away. She'd figured out Dirt's calendar and counting system back on her island. There were twelve months in their solar year. For counting, they used base ten and though she didn't know the names of the numbers beyond ten, she guessed "fifteen" and "twenty-nine" was a lot more than that. She looked up. "Long time, so?"

He gave her a crooked smile. "Long time, yeah." He squeezed his eyes shut and sighed a second time. When he opened them, his expression was faraway and sorrowful. "I found that rock on the same day I found my best friend dead. His name was Frank and we'd been pals since we were eight." He looked at her. "An even longer time."

She nodded once and waited for him to continue.

"Anyway, Frank was a werepanther. A——" He stopped. "You remember upstairs? When I turned into a wolf?"

Assuming he meant the creature with the red fur, she nodded again.

"Well, Frank was like that too, except he wasn't a wolf. He was——" Parker turned to a shelf of books behind him. He pulled one down and flipped through the pages. Finding what he wanted, he held it out to her.

She leaned forward to look. "See?" He pointed to a creature with four legs, a long tail, and a grayish-tan pelt. Its eyes were gold, like hers. "That's a panther. That's what Frank was."

Looking up, she saw Parker staring at the picture. Then he closed his eyes.

Melera sat back in her chair. "How die?"

Opening his eyes, he closed the book and set it on the desk. "He was murdered. Skinned alive. Three humans hunted him down and killed him, just for being what he was." He took a deep breath. "I found him. I mean, I found what was left of him. In the woods, not far from where we both lived. I buried him as best I could and left. It was all I could do."

She raised her brow. "You whack tsem, yes?"

The look on Parker's face turned from sad to incredulous and then angry. "No, I didn't whack them. I...Melera, I was just a kid. What was I supposed to do?"

She shrugged. If it had been her best friend who'd been murdered, those three hu-mans would've been dead in short order—"kid" or not. She didn't know why Parker had let them live but then it wasn't any of her business.

"Anyway," he said in a softer voice, "I wandered around for a long time after that, and while I was walking, I tripped over"— he gestured to the rock with his head—"that. I don't know why I picked it up. I guess because I thought it was pretty." He smiled a little. "No, that's not it. I picked it up because it reminded me of Frank. The brown and gray colors, with those gold stripes. I've carried it with me ever since." Then he sighed. "That's all, Melera." He closed his eyes and pinched the bridge of his nose with his thumb and forefinger.

She stared at him with tightened lips. Her czado had probed while he spoke, so she knew he'd spoken from his heart. But that didn't mean his tale was true. It was like his honest belief he liked the woman he'd been sent to capture. Knowing what the rock would mean to her, Beloc could have planted a false memory about how he'd gotten it. That sort of thing was standard procedure before sending an operative on assignment. Her brow rose. *Wonder how hard it'll be to expose.*

It depends on how deep the lie has been planted in his memory function, her czado said.

She frowned, thinking about the other possibility. If Parker's story was true, it sure as jakk didn't explain how this rock managed to show up on Dirt.

Why would you think his story is true?

Melera didn't answer. She stared at the rock and then looked up to see Parker watching her. "Hu-mans...kill you? Like Frank?"

He nodded. "If they ever find out what I am."

"Why?"

"It's a long story." Tilting his head, he gave her a strange look. "Where're you from, sweetheart? You're obviously not human, so how come you don't know what they're like? I mean, I know in some parts of the world they tolerate us more than in others but there's nowhere I know of where our kind are exactly welcomed." He raised his brow. "And why're you so interested in my rock? How'd you even know it was in that closet?"

She said nothing, debating whether she should tell him. If he already knew, it didn't matter what she said. If he didn't know, then it still didn't matter what she said. Staring at the stone, she was reminded of all she'd lost. *My people, my friends, my clan, my father, my love...* She closed her eyes and started rocking in her seat. "Xia'saan," she whispered. "Home…no more. Gone now. All gone."

Then to her horrified embarrassment, Melera began to sob.

CHAPTER 39

*H*ome…*no more. Gone now. All gone.*

Parker stared at the crying woman with the feeling he'd just stepped all the way through the looking glass. His high school science teacher had told him his rock was a meteorite.

Oh, no. No. Uh-uh. I don't believe it. I won't believe it.

Reality was slipping away. He shook his head hard. It didn't help. Squeezing his eyes shut, he took a deep breath. *Okay, look. I already know Melera can't speak English worth a damn, so she just got her words mixed up.* Opening them, he saw she had curled up in the chair, clasping the rock close. Her tears sparkled as if they held tiny diamonds. Reality started to shift again but he pulled it back into place.

A wave of compassion washed over him. Whatever Melera might be, her wretchedness was clear. Parker rose from his chair, stepped over to her and placed a hand on her shoulder. "Melera…sweetheart."

She didn't respond. He gave her a gentle shake. "Melera, stand up for a minute. Can you?"

She looked up. Clutching the rock, she uncurled her long, golden brown legs. He helped her to stand, steadying her when she began to wobble. He took her place in the overstuffed chair and tugged on her shirt.

"Umpf," he grunted painfully when she collapsed into his lap. She leaned against his chest. Wrapping his arms about her, he kissed her temple and ran his fingers through her shiny black hair. "Tell me," he whispered, kissing her again. "Tell me about home."

Melera had stopped her crying, but she didn't answer for a while. Then, in her broken, halting English, she told him about a planet whose name he couldn't begin to pronounce, which had been located in a distant galaxy whose name he couldn't pronounce either, where a civil war raged between the ruling galactic government and an army of rebels who called themselves something that sounded like fist. She told him about somebody named Beloc, who'd caused her planet to be destroyed—out of spite, it seemed—and about her incarceration in his prison and her subsequent escape.

Twining her hair about his fingers, Parker suppressed a sigh. Her story was fascinating, but there was just one problem. He'd seen the movie only about half a zillion times. "Melera," he said in a low voice, "if there's a war going on in your galaxy and you're in the middle of it, then...why are you here?"

She raised her head from his shoulder. Holding the rock in one arm, she lifted the other and tapped her skull with her forefinger. "Sick. Me head. Beloc—" she paused as if searching for the right word—"fooked wits."

Fooked? He remembered she'd mentioned that word before. Then he understood. "Uh-huh. Okay. This Beloc guy fucked with your head while you were his prisoner and now you sometimes get...sick. Right?"

"Yes."

At least this part's a little more original. "That still doesn't tell me why you're here, though."

Her face appeared troubled. "Pawkher...me not remembuh."

He frowned. "What d'ya mean, you don't remember?"

She stared at him, looking confused.

"Let's try again. What don't you remember? Why you came? Or how you got here?"

She nodded once. "Have ship, yes. Where?" She shook her head. "Me not remembuh."

Parker considered. *Getting better and better...* "Okay. You know you have a spaceship, but you don't remember where you left it. Right?"

"Yes."

"Do you remember why you came here? To Earth, I mean?"

Looking past him, Melera knitted her black brows. "Hide from Beloc," she said after a moment or two, "and Vst. Me know is more but me not remembuh." Then her face brightened. She turned. "Earts? Hu-man name for, yes?"

"Yeah, why?"

She smiled. "Me tsought Dirt."

He smiled back. *Sure you did, sweetheart.* "How'd you end up in Seattle?"

"Not remembuh."

"Do you remember where you've been staying?"

"No."

"Hoo-boy." Parker stared at the wall. Then he sighed. *This is insane. I'm in my study with some psycho bitch who thinks she's a goddamned alien.* He squeezed his eyes shut. *God, how did I get into this mess?*

His eyes popped open a moment later when he'd realized something else. Whether she was psycho or not was the least of his problems. Whatever she might be, Melera said she wasn't the Slayer and his intuition told him she was telling the truth.

How in the world would I prove that?

He couldn't. It didn't take a rocket scientist to figure it out. A serial killer was loose and Melera—some kind of zot no one had ever heard of—couldn't remember how she got here, how long she'd been here, or even where she lived...

She wouldn't have a snowball's chance in hell.

"More difficulty you see?" she interrupted his thoughts.

Parker turned. "Yup. Lots of 'em." He smiled. "Don't worry. It'll be okay. I'm just glad I found you first."

She smiled back. Then she sneezed.

Uh-oh. He pushed her off his lap. "Sit," he said and went to his desk. Pulling out the right-hand bottom drawer, he reached in and withdrew a coffee canister and a pack of rolling papers.

She sneezed a second time.

"Here." He proffered a freshly rolled joint.

Melera shook her head. "No." Her voice sounded raspy. "Need tow-bac-co." She pointed to the joint. "Make me want... fook. No control."

He winked. "What's wrong with that?"

She gave him a long look and then coughed. Screwing her lips, she took the joint and toked on it. She took another two drags before handing it back to him. Her allergic reaction evidently averted, he finished the joint and then doused it in an ashtray on his desk.

They stared at each other. His lips stretched into a predatory grin. "Wanna go upstairs?"

Melera's reply was a slow, wicked-looking smile.

"I think that's a yes." Parker offered his hand and she took it. At the bottom of the stairs, he swept her off her feet and carried her to his bedroom.

CHAPTER 40

Parker woke at dawn. Rolling over, he watched Melera sleep for a while and then decided to get up. Not bothering to put on a robe, he headed downstairs for coffee.

In the kitchen, he took out a can of his favorite French roast, pried off the lid and prepared a pot in his well-used coffeemaker. He pressed the brew switch and waited for the small, round orange light. When it lit, the appliance wheezed and gurgled as if suffering from a rare respiratory ailment. Satisfied the maker was working as it should, he sat at his chrome and white dinette set and stared at nothing outside the window.

Melera says she's some kind of space alien. I—

Why not? his wolf growled.

"You believe her, don't you?"

To humans, we're no different.

He shook his head. "We are, though. They might think of us as aliens but nobody can deny we were all born here. So—"

You blind or something? his beast snarled, sounding exasperated. *You ever seen a zot with eyes like hers? You ever seen a cunt like hers? You ever fucked a pussy like hers?*

"Well—"

No "well" about it, meathead. Here's one for ya. You ever cum like that before?

Parker shrugged. "So? I've felt the earth move and so have you." His brows knitted. *But the rest of it...*

"Okay, let's say she is ET. Where—" His eyes widened. Christ, he'd been banging her for nearly a day. What if he'd caught some weird parasite and it ate out his eyeballs or something?

He clapped his hands over his face. "Stop it. Zots have been cross-breeding since forever—God knows what kinds of mutants are running around out there."

Your point?

Parker balled his hands into fists and slammed them on the tabletop. "She ain't no goddamned alien, okay?"

His *were* said nothing.

He sighed. He already had way too much he couldn't deal with, like Garrett and Kurt. Now pondering whether Melera was a space alien made his head spin.

The coffeemaker had gone quiet. He plucked a dark green mug from a metal tree on the kitchen's work island and filled it. Taking a sip, he made a face. The brew was jet-fuel strong, just the way he liked it. He took a second sip, left the kitchen, and padded to his study.

Parker set his mug on the desk and sat in his old swivel chair. Scanning the bookshelf, he spied his dog-eared book of city street maps. He reached up and pulled it down. Flipping through its pages, he stopped every so often to inspect one that had caught his interest. Then he shook his head and returned the map book to its place. *Melera could be staying anywhere. Guess the best thing would be just to drive her around, take her places. Maybe she'll see something that'll trip her memory.*

Uhrrm. Then we can prove she's not the Slayer.

Yeah, that too. Parker downed a hefty gulp of his now-cooled coffee. Leaning back in the chair, he clasped his hands behind his head and closed his eyes. Tripping Melera's memory was critical but they couldn't traipse around Seattle in secret. He had to figure out a way to explain her sudden appearance in his life. His story had to be plausible but, just as important, unverifiable.

Let's see…Kurt's meeting was the night before last, so she got here sometime yesterday…at least that's true…met her in college? Yeah. Nobody in Seattle knew me then, so that should be okay. He nodded. *A foreign exchange student, definitely…explains why her English is so bad. Now…where's she from?*

A delicious aroma wafted under his nose. His keen olfactory sense told him it was coming from the kitchen. He smiled and waited for Melera to find him.

He was still waiting a few minutes later. Puzzled, he opened his eyes and stood. An overwhelming odor smacked him in the face like a sledgehammer. "Ungh," he grunted, falling back into his chair. He felt dizzy. Shaking his head only made it worse. He began to sweat.

Blood…I smell her blood, his wolf roared in his brain. *Get her!*

Parker-the-human didn't argue. Leaping from his chair, he loped toward the scent, his purpling prick leading the way. Slamming the kitchen door open, he stood just over the threshold, his chest heaving.

Melera looked up. She stood next to the kitchen's work island, holding one of his professional carving knives in her left hand. Her right arm bled and she was cutting a second slice. She gave him a wide smile. "You come," she said, looking and sounding very pleased.

"Not yet," he panted in a voice that wasn't human. "What the hell do you think you're doing?" Closing the distance between them, he snatched the knife, grabbed her by the hair and laid on a brutal kiss.

After he pulled away, she laughed. "Check. Darkfall last, me saw how you like taste me blood. Make you want fook. No control." Tilting her head, she looked at him from beneath her long eyelashes. "Me call, you come. Is good, yes." She grabbed his swollen member and began fondling it.

His jaw tightened. *Just like Kurt.* He slapped her hand away and took a long stride backward. His hot stare had turned icy. "You…don't you ever do that to me again," he said through clenched teeth.

Melera narrowed her golden eyes. "Oh. Me see. Is ohh-kay me you do, yes?"

"What are you talking about?"

"Darkfall last. Al-ler-gy start. Need me tow-bac-co but give you me weed." Melera narrowed her eyes even further. "Me say what weed do. Make me want fook, no control. Give you me weed anyway."

Parker blinked. "But I didn't have any tobacco. I told you that."

"Why you not get some?"

"Now wait a minute. I didn't give—" He stopped. "Okay, okay. I'm sorry. I should've gone out for some cigarettes or something."

She shook her head. "What see-gar-ets is? Need see-gar."

Parker took a deep breath and squeezed his eyes shut, fighting his wolf's urge to give her the big, fat one jutting from his crotch.

He won. He opened his eyes and smiled, feeling a little disappointed by his victory. "Okay. I'll get you some cigars when we go out. Right now, we've got work to do."

Her hard expression turned puzzled. "Do? What?"

"We have to work on a story to explain your being here. You say you're from another galaxy, but I can't go around introducing you as my favorite Martian. I—"

"Is true. What Martian is?"

"Never mind. But if you tell anybody else where you're from, they'll think you're crazy."

Melera stared at him for a long moment. "Like you?"

He didn't reply at first. He thought about the conversation he'd had with his *were* earlier, and about what had happened to them just minutes ago.

"I'm not sure what I think." Taking her hand, he led her out of the kitchen.

CHAPTER 41

Later that morning, Melera and Parker strode to the car in the parking lot of the wearings market he called Nordstrom. Her full lips tightened into a thin line. Their shop-ping trip had humiliated her beyond belief. He'd brought her to a place called the wo-men's department and once she saw the merchandise, she lost her temper. "No," she'd shouted. "Me not put on tsose!"

Parker had clapped a hand over her mouth. "Keep your voice down," he'd said through his teeth. "Why not?"

They'd argued for at least ten or fifteen minutes, Melera acquiescing only because her czado had reminded her they had to blend in with the Dirt people.

Right now, she wore four of their purchases—something the sales-clerk called a bra, and another garment called panties. Over these, she wore a red, figure-skimming dress that came halfway to her knees with a shallow scoop neck and wide straps over the shoulders and a pair of shoes made of strips of something called braided leather.

From the corner of her eye, she watched Parker's jaw set. "I don't understand why you don't like what I bought for you."

"Me tell you—only pleasure-slaves put on these wearings. Dresses, you say. Sandals, you say. Dirt women nutsing but pleasure-slaves."

"That's Earth women and they are not. These kinds of clothes are just what women wear."

"Hmph." But she wasn't going to argue with him. She was not about to run around naked. Going naked was even worse than being a plea-sure-slave. At least pleasure-slaves belonged to someone. Ninturs, or naked people, belonged to no one and were fair game for sex and what-ever else wherever and whenever anyone wanted it. Except for Pawkher,

193

she hadn't seen any naked people on Dirt, so she could only assume there weren't any ninturs here.

He finished stowing the bags in his car. She looked at him. "We go you house now?"

Parker shook his head. "I'm hungry." His voice was curt. "Let's get something to eat, and then we can grab a beer. After all your bullshit in the store"—he glanced at her—"I could use a beer. Maybe five."

Her lips twisted. "Fine."

They climbed into the car and drove away. The feeding station wasn't far from the wearings market. They found seats by the window and a woman all in pink brought menus. Parker seemed surprised she couldn't read it and ordered for her. The food was good, Melera had to admit. After they'd eaten, he paid for their meal and they left the feeding station. "That's better. Now for that beer." He smiled and opened the car door for her.

She frowned. "What beer is?"

He gave her an incredulous look. "You've never had beer?"

"No."

He blew out a small breath. "You've never been shopping, you think all women are pleasure-slaves, you can't read and you don't know what beer is. Sweetheart, where *are* you from?"

"Me tell you already."

He rolled his eyes. "Oh. Right."

They got into the car and rode along without speaking. Presently, they came to a seedy neighborhood. Parker found a space big enough for his vehicle, pulled in and shut down the engine. He turned. "We're here."

"Where?"

"The bar I was telling you about. It's for our kind only—no humans, so you don't have to watch everything you say and do."

"Oh."

They walked back to an alley they'd passed and walked along its length until they came to a nondescript building with a nondescript door set into the siding. There was no sign. Parker pushed the door open and they entered.

It was one large room. The space's most prominent feature was a long counter with a clear shield on top that reached to the ceiling. Behind the shield, she could see rows of liquid-filled bottles. A man stood behind the counter shield. He waved to them. Parker waved back. "That's Mack," he whispered in her ear. "He owns the place."

Melera took in the stains on the walls and ceiling. In a couple of places, the walls sported big dents. A small smile curved her lips. It reminded her of some of the less savory places she'd frequented on Baroe, a space station that served as the social hub for the people who mined the nearby asteroids.

Several people were inside, all drinking something or other. They'd looked up when she and Parker had entered, and now they all stared at her. She ignored them.

"So what do you think?" he said.

The Dark's mercy, I miss Baroe. Melera turned. "Me like."

"Good. Come on. Let's find a seat."

She followed him to a corner booth near the rear of the bar. Parker sat facing the entrance, which meant her back was to it. That made her a bit uncomfortable but she wasn't expecting any trouble, so she shook the feeling off.

He stood. "I'll get us some beer. Be right back." True to his word, he returned in about a minute with a large, condensation-covered bottle in each hand. He handed one to her and took his seat.

He picked up his bottle, raised it until it was about as high as his forehead, then fit the bottle's opening to his mouth and drank. She had no idea what that was all about, but she mimicked him just the same. She took a swallow of beer. It wasn't what she was used to—kind of weak— but it didn't taste bad.

Parker looked her up and down. "You look nice in that dress."

She narrowed her eyes, then let out a minute sigh. "Tsank you."

They were half-finished with their beers when music filled the room. Melera looked up. A man was walking toward their table. Reaching them, he stared at her with a hungry look. "May I have this dance, lady?" he said and glanced at Parker. "If he don't mind, that is."

Her eyes lit up. "Dance?" She looked at Parker. "Dance, yes?"

He smiled. "Go ahead."

Melera grinned. Now the day was shaping up right. She'd seen dancing on the viscreen back on her island while learning about Dirt.

195

It had looked like fun. She was just about to stand up when she remembered her clothes. She wouldn't be able to dance in her dress and shoes. *I'll just take them off, then.* As she undressed, Parker and the man stared at her with unbelieving looks. Once she was in her underclothes, she stood before the man who'd asked her to dance. "We dance now, yes."

Then man's expression turned leering. Then he winked. "Yeah, c'mon baby. Let's dance." He led her across the floor to the room's middle. He stretched out his arms, obviously meaning to wrap them around her.

She smacked the man's chin with a left uppercut that sent him reeling backward. He gave his head a little shake and looked up. "What'd you do—"

"We dance, yes?"

"Yeah—we dance." The man balled his hands into big, meaty fists and rushed her. Melera stepped to the side and tripped him. He went sprawling. Then he jumped to his feet and came at her again. She grabbed his arm, flipped him, and then slammed him to the floor. Disappointment washed through her as she watched him wheeze. "You not dance good."

"Melera, what the hell are you doing?" Parker shouted.

She looked up to see him crossing the room with long strides. He reached her and she smiled. "Dancing."

"That's not—"

By now the man had gotten his wind back. "What is wrong with this bitch?" he snarled. "I'm gonna—"

Parker knelt and put a hand on the man's shoulder. "Naw, man, I'm sorry. She's from Fiji. Her English isn't too good. She didn't mean anything by it. Here—let me buy you a bottle of something. Whatever you want."

The man stared at her for a few seconds through slitted eyes. "Yeah, okay. You buyin' me the most expensive whiskey in the house."

Parker nodded. "Great. Let me help you up. Melera, go put your clothes back on."

Her lips tightened. She'd be damned if she was going to let him order her around. She was just about to say "no" when her czado spoke. *Do not argue. What you did was obviously not the kind of thing Dirt women do.*

She stood and returned to their table. By the time she'd dressed, Parker had come back. "Let's get out of here. But before we do, you go and apologize to that guy."

"Why? We just dance."

"That's not dancing."

"But—"

"Do it, Melera."

Her jaw set. Then she sighed. "Ohh-kay." She walked over to the table where the man sat rubbing his chin and drinking a beer. "Me sorry. Me just try to dance."

The man eyed her. "Don't know what you do in Fiji but over here we don't dance like that." He jerked his head in Parker's direction. "Get yer boyfriend to explain it to you." He lifted the bottle to his lips and turned away.

Parker grabbed her hand. "Sorry again for the trouble, Mack. Come on, Melera." He fairly dragged her out of the bar.

They rode in silence to Parker's house, with a stop to get her more cigars. Before they got out of the car, she turned to him. "Pawkher, me sorry. Me know not me do anytsing wrong."

He didn't answer at first. "Tell you what. From now on, just take your cues from me, okay?"

She nodded.

After they'd put the clothes away, Melera sat on the bed. "What we do now?"

Parker gave her a look. "Now I'm going to teach you to dance." He walked over to a small box and fiddled with it. "This will do." He pressed a button and the sound of drums and other instruments she couldn't identify filled the air. Then he walked to the bed and took her into his arms. "This is how you dance."

Melera decided she liked dancing.

CHAPTER 42

In the wee hours of the following morning, Melera bolted upright in bed, a frisson of stark fear arcing along her spine. She peered into the bedroom's darkness but could see nothing. Why was she so afraid?

Beside her, Parker stirred. "What's wrong, sweetheart?" he said, his voice heavy with sleep.

"N-nutsing. You go sleep. M-me ohh-kay." She began to shake.

The bed rocked a little as he sat up. "No, you're not. What happened?" He snaked an arm over her trembling shoulders. "A bad dream?"

"No. Yes. May-be." She shook her head. "Me know not, Pawkher. Me just wake up scared."

He kissed her hair and pulled her closer. "There's nothing to be afraid of, sweetheart. Not while I'm here."

A small part of her believed him, but the rest of her wasn't listening. Her shaking intensified until her teeth started chattering.

Parker took his arm from around her shoulders. "Lie down," he said, pushing her down on the bed. "Just relax."

She looked up at him. *Easy for you to say.*

He gathered her into his arms and stroked her hair. "My poor sweetheart," he whispered.

His ministrations weren't working. The tremors still rattled through her body. She needed something to take her mind off of her fear.

Then she had an idea. When she was a small child, whenever she had been frightened Tarq would give her a soft, furry wahren to hold. The six-footed, teardrop-shaped animal would lay in her arms, wanting to be rubbed and petted. Doing that had always eased her fear. When she hadn't been scared anymore, Tarq would put the wahren it back into its cage. There weren't any wahrens on this planet and she certainly wasn't a child anymore, but...

She twisted her neck until she was looking into Parker's face. "Woof, please?"

He gave her a leering grin. "Sure."

A moment later, she lay in his wolf's arms. She struggled out of his embrace. Rising to her knees, she straddled the beast's waist and ran her fingers through the pelt covering his massive chest, feeling its roughness. Then she dug deeper until she reached the soft undercoat. She began massaging, grasping fur and flesh, giving it a light tug, and then letting go.

She did this for a long while, then scooted up until she was sitting on the beast's chest. Reaching out, she fondled his ears. She ran her fingers along his face, tracing his snout. Leaning forward, she kissed his nose. He licked hers in return. She giggled.

Moving away from his face, she slid her hands along the wolf's thick, muscular neck in a circular motion until she reached his shoulders. She started her massaging again. About five minutes later, she picked up his left arm and slid her fingers through the pelt, again digging deep until she'd reached the undercoat. Lifting the beast's monstrous paw, she kissed his palm and each of his five clawed fingers. Lowering it to the bed, she then did the same to his right arm and paw.

Melera gazed into the wolf's glowing green eyes and smiled. "Me feel better now. We go sleep, yes?"

He nodded.

"But woof stay."

"Okay," he growled.

She clambered down from the beast's chest, lay beside him and snuggled into his dense fur. His arm encircled her and she snuggled closer. Now feeling calm, warm, and safe, she quickly dropped into sleep.

———————

Parker's wolf stared at the ceiling. *What the hell was that about? I thought she wanted sex.*

Me, too.

Neither wolf nor man said anything for a long while.

No one's ever done that to me before, the beast growled softly. *I felt...*

Felt what?

I dunno. I mean, I'm a killer. A monster. People are supposed to be terrified of me, to hate me, not kiss my nose and give me massages. What she did...it made me feel so good, like... He paused. *Is this what it's like to be loved?*

That's part of it, yeah.

And right now...I'm supposed to be wanting to rip her apart, but I don't. I just want to hold her close, to protect her. The wolf fell silent. *Is that love?*

That's part of it, too.

I'm confused.

Don't think about it, pal. Just go with your feelings.

I'm not supposed to have feelings.

You do now.

The wolf said nothing.

Let's get some sleep. Maybe it'll make more sense in the morning.

I doubt it, but yeah.

The wolf felt his human side's consciousness fade. He stared at the ceiling, his thoughts chasing one another like a cub chasing its tail. Then he gave his head a small shake. *Go with my feelings. Sounds stupid but I guess there's nothing else to do.*

With that last thought, the beast slept, too.

CHAPTER 43

On June seventeenth, Garrett sped west along Duwamish Avenue in her maroon Altima on her way to Balthus Temple. Her lips tightened. *Parker.* It had been two weeks since the night he'd stormed out of KM, Inc.'s party room. She'd worked out another strategy to convince the wolf to join them, but then his college friend had shown up. Her hands tightened around the wheel. *That woman is in my way. If Melera doesn't leave soon...* She shook her head. "Can't do anything about her right now, so stop worrying," she muttered.

She glanced at the dashboard clock and sighed. She was late. She was supposed to have met Paul at the Temple at three, and it was almost three-thirty. She'd been visiting with Ara Kyronos. At one hundred and ten, Ara was the oldest witch in Seattle. Like all witches, her talent had diminished with advancing age and she'd long since retired as an active member of the coven. Garrett hadn't meant to visit for so long, but Ara had a way of making her forget her troubles and the time had flown by.

She barreled along the unnamed service road atop the embankment sheltering the abandoned docks. With a squeal of tires, she rounded the curve and her Altima shot through the open gate. Then she was flying along the track, scattering black gravel in her wake. Slowing to a stop about ten feet from the ramshackle warehouse, she jumped from her car and ran to the main door. She'd just grasped the handle when it was whisked open. Dragged over the threshold, she stumbled into Pinkie's arms.

"Garrett! I'm sorry. I didn't know—"

"Don't worry about it," she chuckled, straightening from the younger witch's unexpected embrace. "I didn't know you were there either, so that makes us even." Then she noticed the dark circles under Pinkie's eyes. She seemed unusually pale, too. Garrett frowned. "Forgive me for asking Sister, but are you all right?"

A haunted look passed over Pinkie's face and then disappeared. She smiled. "I'm okay. I haven't been getting much sleep lately. Got a final in cell biology coming up and I've been studying my butt off." She let out a small sigh. "Sometimes I come to the Temple to work. My apartment house can get pretty noisy, you know?"

Garrett nodded. "Yeah, I remember those days. Just when you need that quiet time, the whole world decides to have a keg party."

"You got it." The two laughed.

"Have you seen Paul?" Garrett said after their mirth had faded.

"Paul's here? I mean, no, I haven't. Why?"

"No reason. He called this morning and asked if we could meet at the Temple's office this afternoon. Said he wanted to talk to me."

Pinkie's eyes widened. "Really? But I thought we'd finished preparing for the summer solstice."

Garrett shrugged. "He didn't say what he wanted to talk to me about. Anyway, I just thought you two might have run into each other."

The young witch shook her head. "I haven't seen him."

"Okay. Paul's always on time, and I'm late, so I'll see you later. Blessed be, Sister. And good luck on your exam."

"Thanks, I'll need it. Blessed be, Garrett." Pinkie stepped outside and skipped down the Temple's stairs.

Closing the door behind her, Garrett headed for the Temple's office. Along the way, she wondered at Pinkie's reaction when she'd told her Paul was here. *She looked almost as if she was scared. And why would she think Paul wanted to talk to me about the solstice?*

Opening the office door, she saw Paul leaning against the metal desk, waiting for her. She pushed Pinkie's odd behavior from her thoughts. "Hi, Paul. Sorry I'm late. I was over at Ara's and—"

"You went to see Ara?" He peered at her with a suspicious look.

"Yes, why?"

"What did you talk about?"

Smiling, she crossed the floor to a large, comfortable chair and sat. "I just went to see her, Paul. I like to keep her up on what's going on with the coven. One of these days we're going to be retired and as for me, I'd like someone to return the favor." Then she noticed Paul looked worn too, just as Pinkie had. "Brother, what's wrong? You look worried about something."

His expression turned grave. "I know what the killer is."

Garrett felt the blood drain from her face.

CHAPTER 44

Garrett stared at him. Paul had said he knew what the killer was—not who. Her heart beat a little faster. "You do?"

He nodded. "Do you know what a uthyrisis is?"

"A what?"

"Doesn't matter if you don't," he assured her. "Outside us demonologists, most others in the Craft haven't heard of it, either." He shook his head. "Anyway, a uthyrisis is an extremely powerful devil. None of the Craft's magickal encyclopedias— the ancient Books of Shadows—say hardly anything about it. It's that bad, apparently. According to what is known, the uthyrisis has a nasty habit of killing the one who summoned it."

She frowned. "What's it look like?"

"It doesn't. Not on this plane, at any rate. It's discorporate. The conjuror has to provide a host body. What type of body doesn't matter, it just has to be alive."

She thought for a moment. "Okay. What you're saying is there's no telling what this—uthyrisis—might look like. It could be a person, an animal...anything."

"Right. But like I also said, it's immensely powerful. The host has to be strong enough to house the devil and live. That's a pretty tall order. Most human and animal bodies can't take it, so the host is usually zot." Paul's brow creased. "And then you have to consider, in this case, whoever summoned it had to have provided more than one host. These murders started last April. Given its power, it's unthinkable that even the hardiest zot could withstand hosting the demon for more than a few days, much less two months. So, given the number and timing of the murders, it means the uthyrisis had to have been summoned at least eight times. And

207

that means…" He sighed. "The odds of finding it start looking pret-ty slim."

Lips pursed, Garrett stared at the carpet, thinking. Then she looked up. "If there's more than one host, how does it get from one to another? Can it just, um, jump? By itself?"

"No. To do that, the uthyrisis must return to its own plane and then be re-summoned." Paul gave her a small smile. "One of its few limitations, I might add."

Neither one spoke for a few minutes. "All right," she broke the silence. "Let's say we do catch the uthyrisis. How do we kill it?"

A troubled look appeared on the elder's face. "I don't know."

Her jaw dropped. "You don't know?"

"No. The Books don't say." He grimaced, apparently at her look of disbelief. "Look, I told you the lore was sketchy. Remember I said the demon has a tendency to kill the conjuror?"

She nodded.

"Well, as far as anyone knows, no witch who has ever called a uthyrisis has survived long enough to figure out how to kill it. And if any of them did, they certainly didn't survive long enough to tell anyone else." Paul sighed again. "Besides, it wouldn't matter. If the conjuror were dead, that's that. Even if we managed to trap the devil, we couldn't send it back. A witch can't undo another's spell."

"So why can't we just kill the host? Wouldn't that take care of it?"

"No, it wouldn't. In fact, I doubt we could even get near it."

"Why not?"

"Because of where it's from. As you know, there are twelve planes of existence—sometimes called dimensions—and we're on the third. The uthyrisis' natural place is on the fifth plane, the fifth dimension. To it, we on the third are transparent, so to speak."

"What does that mean?"

"It means it usually knows our every move even before we do." He seemed to think a moment. "One of my mentors put it this way—'the damned thing can see, hear, and think around corners.'"

"Mother," she breathed, falling back into her seat. What on earth could they do? This whole demon thing sounded hopeless, which made her feel helpless. So she got mad. "Well, dammit—if we can't kill the thing, what the hell happens to it, Paul?"

"I didn't say the uthyrisis can't be killed. I only said I don't know how. The learned consensus is the demon's tremendous energy eventually destroys the host's body. It can't exist here on its own, so it's forced to return to the fifth dimension. If the conjuror is dead, it can't return to the third. So…"

Biting her lip, she thought for a moment and then sat up in her seat. "Paul, do you think a tryst could destroy a uthyrisis?"

"I'd like to think so, but…" He shrugged. "It's true that a tryst taps directly into the power of the ONE and nothing's greater than that, but a tryst is still a three-dimensional entity. Against something from the fifth, a tryst's effectiveness is probably limited. Not that I know," he added. "It just seems logical." He shrugged again. "Anyway, where're you gonna find a tryst?"

"Wishful thinking, I guess." The last thing she needed right now was for Paul to find out she'd taken the first steps to bind herself to Kurt and Parker. There was more at stake than his disapproval or even his anger. As he'd often said, obeying human law to the letter was the only way witches could live in peace. In this, he was rigid as steel. A tryst was illegal as hell.

In her case, the elder would regret it but he'd give her to the humans in a heartbeat.

Garrett leaned back and rested her head on the chair, thinking. She hadn't abandoned her pogrom theory, though she had to admit Paul's hypothesis was sound. In fact, it would explain just about everything. Except why.

Then the whole point of their conversation dawned on her. She looked up. "Okay, Paul. Let's assume you're right about the demon. You know what you're saying, don't you?"

He nodded. "Yes, Sister," he said, his tone grave. "One of us summoned this uthyrisis."

"You can't possibly believe it was one of us, Brother. Who would even think of doing such a thing?"

The elder looked down. Thinking he'd conceded, a superior smile started forming on her lips. Then she realized why he hadn't answered. "You know who it is? Who is it, Paul? Who?"

He shook his head. "I'm sorry, Garrett, but I won't say. I can't."

"Why for Mother's sake not?" she shouted.

Paul's obsidian eyes seemed to burn. "Because I have no proof," he shouted back. He began to pace the carpet in front of the desk. "Garrett, I have to have proof," he said in a quieter voice. "Without it, I might be sentencing an innocent witch to death." He whirled. "You know what would happen. There'd be no trial. Nothing. The humans..." He closed his eyes, his arms hanging stiffly at his sides with hands clenched. "The humans would ask no questions. They'd simply strike the match."

She couldn't argue. That was exactly what would happen to her if she were caught trying to make a tryst.

"And if it turned out I was wrong?" he opened his eyes and glared at her. "Could you live with yourself after something like that, Sister? Could you?"

Garrett looked down at her lap. "No, Brother," she said, her voice low and heavy. "I could not." She wondered whether she should tell Kurt about Paul's suspicions. She decided against it. This was Paul's business and under the Witch's Credo, she had no right to tell anyone about his affairs. To do so would be a mortal sin. Besides, if she did tell Kurt, he would hound the poor man until Paul confessed everything he thought he knew.

And even if he's right, Paul would never forgive me. She closed her eyes.

Feeling a hand on her shoulder, she looked up. Paul stood before her, his face creased by a wan smile. "As soon as I get my proof, you'll be the first to know."

She nodded, her lips tight with worry.

Paul sighed. "I have to get going," he said, backing away from her chair. "Maira will be wondering what's become of me."

"Okay," she whispered.

The elder headed for the office door. "Paul," Garrett called. He stopped and turned.

"Be careful. Please."

Paul chuckled. "Don't worry about that, Sister. I plan to be very careful."

CHAPTER 45

L ate the next evening, Kurt and Daniel, the colony's executor, glided along Underground's deserted brick streets. Daniel had been silent since they'd arrived here and Kurt couldn't contain his curiosity any longer. "What did you want to show me, Daniel?"

"I'd rather not say, Master." Daniel's voice was quiet. "I thought you should see this for yourself."

Kurt frowned, startled that the other had addressed him so. Daniel had been a runaway slave when Kurt had found him hiding in a Missouri swamp in the late eighteen fifties. Upon becoming one of the undead, he vowed never to call any man "Master" again. Kurt, having once been a prisoner in his own dungeons, let it go. Their similar experiences were one of the reasons they'd become friends.

In a flash of insight, he understood. Daniel was terrified. Kurt resisted the urge to stare. He'd never seen Daniel afraid, not even when the other had been alive. And for one so young—just a hundred and fifty years old—he was well on his way to becoming a vampire regent himself. For him to be this frightened...

His lips tightened into a thin line.

The two vampires kept walking. Down in Underground, it was still eighteen eighty-nine. Cast iron lamp posts lined the left side of the avenue. They appeared to burn natural gas but they didn't. The illumination came from witch-light, a cold light more reliable than gas or electricity in that never burned out nor caused fires.

They arrived at a brick building whose visible portion lay four blocks from the center of the Pioneer Square district. Dissolving into mist, they slipped through the tiny opening between the wooden door and the bricks. Inside, it was pitch black. Keeping still, Kurt listened to Daniel's fumbling. Even a vampire was blind in utter darkness.

After a few moments, the day-bright glare from a battery-powered lantern chased away the artificial night. Kurt looked around. The two stood inside a half-tiled vestibule before a door made of sturdy oak with a large pane of glass set into its upper half. Holding the raised lantern before him, Daniel pushed the unlocked door open and stepped inside.

Kurt followed. Neither said a word as they glided to the second floor. At the top of the stairs, Daniel pushed open another half-glassed door. They walked along a hallway until the executor stopped. "Here we are," he said, almost whispering.

Daniel opened this door and the two vampires stepped inside a large room. The first thing Kurt noticed was the smell. Someone had been smoking cigars. He frowned. *Who?* Then he noticed the windows had been painted black, presumably so no light could be seen from the outside. His frown deepened. *Why?*

Underground had been used only four or five times since it had been built but it wasn't deserted. Any zot was free to come here for whatever reason. And then there were the regular maintenance crews, down here at any given time.

Kurt looked around. A hammock had been strung up in one corner. Below it, a few feet away, was a small couch. The rest of the objects were an enigma. A total enigma.

He walked over to a horseshoe-shaped contraption that reminded him of an organ, the kind used in the old vaudeville houses. That was where the resemblance ended. Puzzled, he walked around it twice, inspecting it closely. The back and sides of the—thing— were festooned with holes of varying sizes. Along its top edge was mounted a large, flat screen with three angled sides that reminded him of a television set. His brow knitted. The thing might look like some kind of baroque organ but if that's what it was, he didn't recognize a keyboard.

"This was what I thought you should see," Daniel called from the far side of the room.

Kurt looked up. Daniel stood before a six-foot, elaborately decorated rectangular box with a hinged top. It was open. He walked over and gasped when he saw what the box held. It was full of spikes. Embedded into its top and bottom, the spikes were of different shapes and sizes. Some were round and straight. Others were twisted like bedsprings.

Open at the tops, the holes, like the barbs themselves, were of different shapes—square, round, elliptical—and a few even looked jagged, like the broken end of a rotting tree trunk. The box and its spikes reminded Kurt of one of his favorite torture devices when he was a prince.

He pursed his lips. "When did you find this?"

"Just before I came to get you."

Kurt stared into the box. Then he looked up and fixed the other vampire with a glare. "Leave everything as it is. Post a twenty-four-hour watch on the entire building but don't block the entrances. Anyone going in or out, I want to know at once."

Daniel dipped his head. "Done."

Kurt slammed the box lid shut. He and Daniel regarded each other for a long moment. Then the two vampires left the room.

CHAPTER 46

At ten-thirty a.m. on June twenty-first, Parker and Melera sauntered along Broad Street. The Slayer was still at large, and the city's jittery atmosphere was oppressive. Parker's teeth hurt from all the clenching he'd done lately.

"Where we go, Pawhker?" Melera said. If she was feeling the tension, she gave no sign.

"We're going to the Space Needle."

She shook her head. "Me not stay there. Is too many peoples."

"No, but that's not why we're going. I just want to show you around the city today and the Space Needle is a great place to see it. I figured we could have lunch there, too."

They reached the Needle and Parker bought tickets. "Let's go to the o-deck first."

The elevator that would take them to the top finally arrived and they boarded. It was a long ride up. When they reached the observation deck, he led the way to one of the windows and swept his arm as if to encompass the city. "So what do you think?"

Melera seemed to take in the view of the tall buildings and the ample number of green spaces. "Is pretty. See-at-tell nice."

"Come on. Let's walk around."

They strolled around the observation deck as he pointed out various items of interest. She seemed rapt. That pleased him. After about an hour, he announced it was time for lunch. They took the elevator to the Sky City restaurant. The hostess seated them at a table for two by the window, as he'd requested.

While waiting for their drinks, he took her hand and smiled. "So tell me more about your galaxy. What's your favorite planet?"

Melera smiled back. "Beside home? Prasu. Is planet for everbody. Has sectors so you can have anytsing you want. Want um, waters and sand? It has. Want moun-tains? It has. Too has sector under-ground. Under waters, too." She told him about the sector for families and those for adults only. "Pleasure-slaves there. All kinds." Then there were the sectors for the more adventurous visitors, whether in nature or in an urban area. "City place where peoples in gangs. Might get into fight. Might get killed. Me like go there."

Remembering what had happened the other day in Mack's bar, he could believe it. "Sounds like a great place to visit." *Boy, she's got a helluva imagination.*

Her demeanor turned somber. "Akkad has now. Me not go there again."

He rubbed the back of her hand with his thumb. "Maybe someday you will. You never know."

She nodded. "May-be."

When their drinks arrived, Parker lifted his glass. "A toast. To getting your memory back."

Melera smiled and lifted her glass, too. She downed a quarter of her drink and looked at it. "Is good."

"Yeah. They call these kamikazes."

"Kami-kazes," she repeated and took another swallow.

The waiter brought their food. He ordered wine. He wasn't much of a wine drinker, but he thought she might like some. Since he'd ordered salmon for her, he asked for a glass of white. He got a glass of red to go with his steak. Melera pronounced her meal to be very good.

While they waited for dessert, he told her about what it was like growing up in Arkansas, without mentioning Frank. Then he regaled her with stories of his college days, without mentioning it was then that he'd become a werewolf. He told her about his human grandmother, her Iowa farm, and how he'd inherited half of it when she died.

Parker had never told anyone as much about himself as he'd told Melera. But he found it so easy to talk to her. He was relaxed, a new feeling for him. Being a zot meant always being on guard, ready for anything. With her, he felt he could let his guard down and just be.

After dessert, they left the Space Needle. On the walk to the car, he turned. "Let's try Capitol Hill. I doubt you were staying there, but it's a really nice area and I'd like to show it to you."

She nodded. "Sound good."

They reached the car and drove to their destination. While walking, he pointed out the various mansions.

She gave them all an appreciative look. "Tsey beautiful."

They were strolling along a street nearly all of which was taken up by one house when Parker's stomach rumbled. "I'm hungry. We should go home and eat."

Melera's lips twisted. "Me want stay out."

"Sweetheart, we can come out tomorrow, okay?"

"No."

His temper flared. "Look, it's getting late. We'll come out tomorrow, and—"

"Me say me want—" She flipped her hand. "Fine."

She was quiet during the ride back. He wondered if she was annoyed with him because he wanted to leave and she didn't. He gave a minute shrug. *If she is, she'll get over it.*

They arrived at his house. Inside, he fixed them thick sandwiches and they ate. Melera was still silent, though. *She can't still be mad at me.*

After their meal, she sat on one end of the couch, tucked her golden brown legs beneath her and stared at nothing.

He couldn't stand it anymore. "What's wrong, sweetheart? You've hardly said a word since we left Capitol Hill."

She didn't answer at first. "Pawkher, you tsink me cray-zee still, yes?"

"Well, you have to admit it's pretty fantastic."

"What if me can show you?"

He shrugged. "Okay."

Melera rose from the couch and walked to the middle of the room. He watched her body ripple and then in her place was this blackish-green thing resembling some sort of weird tree. It nearly reached the ceiling.

He got up to get a closer look. A bunch of bright orange tendrils shot out and grabbed him by the neck. *What the fuck?* He fought but more of the tendrils lashed out until he'd been trussed like a turkey. The thing pulled him closer and closer. It opened its mouth, giving him a ringside look at its slimy-looking purple and red maw.

A small part of Parker's mind screamed *it's just Melera* but the rest of him wasn't listening. He was scared out of his wits and redoubled his efforts to escape. *Gimme some help here, pal!*

Shit, I'm trying!

Try harder! Goddammit, this thing's about to eat my face!

Then the monstrous tree spoke. "Gnathn," it said in Melera's deep voice. "Will eat anytsing, but likes best fresh meat." She morphed back and Parker found himself in her arms. She laughed. "Now you believe?"

Stunned, he could only nod. He'd never seen anything like that before and he knew he'd never see anything like that again. And he also knew he couldn't deny it anymore. Melera wasn't loony. She was exactly what she claimed to be—an honest-to-god space alien.

Still in a daze, he stared over her head at the wall. *She's an alien. She's really an alien. Good God, I've been fucking an alien!*

Told you. At least you still have your eyeballs.

What if my dick falls off?

Hasn't yet, has it?

Then another thought occurred to him. *The government! What if they get hold of her? She'll—*

"Is you ohh-kay, Pawkher?" he heard Melera's voice.

He looked down. She looked worried. "Uh…yeah. I'm fine. It was just a shock, that's all."

He led her back to the couch and sat. She climbed onto his lap and lay her head on his shoulder. After she'd made herself comfortable, he wrapped his arms around her and stared at the spot where the tree had been. Jogging her memory was more important now than ever. So was keeping her origins secret. He wouldn't let the government take her.

I won't, either.

Parker's jaw tightened. There was only one place in the city where he knew could hide her and the government would never find her. The place where all zots hid if need be.

In Underground.

CHAPTER 47

On Saturday night, four days after learning Melera was a space alien, Parker sat in a comfortably upholstered chair of an indeterminable color, ignoring the tumult going on around him. He held her across his lap with his arms wrapped about her slim waist. Her right arm snaking around his shoulders made a perfect little hollow at the base of her neck where he'd buried his nose.

He took a long, deep sniff. The pressure in his balls and his bulging prick, already straining his tight jeans, turned painful. He smiled.

Since running her down in Discovery Park, Parker had taken Melera out every day and evening he could. By now the two had rambled through almost a quarter of the city. They'd strolled through various neighborhoods as they had on Capitol Hill, some touristy, others off the beaten track. They'd even made a day trip to Mercer Island. Still, she remembered nothing. It was frustrating, but deep down he was pleased. He hadn't had this much fun in a long time.

Tonight they'd gone to the jam, an irregular, wild, and out-of-control zot party where anything went and usually did. Zots had appetites most humans would never understand and jams were a way for them to let off steam. Tonight's event was being held inside a cavernous warehouse in Seattle's Industrial District.

As a rule, Parker never attended these bashes ever since he'd learned the bands, booze, pills, and everything else except for the sex had been bankrolled by Kurt. To him, the parties were just one more way the bastard maintained his hold over Seattle's zots. He'd made an exception this time only because Melera had wanted to go.

He nuzzled her neck. Since the night he found her, he'd come to like many things about his unexpected houseguest. Her deep voice sent shivers down his spine. Her seeming favorite place to sit was on his lap, whether he was in human or wolf form. And he liked that she was so prickly. As alpha of his pack, most of the city's zots showed him great deference. That was as it should be but he got sick of everyone being so damned agreeable all the time. Melera, on the other hand, would scrap with him at the drop of a hat.

And he loved the lusty tension she aroused in him. She could make him sweat just by walking into the room.

There was no getting around her blood-scent, though. Its tang drove him and his wolf berserk. When she bled, they just couldn't keep their dicks out of her. His grin broadened. They'd bled her a lot since bringing her home.

She hadn't seemed to mind.

Parker listened to the moans and screams coming from the sex pit about fifty feet behind them. They'd walked past it just after they'd arrived. He'd estimated there were at least seventy zots down there, all screwing each other "silly, silly," as Melera would say. It had taken him only a second to decide not to join them. There were a number of very good reasons to keep her out of the pit, but really, he felt unusually possessive tonight.

Her fingers fishing around in his black leather vest pocket brought him back into the moment. She removed a cigar. "Torch, please," he heard her soft command.

He opened one eye. Flaring into his wolf's glowing green, he stared at the brown cylinder and the business end of the cigar blazed orange.

"Tsank you."

"My pleasure." He closed his eye and gave her a small squeeze.

She inhaled several times, then nudged him. He took a few puffs.

"Hey, I thought you didn't smoke that stuff," Tran said.

He glanced over. The beta lounged on a nearby upholstered chaise of the same indeterminate color. Nkele, an Asante princess before she'd become a vampire, lay in his arms.

"Melera's a bad influence," he said, his voice solemn. "I've been thoroughly corrupted."

Tran snorted. "So I see."

Parker watched Nkele give Tran a deep kiss. He smiled. Of all the vampires in Kurt's colony, he knew she was Tran's favorite. He'd had his own favorite vampire until he became alpha of the pack and Kurt's servant. Because of that, he'd had to break it off with her. She hadn't seemed bothered by it but he sure had. In his position, the only vampire permitted to screw him these days was Kurt.

Tran and Nkele's mouths finally parted. She laid her head on his chest and closed her eyes. Smiling, Tran kissed her braided hair and then turned to Melera. "Park says you're..."

Parker noticed Tran now looked at something over the alpha's shoulder and he didn't seem pleased by what he saw. He frowned. "What?"

"Kurt's here."

"Aw, fuck." He turned to see. Kurt was making his way across the warehouse, headed in their direction. It would take him a while to reach them. Zots constantly stopped to greet and have a few words with him, as if paying homage to the lord of the manor.

Tran looked down at Nkele. "Hey, babe, let's go to the sex pit. Or let's dance. Or something." They stood. "See ya, Park," Tran said. "Stay human."

"Yeah. You too, Tran." He gave him a short nod, wishing he could leave with them.

Tran's lips formed a faint smile. Parker understood. As alpha, he was not only giving his second permission to leave but was also letting him know there were no hard feelings about his wanting to get out of there.

Tran and Nkele left. He didn't watch where they went. Turning, he saw Melera's frown.

"Khurt. Vam-pire, yes?" she said while stubbing out the cigar they'd been smoking. "He rule See-at-tell, yes? And you?"

He grimaced and then sighed. "Yeah to all three. At least Garrett's not with him."

"Who Gharrett is?"

"It's a long story. Garrett's freyja of my pack, sorta like a wife. In fact, I had asked her to marry me but..." Parker gave her the short version of his and Garrett's affair, up to and including three weeks ago when she'd told him about the tryst. "That was the night I found you."

Melera didn't say anything for a long while. She stared at him with golden eyes disguised as human-looking, dark amber ones. "Pawkher, what tsey did very bad. Me whack tsem, yes?"

He was too astonished to speak. "Are you crazy?" he whispered after finding his voice. "Sweetheart, you don't just whack a vampire like Kurt. How do you think he got to be the Master?"

She snorted.

"And Garrett, she's a mage. She's got as much juice as Kurt does." He shook his head. "Baby, you'd never get within a hundred feet of either of them."

"Why, Pawkher? Assassin me is, remembuh? Me kill very good, yes."

"But…" He didn't want to insult her but up against those two? She couldn't be that good. He let out a long breath. "Okay. Let's just forget it for now, huh?"

"Good evening, Parker," a familiar velvety voice said.

He turned. The Master had arrived. From the look in the other's eyes, Parker knew he was in, as Melera would say, deep jakk.

CHAPTER 48

Kurt watched Melera lean forward and pick up a cigar-sized joint from the bowl in the middle of the table. Staring down her cleavage, he highly approved of the wolf's visiting playmate.

He pursed his lips. *She's a beautiful distraction but that's no excuse. I got back two days ago.*

The night after he and Garrett had confessed their ruse to Parker, Kurt had left Seattle for New York on business and to attend the gala heralding Manhattan's new Mistress. His and Parker's psychic connection meant the wolf knew he'd returned to Seattle the moment he'd rematerialized on solid ground.

Parker also knew Kurt's rule on visiting zots. Within hours of his return, he should have brought her to be introduced. The rule was a holdover from when he'd been a prince—he'd always wanted to know who was in his territory. His rule wasn't always practical these days but old habits die hard. It had angered him beyond belief that he'd been forced to seek out his servant in order to be introduced to this guest.

He already knew what he'd do about it. First, he'd kick the bitch out of his city and then he'd string the wolf up by his balls.

"Wan' me ta light tha' for yuh, darlin'?" Parker drawled from behind Melera's back.

His tone annoyed him. Parker affected that "down home" Arkansas accent only when he was feeling defiant.

"No, Pawkher," she said, holding one end the cigar between two long and slender fingers. "Do meself." Elbows on the table, she stared at the joint's opposite end and it flared into flame.

While she inhaled, Kurt's eyes widened a fraction and his anger evaporated. "How precise. Very nice, indeed." *Another pyro? Like Parker? Interesting.*

No one said anything. Minutes passed. He stared at Melera, then Parker. Their blatant show of disrespect brought his anger rushing back. His lips tightened. "I'm given to understand you're from the Fiji Islands, Melera."

She didn't answer. She leaned back and held the joint to Parker's lips while he inhaled. He noticed the wolf had unwrapped his arms from his playmate's waist. His hands roamed her torso, with an occasional tease to Melera's large, tantalizing breasts.

"Yes." She didn't look at him.

"What a lovely place to have grown up."

"Yes."

Parker blew out a stream of smoke. Taking the joint, Melera took another drag and then held it to the wolf's lips again.

"Which island do you live on?" Kurt said, still trying to be polite. But his courteousness was about to end.

Parker blew out another stream of smoke. "Ant."

Kurt saw Melera give the wolf a sideways look. "Oh, really?" He stared at her. "Ant, you say? That's odd. I've been to Fiji any number of times and I've never heard of it." He smiled like a fox with a hen in its teeth.

She shrugged and stubbed out the ember in a nearby ashtray.

Kurt narrowed his eyes. *My servant, you will pay dearly for tonight's farce.*

Parker kissed and nipped at his playmate's neck. Then he started massaging her breasts, nearly pulling the top of her dress apart. She giggled.

He frowned. This wasn't like Parker. The alpha might show some attitude but in public, he always behaved like a perfect gentleman. *What in the world is going on?*

Letting go of her breasts, Parker's hands dropped to her waist. "Ah cain' wait no more, darlin'." He lifted her off his lap for a moment and then set her back down.

"Ooo!" Melera squealed. The scent of sex filled the air.

Kurt's jaw dropped. *I don't believe this.*

The wolf bounced her on his lap. "Mmm...Ah'm luvin' this, babe."

Melera leaned forward but didn't say a word. She didn't have to. Her expression said enough.

Parker looked at him, grinning. "Hey, Massa. You wan' a piece? Her other end feels just as good." He winked. "An' we always share, don' we?" The wolf stood, pushing Melera across the table. Now Kurt could see exactly what the other was doing. He'd worked her tight dress above her hips and was giving her the same kind of rough fucking Kurt liked to give him.

Melera opened her dark amber eyes and ran her tongue over her full lips. Kurt needed no further encouragement. He stood and unzipped his trousers. His prick, pale and tumescent, jumped out of its former prison.

The wolf's playmate gave it a scornful look. "She lahkes 'em bigger than tha'," Parker sneered.

"Is that so?" Kurt said. He willed his erection into a monster more terrifying than Parker's wolf's cock. His prick grew to sixteen inches long and nearly seven inches around. He grinned. *Choke on this bitch.* Then he rammed his gargantuan dick down her throat.

She never flinched.

By now a crowd had gathered around the table to watch. Kurt's lips twisted into a tiny smirk. *Well, let's give 'em a show.* He grabbed Melera's hair and ground his hips against her face. Her throat constricted and relaxed, despite his size. More amazing was the fact that she could take all of him in—he'd have thought he'd be in her stomach by now. He closed his eyes. In all of his six hundred and four years, he'd never had a blow job like this one.

"Yeah! Do her Park! Fuck that bitch up good! C'mon, Kurt, you c'n do better than that—you da man!"

Opening his eyes, Kurt saw the crowd that had gathered around the three of them had gotten huge. Hands clapped in a rhythm that matched his thrusts. The noise grew until it seemed to fill the entire warehouse. He gazed at Parker. To his astonishment, the wolf pursed his lips and blew him a kiss. *C'mere*, he mouthed and then licked his lips. Holding Melera by the hips, he lowered her rump a bit and leaned forward.

Kurt placed his hands on her back. Anchored, he leaned forward, staring into the wolf's bright green eyes. If he'd been alive, his heart would have been pounding.

Parker smiled. Kurt wasn't about to deny him. Locking his mouth over the other man's lips, he kissed him, his tongue probing and licking.

He felt as if he were melting inside. *See,* liebchen*? See how good we can be to each other? You have no idea how much——*

The inside of Kurt's mouth tore apart. His eyes flew open. Parker's eyes no longer looked human. He pulled away. Blood ran from his mouth and down his chin. Just like his eyes, his teeth no longer looked human. Horrified, Kurt realized the wolf was chewing on something and that something was the vampire's tongue.

Excruciating pain ripped through his groin. He looked down. His eyes bulged with new terror. Melera had partially morphed into a hideous reptilian creature with a set of teeth a tyrannosaurus rex would envy. And like Parker, she too was chewing.

Blood gushed from where his penis had been. Staring at her outsized jaws, Kurt stumbled backward and fell into the chaise. Parker was laughing. He saw a piece of his tongue fall from the wolf's mouth and land on the devil woman's back.

Parker wasn't the only one who seemed amused by his predicament. Whipping his head right and left, it seemed to Kurt that everyone within eye and earshot was laughing too.

"Hey, Master! You gon' let dat bitch whup yo' ass?" someone shouted with obvious derision.

"Guess she's da man, now," came another raucous voice.

Kurt's royal Stauffen pride asserted itself for all of a split second before fleeing back to wherever it had been hiding. Sick with horror, he watched Melera regurgitate his severed sixteen-inch member. It slithered wetly out of her maw and dropped to the floor.

More than that, he was dying. He could certainly survive the loss of his tongue and penis but Parker's pet monster was now telekinetically crushing his heart and brain. He squeezed his eyes shut just as blood spurted from his nose. *Kill me now. Kill me so this horrid laughter will stop.*

Right before the end, a deep, mellifluous voice thundered through his head. The language was like nothing he'd ever heard but somehow he understood every word.

Jakk with Pawkher again and you will answer to me.

Kurt's eyes flew open. When he'd recovered his wits, he blinked in disbelief. He was intact.

What?

226

He looked around. There was no crowd, no laughter. The jam was going on around him as if nothing had happened. He was thoroughly confused. He'd obviously experienced a horrible hallucination, but...

Why?

He turned to the couple sitting across from him. Parker sat with his playmate perched on his lap, just as they'd been before his terrible vision. The wolf stared at him with a curious expression but said nothing. Then his gaze settled on Melera. She smirked.

Kurt's eyes widened. *She did this?* He was a vampire regent, the Master, yet she'd psyched him as if he were human. *If she can do that to me...*

He stood. "Parker, Melera. I'm so sorry, but I really must be going," he said, his voice showing not a trace of fear.

Parker chuckled. "Oh, gee, that's too bad."

He gritted his teeth, but his pleasant smile never wavered. He turned to Melera. "My dear, it was such a pleasure meeting you. We must talk again soon, hmm?"

"Yes. Me like tsat." She gave him a chilling grin. Then she clacked her teeth.

The Master disappeared in a hurry.

CHAPTER 49

"Damn," Parker said.

He and Melera sat in his old Caprice a few blocks from the jam, which was still going strong. Or rather, Parker sat. Melera draped over him, pawing his chest and gnawing on his neck. He had a fleeting thought they should've waited until after they'd gotten home before smoking that last joint.

He twisted the key in the Chevy's ignition a second, and then a third time. Nothing happened.

"Difficulty, yes?" Melera breathed in his ear. Her hands never stopped moving.

He gave her a sidelong look, his annoyance with his car bleeding over to her feral attentions. "Difficulty, yes," he said, trying to keep his tone neutral. Grimacing, he peeled her off of him, pushed the door open, got out, and walked around the vehicle's rear to the passenger side. By the time he reached it, she was already outside.

Parker let out a heavy sigh. "Come on, let's go back. Someone'll give us a ride home." He started for the warehouse but stopped when she tugged on his arm.

"No. Ride back, me will."

He frowned. He'd gotten pretty good at deciphering her cracked English but this one was beyond him. Melera smiled and pulled him closer. "Me you hold," she said, nodding. That he understood. His arms encircled her waist. "Okay, now what?" To his surprise, she didn't throw her arms about his neck like she usually did. Instead, she kept her hands behind her back where he couldn't see what she was doing.

"Hold tight."

He understood that too. "Sure, sweetheart. Whatever you say." He watched her eyes close.

A blinding flash seared his vision. On its heels came a cold too intense to be called bone-chilling. Another flash and he wasn't cold anymore. Parker blinked, trying to clear the spots before his eyes. When he could see again, his mouth hung open in disbelief. They were no longer across town—they were in his backyard, car and all. "How——?" he began but was interrupted by a fit of shivering. After his teeth stopped rattling, he tried again. "How did you do that?" he said, his voice low and awed.

"Brr-r-r!" Melera squealed and jumped in his arms. She smiled. "We skip tsrough."

"We skip where?"

"Tsrough. You know, like um…" She frowned for a moment. Then her face brightened. "Like door, yes? One room— step—tsen second room tsere in." She gave him a hopeful look.

Parker considered. "Oh, okay. I get it." He crinkled his brow. "But why is it so cold?"

"Is Void. Nutsingness."

"Ah," he said and nodded, though he hadn't a clue to what she'd meant. Then he remembered something about the cold. "Wait a minute. That night we fought in Discovery Park. That's how you got away from me, right? You skipped through."

She grinned.

"Huh," he grunted. "Pretty slick move." Then he cocked his head. "My car's a pretty big thing to skip. Can you skip something bigger?"

"Anytsing, long as me touch it."

"Can you skip something like, say, a planet?"

Melera shrugged. "Never try." She seemed to think a moment. "But prolly not good idea."

"Yeah, I guess you're right." He looked around, then turned to her and smiled. "Thanks for getting us home but there's just one small difficulty."

She frowned. "Yes? What?"

He kissed her ear. "Darlin'," he drawled, "my car should be on the other side of the fence."

CHAPTER 50

While Parker cursed his Caprice, Kurt paced his velvet-lined office, thinking about Melera. She'd humiliated him with that mind-fuck tonight and he'd be damned if he was going to let her get away with it. A vision of himself cowering on the chaise, terrified, flashed through his mind's eye and he again heard the taunts from the jam's raucous crowd of spectators. He shuddered. At least no one else saw his hallucination. Seattle's zots would have been glad to see him die like that.

He halted before the ornate, wall-sized mirror and clenched his fists. "And then she had the nerve to threaten me too," he said to his reflection. His lips tightened. Melera would pay for what she'd done and the price would be her life.

"Should've ripped her throat out right then and there," he muttered, annoyed that he'd been too rattled to do so. He shrugged. No matter. There was always tomorrow. "Yes. Tomorrow. Tomorrow, I'll—"

He raised his brow. "No, I won't." Tearing out Melera's throat in private was one thing but he wanted witnesses. He wanted her to die like she'd made him think he had, bloodied and humiliated before a jeering throng.

Kurt's face brightened. "Well, that's easy enough. I'll just have her brought to one of my warehouses, round up the most sadistic zots in the city, and let them have at her. Of course, I'll be gracious enough to take the last turn." His eyes narrowed. "Yes, indeed. The last face that bitch sees will be mine."

He thought for a moment, then shook his head. It was a wonderful idea, but there was just one problem—Parker. From the way the wolf had looked at her tonight, it was obvious she was more to him than a casual lover. If he had her killed outright, he and Garrett would never get him into the tryst. *And I want that more than I want her dead.*

The man in the mirror furrowed his brow. *Well, wait a minute. Parker doesn't have to know, does he? He teaches those programming classes at the university—what, twice a week? I've heard Melera goes everywhere with him except the men's room but surely he doesn't take her to school. I can grab her while he's out, have my little party and then dump what's left of her into the Sound. And it's not like she'd ever be found. Weresharks are always hungry.*

He paced the antique Turkish carpet again. No, that wouldn't work, either. If Melera disappeared, Parker would be convinced he had everything to do with it. The result would be the same as if he had her killed before the wolf's very eyes—Parker would refuse to make the tryst. And Garrett had been adamant that he couldn't force him to join them. So his hands were tied. If he wanted to have his cake and eat it too, he had to come up with a very good reason for killing Melera. Good enough not to drive Parker further away—and good enough to even bring the wolf closer to him and Garrett.

Kurt strode to his desk, plopped into the burgundy leather executive's chair and slammed his fists against the desk's mahogany top. "This is absurd. Since when does the Master need a reason to kill anyone he pleases?" He glared at the fine wood-grain, then slumped back and closed his eyes. "Since now," he sighed.

How could he have Melera murdered and make her death into a circus spectacle at the same time? He could always say it was because she and Parker had broken his rule requiring visitors to be introduced to him upon arriving in Seattle. He'd done that before. Not always—just often enough to remind the city's zots that his rules were not made to be broken. But using Parker's transgression as an excuse to have Melera killed would defeat his purpose in getting him into the tryst. He had to find a way to turn him against her. *And preferably one that isn't traceable to me.*

He let his thoughts drift back to the time when he was alive and a prince. The territory he'd ruled had been small but prosperous. Because of that, his neighbors had been keen to annex his lands. But they'd failed. Holding onto his realm had been like a never-ending chess game, complete with moves, countermoves, feints, and then checkmate. He'd been very good at the game. He couldn't remember how many ambassadors he'd banished and of his own people, executed.

I won every match except that last one. My dear cousin Reinhardt, may he rot in hell.

Reinhardt had held a large ducal territory immediately to the west of Kurt's and after years of trying, his cousin had finally gotten the best of him. The duke's plan had been so simple he'd never seen it coming. Kurt had been forty-seven at the time, an age when most men in the sixteenth century already looked old. But not him. That had been all the evidence Reinhardt needed. He'd begun a rumor—he'd told Kurt so—and publicly accused him of being *ein seelenlos,* the German term for an exotic in those days. He had known as well as Reinhardt did that he was human but there had been no way to prove it. So he'd been clapped into irons and thrown into his own dungeons. He'd endured the tortures—the strappado, the red-hot pokers, the racks…

Kurt's eyes popped open. *Stop. That's it.* He'd do to Melera what Reinhardt had done to him. He'd start a rumor. Then he frowned. A rumor was fine but it couldn't be just any rumor. It had to be one that would solidly marshal Seattle's zots against her. *Hmm. And Parker, too.*

Rising from his chair, he went over to the liquor cabinet, poured a goblet of wine and took a few sips. He'd been just about to take another when something occurred to him. Glass in hand, he returned to his desk. He set the goblet down next to his computer. Pulling up his chair, he sat and logged on to the internet.

A few minutes later, his lips stretched into a mirthless smile. He settled back in his chair. Unfocusing his gaze, he tuned into Garrett and sent her an urgent telepathic message.

CHAPTER 51

Garrett flung open the door to Kurt's office and strode inside. "I don't know what's so all-fired important you had to call me straight from—"

She stopped when she saw the look on his face. He stared at her bright purple sequined tank top, skimpy red latex skirt, black fishnet stockings, and red spike-heeled thigh boots. "My dear, you look positively whorish." He frowned. "Most unbecoming. Those colors are all wrong for you. You should—"

"Stop it." She glared at him. "You know I'm playing a street hooker at the Stohlman. I ran out right after I got your message. I'm in big trouble with my dresser for wearing this outside." She let out an impatient sigh. "So? You called me over here to criticize my costume?"

"Shut the door, please."

Garrett retreated a few steps and closed it. "Okay, what—"

"I met Melera at the jam tonight."

"You did? What's she like?" she said, her anger forgotten.

Kurt's expression hardened. "Never mind. Just listen. I've figured out a way to get rid of her, a way that'll bring Parker back to us at the same time."

"How?"

"We start a rumor about her."

"What kind of rumor?"

He grinned. "Melera's the Slayer."

She looked at him in disbelief. "That's ridiculous. Why would anybody believe that?"

"I'll show you." He walked over to his desk, motioning for her to follow. "Look here. He pointed at the computer monitor. "What do you see?"

Garrett sat in Kurt's chair. The monitor showed the calendar for last April. "April fourth's been highlighted in blue." She looked up. "So?"

"That's the day the newspapers reported the Slayer's first victim." He scrolled through the calendar to the next week. "Now. Look again." Her gaze followed his pointing finger to another blue square. "April eleventh. That's when the Slayer's second victim was discovered."

"Will you get to the point, Kurt?"

He shot her an annoyed look. "Be patient." He scrolled slowly through the rest of April and then May. Watching the blue squares go by, her jaw dropped a little. "Wait a minute—"

"Right. There's a pattern. Since the first body was discovered, there's been a Slayer murder every seven to nine days. The last one was reported on May twenty-eighth. But—"

"The papers don't know about Katy Drummond," she finished for him. "She was murdered on June fourth." Garrett regarded the blue square a moment and then glanced over the rest of the screen. No other dates had been highlighted. She looked up to find Kurt staring at her. "And today's June twenty-fifth. The Slayer hasn't struck in three weeks."

"Yes, indeed. And from what Parker's been telling everyone, Melera arrived on June fifth. Quite a coincidence, hmm?"

"Mother." She shook her head. "I know what you're getting at. But Kurt, people come and go from Seattle all the time. Why would anyone—"

"Why don't you let me finish?"

Garrett shrugged.

"All right. I'd guess about six hundred zots were at tonight's jam. Let's say about half of them knew I was there and maybe half of those saw Parker, Melera, and me sitting at our table."

She raised her brows.

Kurt smirked. "I *am* something of a celebrity in this town, you know."

Her eyes rolled. "Of course."

He moved from behind the desk and started to pace. "Now. We say something like this. I saw Parker and his college friend with the Master last night. She did something to him. I could see it in his eyes. Whatever she did, if she can do that, what else can she do?"

Feeling uneasy, she shifted in her seat but said nothing.

Kurt didn't seem to notice. "After pointing out the Slayer's three-week vacation, we plant the idea that Melera is our killer and that zots should come to me with their suspicions."

Garrett started in surprise. "Come to you? Except for me and maybe Parker, everyone's afraid of you, Kurt. Why should zots trust you? What's wrong with letting somebody take Melera out independently?"

He sighed. "Because you know how we are. Every little pack, clan, or whatever, always trying to prove each is tougher than the other. What a feather in the cap for one to claim they had slain the Slayer, hmm?" He grimaced. "Garrett, we have to be together on this. It's hard enough for me to keep peace among the zots in this city. You know that. More bad blood will only make it worse. When the time's ripe, I'll hand-pick a delegation to bring Melera to me and then we'll have a public execution, so to speak. That way, no one group can claim superiority. And only if enough of us see her die will everyone else believe she's really dead."

"Wouldn't it be easier just to give Melera to the humans?"

"Don't be silly. What if she tells them she's been staying with Parker? I'd say that would be the end of your tryst, hmm?" He looked at her. "So...what do you think?"

She eyed him. "I think your rumor's got more holes in it than my old leotard. Like I said—why would anybody believe it?"

Kurt smiled. "Because fear has no logic. People are scared, Garrett. When people are scared, they'll believe anything, even utter nonsense." He chuckled. "My dear, I've been around long enough to know. Trust me. It'll work." A few moments passed in silence. "Well?"

She didn't answer at first. "Kurt, what did Melera do to you tonight?"

His smile fled. "Nothing. That's just meat for the rumor. If she's going to be our Slayer, we have to give the impression that no one's safe from her, not even me." He looked away and let out a quiet hiss. "It's terribly embarrassing," he said almost to himself, "but I'm willing to live with it if that's what it takes to kill the bitch."

Her lips tightened. Melera *had* done something to him and Kurt was about as near to invincible as any zot she'd ever known. She looked at her fishnet-covered lap. *Melera's not only in the way, but she's dangerous, too.* Then she remembered her conversation with Paul. Melera couldn't possibly be the uthyrisis but there were other kinds of demons. Not all of them needed magickal help to escape the netherworld.

She looked up. Kurt was staring at her again. "What do you want me to do?"

"I want you to help spread the rumor." He walked behind the desk to a small printer and picked up a sheet of paper. "Here's a list of names. I'm sure you have a spell that can whisper it to them in their dreams."

Garrett looked at the list. There were at least two hundred names. "Yeah, there's a spell, but this is a lot of people. It'll take me a week, maybe more."

"Quite all right, my dear. From what I gathered tonight, Melera isn't going anywhere anytime soon."

She hesitated a moment. "Kurt, this three-week break in the murders…what if Melera showing up isn't a coincidence?"

He nodded. "I've already made a few inquiries into her past."

Standing, she tucked the list in her purse and sighed. "I gotta go. I have to get these clothes back to the Stohlman."

"Of course." Kurt took her elbow and walked her out of his office, down the hallway and up to the door leading to the alley. He bent down and gave her a light kiss on her forehead. "I'm going a-rumor mongering. We'll talk tomorrow, hmm?"

"Okay." She watched him dissolve into mist. Trying not to think about demons, she pushed the door open and stepped out into the night.

CHAPTER 52

Four days after Kurt and Garrett began planting their rumor, there had still been no new murders. Seattleites were jumpier than ever. On the streets, Washington's open carry law was being used to full effect. Everywhere Parker looked, people were packing guns.

He wondered how many of the guns were loaded with silver bullets. He shivered.

Parker and Melera had been roaming the city as usual. As usual, she remembered nothing. The day was unseasonably hot and the heat was raising his frustration level. So as not to take it out on her——the last thing he wanted was to start a fight——he decided it'd be best to get something to cool him off.

"Come on. Let's get some ice cream."

She frowned. "Ice skeem?"

"Yeah. You'll like it."

The ice cream shop was full, with people spilling out onto the sidewalk. Apparently, a lot of other people had the same idea. They walked to the back of the line. Parker could smell the humans' fear. He leaned in close. "You feel it?" he whispered in her ear.

"Feel what?"

He nudged her. "You know."

"Is big badder tsan before but me tsought See-at-tell always like tsis."

"It's never been this bad. If they don't find the Slayer and soon, this city's going to erupt."

Melera said nothing.

"Rick got outed the other day," the woman in front of Parker said. She had a pistol on her hip.

Her companion, also carrying a gun, looked surprised. "Really? Did he disappear?"

"No. He tested human so they let him go." The other woman paused. "It's too bad, really."

"Why?"

"Rick's an asshole."

They moved forward. From behind him came a male voice. "Goddamned zots. You know they're behind this Slayer business. I don't see why we humans just don't kill 'em all."

"We don't know who they are, Harry," he heard a woman's voice.

"We can find out. Give everybody a mandatory GST. You don't take it, you disappear."

Parker and Melera gave each other sideways looks.

They reached the counter. He bought two double-dip cones, chocolate for him and strawberry for Melera.

She took a small bite out of the mound of ice cream. Her face lit up. "Is good, yes."

He felt a warmth flush through his body that had nothing to do with the day's heat. It pleased him that he had pleased her. It was then he realized just how much his feelings about her had changed since the night he'd run her down. Sure, he'd taken her in out of guilt. And once she'd recovered, his feelings had been pure lust. But after spending so much time with her, he felt a deep fondness, like one feels toward a close friend. Even her bitchiness no longer fazed him.

Melera opened her mouth for another bite. He laid a hand on her arm. "No, sweetheart. You're supposed to lick it. Like this." He ran his tongue along the side of his chocolate ice cream mound. "It lasts longer that way."

They started walking, too busy eating their treats to talk. After about a block, Parker looked up from his cone. Now that she'd convinced him she was a space alien, he was curious about what life on another planet was like. Mostly, he was curious about her. "Hey, Melera. So tell me, what were you like as a kid?"

She chuckled. "Troo-ble."

He laughed. "You sound like me. What did you do?"

"Stole me fawtser's flitter for happy ride. End up in lake."

His eyes widened. She'd told him a flitter was a two-seater air vehicle, sort of like a tiny car. "God, Melera—you could have died."

"Almost did."

He shook his head. "Whew. How old were you when you stole his flitter?"

She didn't answer right away. He knew why. He'd taught her to count to twenty but now she had to harmonize the two planets' solar years. She cocked her head. "Twelf, tsirteen your years?"

His estimation of her went up several notches. Stealing cars at thirteen…he'd never been so bold. "I was trouble too, but we—my friend Frank and I, I told you about him—we did stuff like playing dirty pranks on people and breaking into houses."

Melera eyed him. "You get catch?"

He grinned. "Once. Almost. I talked our way out of it." Walking along, they regaled each other with tales from their misspent youth. It didn't surprise him to learn that Melera—along with the rest of her friends, it seemed—had been a daredevil. Compared to her, he and Frank had been about as adventurous as a couple of toy poodles.

They finished their cones and were about to start traipsing around town again when Parker decided he'd had enough for the day. "What do you think of this? Instead of going walkabout, why don't we go to the beach?"

She frowned. "Beech?"

"Yeah. Alki Beach."

"Ohh-kay."

They returned to the car. While driving to West Seattle, it occurred to him they didn't have swimsuits, a beach requirement. He might be able to get away with it but she couldn't. He gave a minute shrug. *Oh, well. We can at least get our toes wet.*

Arriving at the beach, he managed to snag a decent parking space. After grabbing a blanket from the trunk and locking up their personal items, he and Melera crossed the large asphalt walkway to the beach proper. Parker searched for a place where they could lay out the blanket. He had lots of choices. Given the heat, he was surprised there weren't more people out today.

Then something occurred to him. He'd learned from his trip to Nordstrom that a lot of women's underwear—the trendy stuff—looked like swimsuits. And he'd bought some for Melera. If he found a site far enough away from the lifeguards, they might not be able to tell the difference. He looked around and spotted the perfect place, right at the edge of the swimming area. Hardly anyone had camped out that way, either.

He slipped his arm about her shoulders. "Found where we should go. Come on."

She snaked her arm around his waist and they started walking. He wasn't sure when the habit started but these days, they almost always walked with their arms about each other. From the occasional smiles he'd glimpsed from others, it was obvious people thought they were a couple.

If only they knew.

"So tsis is beech," Melera's voice sounded to his right as he spread the blanket and sat.

"Yep."

She smiled. "Like Prasu sector." Her lips tightened and her look turned wistful.

Parker reached over and stroked her hair. "Let's get in the water." He stood and took off his shoes, then shucked his clothes. Melera had stood too, and lifted her dress over her head while kicking off her sandals. He eyed her and grinned. Her underwear, a black strapless bra and black bikini panties, looked identical to the suit a woman was wearing that he'd seen on their way over.

He grabbed her hand and they ran toward the shoreline. Splashing into the cold water, they waded until they were waist-deep. He smacked his hand against the water's surface, sending up a spray that soaked her and laughed. Melera looked surprised for a moment. Her eyes narrowed. Then she did the same to him.

They splashed each other for a while. Parker turned his back to her and bent his knees until the water reached his chest. He swiveled his head to look at her. "Climb on my shoulders."

"Why?"

"Don't ask questions. Just do it. "

She did, and he immediately stood and flipped her off, dunking her. She shot to her feet, laughing. "Tsat fun. Again."

He obliged her. When they'd tired of the game, he suggested they go sit in the sun. They waded to shore and lay down on the blanket close together. Neither spoke. Parker closed his eyes, enjoying the nearness of her.

242

"How you be woof?" Melera's voice sounded to his right. "You say you peoples be hu-man, yes?"

"I drank from a wolf stream when I was in college. Wolf streams look like any other bit of flowing water, except drinking from it changes you into a werewolf."

"Why you drink tsen?"

"Didn't know it was a wolf stream." He paused. "I'll tell you about it sometime."

The sun's heat and the sound of the water gently lapping against the shore made him drowsy. Parker hovered between wakefulness and sleep, his half-conscious state making him feel as if he was floating. After drifting for what seemed like hours, the tantalizing odor of cooking food brought him fully awake. His belly rumbled.

Melera chuckled. "Me hear tsat. You hungry."

Eyes still closed, he smiled. "Aren't you?"

"Yes."

"Then let's go home."

The two rose and dressed. Shaking sand from the blanket, he folded it and tucked it under his arm. Parker held out his other arm and Melera slipped against his side as if she belonged there. His heart stirred.

The trip back was quiet but it was a mellow quiet, the kind that happens between friends who are comfortable with silence. After pulling into his driveway, he reached for his door handle when Melera laid a hand on his arm. He turned.

Her face held an odd look. "Tsank you, Pawhker," she whispered.

"For what?" he whispered back.

"For evertsing."

He leaned over and gave her a peck on her forehead. "No thanks needed. I—"

Something in his heart stirred again. Before he could stop himself, he grabbed her head and laid a brutal, devouring kiss on her lips. After pulling away, he stared into her dark amber eyes in a daze, as if what he'd just done was something entirely new. He gave his head a small shake. "Come on. Let's get something to eat before we starve."

Later that night, after a thoroughly satisfying meal and an hours-long bout of lovemaking that left his body feeling rubber-like, the two lay side by side on the grass in his backyard. An empty bottle of Jack Daniel's and an ashtray containing a half-smoked cigar lay nearby. Hand in hand, they watched the night sky. Or rather, Melera watched the sky. Parker's mind was elsewhere.

I'm an idiot. Come on. Melera's an alien. She's been all over a galaxy and I've only been to Canada. And she's a queen, for God's sake. What do I have to offer her? I should just—

"What tsat one is?" Melera's voice interrupted his thoughts. He turned his head to see her pointing at one of the brighter stars in the west. "Umm..." he frowned a little while digging into his fuzzy memory of the freshman astronomy class he'd taken while in college. "It's uh... Arcturus. I think."

"You not know?"

"I'm pretty sure it is."

"If you not know, you should say so."

He chuckled. "Shall I look it up for you, Your Majesty?"

"Yes."

Silence returned and the minutes ticked by. Parker's mind went back to its churning. *Sure, Melera's a queen but queen of what? Her planet's gone and her people are dead. Maybe I can—no, I can't. Oh, this is so stupid.*

He turned and watched her stare at the sky. "What are you thinking about?"

She didn't answer at first. "Pri-son."

Letting go of her hand, he rolled onto his elbow and peered into her face. "Why?"

She looked at him and gave him a small smile. "Hard to forget."

"Well, let's talk about something else, then." He hesitated, knowing what he wanted to ask, but afraid of her answer. "Do you like Earth?" he blurted.

Melera shrugged. "Is not so different from lots other places."

Was that a yes or a no?

Thinking about his next move made his heart beat faster. "Think you could stay here?"

She snorted. "Me have war to fight, yes?" Then she looked away. "No matter. Me not remembuh ship, me go nowhere."

Parker said nothing. He gazed at her, this courageous woman from the stars who'd endured so much yet had remained unbroken. Hunted by her enemies, he guessed she'd be in hiding for the rest of her life. And Earth, an insignificant planet located in an insignificant galaxy hundreds of thousands, maybe millions or even billions of light-years from her own, was the perfect place for her to do that.

Something in his heart burst like a dam breaking. "Then I hope you never remember a thing," he whispered and kissed her.

CHAPTER 53

Three nights later, at one a.m. on Saturday morning, the uthyrisis stood inside the curved lines that surrounded it. It looked down. It was wearing the Gerald body again. The uthyrisis lifted the Gerald body's arm and peered at it, then did the same to the other. It inspected the legs and everywhere else it could see. No flaky black patches. The Gerald body was holding up well. But something was different. It couldn't sense the Gerald's presence.

Gerald.

Silence.

Ger-aald.

Before the uthyrisis could call a third time, the female who'd summoned it spoke. "I have another task for you."

It smiled. "You wish me to hunt again."

"Yes, but it is a particular life I want you to take." The female closed her eyes. A picture appeared in the uthyrisis's mind. "His name is Paul," the female said. "Gerald met him yesterday afternoon when we were out around town."

The uthyrisis concentrated harder. "Paul is not alone."

"Then I give you two lives." The female waved her arm, and it stepped forward.

The female looked into its eyes. "This is the last time I will summon you. Your work here is almost done."

"What if I wish to return?"

"You can't. Once I send you back, you can only return if I call. And after you complete this task, I will not call you again."

The uthyrisis smiled again. "Then it is best that I not leave." It leapt. Morphing into its fifth-cum-third dimensional form, it wrapped the female in its wings and squeezed. The two crashed to the floor.

"Gerald," the female screamed. "Help me!"

The uthyrisis chuckled. "The Gerald is not here. Only me." Its feeders shot out, penetrating the female's body. She screamed again and thrashed. It thrust a feeder into her mouth and did the same to her other, lower three holes. She thrashed harder. A minute passed. The female went limp.

The uthyrisis morphed back into the Gerald body and stood. A wide grin spread across its face. It was free, now. Free to continue building its epic for the Mighty Ones, a saga that would be the envy of all others.

Giving the female's blood-spattered body one last look, the uthyrisis crossed the remaining lines and disappeared into the night.

The uthyrisis crouched amidst a row of bushes at the edge of a smallish green square. On the other side of the square was a structure the Gerald had said was a house. The lives it was to take were in that house.

Like the Janice had taught it, the uthyrisis had made a plan. It had poked its feeders through the Gerald body, making it bleed a little. It let the Gerald's eyes water until the liquid streamed down the body's face.

The uthyrisis ran up to the house's front. Curling the Gerald's hand into a fist, it pounded on the door.

A male the uthryrisis recognized as Paul opened it. His jaw dropped. "Gerald. What in the Lord and Lady's names are you doing here?" Then he seemed to notice the Gerald was bleeding. "Oh, no. No, no, no." Paul pulled the uthyrisis inside. "Ara," he shouted. "We need hot water, soap, and something to wash him with!"

An old female jumped from her seat and ran into another room. The uthyrisis heard the sound of water running.

"Over here, Gerald." Paul and led it to a chair. The old female held out a towel. He spread it over the seat and pushed the Gerald body onto it. The old female handed Paul a smaller cloth, a bowl of steaming liquid, and a solid, rectangular yellow bar. The uthyrisis watched him dip the smaller cloth in the liquid and rub the yellow bar over it. Then he began wiping the blood from the Gerald body.

Paul gave the uthyrisis a worried look. "What happened?"

"The Slayer," it made the Gerald's voice hitch. "It-it…"

"That's okay. Were you alone?"

The uthyrisis shook its head. "I…I was with a friend. F-from the coven. "You—"

"Pinkie, you mean, right?"

It nodded, making a leap of faith that the young female it had just killed had been called Pinkie. "Then th-this thing comes out of nowhere and grabs me. Pinkie threw some magic at it and it went after her. She told me where you were and…"

"You're going to need more hot water," the old female said. She left the room.

Paul made a couple more passes with the cloth and then stopped his wiping. He stared at the Gerald. "Gerald, how did Pinkie know I was here?"

The uthyrisis grinned.

It leapt at Paul and wrapped him in its wings. Minutes later, he had been drained of blood. Now it was the old female's turn. The Gerald rose from the chair and walked into the kitchen.

Ara stood at the sink. "Feeling better, dear?"

"Oh, yes," the uthyrisis said and leapt. After it had drained her, it grinned again. "I need more tales," it whispered.

CHAPTER 54

Melera woke with a start early Saturday morning. Instead of getting up, she stared at the ceiling.

"Sheet," she muttered a few minutes later and smacked her hand against the mattress. Blowing a heavy breath, she rolled out of bed and began pacing the floor. She'd had a dream. Her father and Ruri had been in it, and so had Beloc. There'd been something else, too—something about music...

She shook her head. "Fook." She'd almost had it. She'd almost remembered.

Feeling Parker's gaze, she turned and saw him leaning against the headboard. Head tilted slightly to the left, his face wore an expression of concerned curiosity. "What?"

Melera opened her mouth but no words came. Her eyes widened in shock. *Ruri used to look at me like that.* And in the next moment, she knew. She loved this Earth-male, loved him with a passionate abandon she thought would never be hers again. But she also knew it could never be. How could it? Parker had a home, his wolfpack, and his friends. She was homeless, friendless, and at war. And her dream could mean only one thing—their time together was running out. What should she tell him?

The two stared at each other, the silence seeming to grow heavier with each passing moment. Her thoughts raced, trying to think of something to say. "Want kof-fee," she said after a moment or two. "Go build." She looked at the floor to avoid Parker's eyes. Then she left the bedroom.

Puzzled, Parker frowned at the empty doorway for a few seconds then got up and followed Melera to the kitchen. He reached it just in time to watch her push the coffee basket into its housing and turn on the machine. Then she rested her palms on the edge of the steel sink and bowed her head.

Walking up behind her, he encircled her in his strong arms and nuzzled her ear. "Tell me, sweetheart."

She didn't answer at first. "Almost remembuh," she whispered.

He froze. "That...that's wonderful," he whispered back after his throat had loosened a little.

Melera said nothing.

He didn't say anything either. He knew her frustration. The longer her memory stayed lost, the shorter her temper became. Sometimes it was all he could do not to throttle her. But her memory was obviously coming back. It wouldn't be long before she remembered everything. And then she would leave.

Parker stared out the window for a long while, thinking. He thought about his human mother and brother, still living in Arkansas. He thought about his wolfpack, whose lives depended on him. He thought about Tran, his closest friend since Frank Suggs. He thought about the life he'd made for himself in Seattle. It had its risks but it was still a good one. Then he thought about the war in Melera's galaxy and what she'd told him about her chances of surviving it. None.

Closing his eyes, he softly kissed his lover's hair. He'd made a decision, and it had been surprisingly easy.

When you go, Melera...I'm going with you.

CHAPTER 55

On Saturday night, Melera decided that "rolling" was the best idea Parker had come up with all day.

He'd been annoying the hell out of her. As usual, they'd spent part of the day making his duty visits. When they'd been alone, if he hadn't been jakking her, he'd been yapping at her, coming up with all sorts of questions about Xia'saan, the war, skipping, and apparently anything else he could think of.

"How long could somebody stay in the Void before they froze to death?" he'd said.

She'd shrugged. "Me not try find out."

He'd given her a sidelong look and shook his head. "Helluva way to get someplace."

"Is too where me rid assassined bodies, yes?"

That had shut him up. Good thing, too—by then she'd been ready to stuff a gag into his mouth.

Parker's arm snaking around her waist brought her back into the moment. The night breeze, warm and soft, tousled her hair and tickled her nose. Looking around, she saw they were heading into Pioneer Square. She liked the area's solid-looking red brick structures—they were Romanesque Revival, he'd told her, though she'd no idea what that meant.

She turned. "We go where, Pawkher?"

"Nowhere in particular. The point of 'rolling is to walk around, see what's going on."

"How long we out?"

"However long it takes, sweetheart."

Arms about each other, they strolled along the sidewalks, stopping here and there to peek inside a club or to admire a window display. Every so often, she caught him staring at her breasts with a hungry look in his eyes. Her cropped, skin-tight top left little to the imagination. A tiny smile stretched her lips. She dropped her arm from his waist and took his hand. He often looked at her like this and she liked it. He made her feel hungry, too.

After a few hours, the two arrived at a corner across the street from a small park. Parker stopped and turned. "This is Pioneer Place Park. It's kind of a central meeting point for us when we're on 'rol. I've already spotted a few of my pack. If you don't mind, I'd like to talk to them a little. See what's going on. Okay?"

"Ohh-kay."

Crossing the street, they entered the green triangle. Per pack protocol, as Parker had explained, Tran—because he was the pack's beta—was the first to greet them. Leaving the three men he'd been standing with, Tran casually walked up to the two of them as if he'd run into a couple of friends. "Hey, Park, good to see you."

"Good to see you too, Tran."

Melera smiled again. Parker had explained the phrase "good to see you" was the standard public greeting among werewolves. The greeting was innocuous enough not to be picked up on by any human within earshot and as for the wolves themselves, it was always good to see each other well and whole.

"You never know what might happen," he'd said. "For us, tomorrow is never guaranteed. Especially these days." Then he'd chuckled. "Besides, you've seen how we greet each other in private. Can you imagine what would happen if one of my pack walked up to me on the street and started licking my mouth? We'd disappear faster than you could even think about skipping."

Standing next to him inside the small, leafy triangle, Melera thought about that conversation. She thought about what had happened in his bedroom that morning and what it meant for the two of them. She thought about the war in Maqu, about how many millions had died already and about how many more millions would die before the war was over, including her.

Tomorrow is never guaranteed.

That was a truth she knew all too well.

CHAPTER 56

Parker and Tran shook hands. Not far from where they stood, he saw Janet and five-year-old Susie sitting on a bench about ten yards away. They seemed to be arguing. He smiled, knowing what was going on. Susie, still too young to understand pack rules, was trying to run over to the three of them.

Janet was barely able to hold on to her squirming daughter. Glancing at his lover, he saw her slight smile. She'd seen them, too. "Melera, you remember Tran from the jam, right?"

Her smile broadened into a toothy grin. "Yes, Pawkher. Ohhh, yes."

Parker thought Tran looked and smelled nervous. "Good to see you too, Melera," he said. His voice sounded as uncomfortable as the look on his face.

What's up with him? This was the kind of thing he hated most about being pack alpha—always having to be on guard, even with friends. Challenges to a death-match weren't always about power. Sometimes a wolf was forced to challenge the alpha for other reasons, like when he'd challenged Slade. He and Tran were close but both knew that neither would hesitate to kill the other to preserve the pack.

God, just not tonight, okay? Then he frowned. It had just dawned on him. There were lots of zots out tonight, not just wolves. Almost all, whenever he'd caught their eye or had spoken with them had seemed nervous, like Tran. *Now that's strange.* He turned. "Tran and I need to talk, Melera. Wait over there." He pointed to a bench about thirty feet away, near where they'd entered the little park.

She raised her brow and stared at him, an obvious "you talkin' to me?" gesture. Without a word, she headed for a bench in the opposite direction, the one where Janet was still trying to hold on to Susie.

"I wouldn't piss her off if I were you," Tran's voice sounded beside him.

Swiveling his head, Parker shot him a puzzled look. "Why? I do it all the time."

"And you're still alive?"

Parker's eyes narrowed. This conversation was getting too weird. "Okay, give. What's the matter with you?"

Tran sighed. "I don't like it."

"Like what?"

"The city's vibes."

"How so?"

Tran waved his arm. "Can't you feel it? Everybody knows the Slayer is still out there but when's the last time you saw so many humans out at night?" He paused. "I mean, look at 'em. All this partying, it's all wrong." His lips tightened. "It's too edgy to be real, Park. I've been out since mid-afternoon and Seattle stinks of fear and even worse, violence."

Parker eyed the ground. Now that he thought about it, Tran was right. He let out a tiny sigh. He was supposed to be on 'rol, but honestly, he'd been too absorbed in Melera to notice what was going on around him. He looked up. "Anybody else nose this out?"

"Yup. Just about everyone I've talked to tonight."

"Mm-hm. Come on."

They strolled over to the pergola, where the three werewolves Tran had been standing with still leaned against the wrought iron. The pergola was an early twentieth- century shelter built over public bathrooms located beneath the street. The bathrooms, no longer in use, were not a part of Underground.

"It's mad out here, dude," the tallest one said. "I don't know what's in the air tonight, but it's scaring the shit outta me."

Parker nodded and turned away. He and Tran visited with a lone wolf who seemed to be admiring the exquisitely carved Tlingit totem pole not far from the pergola. Her assessment of the city's mood wasn't any different.

Walking about, he glanced from time to time to where Melera sat with Janet and Susie. The three seemed to be getting along just fine. His lips stretched into a small smile. Like all zots, werewolves were reserved when it came to meeting new people—Janet more so because of her horrible experience with Slade, the old alpha. Yet now the young mother appeared relaxed, smiling and laughing as though Melera was an old buddy. More surprising, Susie seemed easy with her, too. Slade, his freyja Greta, and their favorites had mistreated the cub almost as much as they'd mistreated her mother.

By the time he and Tran had finished polling the 'rollers, Parker had spoken with twelve of his wolves and all were in agreement. The city's atmosphere might seem giddy but underneath lay something dark and sinister.

"Does Melera know about Underground?" Tran said.

He shook his head. "I thought I'd show her later. Maybe tomorrow."

"Maybe you should show her tonight." Tran glanced in her direction.

Parker frowned. The beta's words belied his expression. He looked as if he'd rather Parker not show her anything at all.

Then Tran did a double-take. "Damn. Do you see that? That's incredible."

He turned. Susie had climbed onto Melera's lap and had fallen fast asleep. His lips stretched into a smile, pleased that at least two somebodies weren't acting like they were scared to death of her.

"That reminds me," Tran's voice sounded. "You still need to choose a new freyja."

Parker turned but said nothing.

"The pack's still divided over Garrett but with the Slayer loose they're pretty much willing to leave things as they are, at least for now." Tran eyed him. "That includes anyone who might be thinking of challenging you, too."

He raised his brow but still said nothing.

Tran stared at him a moment longer and then gave his head a little shake. "Anyway, I've asked around—keeping it on the QT, of course—and it seems most of the pack think Mandy's a good choice."

Parker kept his expression neutral. He didn't give a wererat's ass about what anybody thought about who his next freyja should be. He wouldn't be here much longer, anyway. "Mandy, huh?" He shrugged. "Yeah, well. I'll think about it. Listen, as of now, I'm off 'rol. I need to get Melera home."

Tran glanced over to where she sat on the bench with Janet and Susie. Then he looked at him for what seemed to be a long time. "Take care, Park. Okay?" He turned and walked toward the pergola.

He stared at Tran's retreating back. His second's behavior had been strange, starting with his reaction to Melera. He pursed his lips and then ambled over to where the two women sat on the bench, reaching them moments later. "Hey, there."

Janet stood and lifted the still-sleeping Susie from Melera's lap. "Hi, Al—I-mean-Parker." She turned to Melera. "I'd better take Susie home. It was nice meeting you."

"Yes. We talk again soon, yes?"

A small, shy smile appeared on the young woman's face. "I-I'd like that."

"Wait." Parker gave Janet a questioning look. "You need a ride?"

She shook her head. "No, we'll be okay. Thanks, though."

"Just be careful."

The young she-wolf nodded and walked away. He watched her and her cub for a few minutes. Then he turned to Melera and smiled.

She smiled back. "Go you house now?"

"Yes and no. Tran suggested I show you one more thing before we call it quits tonight, and I'm inclined to agree." She stood and he slipped an arm around her slim waist. "Ready, sweetheart?"

"Yes, Pawkher."

Three blocks later, they reached a narrow alley between two brick buildings. He led Melera inside and stopped when they'd gone just over half the alley's length. They stood before a black metal door set into the brick. It looked like any other entrance used for commercial deliveries.

"What tsat is?" she said, sounding puzzled.

"You'll see." Looking around to make sure no one was watching, he pushed hard on the center brick in the first row above the black door. It depressed about a half-inch and then returned to its place. After hearing a soft click, he opened the door.

Parker turned and grinned. "Welcome to Underground."

CHAPTER 57

With a theatrical gesture, Parker ushered her over the threshold and pulled the door closed behind them. After the witch-lights came on, he slipped past and stepped off the first of a flight of stairs. At the bottom, he pushed open a second door similar to the upper one.

He held it open for her. In the light from the landing where they stood, Melera could see yet another flight of stairs. They continued downward through more doors and stairs.

"Pawkher, where we go?"

"Patience, sweetheart. We'll get there."

He led her down another flight of stairs. When they reached the bottom, he opened a fifth door. Melera stepped inside and halted in her tracks. Speechless, she stood like a statue, her eyes wide in surprise. She'd have thought she'd be somewhere in the building's basement but no—she was standing on a street, a near replica of the one above her.

A gentle push at the small of her back startled her out of her immobility. She stumbled forward a few steps. After regaining her balance, she turned to see Parker standing a few feet away, grinning.

"Like I said, welcome to Underground." His voice sounded as pleased as his smile.

"Khi si'kht a kah," she murmured, looking around. Her brows knitted into a small frown. She had the strangest feeling…

Pain exploded through her skull. Reeling, she let out a little groan and then crumpled, unconscious before she hit the brick sidewalk.

What the hell? The shock from his lover's sudden collapse paralyzed him. "Melera," he shouted when he could move again.

Parker was at her side in two bounds. Pulling her into his arms, he sat her up. With his thumb, he raised her eyelids one at a time but instead of whites, he saw iridescent gold. They didn't spin, so he knew she was out cold.

He looked around. Slipping an arm beneath her knees, he carried her to a sidewalk bench he'd spotted. Laying her flat, he knelt and peered into her face. "Melera." Seeing no reaction, he lightly slapped her cheeks. "Melera, honey, wake up. Wake up, baby."

Her eyelids fluttered once and then opened. "Pawkher?"

"Yeah, sweetheart. I'm here."

Her golden irises began spinning fast. "Pawkher," she said, bolting upright. He leaned backward just in time to avoid a cranial collision. "Me remembuh. Remembuh evertsing."

"No kidding?"

Melera stood. "Come. We go." She began striding down the street.

He jumped to his feet. "Wait! Where are you going?" He trotted after her.

She grabbed his hand after he'd caught up and gave him a little tug. "Come." They moved east, opposite from the way they'd been going while topside.

Melera filled him in while they walked. "Tarq Shen'zae— me fawtser—back Vst in war. Promise he Xia'saan battlefleet— starships, yes? Only way tsem can fight Akkad." She paused. "Akkad find maybe Xia'saan fleet in Maqu and take, yes? One time, learn Tarq about wormhole to here, give him idea, yes?"

Parker frowned. Given her terrible English, it took him a while to figure out what she'd said. He nodded when he had. "Okay. Your father promised to give the battlefleet to—whoever you said they are—so they'd have a better chance at winning the war. The problem was the— whatever—might take it for themselves. So your dad finds this wormhole thing by chance and..." His frown deepened. "And what?"

She took a breath. "Pawkher, listen you. Inside Earts solar system Xia'saan fleet hides."

He stopped in his tracks. "Hide? How d'ya hide something like that?" He shook his head. "Look, I know us Earthers are a bunch of primitive techno-apes compared to you, but there're all sorts of telescopes and satellites up there in orbit and a lot of 'em can see out way farther than just this solar system." He raised an eyebrow. "A fleet of spaceships? Don't you think somebody down here would've spotted it by now?"

She pursed her lips. "No. Have program, ships do. Like, um—" she frowned a moment—"shield, yes? See not, tsen."

He rolled his eyes. "Of course. How stupid of me."

They started walking again. A short while later, she stopped in front of a brick building. He looked up and down the street, guessing they were about four blocks from Pioneer Square's tiny park and about a hundred feet below it.

Melera opened the door. The blackness inside was absolute. Stepping over the threshold, she disappeared into the abyss with Parker right on her heels.

CHAPTER 58

While Parker tried to revive Melera in Underground, Kurt finished chaining Garrett to the black leather mattress.

This was one of the things he liked about her. She was deep into the scene and they entertained themselves with one of their little games as often as they could. He smiled. The two had been engaging in their romps for almost as long as they'd known each other, nearly fifteen years. Garrett might look like a fresh young thing just out of college but she was in her early forties.

Bound, she looked up at him with hazel eyes wide, her face full of anticipation. Kurt affixed a black leather mask to her head. "You know the rule," he whispered as he mounted her. "Silence, or you'll be punished." Then he rammed his dick into her and fucked her hard. This was another thing he liked about Garrett. She liked rough sex.

He could feel her scream building. Thrusting harder, he was deciding on her punishment when—

Kurt! Get down here! Now!

I'm busy, Daniel!

No! Now! I'm in Underground!

He immediately pulled out of her. "My dear, I've got to go. A bit of an emergency."

"What?" she cried. "Kurt, wait—you can't just leave me—"

"I'm terribly sorry, but I really must go." He chuckled. "Don't go away. I'll be right back." He dissolved into mist and left the playroom.

"Kuuurt," he heard her scream as he sped along the hallway.

Following his link with Daniel, he materialized in the room from where the other had called. Kurt gave him a baleful stare. "This had better be good, Daniel."

"It is. I saw Parker and a woman I've never seen before—I assume it's that college friend of his—go in the building across the street."

His anger evaporated. "When was this?"

"Just now."

A tiny smirk twisted his mouth. His digging into Melera's background during the past week or so had turned up exactly nothing. No birth record, job records, credit history—and no record of her ever having attended Parker's alma mater. It was as if she'd simply materialized out of thin air. That had only fueled his suspicions about her connection to the Slayer. *And it seems I was right.*

"Kurt," Daniel said.

He looked up. Daniel's expression was somber. "You think Parker knows anything about who—what she is?"

Kurt pursed his lips, considering. That bit about Melera being a friend from college was a bald-faced lie but... "No, Daniel. I don't think he does." He paused. "My servant is many things but stupid isn't one of them."

"Whatever you say. I don't know him nearly as well as you do."

His eyes narrowed. "You don't trust my word, Daniel?" he said, his voice soft.

Daniel rolled his eyes. "Oh, come off it, Kurt."

He smiled. His relationship with Daniel was more than just friendship. Within a century after Daniel's rebirth, it had become obvious that the other could someday become a vampire regent as great as he, the rarest of their kind. Daniel was young but in Kurt's mind, he was already an equal.

Daniel cocked his head. "So what now?"

Kurt shrugged. "I'm going after her, of course. If Melera is who we think she is—"

"Need some back-up? I'll call—"

"No."

Daniel eyed him. "You forgot she killed a morran?"

He arched his brow. "I've killed morrans too, Daniel. Quite a number of them over the years."

"But—"

Kurt waved his hand. "Oh, stop worrying. I won't be alone. If it makes you feel better, Parker's in there too, remember?" He curled his lip, thinking how lovely it'd be to force the wolf to turn—murderously so—on his friend. Unfocusing his gaze, in seconds he'd established a telepathic link with Parker. Now he could see exactly what was happening with the wolf.

Parker and Melera stood before that horseshoe-shaped thing he'd seen the other day. Giving a hard mental shove, he bulled his will into Parker's body. As usual, Parker fought the intrusion. This time though, he noticed the wolf's will seemed much stronger than it ever had before. "I'm sure," Kurt said through clenched teeth, "that between the two of us, we can take her."

Parker's will finally collapsed. He took control of the wolf's body, manipulating him like a puppet on a string. In his mind's eye, he watched Parker's hands reach for Melera's neck.

"*Scheisse,*" he hissed a few minutes later. His jaw set. *I'm going to take care of that bitch myself. Right now.* He was about to dissolve when Daniel grabbed his wrist. Kurt glared at him. "Let go of me, dammit."

"Kurt," His voice was grave. "Be careful."

Kurt didn't answer at first. He stared at his executor. "I will," he finally said. "I will."

CHAPTER 59

While Daniel watched from across the street, Melera and Parker entered the pitch-dark building. They felt their way up the stairs to the second floor and then along the hallway. She groped for the doorknob. Finding it, she opened the door to her temporary base and stepped inside.

"Fook." The four tube lamps, each standing in a corner of the room, emitted a soft glow. "Fook, fook." Now the lights were at half power.

Melera scanned the room. *Good.* Everything was just as she'd left it. She started across the hardwood floor, Parker's footsteps echoing behind her. Then she heard only her own.

She turned. He'd halted about four feet over the threshold. Seeming confused, he frowned when he saw the siitheer but said nothing. Then he focused on her hammock and small couch.

She watched his expression change from puzzled to incredulous. "Wait a minute. You mean you were staying down here the whole time?"

Now it was her turn to look puzzled. "'Splain you?"

"Before I found you that night in the park. You were here?"

She blinked a few times. "Yes, why?"

He stared at her. "How...how'd you get in?"

"Same way we did, yes?"

"Well, yeah, but..." He stared a moment longer and then waved his hand. "Never mind." His jaw dropped a moment later as if he'd just realized something else. He looked around the room again. "Damn, Melera. This is wild."

"Wild?" She peered about her base. There wasn't anything in here that needed taming.

Parker must have seen her confusion. "I'm sorry, sweetheart. This is so…I mean, I've never met…I mean, nobody's ever met a space alien before, and…" He looked around the room a third time. "It's…it's just… wild," he said, his voice sounding as awed as the look on his face.

Melera shrugged.

"What's this?" He pointed at her siitheer.

"Tsat? Is siitheer. Music, um, box. Me use to break code."

"How does it work?"

"Come. Show you."

She walked over to the instrument and checked the large battery she'd brought. Satisfied it carried enough charge, she pressed the orange power switch. The machine hummed for a second. Its three flat screens came to life showing Tarq's code. They also showed where she'd left off trying to break it—in the middle of the fourth movement. She stared at the screens. A tear formed in the corner of her eye. It was all she had left of her father.

"What's that?" Parker said.

"Code."

She felt his arm slip around her waist. "Play it for me?"

Nodding, Melera bent over the keyboard. She played only ten lines of the score at first. Then, unable to resist, she began singing the remaining five.

"No!" Parker roared in her ear. "I. Will. Not!"

She jumped. "What the jakk is the matter with you?" she yelled in Xia'saan. Then she noticed his violent trembling. Her brow creased. "Pawkher? What wrong?"

He didn't answer. His eyes bulged from their sockets and a ghastly smile stretched his lips. His muscles began rippling beneath his skin like water. Her frown deepened. He looked as if he was in the midst of one of her seizures.

"Pawkher—"

Before she could say anything further, his hands closed around her throat.

CHAPTER 60

Parker sensed rather than saw Melera's startled movement beside him. *Wha—Kurt, you motherfucker, stop it!*

Shaking with effort, he struggled to keep his hands at his sides but the next thing he knew he was throttling the woman most important to him. "Get out," he shouted in her face. "Get the fuck out of me!" Parker and his *were* fought the Master like demons.

Kurt won. Parker's hands tightened around Melera's neck. "Noooo," he screamed.

It didn't do a bit of good.

Melera's czado took over instantly. She ripped Parker's hands away from her throat with ease and leapt backward.

He came at her.

I don't want to kill him.

We may have to, her czado said.

She feinted to her left. When Parker went for her, she jumped in the opposite direction and landed on the other side of the room. He came at her a second time and she executed the same move.

Melera had yet to lay a finger on him, keeping her distance until she figured a way to drop him without hurting him too much. She dodged him a third time. *Ohh-kay. I know.*

When Parker rushed her this time, she was ready. She let him get within an arm's length and then went into action, pelting him on his neck, chest, spine, and the backs of his knees in an orchestrated sequence. He couldn't react fast enough to counter her attack. She'd used this technique on Tyrocsins to knock them out cold without causing pain.

Except it wasn't working.

Damn. Parker should have gone down after she'd hit all the pressure points once, but he didn't even seem fazed. From what she'd learned from him, zots were about as physically close to Tyrocsins as two different species could get. But obviously, they weren't close enough.

She tried again with the same result—nothing.

Sheet!

Melera balled her hands into fists and delivered two hard punches, one right between his eyes and the other to his jaw. He dropped like a stone. She stood over his unconscious body, panting a little. "What the jakk was that all about?" she said in Xia'saan.

Just then, her keen senses told her she and Parker weren't alone. She looked up. Her eyes narrowed. "Tse Master," she sneered. "Fook Pawkher's head so he kill." Straightening, she took a step backward and chuckled. "Tsink you master me?"

The Master flew at her.

CHAPTER 61

Back in Kurt's playroom, two levels below Last Chance's dance floor, Garrett saw the whole thing. Her telepathic link with Kurt let her watch through her third eye, like a movie.

Kurt and a tall, muscular woman with long black hair—*that has to be Melera*—faced one another in a large room. Behind her, Parker lay sprawled on the floor. He looked to be unconscious. She turned to Kurt. He looked furious.

Melera didn't seem frightened at all. Her lips stretched into a sneer. Kurt leapt at her like a tiger. Garrett knew from experience that his movements wouldn't have been visible to her if she'd been watching with her own eyes. Yet Melera must have seen it because she stepped out of the way.

That's...that's impossible. Kurt never said she was a vampire.

She gasped when she saw Kurt crash into the wall. Picking himself up off the floor, he faced Melera again but made no move toward her. She could sense his power building until his body glowed with it. Then he hurled it toward the strange woman in a blast of light that completely enveloped her.

Garrett gasped a second time. Kurt had hit Melera with enough heat to melt stone, yet she was unhurt. She beckoned and Kurt flew at her again. This time the other woman stood her ground. When he reached her, she grabbed him by the throat with one hand and threw him across the room.

"Motherdamn," she whispered in disbelief.

Goggle-eyed behind her leather mask, she watched Melera and Kurt's fight. When he dissolved into mist, she morphed into a column of fire. He assumed the shape of an enormous spider. She transformed into a nightmare with an impossible number of tentacles and imprisoned him in her coils. He broke her hold by changing into a wurm, but no matter what form he took, she countered him with ease. Judging from the look on her face, Garrett had the feeling she was just toying with him.

Melera gripped Kurt's throat and lifted him high so his feet dangled. Then, in a lightning move, she slammed him to the floor. With one hand around his throat and her knee on his chest, she stretched out her arm. Something flew toward her from the left and then a four-inch rod of lavender light appeared in her other hand. She brought the light close to Kurt's face.

It was the first time Garrett had seen him show fear. "Nooo," she cried, struggling against her bonds.

But she was far from helpless. She concentrated a moment. The chains holding her down burst apart. Ripping the leather mask from her face, she leapt off the mattress and bolted for the door. Moments later, stark naked, she ran along a deserted Underground street. Chain links clanking on wrists and ankles, her bare feet flew over the brick sidewalk. Fear and magick bolstered her speed.

Following her telepathic link with Kurt, Garrett ran for his life.

CHAPTER 62

Parker came to, feeling like he'd been hit by a couple of semis. *Ugh. What did she do to me now?*

Deep, mocking laughter brought him fully awake. He opened his eyes to see Melera, her arm outstretched, holding Kurt up in the air by his neck with one hand. He struggled but her grip was firm. Then she hurled him to the floor.

"I'll be..." he muttered. He couldn't believe what he was seeing—Melera was trashing the Master. Her hand still gripping Kurt's neck, she knelt with one knee on his chest. From out of nowhere, a small flashlight materialized in her left palm. She flicked it. A slender length of lavender light appeared. Its glow was soft, almost inviting.

"Tell you what happen you fook wits Pawkher one more, yes?" Her tone sounded low and dangerous.

He started in surprise. *She did? When?*

"The wolf is my servant," Kurt shot back. "Damn you and your threat. He's mine to do with as I please."

Melera circled the glowing stick over his face. "No. Me tsink not." She chuckled. "Tsis laser-knife, yes? Pawkher tell me how make you die. Heart or brain, he say. Me choose brain."

Her smile made Parker's blood run cold. She raised the knife.

No, Melera, no! He couldn't let her do it. Killing the Master would create a power vacuum in the vampire colony. A struggle for succession would be inevitable and an all-out zot war was almost guaranteed. That would be bad enough in even the best of times but with the Slayer still loose, it'd be disastrous.

He started to stand, but he knew he'd never get to the two of them in time. *I'm sure she thinks I'm still out.*

He'd just drawn a breath to let fly a rebel yell when the door crashed open.

Garrett saw the shining purplish rod descend toward Kurt's face. Without conscious thought, a ball of glowing red energy filled her palm.

The ball was one of the most lethal weapons in her arsenal. Drawn from the ONE, only mages could wield it without destroying themselves.

She drew back her arm.

CHAPTER 63

Parker whipped his head around when the door crashed open. In a split-second, he realized Garrett's flaming red ball was aimed at Melera. *Shit! She's gonna—*

He leapt. A burning sensation in his shoulder barely caught his attention. He crashed into Garrett and they fell to the floor. Her red ball of destruction went wide and exploded against one of the large windows. The glass and its frame vaporized, leaving a great, smoking hole where the window had been.

"Get off me, motherdammit," she yelled. Parker felt her small hands pushing at him. Ignoring her, he looked over his shoulder. Melera still knelt on Kurt's chest. She stared at the two of them with a curious expression.

He blew a sigh of relief. Kurt looked as if he was about to faint but at least he was alive.

"Parker, move!" Garrett yelled again.

He rose from the floor without a word.

Garrett jumped up and started for Melera and Kurt. She'd taken one step before he scooped her up in one arm. Holding her against his waist, he dangled her like a rag doll.

"Put me down," she yelled a third time, kicking and punching the air.

"Shut up."

Garrett shut up.

Parker gave his lover an anxious look. "Are you okay, sweetheart?"

Releasing Kurt's throat, Melera stood in one, fluid motion. "Yes, Pawkher." A half-smile appeared on her face. "You not."

He looked down. A deep gash in his shoulder was already healing.

He raised his brow, remembering the burning sensation just before he'd crashed into Garrett. Melera must have thrown the laser-knife when she had burst through the door. His brows shot up. She wouldn't have missed her target. Garrett didn't know it but he'd just saved her life.

"You duck faster next time, yes?" Melera said, sounding amused.

Parker didn't answer. He sniffed and smelled charring wood. It had to be the laser. He set Garrett on her feet. "Where's the knife?"

Melera shrugged and held out her hand. There was a purplish flash and then she was holding it. She thumbed it and the laser rod disappeared. Then she looked up and pointed. "Pawkher, who?"

He turned in the direction of her pointing finger. His jaw dropped. In all the excitement, he hadn't noticed Garrett was naked. He took in the leather restraints and the broken chains. "What the hell you got on? You never told me you were into—this."

"Got a problem with it?" she snapped.

"You owe him no explanations, my dear," a familiar velvety voice said from behind him.

Parker looked over his shoulder. Kurt had risen from the floor, obviously trying to act as if nothing had happened. Kurt, he saw, also sported leather wrist cuffs though without chains.

His head snapped around. "Oh, I get it. I'll bet you were doing—" he looked Garrett up and down—"him the whole time you were with me, weren't you?" She opened her mouth but he spoke first. "You like BDSM? Should've said something. I'd have been more than happy to beat the shit outta you."

"How dare—"

"Fuck you, sweetheart," he said, thoroughly sick of the vampire-mage-werewolf triangle he'd never wanted to join.

"Pawkher, who?" Melera said, sounding impatient.

He turned. "This is Garrett. The one I told you about." He watched her slowly look over Garrett's slender, boyish body and then at herself. Arching her brow, she turned to him and stared in disbelief.

Her look made him squirm. With a crooked smile, he glanced at the ceiling and shrugged.

"You—" he heard Garrett start.

Melera's deadly expression silenced her.

Parker stared at Kurt. "So what did you think were you doing, trying to make me kill Melera like that?"

"I could ask you the same thing, Parker."

"Huh?"

Kurt, apparently recovered from Melera's assault, twisted his lips into a smirk. "Who is she really, Parker? None of us believes that story you've been telling about her being a friend from college."

"But—"

"And I suppose you haven't noticed that—thing—over there." He pointed to the pipes of Melera's music box. "Look at it. It's just the right size to hold a body. And those tubes—all of them different shapes and sizes. Remember those pictures Mandy showed us? Remember how those bodies looked?"

Parker's jaw dropped at Kurt's implication. "No, she's not," he shouted. "She's—"

"Khurt and Ghar-rett," Melera said. All three turned to look at her. "Me be from Maqu." Kurt and Garrett looked confused. "Maqu," she repeated. "Not Earts. Maqu. Nutser galasky, yes?" Parker watched the two's expressions change from startled to incredulous. Then Garrett's turned furious. "That's bull," she shouted. "You're the Slayer!"

"She isn't," Parker yelled.

"Prove it," Garrett shot back.

"No," Melera said, now sounding annoyed. "Me not your Slay-er. Kill me will, yes. Leave bodies to find, never." She gave each of them a long look. "Have"—she seemed to stop to think for a moment—"have difficulties, you tsree. Do nutsing wits me. Fight out, yes." She sauntered over to her music box. Picking up a cigar, she stared at it until one end flared into flame. She took a long drag and blew out a heavy stream of smoke. A few seconds later, she took another drag. And another. She didn't say a word.

Her silence made Parker uneasy. "Sweetheart?" he said, his voice tentative.

She turned.

"Sweetheart, I'm—"

Melera shot him a withering look. Then she vanished.

CHAPTER 64

At six a.m. Sunday morning, Parker woke up in bed alone. A sleepy smile stretched his lips. *Build kof-fee, yes.* Rolling over, he buried his face in the king-sized pillow Melera had used and took a deep breath. Her blood-scent gave him an instant boner.

Melera's disappearance last night from her temporary base in Underground had scared him. She'd looked pretty pissed. After she'd gone, he'd bared his fangs at Garrett and Kurt and raced home. To his relief, she'd returned to his house. He'd found her coiled on the over-stuffed study chair and staring at the Xia'saan rock on his desk, waiting for him. Her expression had seemed troubled but he'd paid no attention.

Parker had swept her into his arms. "I love you, Melera," he'd whispered, covering her face with kisses. After pulling away, he'd gazed into her whirling, golden eyes. "I...wherever you go, sweetheart, I'll be there." He'd started kissing her again. "Whatever you want me to do, I'll do it...please...just take me with you...I love you..." Melera hadn't said anything, but he'd ignored that, too. Then he'd picked her up and carried her to bed.

They'd made love for the rest of the night. Sometimes sweet and tender but mostly hot and raw, they'd bled each other mercilessly. With her five voices and his one, they'd songed over and over until he'd felt as if they *had* merged to become one person.

His smile broadened. He loved singing in her choir.

Then he frowned. Right now, something was wrong. He smelled her but he didn't smell any coffee. He sat up and sniffed. Her scent was in the air, but not strong. Not like it should have been if she were in his house. His eyes widened. He wasn't just alone in bed. He was alone, period.

Parker bolted from under the sheets and ran to his closet. Throwing open the door, he peered inside the darkened space. Every piece of clothing he'd bought for her was there, neatly aligned on hangers.

No!

He threw on a pair of jeans and a shirt, leaving the latter mostly unbuttoned. Stuffing his bare feet into a pair of loafers, he fled his bedroom. He was down the stairs in three bounds and at the front door in two more. Snatching his keys from the nearby hook, he raced out of his house.

Reaching his car, he nearly tore the old Caprice's driver side door off its hinges. He leapt into the drivers' seat and slammed the door hard enough to rattle the windows. Shoving the key into the ignition, he gave it a savage twist and glanced into the rearview mirror. His face was streaked with last night's blood.

Fuck it!

The motor roared to life. Stomping on the accelerator, he peeled out of his driveway and headed downtown. If he ran over something or someone, too bad—it shouldn't have been there in the first place, or it should've moved faster. Reaching his destination, he screeched into the closest parking space to the building where Melera had made her Underground base. Even on a Sunday like today, a drive to Pioneer Square usually took at least twenty minutes. He made it in ten.

The Caprice still rocked on its tires when Parker jumped out. Racing along an alley, he skidded to a stop before one of Underground's hidden entrances. Finding the brick that would unlock the door, he banged his fist against it. A couple of seconds passed. Nothing happened. "Come on, come on," he breathed. When the lock finally clicked open, he tugged on the handle but the door stayed shut. "What the...?" He grabbed the door's handle again and tugged harder. It didn't budge.

Parker slit his eyes and clenched his teeth. No goddamned door was going to keep him from getting inside. Gathering his strength, he wrapped both hands around the handle. Then he placed one foot against the brick next to the door's lock and wrenched. The door flew open. He stumbled backward and fell on his butt from its unexpected speed. Jumping up, he dashed inside.

He rushed down the steps without waiting for the lights. Stumbling after the third one, he rolled the rest of the way to the bottom. Unhurt,

Parker sprang to his feet and ripped open the door that led to the second set of stairs. He ran down the flights until he came to Underground proper and sprinted along the brick sidewalk. Arriving at Melera's building, he barreled through the main entrance, unslowed by the complete darkness. Navigating from memory, he took the stairs three at a time to the second floor.

Parker didn't have to remember which room she'd occupied. He could smell her.

Faint light spilled into the corridor from underneath the door hiding her base. His heart leapt. *She's still here!* Reaching her door, he flung it wide and sped within. "Melera! I—"

She spun around and let out a startled gasp.

He stepped further inside and stopped. Except for Melera and what looked like a miniature emergency lamp in the middle of the floor, the room was empty. His eyes narrowed. "Where do you think you're going?"

"Me..." She shook her head. "Me tell you from beginning. When remembuh come, me must go."

"Why? You told me your side wants you dead as much as the other side does."

"Troots, but find me battlefleet first."

"That's right. Your fleet is here. You're going—why? It doesn't make sense."

Her expression hardened. "Pawkher, make this difficult not more, yes? Me must go."

"And I'm asking you why."

She looked down and then up. "Call me Vst did. Need me tsey do for...um, job."

"They need?" he cried. "These fuckers whistle and you come running? What about me? Melera, I need you too!"

"Pawkher—"

He closed the distance between them in two long strides. Grabbing her by the shoulders, he shook her hard. "Who the hell do you think you are, Melera?" he bellowed in her face. "You come waltzing into my life and now you think you can waltz right out again? Dammit, I won't let you!" With a brutal jerk, he slammed her against his chest and then savaged her mouth.

On releasing her, he saw her eyes had filled with silver-flecked tears. "Me must go, Pawkher," she whispered.

He stared at her for a moment. Then, shaking his head in frustration, he dropped his hands from her shoulders and started to pace the room. *God, how do I get through to her?* He turned. "Look, Mel—"

Melera's hands balled into fists. "No take you," she screamed. "Me tell you, me not see war end." She stabbed at him with her index finger. "Bring you, be murder, yes!"

Parker was speechless. "Murder?" he shouted after he'd found his voice. "You know how ridiculous that sounds? Coming from you? Her Majesty the fucking assassin?"

Neither said anything for a long moment. He let out a heavy sigh. "Okay, Melera. You say bringing me with you would be murder. Maybe it is to you but shouldn't that be my choice, not yours?"

She crossed her arms under her breasts and turned away.

Parker threw up his hands and began pacing again. A minute passed. He whirled. "Melera, do you want me to beg? Is that what you want?"

She turned back to him. Tears rolled down her cheeks but she said nothing. He sank to his knees. "Look at me, Melera," he said, his voice soft and tight. "I love you and I'm begging you. Take me with you. Please. Don't leave me."

Squeezing her golden eyes shut, her face looked a mask of pain. "Me sorry, Pawkher. Me must go." She opened her eyes. Then she closed them again.

Parker jerked into a squat. "Not without me, you won't!" Even as he leapt, he knew he was a second too late. He felt a blast of cold, and then his arms closed around empty air. He hit the floor, rolled onto his shoulder, and ended up on his back.

A minute later, he slowly got to his knees. A strangled growl started low in his throat and quickly grew into a full-fledged howl. "Melera...oh, God, no!" He stared at the spot where she'd stood only moments before.

Toppling like a newly-sawn oak tree, Parker doubled over and buried his face in the crook of his right arm. His broad, muscular shoulders shaking with his sobs, he pounded the plank wood floor with his fist.

"No...no...oooh...noooo!"

CHAPTER 65

"Can you believe it?"

"What do you think'll happen now?"

"Isn't it obvious? There's gonna be a pogrom."

"How—no way we'll be able to stop something like that."

"Paul, Ara, pogroms...Mother, please tell me this is not happening."

"It *is* happening," Garrett said loud enough for everyone to hear. She'd gotten the coven's attention. "Everyone sit down. We haven't much time."

After recovering from the horror of the morning newspaper's headline, she had immediately called Georgia, initiating the Round Robin. Not all witches are telepathic. The Round Robin tasked each covener to reach out to specific witches until all had been contacted.

She gazed at the faces ranged around her. Some appeared to be in shock. Others wore angry looks or were crying. A few, like her, were having a difficult time stemming the tears. Everyone had loved Paul's kindness, his quiet authority, and his dry wit.

Twenty-six of us now. She counted heads in the room and then frowned. There should have been twenty-six witches but right now there were only twenty-five. She turned to Annamarie. "Where's Pinkie?" Pinkie was one of Annamarie's contacts.

Annamarie shook her head. "I don't know, Sister. I called three times, got no answer, then went over to her apartment and..." she shrugged.

Her lips tightened. "We'll have to start without her, then." *Dammit, Pinkie—where are you? We need all the help we can get.*

Dana, who'd been staring at the floor, looked up. "Are they sure it was the Slayer that killed Paul and Ara?"

Sam turned. "How can it not have been? Didn't you read the paper? The bodies had been covered with those holes and nearly all their blood had been drained."

"Just like the others," Robert said, his voice soft. Then louder, "Has anyone figured the time of death?"

"According to the paper, it was sometime early this morning, which means they were probably attacked sometime yesterday," Sam said.

Georgia shook her head. "Why'd they even report it? Humans don't care what happens to us."

"That's easy," Maureen spoke up. "When she wrote the story, the reporter didn't know Paul and Ara were witches. The GSTs hadn't been run yet and she wanted a scoop."

Jolene frowned. "I don't understand something. How did the Slayer get Paul? I mean, Ara I can understand. She doesn't—didn't—have much talent left. But Paul?"

The Lair was silent. "It's not that simple," Garrett said, straightening her back. "The last time I saw Paul was one day last week. He said he needed to talk to me. So I met him here, in the Temple office." She looked around. "Paul told me he knew what the Slayer was. Not who, but what."

The coven erupted into a chorus of babbling disbelief. Garrett held up her hand.

"So what is the Slayer, then?" Robert said after everyone had quieted.

"The way Paul explained it, the killer is a uthyrisis, a kind of demon—except it's from the fifth dimension. Not ours."

A few of the coven reacted with horror, while most looked confused. Seeing this reaction, Garrett related everything she could remember of what Paul had told her. "Worst of all, nobody has a clue how to kill it."

"Wh-what do you mean no one knows how to kill it?" Sam sputtered.

"Just what I said."

"What I'd like to know is why Paul would have been at Ara's in the first place," Maureen broke in.

"I can tell you," Raymond spoke up. "A lot of you wouldn't know, but Ara is—was—a demonologist, like Paul. If anyone knew anything about this uthyrisis, it would have been she."

"Did Paul tell you who summoned this abomination?" Robert said.

Garrett looked up and shook her head. "No, he didn't." Then she sighed. "Believe me, I tried, but he refused to say because he hadn't any proof." Her eyes welled with tears. "When we parted," her voice hitched, "that was the last time I saw him." She gazed down at the floor and blinked. *Our Credo...if I hadn't been so concerned about our Credo.*

No one spoke for a long while.

"Pinkie's a demonologist," Annamarie whispered. In the Lair's silence, she may as well have shouted.

As one, the coven turned and stared at her. "But I thought Pinkie didn't have a specialty," Gene said. "She told me she was a generalist." Others murmured in agreement.

Eyes like saucers, Annamarie shook her head. "Uh-uh. It was when, you know, she first got here from Pennsylvania. We were eating lunch on campus. Anyway, she'd started talking that revolutionary stuff and asked me what my specialty was. I said it was weather and..." She paused for a long moment. "She said hers was...demonology."

The witches all looked at one another. Garrett's eyes widened. *Could she be the one Paul was talking about?* Then something else dawned on her. When she and Paul had talked about someone from Balthus having summoned the demon, the one question he couldn't answer was why. Now she thought she knew. Nobody was trying to spark a pogrom—it was far worse than that.

"We gotta find Pinkie," Sam blurted.

"Does it matter?" Gina said. Everyone turned to stare at her. She held out her hands. "I mean yeah, if she did this, only Pinkie can send the demon back to whatever dimension it came from but that's only part of it." She looked around. "The real question is—when will the pogrom start?"

The coven began talking all at the same time. "Wait," Garrett said. "We might not have the power to stop a pogrom after it starts, but with luck, there might not be one. Don't forget the Pax Omnia cast last April." She turned to Anna. "Will it hold?"

Anna shrugged. "Hard to say. It's still early for a Sunday but once the humans all learn about Paul and Ara"—she shook her head—"their combined negative psychic strength will probably go through the roof."

Garrett's heart sank. "Is there anything we can do?"

Anna's lips pressed into a grim line. "The eight of us," she said and nodded at a knot of seven of their coveners sitting nearby, "can work to shore the Pax Omnia up. No guarantees, though."

She nodded. "Do your best."

Picking up her pillow, Anna walked over to her small group. She dropped her pillow on the floor and sat. Garrett saw Anna's lips moving. She couldn't hear what her covener was saying but she saw the other seven witches' expressions turned grave.

The rest of the coven made ready to leave. She stood and let out a small sigh. *Let it hold, Mother*, she prayed. *And please, let us find Pinkie, too... soon.*

Giving Anna and her group one last look, Garrett headed for the Temple's main doors.

CHAPTER 66

Outside, Garrett pulled out her cell phone. With Anna and her seven witches working on the Pax Omnia, that left only seventeen—including herself—to scour the city for Pinkie.

The coven couldn't rely on magick to find her. If Pinkie were the one behind this madness, she'd know enough to cast an obscuring spell. If she had, no amount of magick in the world could uncover her. One thing was clear. They needed help.

She called Parker first but there was no answer. Frowning, she punched in Tran's number.

He picked up the phone. "Yeah?"

"Tran, it's me, Garrett." She heard his surprised gasp and smiled. Pack freyja or no, she'd never called him before. "Listen. You heard about the murders last night, right?"

"Oh man...yeah."

"Well, they were witches. One active, the other retired."

"What?" he shouted.

"You heard me. But I gotta bigger problem. One of my witches is missing and I'm sure she's connected to the Slayer."

"Shit...who?"

She told him and gave a description. "Can you get the pack to go out and look for her? The coven has already started looking but there aren't enough of us to look everywhere."

"We're already gone freyja, but we'll only be a dozen or so. The full moon's a coupla days away, so most of the pack has to stay indoors, you know?"

"Oh...yes." She'd forgotten. Unlike Parker and other top-ranked wolves, lesser wolves began changing, off and on, two and even three

287

days before the full moon. For them, going outside would be suicide.

"You talk to Park?"

Tran's question jerked her back into the moment. "No. I tried but he didn't pick up."

"Okay. No problem. I'll get word to him."

The mage-cum-pack freyja smiled. "Thanks, Tran. Blessed be." She cut the connection.

Stepping off the Temple stairs, Garrett headed for her car. She frowned a little. She'd had to use the telephone because she couldn't reach Parker through their telepathic link. Since the night of the meeting—*since Melera had shown up*—Parker had somehow been able to shut her out. And keep her out, as if their link had never existed.

Reaching her car, she leaned against the driver's door and sighed. *Park or no Park, at least the pack's out there looking.* Then her brows rose. Maybe Kurt's vampires could help. She shook her head. Vampires were fine hunters but right now they were all asleep. *Motherdammit, where's a good bloodsucker when you need one?*

Tight-lipped, she got into her car and drove away. At a stop sign, she had an idea. Checking the dashboard clock, she saw it was just after eight-fifteen. She glanced at her cell phone sitting in its holder. "Kurt." The phone beeped as it placed the call. Though the colony was asleep, Kurt might be awake. He'd told her once he was an insomniac. She'd been surprised. She hadn't thought vampires could be insomniacs. They were dead.

"Hellooo," his voice purred just after she'd stepped on the accelerator.

"Kurt," she said, relieved. "It's Garrett."

"I know very well who you are, my dear. And on such a lovely morning, made even lovelier by the sound of your voice."

She gritted her teeth. She hated when he started with that crap. Normally she would have told him to stop being silly but decided to ignore it this time. There were far more important things at stake right now. She took a breath. "Kurt, I need help."

"I'm sure you do. I saw the paper. Two of yours, right?"

"It's worse than that." Garrett told him about Pinkie, Paul's suspicions, and the demon.

"Melera's a demon?" he said. He sounded horrified. "No wonder she kicked...dammit Garrett, I—"

"Wait, wait! I wasn't talking about Melera. I mean, she could be, but—"

"If she isn't...witch, why the hell didn't you say anything about this sooner?"

"I'm sorry, Kurt. I wanted to, but our Credo—"

"Your Credo might be the reason why Paul and Ara are dead."

She didn't answer. Tears streamed down her cheeks. "I...I know," she said, her voice small and choked with emotion.

Kurt sighed. "So what about this Pinkie person?"

"She's missing." The telephone was silent. "The coven's out looking for her and so are the wolves. I don't know how to contact any of the others. The eagles, the rats, elves—you know. Could...will you help?"

"Of course I will," he snapped. "There's a damned demon loose in *my* city." He paused. "Were you on your way over here? Because if you weren't I'd suggest you ought to be."

"But I need to—"

"*Ja,*" he assured her. "We'll look for her together. *Auf Wiedersehen.*" He hung up.

Garrett stared at the phone.

Together?

CHAPTER 67

Half a world away from See-at-tell, Melera took one last look around her island base and sighed. Most of what she'd brought would have to stay. Her corvette wasn't big enough and the transport she, Tarq, and Ruri had used to haul all this stuff to Dirt was in Maqu.

She wondered if anyone would ever find it. Her shoulders twitched. *Doesn't matter. I'm not coming back.* She had her siitheer and that was all she really needed to finish breaking Tarq's code.

A wave of annoyance washed over her. *Damn this thing.* Her black setsul—travelsuit—itched and so did the golden neck collar beneath it. Tugging at the garment this way and that, she tried to make it more comfortable but it didn't work. *Jakk this.* She reached for the suit's closure just below her chin and pulled it open, down to her stomach. There—that was better.

Melera started for her corvette's lowered boarding ramp, thinking about what the Vst was asking her to do. *Hope I don't have a seizure in the middle of it. I'm lucky I didn't have one while I was with Pawkher.* But she knew her luck couldn't hold much longer. The fact she hadn't had a seizure in—what, a standard Dirt month?—only meant the next one was way overdue. She shook her head. Her mission, her seizures—they were all the more reason to leave Parker behind.

Another sigh escaped her. Plodding across the cavern floor, the weight of her dejection pushed her head down until she stared at her feet. Her eyes burned with unshed tears. She didn't want to leave. Dirt had its problems—its people were xenophobes, for one—but no planet was perfect. *Pawkher asked if I could stay here. Yes. Yes, I could.* She took a few more steps and then stopped. Her head snapped up. *No. I won't go back to Maqu. Let the Vst lose this jakkin' war. I've already lost everything. Why should I——*

Pure agony as from a high voltage shock blasted through her. Feeling as if she'd been turned inside out, Melera collapsed, her scream echoing about the cavern. She crouched on the cave's smooth floor for a few moments, then looked up, bleary-eyed. The spasm had lasted only a second.

You have forgotten we are ka-bound to the Vst? her czado said.

Wiping the tears from her eyes, she rose to her knees. "No," she panted. "Just…testing it."

A stupid thing to do. We cannot escape. We must give whatever aid the Vst asks of us or the ka will take our mind.

"Consider me…reminded." She climbed to her feet and waited for her tremors to disappear. When they had, she resumed walking. Depression settled over her again. "What the hell. Might as well go back. Being ka-bound, the seizures, the Vst, Beloc…anyway you look at it, we're jakked, right?"

Her czado said nothing. Reaching her corvette, she leaned against one of the ramp's vertical supports and squeezed her eyes shut. "Why did we have to remember anything at all?"

We would have eventually. The ka is like that. It is why we always remember.

Melera didn't reply. She walked up the ramp and stepped through the outer hatch's opening. "Bas." The door closed. She stepped through another opening. "Bas-tu." This door also swung shut. Now inside her ship, she waited for the familiar double chime. *Bing-bing.* She nodded once. The airlock had been secured. She was ready to leave.

Once on the corvette's compact bridge, she settled into the command chair and glanced at the lights on the instrument console. All systems were ready to go, except for one. The stealth shields. She drummed a simple tattoo on a round, black depression on the console. It lit up, its glow rippling through the spectrum until it blazed yellow. There—the stealth shields were up. Her ship was now invisible to the outside world.

"Ke'je." The corvette's four drives hummed. She drummed a different tattoo on a lighted purple square. The humming turned into a roar. She listened to the drives for a while. Then her lips tightened. *Better get out of here before the rock melts.*

Reaching overhead, her fingers closed over a toggle. She threw the switch and watched a huge section of the mountain's interior dissolve.

The switch activated the disruptor, a device that temporarily scrambled the molecular structure of anything at which it was aimed, causing it to disappear. A force field held the rest of the rock in place and once she was safely outside, that part of the mountain would rematerialize.

Melera stared at the clear azure sky beyond the cave entrance. "I love you, Pawkher Bekhensson," she whispered in Xia'saan. A single tear trickled down her cheek.

She took a deep breath. Then she took off.

CHAPTER 68

While Melera streaked into the stratosphere, Kurt paced his velvet-lined office, thinking about this demon Garrett had described. "If she's right, we are in deep *scheisse*," he muttered.

He'd been in exactly this kind of situation in the mid-seventeenth century. A spell the local coven had cast had gone wrong and one of these nether creatures had slipped through the magick circle. It had been one of the few times in his long un-life he'd seen zots and humans work together to send the thing back to whatever hell had spawned it. It hadn't been easy, either.

Unconsciously, Kurt ran a trembling hand over his cheek. Demons possessed powers beyond imagining. Compared to them, even a vampire regent was as helpless as a newborn human. He stopped his pacing. Last night, Melera had pounded him into the ground as easily as he might have crushed a bug under his heel. If she was a demon, he was lucky he wasn't twice-dead.

And if it hadn't been for Garrett, I would be.

He pursed his lips. *No. Melera's got to be our demon. It's the only explanation. Parker has no idea what he's dealing with and if he does, he's completely out of his damned mind.*

A soft knock on the door made him look up. "Come." The door opened. It was Gordon, one of his human servants. He looked nervous. "Master, have you seen Gerald lately?"

"No. Why?"

Gordon hesitated. "Nobody's seen him since Friday." His voice held a slight tremor.

Kurt's eyes widened. "Since Friday?"

He nodded. "Moira said she saw him leave here around four that afternoon."

"Was he alone?"

"No, Master. There was someone else waiting in a car but Moira couldn't see who it was."

"Well, did she know who the car belonged to? What color was it? Was it big, small, or in-between?"

Gordon appeared confused. "I-I'll ask, Master, but I'm pretty sure she doesn't know."

Kurt narrowed his eyes. "Get out, Gordon," he said, his tone soft and dangerous. Gordon left in a hurry. His lips tightened. *Gerald missing... dammit, I do not need this.*

He began pacing again, faster this time. Could Melera have gotten Gerald? He shook his head. *No. Parker would've known unless...wouldn't he?* He ran his hand over his cheek again. Now was just as good a time as any to see what the wolf was up to. He walked over to his desk and leaned against it. Closing his eyes, he opened his mind and tried to tune in to his servant.

Nothing.

Brows knitted, he tried again. Still nothing.

Kurt's eyes flew open. *Oh, no...*

"Garrett," he whispered, "you'd better get over here—right now."

CHAPTER 69

Garrett knocked on the door to Kurt's office and then opened it. Standing by his desk, he whirled in her direction. "Come on, let's go."

She frowned. He looked ready to explode. In all the years she'd known him, she'd never seen him like this. "Kurt, what's the matter?"

"You have a missing witch?" He brushed past her out of his office. "Well, I'm missing a werewolf...maybe two."

Her jaw dropped. Rooted, she watched him stride along the hallway. Things were looking darker by the moment. "Wait," she called, running after him.

He waited. She caught up and peered into his blue eyes. "What are you talking about? You said you'd go with me to look for Pinkie. What's this about missing werewolves?"

"Gordon just told me Gerald's missing. Nobody's seen him since Friday afternoon."

"So who's the other?"

Kurt didn't answer her question. "Let's go."

"Okay, fine. We'll go look for Pinkie and now Gerald, too. But Kurt..."

He gazed at her expectantly.

She stared at him. "It's nine in the morning."

"So?"

"You can't—"

"Yes I can, Garrett." His hard expression softened. Smiling, he bent down and planted a light kiss on her brow. "Let's go now, shall we?"

With an incredulous sigh, she followed him up the stairs to the street.

By eight in the evening, Seattle felt ready to burst. On the street, two women got into a shouting match over being jostled. One man pulled his gun and brandished it at the couple walking behind him, warning them not to get too close. Toddlers and babies wailed and could not be consoled. Faces were grim.

Garrett tightened her lips. Anna and the others might be doing everything they could but the Pax Omnia wouldn't hold much longer.

She glanced at Kurt. She'd been skeptical when he'd led her outside this morning, but they'd been out all day and he appeared absolutely fine. She stole a glance at him. *More than fine.* The vampire, with his beautiful blue eyes and golden curls, shone like a god.

"How much longer shall we look, *liebchen?*" his smooth voice interrupted her thoughts.

She sighed. "I dunno, Kurt. I mean, it's possible they're not in the city anymore. But if they are, I can't believe in all the time everybody's been looking no one has found either of them."

He nodded. "Yes." A thoughtful look crossed his face. "Tell you what. Let's try this street here and if we still don't find anything, we'll go back to Chance and rethink our strategy. Besides, I'm sure you haven't eaten today and I'm feeling a little peckish myself." He lifted her chin with one index finger. "Agreed?"

Garrett melted, dazzled by his sunlit beauty. Then she caught herself, realizing what he'd just said. Her jaw dropped. "Eat? But—you—vampires don't..."

Kurt closed one eye and squinted at the sky, his lips pursed as if deep in thought. Then he looked down at her. "How does eggplant lasagna sound to you? Maybe with a nice salad, hmm?"

Her jaw dropped further.

He grinned. "And after we eat, I'll have Gordon and the others start setting up the buffet."

Her jaws snapped shut. This was too much. "Kurt, don't tell me you're planning to open the club tonight."

He looked surprised. "Why not?" Before she could answer, he shrugged. "True, there might be a demon on the loose and the city might be about to blow up, but"—he shrugged again— "business is business, hmm?"

She stepped back, feeling horrified and bewildered. For as long as she'd known him, she'd never understood his callousness, his... *It doesn't matter,* a little voice echoed inside her head. *Admit it. You love him, even though he doesn't and will never love you.*

"Yeah," she muttered.

"What did you say, my dear?"

"Um, nothing. Come on."

Kurt caught her arm. "I was kidding about opening up tonight. I would but there's no use wasting time and money if you know no one's going to show."

She curled her lip, disgusted she'd been sucked in so easily. She stared up at him. "And the lasagna? Were you kidding about that, too?"

He gave her an innocent look. "No."

Garrett blinked a few times but said nothing. Smiling, he took her hand and led her along the street. They were halfway down the block when she stopped in her tracks. "This is it, Kurt. Pinkie's here...somewhere."

"What makes you think so?"

"I'm a mage."

"Ah. I see." He tilted his golden head. "What do you feel?"

"My skin is prickling. And the spell...somebody's killed the cat. There's a building on this street that's been warded against curiosity." She closed her eyes and concentrated. "The spell has Pinkie's magickal signature."

"Let's find it, hmm?"

The two strolled along as if they hadn't a care in the world. "Here," she whispered, halting them before a small warehouse.

Kurt drew her close. "You sure?"

Ordinarily, Garrett would have bristled at a question like that. But these weren't ordinary times. "Yes, I'm sure." She tugged on the door and was surprised to find it wasn't locked. Her heart sped up, her uneasiness growing.

As soon as they'd entered, the magick hit her so hard she nearly fell.

299

Then Kurt's hands were about her shoulders, steadying her. "All right, my dear?"

She nodded and began to pace. The magick in here was different than the type warding the building. Her skin had stopped prickling. A warm, sick feeling flooded her belly, making her nauseous. It wasn't like anything she'd felt before from a spell but she didn't have to guess what it was.

Garrett looked up and saw a black door, not unlike the ones that led to Underground. "There, Kurt. Through that door."

They ran over to it. She pulled on the handle but the door didn't budge. Giving the door a quick once-over, she saw it wasn't aligned on its hinges and it was too heavy for her to pull. She'd just started chanting a lightening spell when Kurt interrupted her.

"Let me."

She moved out of his way. With his preternatural strength, he ripped the door open.

Garrett gasped. Pinkie lay sprawled half in, half out of a green and white magick circle, her body riddled with holes. "Pinkie," she shouted and ran over to her. "Kurt, she's alive!"

Kurt was right on her heels. "How? Her blood's been drained."

Kneeling, she cradled the dying witch. "Magick, Kurt. It preserves the one who owns it, at least up to a point." She leaned closer to Pinkie's face. "Pinkie, it's me, Garrett. Can you hear me? Can you talk?"

"Yeah," Pinkie whispered.

"Please, Pinkie. Please tell us how to kill the uthyrisis."

"No."

"Pinkie, please!"

The young witch didn't answer.

Tears welled in Garrett's eyes. "Why did you do this, Pinkie? Why? Didn't you know the uthyrisis would kill you?"

A tiny smile stretched Pinkie's lips. "The revolution started on a Sunday..."

Then she died.

CHAPTER 70

Parker had no idea how long he'd lain crucifixion-like on the floor, staring at the ceiling. He didn't care, either. But some other part of his psyche did.

Get up, an inner voice commanded.

He didn't move. "No."

You have to.

"Why?"

You have a pack to take care of.

"Fuck the pack."

Then how 'bout getting your ass up 'cause I'm hungry? his wolf growled.

He blinked a few times. "Okay," he muttered a moment or two later. He got to his feet. The small light Melera had left behind had gone out but the room wasn't completely dark. Ambient light from the old-fashioned street lamps outside shone through the hole in the wall Garrett had blasted out last night.

Shuffling across the room, he reached the open door. The hallway was just as black as it had been earlier. He stood in the doorway, trying to remember where the stairway lay. *Just go,* that inner voice said. He nodded and stepped into the corridor. His feet scuffed the floor as he walked. *First Garrett and now Melera. Why? What did I do that was so damned wrong?*

A second later he smacked face-first into the half-glassed door guarding the stairway. Barely aware that his nose hurt, Parker stumbled down the steps onto the Underground street.

"All I did was love them," he whispered, shuffling along the sidewalk.

His mind went blank until he'd reached the street topside. Looking right and left, he didn't see his car. He wondered where he'd left it. "Fuck it," he muttered and started walking.

I loved her too, his wolf growled after they'd wandered a couple of blocks. He nodded but said nothing.

Then he heard a shout. "Park," someone yelled.

He turned. Tran was running toward him. The beta caught up to him a few seconds later, looking pissed. He glared at his alpha. "Where the hell you been?"

Parker blinked. "Underground."

Tran's angry expression turned incredulous. "All day?"

Parker looked up. He hadn't noticed it had gotten dark. He shrugged. "Guess so."

Tran's angry frown reappeared. "Dude, you..." He peered into Parker's face and his angry look melted into concern. "You okay?"

Parker shook his head. Tears welled in his eyes and he looked away. "Melera's gone."

Tran said nothing for a minute. "Look, I'm sorry. But there's a whole lotta shit goin' down right now and we're in the middle of it."

That got Parker's attention. "What shit?"

Tran quickly filled him in. "The Slayer got two more this morning." He paused. "You know that?"

"No."

"Jeez!" Tran spat, throwing up his hands. He took a deep breath. "The two this morning were witches. One of 'em had almost as much juice as Garrett." He gave his head a shake. "Anyway, the Slayer seems to be some sort of demon one of the coven's witches conjured up. She's dead now, too, which makes three dead witches. And the thing's still out there."

He took another breath. "Park, the humans are going berserk. You saw last night how edgy they were. Word about the first two witches hit the street this morning and since then the humans've killed a bunch of us as well as their own and that's with the witches workin' like dogs to keep the lid on."

Parker was dumbfounded. "Damn," was all he could say.

"Oh, and on top of all that, Gerald's still missing."

Parker's stunned expression melted into a frown. "Missing? What d'ya mean Gerald's missing?"

"Just what I said. Kurt's vampires and human servants say they haven't seen him since Friday afternoon."

Parker squeezed his eyes shut. Tran was right. All kinds of shit was going down. Opening them, he saw the other's lips tighten. "You know, there are lots of folks who think Melera is the Slayer."

"No, she isn't," he growled.

"Dude—"

"You said the humans are going berserk, right?"

Tran nodded.

"So how many of the pack are in Underground?"

"About a quarter of us."

"Why?"

The next thing he knew he was sitting on the ground, his chest hurting from Tran's punch. The other man loomed over him, his eyes blazing his werewolf's orange.

Parker felt his wolf respond. "What the—" he snarled.

"Jesus fuck, Parker," Tran roared. "The full moon's less than forty-eight hours away. You—" He stabbed the air with an index finger. "I'm sick of your shit, Park. If you'd bite your own bitches instead of God-knows-who, maybe you'd know what the fuck's going on around here." He narrowed his glowing eyes. "Dude, if you don't wanna be alpha anymore, then I will!"

Parker's face went very still. When he spoke, his growl was very soft. "Tran, are you challenging—"

Before he could finish, three explosions, followed seconds later by a fourth, rocked the city.

Seattle was plunged into darkness.

CHAPTER 71

The shock waves generated by the four explosions pitched the ornate chandelier in Last Chance's private dining room. Then everything went black. Sirens, echoing from all over, set up an ear-splitting wail.

"Kurt," Garrett cried. The vampire's name had hardly left her mouth when the room's windows shattered in a hail of bullets.

"Get down!"

He pulled her out of her seat as the table at which they'd been eating crashed to the floor. Crystal shards from the chandelier rained down on her head. "Kurt?" she whispered, feeling her scalp for cuts.

"Shh."

They waited in the darkness. No more shots came through the windows, though she could hear them in the distance. There were no more explosions.

"All right," Kurt said. "It's over. For now, anyway."

He helped her sit up. She heard him feeling around for something. "What—"

There was a snap and suddenly she could see. The candle that had graced their table burned brightly beside him.

"Obviously someone's blown up the city's power plant. And can you believe it? A drive-by?" He sighed. "I suppose this means Pinkie's revolution has officially begun." He peeked over the rim of the fallen table and looked around. "Dammit, I just had this place redecorated."

Garrett let out a little gasp. Those bombs, those guns... And what had Anna said this morning about the humans' combined psychic power going through the roof?

"Oh, no," she whispered. "Oh, no...Anna!" She scrambled to get up, ignoring the crystal shards biting into her hands. Tears fell from her eyes.

"Garrett, stop." Kurt tugged at her skirt. "Where do you think you're going?"

She kept struggling. "The Temple, Kurt. I've got to get to the Temple."

He yanked on the cotton material, forcing her back to the floor. "Sit down, witch. You go out there now and you're liable to get yourself killed."

"But—"

"But nothing, Garrett. Outside is not some child's video game."

She squirmed. "I'll use an obscuring spell. Kurt, I have to go. Now!"

He grabbed her by the waist and held tight. "Fine. No one will see you. But will your spell protect you from a stray bullet? Garrett, you want your damned tryst, don't you? Stay inside."

Garrett collapsed. Of course there was a spell that would protect her from bullets but she couldn't remember it.

"Why are you so hell-bent on getting to your Temple, anyway?"

"The Pax Omnia's broken."

"No. Really?"

She squeezed her eyes shut. "You don't understand." She explained what her eight coveners had been doing all day. "You felt it when we went out this morning. The tension was bad enough then, and as the day went on, it just got worse. So they would've had to increase the spell's power to keep its hold over the city. By now, the level of energy they must've been channeling, the human psychic power spike after the first three blasts, and then...then that fourth one...it had to have been the Temple."

Kurt pulled her against him and gave her a little squeeze. "Oh, Garrett—I'm so sorry."

She didn't reply. She hadn't felt so bereft since she was a child, since that night in Kilkenny City when the slavers had come for her and her family and she was the only one to escape.

Garrett buried her face in Kurt's chest and sobbed.

CHAPTER 72

"What the—" Tran said.

In the moonlight, Parker noticed someone on the roof throwing an object the size of a peach toward them. He leapt to his feet, grabbed Tran's arm and yanked. Dragging him at werewolf speed, he threw Tran into a recessed doorway twenty feet from where they'd stood. Then he squeezed inside, too.

Face-to-face, Parker pressed against the other man. He heard an explosion, followed by the smell of brick and concrete dust. Tiny granules of mortar dislodged from the bricks overhead sprinkled over his neck.

"Aagh!" He pressed harder against Tran.

"What's happening?" Tran whispered.

"Something just sliced my back."

A second later, he heard machinegun fire. It was very close. "God," he whispered, "please don't let there be anyone across the street."

The bullets rained down for no more than three minutes but to him, it seemed like an eternity. After the shooting stopped, he turned. His back pressing against Tran's chest, he leaned forward until just his head was visible from the recess.

Parker looked up, and left and right. "Okay," he said in a low voice. He took a small, careful step forward. "I think we're clear. I'll go out first. Stay against the wall but be ready to run."

He moved to the left and keeping his back to the brick, inched along the bullet-pocked sidewalk, looking up at every other step. Tran did the same. He heard more explosions in the distance. Though the streetlights were out, there was enough moonlight that he could see clearly.

"What happened back there?" Tran said, his voice quiet.

"Just after the lights went—when I was sitting on the ground—I saw somebody on the roof. Then I saw him throw something. I wasn't sure, but it looked like he was aiming for us."

"How did you know it was a grenade?"

Parker stopped and looked at him. "I didn't. But if somebody's up on a roof at night with the lights out and throwing things at people on the street, you can be pretty damned sure it ain't diamonds."

Tran said nothing.

The two wolves inched their way to the corner. This particular stretch of street was quiet but the next block looked to be on fire. Parker peered around the building. The flames illuminated people running back and forth.

He turned. "Okay. We've got to get the others to Underground. You told me about a quarter of us were already down there. I'm assuming they're the ones on the clean-up roster for this week. Off the top of my head, it's Donny, Harold, and Shirley—I also assume they've got their cub with them—Leona, Jackie, Devon, and..." He thought for a moment. "Oh—Sarah, Tasha, Jim, and Gary. So that's eleven."

Tran raised his brows.

He gave his second a smug look. "Hey, just because I haven't been biting my own bitches doesn't mean I don't know what's going on around here." Then his smug expression disappeared. "Um...Tran? Uh...just what is going on around here?"

Tran shrugged. "Garrett said it's some kind of revolution. That witch—the one who brought the demon? She was part of it. I dunno—something about forcing humans to recognize us as human."

"But we're not."

"Hey, don't make no sense to me either, dude."

Parker rolled his eyes. "Crazy." Then he flipped his hand, dismissing it. "Okay. Back to where we were. Am I missing anybody who's underground right now?"

"Yeah, but just a few. Jill, Garland, and Janet. Susie's down there, too."

"I don't remember seeing Janet on the list."

"When Garrett told me this morning what might be going down tonight, I went and got them first thing. They're way out on the south side." He glanced at the next block. "If things got nasty, they'd be the hardest to get to, you know?"

Tran frowned. "Speaking of Janet and Susie, I had a little trouble getting in Underground this morning when I had them with me. The first two doors I tried were...I dunno, locked or something." He peered at his alpha. "Did you have a problem getting in?"

Parker's expression turned thoughtful. "Yeah, I did..." He squeezed his eyes shut. "Great. Exactly what we need. Doors that won't work." He opened them and blew an explosive breath. "The door I was at? I got it open by hauling hard on it—and I mean hard. Try that."

He looked away and back at Tran. "Anyway, you take the east side and I'll take the west. Start with those living closest to Underground and bring them here. Keep your groups small. The fewer there are, the easier it'll be to hide. If the street looks quiet, tell the pack to stay inside and head for the basement." He listened. "Got a bad feeling it won't be that easy, though. Those blasts—the ones that sounded kinda far away..."

Tran nodded. "Know what you mean."

Parker eyed him. "If you see any Firsts or Seconds along the way, tell 'em to get going—we need help." He turned to leave.

"Park," Tran said.

He looked over his shoulder.

"Listen. Back there, when that guy—"

Parker did a full one-eighty. Licking Tran's lips, he planted a quick but solid kiss on his second's mouth. "Hey, dude. What're alphas for?"

Then he loped away.

CHAPTER 73

By midnight, Seattle was a sea of chaos.

Kurt, in mist form, flew over his city watching the revolution unfold. Everywhere he looked, fires blazed out of control. The streets had become war zones. Death lurked around every corner, in every alley, from the rooftops, and even in the windows of seemingly deserted buildings.

Seeing this set off a rage in him that bordered on madness. In the moonlight, he spied four revolutionaries on the street, identifiable by the camouflage they wore and the rifles they carried. Zeroing in on the closest one, Kurt swooped downward. He would wring her neck and then all the others. He had almost reached them when—

Stop, a voice shouted in his head. *Stay on target!*

The inner voice pulled him up short. He swerved away from the four and materialized behind a small office building. Back to the concrete, he pressed himself tight against the wall and clapped his hands over his face. Through monumental effort, he willed his rage to dissipate. Five minutes later, he'd finally calmed. He dissolved into mist and took flight again.

He thought about his mission, as he called it. After the city had blacked out, he and Garrett had hurried to Underground. There were bound to be casualties, and she needed to be there to heal them. About ten minutes after they'd arrived, the refugees began trickling in. Several had told him about Underground doors that wouldn't open, even after the locks had been disengaged. A refugee showed him one. He'd tried to push it open. To his surprise, it had stayed shut. Doors to Underground only locked from the outside.

Garrett had stepped up next to him. Raising her arms, her hands hovered over the door from about an inch away. "It's been warded again.

The ward against human discovery already there has been overlaid with a standard locking spell." She'd looked up at him.

"Can you tell who did it?" he'd said.

She'd pressed her hands on the door and concentrated. "Someone named Oto." They'd tried other doors. Some had opened, some had not, but all the locked doors had been warded by Oto. She'd pressed her hands against the twentieth locked door and turned. "This one's been warded by Slick."

That was all Kurt had needed to hear. It would be like looking for two needles in the proverbial haystack but he was determined to find them.

Flying over the city, he opened his mind. The sudden cacophonic blast—screams, gunfire, explosions—almost knocked him back into solid form. It took hard willpower to right himself. Once stable, he focused on a particular set of vibrations—Oto's.

On and on he flew, searching for Oto's magickal signature. Flying along a deserted street, he heard the tell-tale buzz that he'd found him. He looked down. A man with a sniper's rifle was walking along its middle. He started his descent and had almost reached solid ground when a phalanx of police in full riot gear rounded the corner.

Oto unslung his weapon. The cops pumped him full of lead before he'd had a chance to curl his finger around the trigger.

Kurt waited for the police to leave. Once they had, he materialized next to Oto's bullet-riddled body. He stared down at the corpse. "You were very, very lucky," he murmured. Then he misted again and went in search of Slick.

It didn't take him long to find the other revolutionary. Not far from where Oto had been shot, Slick stood atop a low-rise office building, his arm drawn back. He held a grenade. Kurt waved his hand. Slick tossed the bomb and threw himself flat on the rooftop.

There was no explosion. Kurt disabled the grenade. He glided over to where Slick was now getting to his knees, grabbed him by the collar and yanked him upright, lifting the other man so that his feet dangled.

"What the fuck?" Slick yelled, struggling to break Kurt's grip.

Instead of answering, Kurt let Slick dangle for about a minute longer. "You might as well stop. You can't fight me," he finally said in his silky smooth voice.

Slick stopped his struggling. "Who the fuck are you?"

He set the other man down on the rooftop and turned him so they were face to face. "Oh, just the Master of Seattle."

Slick's eyes bulged. "Wh-what do you want?"

Kurt cocked his head. "A silly question, wouldn't you say? I want you." He glared at the other man. "Not only do you have the gall to destroy my city but you also endanger what is mine by sealing off those Underground doors. It's unforgivable. And you will pay for your crime."

"What're—what're you going to do?"

He waved his hand again.

The look on Slick's face turned terrified. "Wait—wait! I can't move," he cried.

"Indeed you cannot. I've placed you under a stasis. You can't move but I'm allowing you to speak."

"Wh-why?"

Kurt lifted his hands and morphed his fingers into razor-sharp claws. He stepped forward. A wide, mirthless smile stretched his lips.

"Because I want to hear you scream."

CHAPTER 74

While Kurt ripped Slick to shreds, Parker ran uptown, headed for Oren and Maggie Wilson's house. They and their three cubs were the last of his pack to check on and get into Underground.

After parting from Tran, he'd decided to chance driving to round up the spread-out pack. Skirting the burning streets and keeping to the shadows, he'd returned to where he'd left his Caprice. It was in flames.

Goddamn those sonsabitches!

He'd have to do this the hard way—on foot. Even so, he'd been pretty sure the Wilsons would be okay. Maggie was scrum but Oren was a First. Oren, better than anyone but Tran, would know how to hold out under attack. They were also the furthest from Underground, so he'd saved them for last.

As Parker sprinted toward Linden Drive, he could see the tell-tale orange glow of a fire burning out of control. "Oh, no," he murmured. A hundred feet further, he could see three houses in flames—and one of them belonged to Maggie and Oren.

"Shit." He ran faster. Turning the corner, he saw a crowd of humans milling about in the street. He cut around them and ran across the backyards until he reached the Wilson's. A figure lay in the grass.

It was Maggie. Parker knelt beside her. In the firelight, he could see how badly she'd been beaten. Her beautiful chocolate face was nothing but lumps and her smashed left eye hung partially out of its socket. A torn-off lower lip showed what was left of her teeth. Blood drenched the front of her dress. It was hard to tell if she was still alive.

"Mags," he said in a low voice. "Mags, can you hear me?" Not expecting anything, he was surprised when Maggie's one eye fluttered open.

"Park," she croaked. A small smile turned up on the corner of her mouth that hadn't been damaged. "Good…to see… you…"

He returned her smile while holding back his tears. "Good to see you too, Mags." His throat tightened and he couldn't say anything for a moment. "Mags," he said when he could speak again. "Where are Oren and the cubs? Did they make it?"

A tear appeared in the corner of her good eye and trickled down the side of her nose. "No," she whispered. "They…killed them…forced me to watch…then…it was my…turn."

He squeezed his eyes shut. If he'd been here… "Oh, God—Mags, I'm sorry."

"Nothing you—"

"Hey," a rough male voice shouted from behind them. Parker shot to his feet and turned. His mind reeled. Walking toward him was none other than Pitt Jackson, the murderer of Frank Suggs.

Childhood memories flooded through him. He heard again Pitt's boasting around town about his skinning the young werepanther and showing off Frank's pelt. He relived the Judge's harsh interrogation about whether he knew Frank was *were*. He heard again his repeated denials that he'd known and his silent prayers the Judge wouldn't see through his lies. The Judge had been a hard and brutal man and there was no telling what he would have done had he discovered the truth—even to his then fifteen-year-old human son.

What's Pitt…how?

"What're you doin'? Dontcha know she's one a' them?" Pitt's tone was suspicious.

His questions jerked Parker out of his shock. If he'd any doubt before, he didn't now. He would have recognized that scar splitting Pitt's face anywhere.

Pitt looked him up and down with a puzzled frown. Then the light of recognition spread across his deformed features. "Well, well, if it ain't Parker Berenson," he sneered. "Been a long time, boy. Yuh done all growed up."

"You haven't changed a bit." It wasn't a compliment.

Pitt chuckled. "Hey, boy—yuh remember yore buddy Frank, dontcha? I still got his pelt layin' on mah floor back home. Moths got to it a while back, but it's still a good-lookin' piece a' panther hide."

The sound of Frank Sugg's name coming from Pitt's misshapen mouth triggered a rage Parker thought he'd long-since buried. The gut-twisting, impotent rage of a fifteen-year old boy whose best friend had been murdered and there wasn't a damned thing he could do about it. He could do nothing about the men who'd killed Frank, much less anything about the man who'd ordered the killing—Judge George Eric Berenson. His father. His own goddamned father.

He set his jaw. Well, he wasn't fifteen anymore, and this time he would do something about it, and that was to torch Pitt where he stood. He'd just begun focusing his pyro energy when from the corner of his eye, he saw at least twenty men and women round the edge of the burning house. They stopped about ten or twelve feet away, watching the two men. *Dammit to hell.* His chance to do something had gone.

Pitt looked down at Maggie. "She still alive?"

Parker shrugged, trying to ignore the tightness in his chest. "Yeah, barely."

Pitt eyed her and then looked up with a malevolent, gap-toothed grin. "Mah nephew tol' me her name's Maggie. I 'ont care if she's the Queen of England—dis here *were* girl got some mighty fine pussy."

He was hardly able to restrain himself. Then he saw another frown appear across Pitt's face. Pitt looked him up and down again, apparently seeing more than just the Parker Berenson he'd known fourteen years ago but now "all growed up." He seemed to take in Parker's size, physique, and the dense body hair peeking out from his torn shirt.

He knew what was coming. Pitt was a sniffer, a human with the innate ability to tell zots from humans. It was why his father had often used the homely backwoodsman to ferret out and then eradicate zots living in the county where Parker had been born.

Pitt peered into his face. "Berenson, I knows for a fack yuh was born human. But I also knows things change and when they do, sometimes they go straight to shit." He paused, giving him a meaningful look. "Sure you ain't one a' them?"

Parker stared Pitt in the eye. "No," he said in a steady voice loud enough for everyone to hear. "I'm not. I'm human, Pitt. Like you." He felt as if he'd just betrayed Frank all over again.

Pitt pulled a hunting knife with a silver-coated blade from its sheath clipped to his belt. "If you ain't *were*," he said in a soft but threatening tone, "why 'ont yuh finish the werebitch off?"

Parker stared at the weapon. If he didn't take it, he wouldn't make it out of Maggie and Oren's backyard alive.

You have a pack to take care of.

He took the knife.

Turning, he took a step and knelt next to Maggie. From the look in her good eye, he knew she'd heard every word. *Forgive me, Mags,* he mouthed, tears welling in his eyes.

Maggie gave him a slow wink.

Then he slit her throat.

"Now. Dint' that feel good?" Parker heard Pitt's voice behind him.

Pitt Jackson, you are going to die.

Timing, though, was critical.

He stood. Dropping the knife, he somehow managed to keep his nausea at bay. He turned to Pitt and shrugged. "Nah. I mean, it was alright, but..." He winked. "I know something a lot better."

Pitt seemed to get excited. "What?"

Parker grinned. "This!"

He leapt. Morphing his human head into his wolf one, he tore off Pitt's skull with his teeth. Then he took off running, as fast as his *were*-strength would allow. The humans chased him but he knew they'd never catch up.

Sprinting downtown, Parker morphed his wolf's head back into his human one. Tears streamed from his eyes. Tears of sorrow for Frank and Maggie, tears of joy at Frank's finally getting justice. Tears at his having avenged the Wilsons' deaths, at having avenged all the zots he knew Pitt had murdered while he was growing up and all the zots Pitt had surely murdered since then.

"Pitt," he said with a laugh. "Now that—that felt real good!"

CHAPTER 75

The uthyrisis was having a fine time. Tonight, it had eaten many, many of these three-dimensional humans and it was hungry for more. *More tales for the Mighty Ones.*

The uthyrisis was always hungry. The blood it fed on sustained the host. Without it, the body would die. The uthyrisis didn't need blood to eat. It fed on emotions—hate, fear, and despair, among others. It had been delighted to discover the three-humans always made plenty of food. If it weren't for the host's body, the uthyrisis wouldn't have to approach the three-humans at all.

But it did—and not just to feed. The uthyrisis liked the three-humans. When it had wrapped one in its wings, the terror it ate was ambrosia. And it liked the feel of a three-human's struggling, especially after the Gerald had shown it the holes they had in their bodies where they would sometimes join together. When it put its feeding tube into one of those holes, the three-humans struggled even harder. That made its meal all the sweeter.

"Here is one," the uthyrisis whispered. It watched the three-human approach. Though wider and rounder, it had a shape similar to the Gerald so the uthyrisis knew it was male. That meant he had only three holes instead of four. Three holes or four, it didn't matter to the uthyrisis. It liked them all just the same.

The male turned and walked into the grassy area near the bush behind which the uthyrisis was hiding and stopped only a few feet away. His back faced the bush. The uthyrisis heard something rasp and then the sound of liquid hitting the ground. It leapt, flattening the Gerald's body as it did so.

"Hey," the male shouted when it had wrapped him tight.

Attacker and victim crashed to the ground. Face in the dirt, the male could no longer speak. The uthyrisis dissolved the other's outer skin. Then its feeders emerged in full. Finding the larger of the male's lower two holes, it shoved one of its tubes inside, then did the same to the smaller one.

The male thrashed and managed to roll them over. He tried to cry out, so the uthyrisis thrust a tube into his topmost opening. It chuckled. "Like it, do you? The Gerald said you would. The Gerald said all you three-humans like it."

The male grunted.

The uthyrisis savored his terror while the Gerald savored his blood. Then it laughed and kissed the male's neck.

It liked it, too.

CHAPTER 76

Parker had gone insane.

Having to kill Mags had been bad enough. But when he came across the torn and mutilated bodies of First-ranked Jane Roberson and five of the lesser wolves in his pack she'd been leading to Underground, it was the last straw. Her group had been too large but Jane was smart and savvy, so he was sure there'd been a reason for it. From the burn marks, it was obvious the humans who'd done this—it had to be—had been armed with silver.

After discovering this massacre, he let his wolf take over. He didn't change completely, but his hands had morphed into wolf paws. He attacked every human he saw. He jumped into the middle of every street battle he came across, hungry for bloodshed.

Halfway to downtown, he ran into a battle between a gang of humans and a small troop of elves. He could tell the elves were using glamour but it wasn't enough. There were just too many of the enemy.

"Aaahhhhrrrr," his wolf roared. He leapt into the fray, slashing and tearing at anyone who came within reach of his claws. His presence—and bloodlust—tipped the balance. At one point, he felt a knife plunge into his left side. Made of steel, it had barely hurt. He whipped around. A human still held its hilt.

"Wrong blade, dude," Parker snarled. Then, planting his claws through the man's forehead, he tore off the other's face.

By the time he had made it to Pioneer Square, his need and his wolf's need to kill had been sated. It was time to see about the rest of his pack. Instead of going after any human he spotted, he skirted them. Zigzagging his way through the historic district while heading for Underground, he rounded a corner and saw a mob of humans, some with torches, coming his way. He and his wolf were formidable, but...

The mob spied him. They ran for him, screaming.

"Shit." He turned and ran in the direction from which he'd come, looking for any place he could hide. Looking over his shoulder to see if he'd put some distance between him and the mob, he was grabbed by the arm and yanked into an alley.

"Park," he heard an urgent whisper. It was Sheila Graham, the leopard queen. Her face was streaked with blood and tears. "We can't get into Underground. Most of my leap is dead because every door we've tried won't open and then we've had to fight and"—her voice hitched—"and I don't know what to do anymore."

"Is there a door here?" he said, keeping his voice low.

Sheila nodded. "Back there, but it's locked too." Shouts and feet pounding on the pavement were followed by the smell of burning wood. "They're coming. Oh, God-Khensa, they're coming."

"Shh. Come on." Parker and the leopard queen ran to the back of the long dead-end alley. When they'd reached it, he saw Sheila hadn't been kidding about her leap. They'd been devastated. Not one of her catmen or women was whole. Some had partially morphed, obviously from their pain. Brian, the queen's consort, was cradling a catwoman who'd lost so much blood Parker thought she had to be dead.

"Last stand, huh, babe?" the catman said. He glanced in the direction of the noise that was getting louder.

"Not if I can help it." Parker stepped over to the door. Bracing his foot on the wall next to the jamb, he wrapped his hands around the handle. Gathering his strength, he pulled.

Nothing happened. He tried again—with the same result.

By now the human mob had reached the alley. "Look," someone shouted. "There's more of 'em!" They ran along the bricks, their fire-lit faces filled with murderous intent.

"Parker," Sheila whispered.

Brian propped the catwoman he'd been holding against the wall and stood. He turned to Sheila. "I love you," he murmured and caressed her jaw.

This is your last chance, dude. Parker marshaled all his *were*-strength and hauled on it. The door flew open. "Quick. Get inside," he said to the others. They worked fast. Those who could walk half-carried, half-dragged those who couldn't.

He pushed the last wereleopard into the vestibule. Then he leapt inside. From the corner of his eye, he saw movement. Whirling, he slammed the door shut just in time to sever the first three fingers belonging to the first human who'd reached them.

Once Underground, Parker went looking for his pack. He found twelve of them. They gave him a casualty report, as much as they knew. It was grim.

Then he went looking for Kurt. He threaded his way through the crowded streets, asking for information. No one had seen him.

The longer he looked, the more his anger and frustration grew. At this rate, he'd be looking all night and the next day. He was about to ask again when he decided he'd had enough. Hands clenched into fists, he stood in the middle of Underground's main street and tilted his head back. "Has anyone seen the fucking Master?" his wolf roared. His voice echoed among the buildings.

Underground went silent. Everyone within earshot stared at him.

About five seconds later, Parker heard a small, frightened voice. "I have."

He turned toward the sound. A girl, not more than eight, stood ten feet away. He got down on one knee and beckoned the child closer. As she neared him, her look grew even more scared.

"Where'd you see him, sweetheart?" His voice was gentle.

The girl pointed across the street. "He was over there. He and a little skinny lady went that way." She pointed to her left.

He swiveled his head to look and turned back to the girl. He smiled. "Thank you, honey. You've helped me more than you know."

The little girl smiled, too. She backed away and a moment later was enveloped in the arms of a woman he assumed was her mother.

Parker stood and started walking. His smile widened into a feral grin.

He knew exactly where to find Kurt.

CHAPTER 77

As Parker and the wereleopards made their way into Underground, Garrett had just finished healing an elf with two broken legs when she saw Kurt's legs materialize next to her. She looked up. He gazed down, expressionless. "Come. We need to talk." He turned and began walking along the brick-paved street. She rose without a word and followed.

He led her to his red velvet office underneath Chance. "I found the two who'd sealed the doors."

"Where are they now?"

Kurt's lips stretched into a chilling smile. "They're dead. One had been shot by the police and the other..." His smile widened. "The other fell to me."

Garrett shuddered. She didn't want to even try and imagine what he had done to the culprit, no matter how much he deserved it.

His smile faded. "So many of us," he said in a soft voice.

"So many of us," she echoed, her voice just as soft. "From what I've been able to gather from the zots down here, there are at least eight hundred dead topside and probably more. Brother Tom..." She tried to swallow the lump in her throat. "Brother Tom says five more of the coven are gone."

Kurt seemed to gaze at the wall. A pained look crossed his beautiful face and his blue eyes seemed to shine. "A good part of my colony is missing." His low tone carried a slight rasp. "Including most of my justborns." He looked at the floor but said nothing further.

Surprised, Garrett stared at him. In all the years she'd known Kurt, she'd never seen him display such emotion. She hadn't thought him capable. Then her lips set into a line. "Kurt, we have to make the tryst. It's the only way to stop this madness."

He looked up. His eyes were no longer shiny but they seemed troubled. "I don't know if we can."

She frowned. "What do you mean?"

"I mean I think Parker might be among the dead."

Garrett thought her eyes would pop from her head. "What?"

"I can't call him," his voice rose. "I've tried and tried, but there's nothing. I can't even feel him."

Her knees went weak.

"It's the only explanation. Parker's my servant. He can't just shut me out."

Just then the door to the office was kicked open. The two turned as one. "Parker," Garrett said. "We were just…" Her eyes widened when she saw his torn and bloodied shirt.

"You goddamned sonofabitch," he snarled. He stared at Kurt with undisguised hatred. Then he launched himself at the vampire.

"Parker, no," Garrett screamed. A ball of witch-power appeared in her left hand. She threw it at the same time Kurt's hand chopped the air.

The werewolf crashed to the floor.

CHAPTER 78

Kurt watched Parker get to his feet, his face grim. His relief at seeing his servant alive didn't mean he'd suffer the other to attack him. "You just took an incredibly foolish chance, wolf."

Parker opened his mouth to say something, but Garrett beat him to it. "Park, wait."

"The hell I will." He glared at Kurt with eyes like green ice. "I lost over half my pack tonight because most of 'em couldn't get into Underground. They died because of you. I thought——"

"Parker, shut up," Garrett shouted.

The wolf stopped his tirade. Turning, he stared at her through narrowed eyes.

She took a breath. "The doors wouldn't open because they'd been warded. They'd been warded with a locking spell."

"Bullshit," he shot back. "I got 'em open. It took some doing but I got them open."

Kurt's jaw almost dropped. Even he, the Master, couldn't break a witch's spell. *My word, if Parker can do that——*

"You broke through a witch's spell?" Garrett said, her voice faint.

"I don't...why should I believe you about some damned spell?"

"Because it's true," Kurt said. "Ask any witch down here. They'll tell you the same thing."

Parker didn't take his eyes from Garrett. "Who did it, then? Don't tell me it was one of yours."

"Don't be ridiculous."

"There were two of them," Kurt cut in. "Revolutionaries."

Parker looked at him. "Where are they?"

"Dead. One was shot, and the other"——he smirked and raised his hands——"I took care of."

The wolf stared at the bloody cuffs on Kurt's shirt and jacket. His lips tightened. "Okay. Let's say I believe you. What do we do now? Wait down here for this—" he waved his arm—"revolution to end? Tran told me about this demon thing. What's going to be done about that?"

"Where's Melera?" Kurt said.

A pained look crossed Parker's face. "Gone. She left this morning."

"Gone where?"

His pained expression disappeared and his eyes narrowed. "I don't care what you all think. Melera isn't the Slayer, okay?"

Kurt raised his brow. "Are you sure about that?"

Parker opened his mouth but Garrett spoke first. "Park, we have to make the tryst."

"No way! Are you two crazy? Do you really think I'm gonna join you after all the shit you've pulled on me?"

"Parker," Garrett shouted. "It's not about you anymore. How many of us do you think are still up there?" She pointed toward the ceiling. "If we don't make the tryst, how many more of us are going to die tonight?"

He turned away without a word.

Garrett's expression turned furious. "Motherdammit, Park, we don't know how long we're going to be down here. We're all in shock right now but eventually most of us will heal." She blew an explosive breath. "We don't get along with each other as it is. If we can't leave, how do you think that's going to work?"

Parker's silence was maddening. "What about food, Parker?" Kurt said, trying to maintain a reasonable tone. "Chance's freezers are full right now but the food will eventually run out, especially given the way you *weres* eat. What do you think will happen then, hmm?"

He turned his head a little. That slight acknowledgement gave Kurt a thrill of satisfaction. The wolf knew what would happen as well as he did. The predatory *weres*—like Parker—would start viewing the non-predators as lunch.

"And then there's the Witch's Credo," Garrett said in a soft voice.

Parker whirled. "I don't give a damn about your Credo."

"Then think about your pack," Kurt snapped. "Aren't you supposed to be the one to take care of them?"

Parker stared at him a moment, then shook his head. "No. There's gotta be another way. You two have fucked with me enough as it is and the last thing I need—"

Kurt heard the muffled whmph! of something exploding on the street above them, close enough to make the building shiver. The three looked up at the ceiling. He saw a tiny crack appear in the plaster above Parker's head and then lengthen until it reached the top of the room's far wall. He looked at Parker. From the expression on the wolf's face, he'd seen it, too. Kurt cocked his head. "Well, Parker?"

He didn't answer. The minutes ticked by. "Okay." His shoulders slumped. "You guys win. I'll do it."

Kurt nearly sighed in relief. Between Pinkie's revolution and their rampaging demon, the situation topside was bad enough. A second war erupting in Underground would have been a nightmare. He'd witnessed enough wars to be no stranger to combat but nothing he'd seen in his centuries-long life had ever changed his opinion that bloodshed was bad for business, especially his. This insanity had to be stopped, the sooner the better, and he'd use any means at his disposal to do it. He turned to Garrett. "Can we make the tryst from here?"

"No. The spell we cast has to spread over the city. To do that, it'd be best if we were someplace up high, especially now that the Temple's"— her voice hitched—"gone." She turned away and hid her face in her hands.

Parker frowned. "What do you mean the Temple's gone?"

She didn't answer.

"The coven's Temple blew up," Kurt answered for her. "Eight of her coveners were inside making magick, trying to keep the Pax Omnia together." He paused. "Remember when all this started? Those three explosions followed by a fourth?"

Parker nodded.

"The fourth was the Temple."

The wolf said nothing.

"So you see," Kurt said, "you aren't the only one who's lost loved ones tonight."

Parker shot him an odd look, then turned to Garrett. "Garrett, I'm—"

She spun around. Her eyes were wet. "Like I said," she cut him off in a clear, strong voice, "we need to go someplace high up."

329

No one said anything. "So where would that be?" Parker said.

Realization dawned on all three faces at the same time. They looked at each other.

"The Space Needle," they said as one.

CHAPTER 79

"How do we get there?" Parker said, looking from one to the other. "The Needle is across town. We'll never make it alive."

Kurt stretched his arms. "That's easy. Come, both of you. Take my hands and hold on."

They did. After a moment, Parker felt a sensation of flight and then they were in the Space Needle.

He immediately dropped Kurt's dead-cold hand and stepped away. They'd materialized in the reception area of the Sky City restaurant. Above them was the Needle's observation deck and above that, darkness and thin air.

Except for the three of them, the restaurant was empty. He crossed the plush carpeting to the elevator. Putting his ear to the door, he listened for the sound of working machinery. The Needle was silent. If there was anyone else around, his wolf-hearing didn't pick them up.

Parker stepped backward and relaxed a little. *Good. I'd hate to have to explain what the three of us are doing up here.* He walked over to one of the windows lining the entire room. The only light came from the moon. Maybe that was enough—it was for him—but... "Uh, anybody think to bring candles?"

Garrett held up her hand. "No, but that's not a problem."

He watched a ball of witch-light form in her palm. When it had grown bright enough, she tossed it into the air where it hung like a glowing bluish-white balloon. Then he thought about how Kurt had brought them all here and shuddered. The way his body had evaporated and then later coalesced had felt creepy. "Like skipping, only worse," he muttered.

That reminded him of Melera. He didn't want to think about her, so he gazed out the window instead. From up here, the fires in the city formed a loose checkerboard. Being so high, the raging flames had been reduced almost to a soft glow. It was sort of pretty. But that was from up here. Parker knew how very, very ugly it was down in the streets. He frowned. *The one time we could really use some rain and it doesn't happen.*

"What now, Garrett?" Kurt said, breaking through his thoughts. He turned. She was still hanging on to the vampire's hand. He shuddered again. *How can she stand it?*

"Becoming a tryst is in a way like casting the Saperet," Garrett said. "We—"

Parker's eyes widened. He knew what that meant. "Hold it. Lemme get this straight." He jerked a thumb over his shoulder. "Seattle's going up like the fall of Rome and you wanna screw?"

Garrett glared up at him. "Yes, I do. Sex is the most potent magick of all, something you oughta know. Making the tryst is about merging our power, Park. I told you that, remember? Our psychic walls break down and we merge to become one."

His jaw tightened. He remembered, sure. But after all he'd been through today, he wasn't in the mood to fuck anyone, much less Garrett. And he damned sure didn't want to fuck Kurt. Then, with a tiny sigh, he pinched the bridge of his nose between his thumb and forefinger. Considering the holocaust on the streets below, his personal feelings no longer mattered. "Okay. I said I'd do it, so let's just get it over with, huh?"

"You don't sound like you want to do it." Garrett sounded angry. "Parker, you have to be willing to join with us or at best it won't work and at worst you'll get us all killed."

He gritted his teeth. "Listen, sweetheart. This is as good as it gets, so take it or leave it." He ripped off his bloodied and tattered shirt. Garrett had been right again. Damned straight he didn't want to do this, but he didn't see he had a choice. As for whether his attitude killed him or all of them...

Too bad.

A memory of Melera flashed through his mind while he unzipped his jeans.

Merging...

Parker went still for a moment. "Making song," he whispered and then squeezed his eyes shut. Maybe killing the three of them would be best.

Taking off his jeans, he winced when he saw his ruined loafers. He turned to the others, trying hard to shake his feeling of being trapped. Garrett and Kurt were still dressed. They'd been busy watching him. Parker let out an impatient breath. "Well? Are we gonna do this thing or aren't we?"

Glaring, he watched the other two strip off their clothes.

CHAPTER 80

Garrett unbuttoned her blouse, trying not to panic. *It's all wrong!* Peeling the sleeves from her arms, she folded the shirt neatly and then placed it on the floor. She would've never believed her dream would turn out like this.

Shimmying out of her tight beige skirt, she doubled it and laid it on top of her white blouse. When she straightened, she saw that Kurt, like Parker, was naked. She looked down at herself and then eyed both men. "We need to wash off this blood." She hoped she sounded matter-of-fact.

Parker tilted his head at Kurt. "What about him?"

The vampire chuckled. "Oh, water doesn't bother me."

Parker stared at him with an expression of utter disbelief.

Kurt winked. "C'mon. You wash my back and I'll wash yours."

The werewolf said nothing. He stared for a moment longer and then turned back to Garrett. Instead of disbelief, now his face held betrayal, thinking she'd tricked him again.

His look put her on the defensive. She held out her hands. "I didn't know water won't harm him." It was true. Until today, there were a great many things she hadn't known about Kurt.

With a heavy sigh, Parker turned and headed for the men's room.

Inside the women's room, she snatched a few paper towels from the dispenser and wet them with soap. Scrubbing her face, she avoided looking into the mirror so as not to see the fear in her eyes. The magick the three of them would draw tonight made the Saperet look like an ordinary, everyday spell and none of them were ready.

Garrett had planned carefully. Over the past year, she'd squirreled away the paraphernalia she'd need to prepare for the rite in various places throughout the Temple, so no one—especially a more experienced witch like Paul—would discover her stash and put two and two together. She'd studied the calendar, selecting a ten-day period when the Temple would not be in use.

She would have spent over a week in seclusion, fasting, praying, and taking cleansing baths. She would have purified the Lair's atmosphere by burning incense and candles twenty-four hours a day. Two days before the ritual, she would have summoned Parker to the Temple for fasting and bathing. On that final day, before consummating the rite, she would have summoned Kurt to be rubbed down with sterilizing herbs and tinctures.

Then again, if I'd known he could do all I've seen him do today, I'd have not only made sure he'd fasted but I'd have dunked him into the bath, too.

Garrett scrubbed at a blood spot on her ankle. It was bad enough they were unclean. They might not be able to call the magick. Worse, they had no mandala. Without the circle holding the spell together the three's energies might dissipate, leaving them in a vegetative state. Worst of all was Parker's reluctance to go through with the ritual. That could have consequences she didn't even want to think about.

Just then, the warning Goddess had imparted the night of the Saperet ritual last February echoed through her brain.

IT IS A MOST DANGEROUS GAME YOU PLAY, DAUGHTER. HAVE A CARE—IT IS NOT ONE YOU WANT TO LOSE.

Her head jerked up. She stared at her reflection in the mirror. "Yes, Mother. I know. I've already lost the game. More than that, I also know I'm about to commit the greatest of all sins against You—not only am I about to take my own life but I'm about to take the lives of two inno-cent others." She paused. "But I have to go through with the tryst ritual, Mother. I have no choice. To save our own, I have to try." Her eyes closed. "Great Mother, have mercy upon my soul."

Garrett cleaned the last of the blood from her body. Taking a deep breath, she then left the ladies' room. Stepping into the reception area, she saw Parker and Kurt were already there, waiting for her.

She walked over to the two men. "Okay. This is what'll happen…"

CHAPTER 81

Parker tried hard to stay focused on what Garrett was saying but thoughts of Melera kept getting in the way.

"I'm the conduit, right?" she said. "Your power will flow through me and back into both of you. That's called 'the mixing.' Once that's done, we'll cast the Eall Tholia spell. Like I told you before, it's similar to the Pax Omnia, but the difference is the Eall Tholia can't be broken." She paused. "Anyway, after it's over, we'll have established a mind-body link with each other. A lot like telepathy, except much more intense. We'll also be able to pool our power whenever we need to." Her lips stretched into a small smile. "Let's do it."

Garrett and Kurt settled themselves on the thick carpet. Parker watched her fondle the vampire's cock. Kurt's boner was almost immediate. Then she climbed on top. *At least the sonofabitch picked someplace halfway comfortable.* He would've hated having to do it on the o-deck's cold, hard floor.

He watched them for a while. With a jolt, he realized he felt nothing. No jealousy, no rage over the fact his freyja was screwing the man he despised most in all of Seattle. Then he realized he felt nothing for Kurt either. As far as he was concerned, those two could have each other.

His revelation wasn't doing anything for him, though. His dick stayed limp. Not even his wolf seemed to be interested.

"Come…come on, Park," Garrett panted.

Parker looked up and shrugged. "Can't. Dexter doesn't wanna play."

"Then…think of something."

Unbidden, a vision of Melera appeared in his mind's eye. She lay on his bed with her legs spread wide, caressing her dripping, red-swollen cunt. Then she slipped an index finger inside and slowly drew it out. With a lascivious smile, she held it up for him to taste.

"Uhhm," he whimpered.

The vision worked. He was hard as a rock now. Holding the image in his mind, in two bounds he reached the spot where Garrett and Kurt were panting over each other. He knelt behind her. Then he shoved his cock into her ass and pumped her hard.

On his inner movie screen, he watched Melera open a long gash between her neck and shoulder with slow and deliberate sensuousness. The olfactory memory of her blood-scent drove him berserk. He saw himself leap onto his bed, ram his dick into her and worry at her wound.

Melera's deep, slightly mocking laughter echoed through his brain. "Yes," he heard her gasping whisper. "Do me Pawkher, do me…yesss… aahhh!" she screamed. Forgetting himself, he morphed his hand into his wolf's paw and sliced open Garrett's shoulder. He bent down to lap at her blood.

His first taste brought him back to reality and he opened his mouth to howl in despair. Just as he'd taken a breath, he noticed a bluish-green light flickering along his fingers. He closed his mouth and frowned. Looking up, he saw Garrett's back had begun to glow, too. Moments later, the three were enveloped in a blue-green blaze.

Parker felt a lurch in his mind and body. Before he could wonder about it, he was no longer himself.

CHAPTER 82

Kurt felt hollowed out, like an ancient birch canoe.

It was more than being mentally aware of Garrett and Parker. He heard her chanting, and he'd felt Parker's disappointment that his dream of fucking Melera hadn't been a reality. His telepathic links to the two of them would have allowed him to sense these, anyway—before today, that is. No, it was something else, something he couldn't quite figure out. He listened to Garrett's mental intonations and frowned in puzzlement. Her voice didn't sound normal. It sounded much more...

Then he felt Parker's cock sliding into his ass. He gasped with pleasure and promptly forgot about everything else. *So... good*, liebchen.

Kurt opened his eyes and gasped again. He'd gone mad, he was sure of it. Aside from the brilliant blue-green radiance bathing them, he couldn't see worth a damn—everything looked inverted, everted, and reverted at the same time. He panicked. *Which way is up?*

In his mind, he heard Parker chuckle. *Relax. You'll get used to it.*

A moment later, he understood. What he was seeing were three different perspectives of the same view superimposed on one another. Through his own eyes, he looked upward. The view coming from his chest belonged to Garrett and the one looking down at him belonged to Parker. From his tri-perspective, Kurt stared into the wolf's bright green eyes, at his own blue ones, and at his throat.

Parker had been right. It hadn't taken long for his dizziness to disappear but having trifocal vision still felt very strange. He closed his eyes, swept away by the feeling of the wolf's prick inside him while he was inside Garrett. Her rhythmic intonations reverberated through his body.

I love you, Parker, he blurted. Opening his eyes again, he saw Parker raise his brow. Then he felt the other's especially hard thrust.

Bullshit.

Kurt saw himself nod. *It's true. I—*

Just then his awareness shifted. His triple vision had expanded to encompass his sense of touch. In his tri-tactile state, he felt the wolf pull out of his ass. At the same time, he felt Parker's arms slipping about Garrett's waist. From her sensory perspective, he felt her being rolled onto her back. Her legs were forced apart and then Parker was slamming into her as if he wanted to hurt her.

Her? Me? Us?

The tri-tactile sensation of fucking and being fucked sent him into ecstatic overload. Unknowingly, he rolled over and shoved his dick into the wolf's ass. He laughed in delight. Through his-Garrett's-Parker's eyes, he saw the witch-light had changed. Now, the wolf glowed green, the mage bright blue, and himself, red.

Red. How fitting! said a small voice in his head—his? Parker's? Garrett's? The colors swirled, bouncing off one another, now writhing like live snakes, now penetrating each other...

Kurt felt himself and the others, now a part of him, being rocketed higher and higher. Just when he thought they'd reached the heavens, he felt a mighty vortex suck the three of them into its invisible maw.

Then they exploded.

CHAPTER 83

Garrett Larkin, the mage, was no more. She no longer had an identity. The magick had blown her persona out of existence. Tiny bits of her mind rained through the ether like twinkling blue stars. If she'd been able to see, she would've noticed the red and green stars raining along with hers.

Her mind-bits became conscious of a force pulling them back together. Clumping here and there, her persona accreted like planets forming in a solar system. A sense of self soon crept into being. When it had, she was no longer just Garrett Larkin. She was Parker Berenson and Master Kurt, too. The three's psychic walls had been broken. She opened her eyes and saw through Parker, Kurt's, and her own that they lay on their backs, their feet forming a triangle.

They sat up as one, each surrounded by a halo of blue, green, and red. "It worked," they said in unison. Their individual voices had blended as well. Garrett's soprano, Kurt's high, and Parker's full baritone issued from all three throats.

"Quickly," they said and stood. "This phase won't last long. I haven't much time." Facing each other, the three raised their arms and touched hands, palms and fingers pressed together. "Eall tholian ofer ma vela," they intoned. While they chanted, the fingers of each, pad to pad, engaged in an intricate dance. This particular dance described three, one of the universal sacred numbers in all of its manifestations.

"Eall tholian ofer ma vela..."

The auras surrounding each of them began flowing into the center of the triangle. A compact ball of swirling hues at first, it quickly grew into an amorphous blob of blinding light and color large enough to encompass the three who'd created it.

"Eall tholian ofer ma vela…"

Their chanting grew louder. The blob began to lengthen. By the time they were screaming the ancient words, the dazzling, tri-colored splotch reached the ceiling.

"Vela!"

With an ear-shattering roar, the column of densely concentrated magick hurled itself through the roof. The witch light went out.

Garrett, Kurt, and Parker fell to the floor in a dead faint.

CHAPTER 84

For anyone with eyes to see, the light show emanating from the Space Needle was spectacular. The entire structure was bathed in a bright white glow that pulsed so fast the tower appeared to vibrate. Light throbbed in the windows near its summit. The red, green, and blue colors chased one another in a manic game of tag. Beams shooting through the glass made the deck seem to spin. The Seattle landmark looked as if it were about to launch itself into space.

Moments later, the tri-colored radiance burst from the Needle's tip like water gushing from a fire hose. Pointing straight at the heavens, its zenith widened into an inverted cone. It spread, faster and faster, until it became a disc of spinning light parallel to the ground. Then the disc began to expand and kept growing until all of Seattle lay beneath its umbrella.

Zots and humans on the streets stopped in their tracks. Staring and blinking in confusion, they looked at the torches, clubs, and guns they carried as if wondering what these weapons were and why they were carrying them.

With hardly a word spoken, most of them turned around and began heading home.

The uthyrisis didn't know what was happening. Its emotional feast of hate and fear was fast disappearing. Not only that, the Gerald's food was disappearing too. The few three-humans it had eaten lately weren't nearly enough to sustain the host.

The uthyrisis decided to return to the place where it had taken its first morsels tonight. There had been lots of three-humans around then. Maybe they were still there.

Troubled by this turn of events, the uthyrisis headed for Discovery Park.

CHAPTER 85

Parker, Garrett, and Kurt came to at the same time.

Parker immediately sensed he was back in his own skin. Well, mostly, anyway. He could still sense Garrett and Kurt inside him but not as intensely as he had a few minutes ago. It was like having half of an out-of-body experience. "God," he whispered and struggled to sit up. He had a pounding headache. Upright, he pinched the bridge of his nose with a thumb and forefinger.

Umph, he heard Garrett's grunt in his mind.

Agreed, Kurt thought.

Parker cautiously opened his eyes. In the moonlight, he could see he was looking through only one pair—his own. A wave of relief washed over him. That trifocal vision would've driven him bananas. He turned to Garrett. "Did it work?"

She didn't answer, but he could feel her uneasiness. "I don't know."

His brow furrowed. "Whaddaya mean, you don't know? What was all that we just did, then?"

"Wait—what I mean is that I don't know how well our trysting worked. That glowing with the three colors—the one that went through the roof?" She looked at him and Kurt. "It should have been violet. Like an ultraviolet light." A tear formed in the corner of her eye and trickled down her cheek.

Parker felt her tear tickle his own cheek. He wiped it away without thinking.

"And if it had worked completely, we'd be able to feel a lot more of each other than we do now."

He looked at the floor. He did feel Garrett's despair at having failed to make a full tryst. Not as much as she was feeling it, but...

"And the Eall Tholia? How long will it take to tell if that worked?" Kurt said, rubbing his hand over his cheek as if to wipe away Garrett's tears.

"We should be able to tell something right now, though it'll take a few days for the spell to completely settle." Her expression turned pained. "But that won't matter much if human attitudes toward us change only a little bit, right?"

Parker's lip curled. *All that bullshit for nothing.* He gave his head a minute shake. "So what's happened to this demon thing? What would the spell have done to it?"

Garrett looked at him. "I don't know. The way Paul explained it, the uthyrisis is a fifth-dimensional being. So even if the tryst and the Eall Tholia worked one hundred percent, they still operate in only three dimensions, and that's their limitation."

No one spoke. Then Parker sighed and stood. He spied his jeans and put them on. There was no point in even trying to wear his tattered and bloodied shirt. *Or my shoes, either.* He turned and headed for the elevator. Pushing the call button, he heard the machinery crank to life.

"Wait a minute," Garrett cried. "Park, where are you going?"

He looked over his shoulder. "Gonna catch me a demon. Even if humans end up loving us to death, there's no point to any of this if that thing's still out there, right?"

"Parker, you can't just...look, we have to come up with some sort of plan or you could kill us all. We're linked now."

He didn't reply at first. "Yup." A small smile appeared on his lips. "But I guess you should've thought of that before you got me into your damned tryst."

Parker stepped into the elevator cab and was gone.

Once back on the street, he saw Seattle was still burning, judging by the orange-white glow he could see against the night sky. Sirens continued to blare, broadcasting the city's plight. But for all that, a sense of calm pervaded the atmosphere.

Spell must've worked. Wondering where he should go, he realized he hadn't a clue how to go about finding the demon. The thing might be downtown. Or it might be uptown. Or it might be a thousand miles from here.

Parker snorted. *Well, hell. Why not try—*

He cut off the thought and started walking. Subconsciously, he knew exactly where he was going— Discovery Park. There was no reason for him to think the demon was there but that was where he and Melera had first met, so maybe, just maybe…

Reaching the first street corner, he turned and trotted north.

It never occurred to him that he could have just borrowed Kurt's ability to morph himself into mist and flown there.

CHAPTER 86

"What does he think he's doing?" Garrett cried.

Kurt turned. "You heard him. And if that's what he intends, I should think he'll need all the help he can get. Let's go."

Without another word, they dissolved into mist and left the Needle. From their airborne view, both could see Seattle was still on fire. But there was something else. *Listen to it out here, Kurt,* Garrett thought at him. Neither of them could speak while in mist form. *Parker was right— the rioting has stopped.*

Yes, it seems so.

Parker was nowhere in sight but that didn't mean they didn't know where he was. Through their trystic link, they followed him uptown.

Where do you think he's going? Garrett thought.

I've no idea.

The wolf moved fast, Kurt had to grant him that. Within forty minutes, he was turning off the street and into Discovery Park. Once inside, he headed straight for the bluff overlooking the Sound.

It's interesting that though we're linked, we can't hear him make his decisions about where to go, hmm? Kurt thought.

Yeah. I don't hear a thing from him except a kind of white noise. It's like he's not thinking at all. He's just doing.

Is he shutting us out?

No. He can't. If he was, we wouldn't hear anything, not even the white noise. He's just...blank.

Kurt thought nothing. Then he sensed Garrett hesitate. *That might be it,* he heard her think.

What?

She hesitated again. *Paul told me one of the reasons the uthyrisis is almost impossible to beat is because it's from the fifth dimension, not the third.*

You mentioned that. So?

It means the demon can perceive us on all levels of our existence better than we can. It can see our thoughts before they take form in our minds.

And?

Don't be dense, Kurt. If Parker isn't thinking, it can't know what his next move will be.

They mentally and physically felt Parker stop in his tracks and stare in surprise. The two looked down. Both did a misty double-take.

Gerald? the three thought as one.

CHAPTER 87

Parker couldn't believe what he was seeing. Gerald stood in the grass ten yards away, looking lost. "Gerald?" he called.

The young scrum werewolf turned. "Alpha," he shouted and ran toward him.

Parker met him halfway. The two crashed into each other and nearly toppled to the ground. He enveloped his lowliest packmate in a bear hug. "Thank God you're all right. Tran told me you were missing and when I couldn't find you in Underground, I thought you were dead."

Neither werewolf said anything for a long moment. A minute frown creased Parker's brow. Gerald didn't smell right. Disengaging from their embrace, he peered at the scrum's face. Gerald's eyes seemed different, too. A thought tickled at the back of his mind...

Gerald took a few steps back and stared at him but said nothing.

Without realizing it, Parker stepped back a pace, too. "Why aren't you Underground, Gerald?"

The scrum werewolf smiled. "Because."

That one word was all it took. He knew exactly what stood in the grass talking to him.

The uthyrisis leapt. He dove out of its way without thinking. Rolling on the turf, he morphed into his wolf and crouched on the ground, un-moving. He decided to torch the thing. Staring at it, he narrowed his eyes and concentrated for a second. He hurled the bolt of fiery power at where the uthyrisis stood—

—to find that he'd somehow missed. The only thing on fire was the grass. The uthyrisis was standing three or so feet from where it had been previously.

What the...? Parker blinked in confusion. He hadn't missed a target that big in years. He tried again with the same result.

Before he could try a third time, the uthyrisis grinned and leapt at him. It had morphed Gerald's human arms into his wolf ones, and it had also morphed to a height matching his.

He would have tried torching the uthyrisis again but he was too busy fighting for his life.

They slashed at each other. Gerald ripped into Parker's chest. He landed a kick to the other's stomach, opening five deep gashes. The uthyrisis rushed him. He waited until it was at arm's length, then gave it a hard punch in the face and another to its wounded midriff. Gerald stumbled backward, then doubled over and howled. Parker leapt forward to tear off the other's head but the demon unexpectedly straightened. Managing to change his trajectory at the last minute, he landed behind it, leaving ten long gouges in Gerald's back. The battle raged on. Parker fought mindlessly, a killing machine intent only on destroying his opponent.

Then the unthinkable happened.

CHAPTER 88

Materializing about twenty feet behind Parker, Kurt and Garrett watched him run toward Gerald, both feeling just as shocked and surprised as the wolf did. A few minutes later, they felt Parker's uneasiness about the young man. The two let go of each other and stepped back. It looked like the two wolves were squaring off.

They saw Gerald smile and like Parker, knew they'd found the uthyrisis. The otherworldly killer wearing Gerald's body lunged at him.

With an instinct born of their trystic link, Kurt and Garrett thought nothing further. They poured their own psychic energy into Parker's mind and body. Though they felt each hit he received, they ignored the blows the two inflicted on one another.

The wolf moved faster than either of them had ever seen before. The demon was using Gerald's fighting skills and while the scrum werewolf had been good enough, he'd never been a match for Parker. He'd torn the uthyrisis in at least a dozen places and while he wasn't unmarked, he was in much better shape than the demon.

The uthyrisis launched itself toward Parker, morphing into what looked like a giant butterfly. Parker stood rigid, staring as if transfixed. Then he dove to the right but he'd hesitated a second too long. The uthyrisis wrapped him in its wings. They plummeted to the ground.

"Arrggh!" Parker roared. At the same time, Kurt felt myriad sharp hollow needles punch through his skin. Garrett, he knew, felt it too. Magnified by their shared tactile sense, the pain was unbearable. As one, they dropped to the earth. Then he felt one of those needles slide into his anus and another one into his urethral opening.

Parker screamed.

Garrett screamed.

Kurt screamed. Parker's thrashing only made things worse. He felt the hollow needles greedily sucking the wolf's blood. The uthyrisis squeezed his victim tighter. Kurt felt as if he was being crushed. He couldn't feel Garrett anymore. Rolling on the grass, he tried with all his psychic might to help Parker dislodge the thing. It did no good. The uthyrisis had them all.

His vision turned fuzzy and dim. Blood spurted from his nose. It was funny, in a way. Though it had been a hallucination, he was dying in just about the same humiliating manner as Melera had made him see. The only difference was that no crowd was here to witness it.

He heard a distant roaring sound. Then it began to fade.

I wanted to live forever...

Garrett had never felt such pain. She writhed on the ground, trying to chant a spell that would render her, Parker, and Kurt numb. Her agony kept her from concentrating on the words. Then she tried to summon a red ball of destruction to throw at the uthyrisis but she couldn't do even that.

She felt herself dying and she could feel Parker and Kurt's imminent deaths. She tried again to cast a protective spell, though she knew it was futile.

Mother, please help us, she cried in desperate prayer. With her life almost gone, it was the only thing she could do.

But Goddess didn't answer.

Parker was barely conscious of the crushing pressure from the uthyrisis's wings wrapped around him. He'd fought for as long as he could. It was just as well. Once he'd decided to go after it, he'd figured his chances of surviving their meeting were slim to none, anyway.

The pressure on his body disappeared but he was too far gone to wonder why. He felt himself drawn deeper and deeper into the darkness of death.

Then he felt nothing.

CHAPTER 89

A blinding flash of light and a blast of frigid air startled the uthyrisis into dropping its morsel and caused it to morph back into the Gerald body.

What?

Before it could wonder what had happened, its head was wrenched to the side and it was flying through the air. The uthyrisis landed with a hard thud. Leaping to its feet, it saw nothing. But there was something out here. It peered deeper into the night. It cocked its head, listening. It couldn't hear any thoughts, either. The uthyrisis shook the Gerald's head. *Perhaps it was just a passing spirit.*

It had just taken a step to finish its meal when something kicked it from behind, sending it sprawling. It leapt to its feet again and whirled in time to see a shadow dart off to its right, toward where its meal lay unmoving in the grass. Anger surged through it. *No. He is mine. You will not spoil my tale.*

The uthyrisis charged but it didn't get very far. A hard blow to the Gerald's stomach doubled it over. Pain lanced through the body. Before it could cry out, something whacked it on the chin. The uthyrisis arced backward and stumbled. It had just regained its balance when the shadow appeared, lifted it bodily and threw it to the ground. Dazed, the uthyrisis closed its eyes.

The next thing it knew, a heavy weight had settled on the Gerald's chest and a hand was gripping its throat. It opened its eyes. A female three-human stared down at it. The uthyrisis smiled. *Another tale to tell.*

Then it noticed this female's eyes were different from all the other three-humans it had seen. Instead of a round spot in the middle of a sea of white, this one had golden eyes with a slit down the middle. They seemed to spin. A dim golden halo appeared around the female and then brightened until it glowed.

The uthyrisis gave a little shrug. It didn't matter. Strange eyes, halos—as far as it was concerned, here was more food. *And I am still hungry.*

In an eyeblink, the uthyrisis morphed and wrapped the female in its wings. Knocked out of position, she now lay flat, face to face with the Gerald. Grinning now, the uthyrisis secreted its clothes-dissolving acid.

Except it didn't work. A frown creased the Gerald's brow. It tried again. The female's clothes still didn't dissolve. Puzzled, it stared at her.

The female stared back.

The Gerald's jaw set. *Very well—I will just feed.* The material would slow the three-human's blood-flow but that would only prolong its meal and the female's agony. The uthyrisis thrust out its feeders. Like the acid, they too couldn't penetrate the female's clothes. It tried a second time and then a third. Her clothes remained intact. Then the uthyrisis realized something else. Unlike the other three-humans it had eaten, this one wasn't terrified.

The female smiled.

The uthyrisis was blinded by another light-flash. On its heels came that blast of bitter cold. Sucking in air from the shock, it morphed back into the Gerald body. When the spots before its eyes cleared, it was someplace it had never been before. It floated in an ocean of night. The stars and moon had disappeared. The only light, little that it was, came from the strange female's glowing halo. As far as it could tell, there was nothing to see. And it was mind-numbingly cold.

An instant later, the Gerald body froze and died. The uthyrisis was thrust out of the carcass. It watched the three-female kick the Gerald away from it. For a few seconds, by the light of her halo, the uthyrisis saw the body tumbling away, weightless. Then it disappeared into the blackness.

The female still smiled. Then she punched the uthyrisis in its fourth eye.

Sharp, bright, pain. Enraged, the uthyrisis lunged and lashed out with its now-flexible feeders. Whipping them around the female, it pinned her against its misshapen, balloon-like body. She struggled but soon stopped. There was no point. The uthyrisis stared into her face with its primary eye, expecting to feast on her terror.

Her smile never wavered.

The uthyrisis let out the breath it had been holding and tried to take another. *There is no air!* For the first time ever, it felt its own fear. It started to panic but then calmed. *It is all right. I will be pulled back into my home dimension at any moment now.*

But it wasn't. It floated with the female in the dark, airless place. A second passed. And another. Then it understood. There was no going back to the fifth dimension from this place, wherever it was. It was trapped here, just like the female.

One of its feeders froze. Abysmal cold rocketed through its body, freezing every cell. The uthyrisis stared at the female, horrified at the imminence of its own death. It took small comfort in the fact she was dying, too. Her golden halo, so bright when they came to this place, was now dim, almost gone.

The cold burst through the uthyrisis's brain. The last thing it saw before it died was the strange female's frozen, smiling face.

CHAPTER 90

Garrett couldn't find the Light. She swam purposefully through the Eternal Night, searching for the glow that was the portal to the spirit realm. There, she would rest from the trials of her most recent lifetime and prepare for her next one. Perhaps she would return to the plane she'd just left, or perhaps not. It didn't matter. She swam on and on through the darkness but didn't panic. She was beyond that or any other emotion. All had been left behind when she died.

The Light appeared like a brilliant pinpoint, a lone star in the blackness of space. She swam toward it. A moment later, she was surrounded by and floating in its fiery glow. Soon would come the pull that would take her spirit to her new home, wherever that might be. But it didn't come.

YOU MUST WAKE, DAUGHTER, a familiar whisper echoed. *WAKE. THERE IS A LIFE HANGING IN THE BALANCE.*

Mother? her spirit called. *I'm coming, Mother. Wait for me.*

WAKE, DAUGHTER, the whisper repeated. *A LIFE...IN THE BALANCE...*

The next thing Garrett knew, she was back in her body. "Ummm," a thin moan escaped her throat. Her brain ached, as did everything else. And she was so tired. *Sleep...I need to sleep.* She started drifting off.

A life...in the balance...

Her eyes flew open. "Kurt," she whispered. A jolt of adrenalin surged through her, banishing her pain and fatigue. She sat up and swiveled her head. Kurt was lying about ten feet away in the moonlit clearing. Beyond him, she could see where Parker lay sprawled, his body pocked with holes and bleeding. Her trystic link informed her that the others were both alive but Parker's life was ebbing fast. Her instinct was to save him first. She scrambled toward him but stopped after realizing she would not be able to do it alone. She could always draw power from Kurt but doing so while he was unconscious might kill him. *Okay. Kurt first. Between the two of us, we should have enough strength to save Parker.*

She crawled over to where Kurt lay.

I hope!

Kurt heard someone calling his name, over and over again. Whoever it was, she sounded far away. He listened for a while. *I never would have believed it. Vampires have an afterlife. Interesting.* Then he noticed something else. He couldn't quite put his finger on it but somehow he felt...diminished. He made a mental frown. *Why would I feel—*

"Aggh," he yelled. What felt like a bolt of lightning ripped through him. His body was on fire, burning from the inside out. He screamed again. Then, as suddenly as it had appeared, the burning sensation was gone.

"Kurt," a voice shouted. "Kurt!"

His eyes popped open. Garrett's face hung inches from his. "Kurt. Oh, Mother, Kurt...you're all right."

"Garrett," he whispered. Then he remembered the demon. His eyes went wide. "Parker. Where's Parker?"

That was when he realized that Garrett knelt over him, her hands on his chest. She dismounted and pointed to her left. "Over there. Come on."

He sat up and looked around. The wolf lay sprawled in the grass about fifteen feet away. *Oh, no...* Holding each other up, they stumbled to Parker's side. Kurt let go of her and looked down. Parker seemed very still. He turned to Garrett but she was already on her knees. "He isn't—"

"No, but he will be if we don't hurry. And we'll go with him. Help me get him into position." She pushed at the unconscious wolf, trying to roll him onto his back. Kurt dropped down beside her and between the two of them, they managed it. "Garrett? What do you mean, we? You're the healer."

"The tryst, Kurt—the tryst. I need your energy. I can't heal him without you. Don't argue with me. Pull his arms out to the side." Turning her back to him, she began straightening Parker's legs.

Kneeling behind Parker's head, Kurt dragged each of the werewolf's arms toward him. By the time he and Garrett had finished, Parker lay crucifixion-style in the grass. Garrett straddled him and pressed her hands over his heart. "You need to be touching him, Kurt."

Kurt edged closer. Tucking his legs beneath him, he gently placed the wolf's head in his lap. He looked up. "Now what?"

"While I'm weaving the healing spell, I need you to channel your energy into him."

He frowned. "How do I do that?"

"Just visualize it. Or think it. It doesn't matter. It's the intent that counts."

"Like how one vampire rebirths another." He nodded. "All right, ready when you are."

Garrett closed her eyes and took a breath. "Haela se novae menos et corporus, haela se novae menos et corporus," she chanted.

Staring down at Parker's eyes, now closed, Kurt began stroking his forehead. *I love you, wolf. No matter what you think of me, I love you. Live, Parker—live. I want you to live. I need you to live. I want you to live...*

He felt his energy begin to flow.

CHAPTER 91

In the moonlit clearing, Parker slowly opened his eyes to see Kurt's ghost-pale face looming upside down above his own. He didn't understand at first but then realized his head lay in the vampire's lap. With a jerk, he struggled to get up. Kurt already had his dick up his ass once tonight and he wasn't about to give the bloodsucker a blow job on top of it.

Kurt forced him back down. "Easy, wolf." He smiled. "That's not—"

Still reading my mind, asshole?

Kurt stopped his caresses and his smile died. "We trysted, wolf. Remember? I can hear everything you think without even trying. Until we figure out how to gain at least some privacy from each other, try to be a little more charitable in your thoughts, hmm?"

"Parker," he heard Garrett's voice.

His gaze shifted. The mage straddled his waist, her delicate hands laying directly over his heart. From her position, it was obvious she'd magickally sped his healing process. "You'll be okay, Park. You've lost a lot of blood, but you'll—"

He tuned her out. Sure, he'd live. But without Melera he was not okay and without her, he didn't want to be okay. Then he frowned. "Wait a minute. Where's the demon? How come I'm still alive?"

"Those are very good questions, dear Parker," Kurt said. "Personally, I have no earthly idea. What do you remember?"

He thought for a moment and then shook his head. "Last thing I remember was it letting go of me. After that..." He shrugged. "What about you two?"

"I don't know," Garrett said. "I mean, when the uthyrisis had you, it had us, too. I don't remember blacking out and I guess Kurt doesn't either, right?"

Kurt nodded. "Though I do remember this odd roaring sound. But I thought I was just dying."

Parker sighed. "Well…at least it's gone."

Garrett dismounted and sat on her knees by his side. She peered at him. "How do you feel, Park?"

He glared at her. "Like shit. How do you think I feel?"

She drew back as if stung. "We need to get to Underground."

"Garrett's right, Parker," Kurt said. "The city might be quieting but it's not over yet. And I'm sure your pack needs you right about now, hmm?"

Parker blew a heavy breath. "Yeah. Okay." Now that Garrett had climbed off him, he sat up and looked around at the burned and trampled grass. His brow creased. "I don't get it. I mean, why would the demon let me go? What hap—"

His eyes widened. It had just dawned on him. Something Kurt had said about Earth… He looked at Garrett, then Kurt. "Wait. How long have I been out?"

Kurt rubbed his chin. "Hard to say. Garrett and I came to…oh, about five minutes ago, and—"

Parker leapt to his feet, ignoring the nausea that threatened to bring him down. "Melera," he shouted. He ran deeper into the clearing, searching with his eyes and nose. There was nothing. "Melera! Get out! OhGod—getoutgetoutgetoutoftheVoid," his words tumbled out in a rush.

He sensed Garrett and Kurt come up behind him. "Is Melera here?" Kurt said, sounding as alarmed as Parker felt. "Where—"

An abrupt flash blinded him. When his vision returned, he saw a white figure appear out of nowhere, fall, bounce, roll over the grass, and finally come to a halt. "Melera," he shouted again and ran to her inert form. He could feel the cold radiating from her body from five feet away.

He reached her. Falling to his knees, he lifted her in his arms but immediately dropped her. The cold was so intense it had burned him. He morphed into his wolf and tried again. There—that was better. The cold still scorched but at least his pelt absorbed the worst of it. He stared into Melera's face. She looked dead. Her golden brown skin was only a shadow of its usual color and her lips had turned blue.

I have to get her warm. Sitting cross-legged, Parker pulled her onto his lap and tucked her frozen legs between his. Then, twining his arms about her, he pulled her close so that her head rested on his broad, pelted chest. He looked down. Cradled by his eight-foot wolf, Melera seemed so small and vulnerable.

The summer's heat melted the frost covering her from head to toe, leaving him feeling damp. "Melera," he snarled a while later.

She didn't answer.

"Melera," he tried again, growling louder. She still didn't answer.

Minutes passed.

"Parker," he heard Garrett's soft voice. "I'm sorry——"

Her pity angered him. "No," he roared. Shoving Melera to the ground, he then straddled her hips. He towered over her. "Dammit Melera, wake up," he bellowed, backhanding her across her cheek. "You didn't come all the way back here just to die on me. Now wake up, bitch. Wake up!"

He slapped her again and again.

Nothing.

Parker, still in wolf form, finally sat back. *Garrett's right. Oh, God...* He lifted Melera's body and held her, staring into her dead face. Hot wolf tears from his glowing eyes fell upon her like rain.

A few minutes later, her skin flushed. He forgot to breathe. After what seemed like an eternity, she opened her golden eyes.

"Pawkher?" she whispered.

Unable to answer, he covered her face with rough wolf kisses, bathing her with his long tongue. "Yeah, sweetheart. It's me," his growling voice hitched after his throat had loosened. "I'm here."

She gave her head a little shake. "What fook tsat was?"

"A demon." He nuzzled her nose with his wolf one.

"A what?"

"The Slayer."

"Oh."

She began to shiver. Parker rose from his knees and sat cross-legged on the ground beside her. Pulling her into his lap, he held her close as he had before when he'd first tried to warm her. He closed his eyes. Resting his wolf's jaw on top of her head, he slowly rocked back and forth.

Five minutes later, Melera stopped her shivering. He lifted his chin. She looked up at him. Morphing back into human form, he gazed into her whirling, golden eyes. He had so many questions, like what had happened while she and the demon were inside the Void? And how had she managed to survive for so long? But he had one question that came before all the rest. "Melera, why did you come back?"

That sly grin he loved so much spread across her face. "Need see-gars."

He snorted. "Figures." Then, with a quiet chuckle, he gave her a deep kiss. He felt Garrett and Kurt standing somewhere behind him and knew they felt exactly what he was feeling, with his lips locked on hers. Ignoring them didn't work. He could sense their growing impatience, just as they could sense his growing irritation. *Kiss my ass,* he thought, knowing they'd hear him.

"I hate to intrude on this happy little reunion, but…" Kurt said, his voice dripping with sarcasm.

Parker scowled over his shoulder.

"I really think we ought to be going, hmm? I'm sure you weren't paying attention, but I heard voices coming from over that way." He pointed to his right.

"So leave."

"Parker," Garrett snapped.

Melera struggled to rise. Parker helped her stand, steadying her when she began to wobble. She took a few steps backward and faced him, her expression unreadable. "You still come Maqu wits me, yes?"

He didn't hesitate. "Yes."

"You come, you die."

"Everybody dies, sooner or later."

Her look softened. She leapt into his arms. Catching her by the waist, Parker held her tight. "Me love you, Pawkher," she said, her face buried in his neck.

He closed his eyes, drowning in her delicious scent. "I know, sweetheart. That's why you came back for me."

"And see-gars, too."

Parker smiled into her hair. "Okay. And cigars, too."

A moment later, Melera stepped out of his arms. She took him by the hand and gave him a little tug. "Come. We go now." She started walking. He followed.

"Park," he heard Garrett's shout behind him. "You can't... what about us?"

He turned. "What about you?"

"Stop it, Park. You know damned well we're too linked to get far from one another."

Parker rolled his eyes and turned to Melera. "Honey, I..." He quickly explained what he, Kurt, and Garrett had done. During his narrative, her eyes grew bigger and bigger.

"Take wits us?" she cried, pointing a finger at Garrett and Kurt.

"Well...hell, sweetheart. It seemed like a good idea at the time and besides, how was I to know you were coming back?"

Melera stared at the other two with a disgusted expression. Then she looked at him. "Ohh-kay," she said, her tone full of sullen resignation. She looked at the three of them in turn and let out a heavy sigh. "Come." She spun on her heel and started walking.

"Wait," Garrett said. "Where—"

"Ride back me will," Melera snapped over her shoulder. "But go now we must."

"Be real, Garrett," Parker said. "She's gotta park her ship somewhere. We'll be back. Come on."

Kurt stared at Melera as if he'd realized something momentous. "Parker, are you...are you saying Melera actually has a spaceship?"

"Sure. What else would an alien have?"

Kurt looked as if he'd faint. "So she...she really is a..."

Parker blew an explosive breath. "Yeah, Kurt. Weren't you listening last night when she told you what she was?"

Kurt, apparently trying to take it all in, said nothing. Garrett stood open-mouthed.

Dismissing them, Parker turned to his lover and affected a serious look. "You do remember where you left your ship this time?"

She gave his cheek a playful slap. "Me remembuh, ass-smart."

He grinned. "That's smartass, sweetheart. If you're going to call me names, get it right." He glanced around him, then looked at her. "So... where is it?"

Melera reached under her chin and partially opened her form-fitting black suit, revealing a wide, golden neck collar. She smiled. "Ke'je."

The collar flash once. A brilliant, blue-white blaze lit up the night sky behind the trees to his left, accompanied by a low humming sound that vibrated his bones. Its light shot through the gaps in the foliage, casting stark shadows across the clearing where they stood. "Wow," he said, eyeing the radiance. "Guess that answers my question." He stared a moment longer then looked at Garrett and Kurt. "You guys coming?"

"I...uh," Kurt said, his blue eyes like saucers.

"W-we..." Garrett stammered.

Parker shrugged. He turned to Melera and gave her a wolfish grin. "Fook them. Let's go."

Hand in hand and laughing, the alpha werewolf and the alien warrior ran into the light.

TO MY READERS

Hello, and thank you so much for reading *The Underground!*

I've been asked how in the world did I came up with the idea for this book. Well, one day I was thinking about werewolves and what they would have to do to survive in modern society. If there's more than, say, five, would they band together or would they go it alone? What—or who—would be their prey? If they lived in the countryside maybe they'd hunt deer or grab a cow. But what if they lived in the cities? That raises a whole host of other issues—jobs, secrecy, and so on. Since I like to play mind games with myself, I took up the challenge!

I'd love to have you along on my writers' journey! To get on board, you only have to join my email list at www.roxannebland.rocks. You can stay updated on my works-in-progress, enter contests for nifty swag, and don't be surprised if I ask for your feedback on a project! More than that, by signing up you'll get a FREE copy of my ebook *The Final Victim*, a companion novella to the dangerous world of *The Underground*, where the drama unfolds from the elven point of view. What's more, *The Final Victim* is exclusive to me and is not available anywhere else! For your convenience, I can provide the novella in .epub, .mobi, or .pdf formats. If you'd like to spend more time in *The Underground* world, you might want to take a peek at *Invasion*, its sequel. Both novels are available in online and print formats.

One more thing—please consider leaving a review of *The Underground* on the platform where you purchased it, on your favorite readers' website(s), or recommending it to a friend. I'd appreciate it!

Thanks again for your support!

Roxanne Bland

Made in the USA
Middletown, DE
10 April 2023

28465810R00224